Maria Louise Pool

The Two Salomes

A novel

Maria Louise Pool

The Two Salomes
A novel

ISBN/EAN: 9783337000257

Printed in Europe, USA, Canada, Australia, Japan

Cover: Foto ©Andreas Hilbeck / pixelio.de

More available books at **www.hansebooks.com**

THE TWO SALOMES

A Novel

BY

MARIA LOUISE POOL

AUTHOR OF

"ROWENY IN BOSTON" "MRS. KEATS BRADFORD"
"DALLY" ETC., ETC.

NEW YORK
HARPER & BROTHERS PUBLISHERS
1893

TO

CAROLINE M. BRANSON

THIS STORY

𝕴𝖘 𝕯𝖊𝖉𝖎𝖈𝖆𝖙𝖊𝖉

WITH THE LOVE OF

MARIA LOUISE POOL

CONTENTS

CHAP.   PAGE

    I. A PROPOSAL 1

   II. TWO KINDS OF LOVERS 17

  III. ANTINOUS 36

  IV. "SLEEPERS AND BUFFETS" 55

   V. MISS NUNALLY 74

  VI. MR. MAINE "FLAXING ROUND" 94

 VII. AN AMANUENSIS 114

VIII. "MATERIAL" 132

  IX. "FOR LOVE" 153

   X. A LITTLE TENNIS 171

  XI. CONFESSION 189

 XII. THE MOTHER 208

XIII. AN ENGAGEMENT 227

XIV. TOUCHING TRUTHFULNESS 247

 XV. "HOW SHOULD YOU THINK OF YOURSELF?" . 264

XVI. QUESTIONING 283

XVII. TIRED 301

XVIII. "AND NOW THERE IS NOTHING BETWEEN US" . 319

XIX. "AS FOR ME, I LOVE HIM NOT" 338

 XX. "HE WILL COME BACK?" 358

THE TWO SALOMES

I

A PROPOSAL

"Have they found out yet what's the matter of Salome Gerry?"

"Yes; I heard Mis' West tell what the doctor from Boston said it was."

This reply was given with an air of some importance, and the speaker waited to be questioned still further before divulging what she knew about the ailments of Salome Gerry.

"Well," was the somewhat impatient response, "ain't you goin' to tell? I s'pose 'tain't no secret. Not that doctors know much of anything; though 'tis a relief to have um take the responsibility off your shoulders when you have sickness in the fam'ly. I remember when Elnathan was took with the fever 'n' ague the first time, his mother—she was stoppin' with us that fall—would stick to it that she'd doctor him herself. 'N' I remember—"

The two other women present here exchanged glances of despairing commiseration, and one of them exclaimed, desperately:

"We all know 't Elnathan's mother was an awful

1

good nuss. There wa'n't nobody like her. Folks used to come from all over for her if anybody was taken sick."

Then the third woman hastened to ask again:

"What 'd the doctor from Boston say about S'lome Gerry, anyway? She's ben kind of pindlin' s'long I sh'd think her folks 'd be almost discouraged."

"I guess they be. 'N' I should think they'd feel worse now they know what 'tis that ails her," with still more importance.

"I s'pose you'll tell when you git ready," now said the thin-faced Mrs. Lamkin, hunching her high shoulders yet higher in her irritation.

Mrs. Sprague responded that she was just as ready now as she ever should be, and she didn't know as she was keeping anything back. The two other women were aware of a keen apprehension lest Mrs. Sprague should again refer to Elnathan's mother and her capabilities as a nurse. Elnathan was Mrs. Sprague's husband, consequently Elnathan's mother stood in the relation of mother-in-law to Elnathan's wife. And to be mother-in-law to "she that was Emmeline Rusk," was to stand in a position requiring great gifts of tact and amiability.

"Mis' West said the doctor from Boston," now began Mrs. Sprague, "told the Gerryses that Salome had incipient thigh-sis."

"Mercy!" cried Mrs. Lamkin, sharply, "what's thigh-sis? Is it ketchin'?"

"Incipient thigh-sis, I said," corrected Mrs. Sprague. And she added, more carelessly, "I'm sure I don't know whether it's ketchin' or not. But I guess 'tain't, or the rest of the Gerryses would have had it long ago."

The third woman, whose name was Scudder, and who

had thick gray hair arranged in long folds on each side of her face, and whose large, protruding eyes were of the same gray as her hair, now said gently that she s'posed it must be some new disease. Folks were getting up new diseases real often nowadays. For her part, she thought the old ones were more than anybody could manage.

Here she chuckled quietly. She drew the folds of her brown "Stella shawl" higher over her ample shoulders, and inquired if the doctor told the Gerryses what to do 'bout S'lome.

Again Mrs. Sprague quoted Mrs. West as her authority. Mrs. West had said that S'lome's mother was all broke down about it.

"If 'twas my girl," went on Mrs. Sprague, with decision, "I should call it consumption, or something that would be consumption in time. But if anybody'd ruther have thigh-sis, why, let 'em have it."

"Are they going to do nothing about it?" asked Mrs. Scudder, in her soft way.

"Mis' West said the doctor said medicine wa'n't of no count in such cases," continued Mrs. Sprague. "He said the winters here were too severe for her. He advised 'em to take her to Floridy."

"Gracious!" said Mrs. Lamkin. "To Floridy? They can't do it, can they? Her father ain't very 'forehanded. I don't believe he's got a cent in the bank."

"I'd know, I'm sure. Mis' West said she understood they were goin' to try to send S'lome and her mother some way or other."

"I want to know," responded Mrs. Lamkin, sitting up very straight in her surprise. "I don't see how they're goin' to do it. They'll have to moggidge their place, won't they?"

"If they do moggidge, I for one can't see how they'll ever lift the moggidge. Mr. Gerry never was so scrabblin' as he might be."

"Mebby the church'll help 'em some," suggested Mrs. Scudder, now taking out the long pin with which she had just fastened her shawl.

"Well, then, you jest bet the church won't," retorted Mrs. Sprague. "The church's got enough to do with foreign missions, 'n' rasin' the minister's salary, 'n' the bell's cracked, too, you know. It sounds awful when they ring it. I'm ashamed every Sabbath to have the Baptists, 'n' the folks that don't go to meetin' anywhere, hear our bell. We don't think enough of the Lord's work."

Mrs. Scudder did not wish to continue the subject of the cracked bell, so she ignored the words referring to it. She asked :

"If S'lome Gerry goes to Floridy what'll become of her beau ?"

Mrs. Lamkin here gave a little shrill laugh, and inquired,

"Which beau you mean ?"

"I didn't know she had more'n one reg'lar beau, and that's Dick Chapin, ain't it ?"

"Now, I should have said 'twas Walter Redd," remarked Mrs. Lamkin.

Then the three women looked at each other and began to laugh.

It was Mrs. Scudder who ceased laughing first. She found her pocket in the folds of her skirt, and drew her handkerchief from it. She carefully wiped the corners of her mouth. Then she patted the large bow in which the ribbons of her bonnet were tied. For she and Mrs. Sprague were making a "set call" on

Mrs. Lamkin. And in a set call people always wear their Sunday bonnets.

Mrs. Scudder also had on her best gloves. They were of black kid, worn white on the tops of the fingers and thumbs. They were also somewhat baggy across the back. But the wearer of them was conscious of being much dressed. And this consciousness surely is among the first effects to be desired from wearing clothes.

Mrs. Sprague wore a black cape, with square ends in the front and a deep point behind. It was lined with black flannel, and since gimp had come into fashion again for trimming, the narrow folds which had once adorned it had been removed to give place to the gimp. The garment was now considered as specially appropriate for spring and fall wear.

Mrs. Sprague did not know that Mrs. Lamkin had once told an intimate friend that she thought Emmeline Sprague looked like the Old Harry in that cape.

It may be called a wise arrangement of the universe that we are usually ignorant of such little remarks made by our friends concerning us. Ignorance is sometimes a great strengthener of friendly feeling.

After they had all laughed concerning Salome Gerry's beau, the three made an attempt to talk about a new recipe for sweet pickle which Mrs. Lamkin had been making. That lady went into the buttery and came back with two pink sauce plates. Each plate held a teaspoon and some of the sweet pickle.

The two callers tasted with grave deliberation.

"It's a grain too clovey, ain't it?" anxiously inquired Mrs. Lamkin, looking from one to the other.

"I should say," said Mrs. Sprague, "that it was a

little, just a little, too sharp with vinegar. I guess your vinegar's got ruther strong by this time, ain't it, Mis' Lamkin? What do you think, Mis' Scudder?"

Mrs. Scudder was pressing her lips critically together. She waited a minute before replying.

"I call it jest exactly right for cloves," she said. "But I guess you used brown sugar, didn't you?"

Mrs. Lamkin confessed that she had done so.

"That's it!" triumphantly exclaimed Mrs. Scudder. "I always use granulated. 'Tain't none too good. But this is first-rate, Mis' Lamkin; I don't find no fault with it."

As if to emphasize her words, Mrs. Scudder took another and quite liberal taste of the concoction upon the plate which she held between her gloved fingers. She had a sense of being very "dressy," holding the plate in that way.

" I was goin' to send some over to the Gerryses," said Mrs. Lamkin, "they all like it so, and Mis' Gerry ain't had no chance to make preserves nor nothin' this fall, she's been so worried, she told me. She thought mebby S'lome would come over this after-noon, 'n' if she did I was goin' to have her carry back some of this. But, p'raps, bein' made with brown sugar, so, Mis' Scudder, 'tain't what one would like to send to a neighbor."

The speaker looked with a challenging humility at the large face framed in the gray hair. The owner of the face and the hair smiled indulgently.

" Lor'," said Mrs. Scudder, " you know better than to talk like that. But is S'lome able to be out this weather? There was a white frost last night, even on the uplands."

"Oh, she ain't so low as that," was the answer.

"She seems to be pretty well a good deal of the time. She goes everywhere. She's real cheerful."

Mrs. Sprague shook her head when she heard this last remark.

"It's a bad sign for consumptive folks to be cheerful," she asserted. "For my part, I'd ruther see um blue as indigo."

Here she happened to glance through the window. She started.

"Who be they?" she asked, quickly.

They all looked eagerly into the road. Coming down the hill, sauntering slowly in the late October sunshine, were two people, a girl and a young man. They were not talking, and they were not walking near each other, nevertheless there was an undefinable air of intimate acquaintance about them.

"I declare if that ain't S'lome herself!" exclaimed Mrs. Lamkin. "I guess I'll thump on the winder, and ask her to take home some of the sweet pickle. What feller is that with her?"

"It's Dick Chapin. He wears a blue suit like that," promptly answered Mrs. Sprague.

Meanwhile Mrs. Lamkin had "thumped on the winder," and the two in the highway had paused and looked up at the house. The woman beckoned vigorously.

The girl said a few words to her companion, then she walked quickly up the path to the door. The young man did not follow her. He lounged against the fence, waiting.

The next moment the door of the sitting-room opened and Salome Gerry entered.

The three women looked at her with the most intense interest. She was not only Salome, the girl whom they had seen grow up among them, she was a person who was said by a doctor from Boston to have incipient phthisis, and who was consequently recommended to go to Florida.

Perhaps the girl felt something peculiar in their glances, but she bore the scrutiny with considerable fortitude.

She had a slight, lithe figure, and a thin, sensitive face—a face that looked as if it would flush easily, and one was greatly surprised to know, on acquaintance, that it did not thus flush. Acquaintance also revealed that, instead of the skin's showing any emotion, the eyes had a way of suddenly kindling with a quick, rising fire, and then as suddenly becoming calm again. But she was a very calm looking girl now as she stood just within the sitting-room. She smiled at Mrs. Lamkin, who hastened to say:

"I'm real glad I saw you, S'lome, for I was jest wondering how I should send some of my sweet pickle to your mother. I know she's awful fond of it when it's made of them Bicknell pears, as mine is. I'm going to put some in a pail. Se' down a minute, S'lome."

The girl walked towards the nearest chair and placed herself in it.

"Mother'll be ever so much obliged," she said, cordially. "It's so good of you, Mrs. Lamkin, to think of it."

Mrs. Lamkin turned at the door and looked at Salome, smiling as she did so, and her smile was different from those she had given her "set callers."

"I guess I sha'n't hurt myself with goodness," she responded; "you needn't worry about that one bit."

Whereupon she disappeared through the door which led into the kitchen.

The two women remaining continued to gaze at Salome, who made some remark about the frost of the night previous. The two responded to it in an undefined murmur.

Mrs. Scudder made a movement as if she were drawing her gloves on still farther. But she kept her gaze on Salome. At last she could be silent no longer.

"Mis' West was tellin' Mis' Sprague," she said, "that your folks had had a doctor out from Boston to see you, S'lome."

"Yes, mother and father both thought best to have Dr. Bowdoin," answered the girl.

"Wa'n't it dretful expensive?" inquired Mrs. Sprague, with ill-concealed eagerness.

"Yes, it was. But they said they shouldn't feel easy if they didn't have him. They said they felt they could have confidence in what he said."

"Do you know how much he did charge?" asked Mrs. Sprague, bending forward a little as she spoke.

"Father didn't tell me," was the reply.

The girl did not add that Mr. Gerry had purposely refrained from giving this information so that his daughter should not be able to gratify just this kind of curiosity.

Mrs. Sprague sank back in her chair. She drew the ends of her cape closely about her.

Salome laughed slightly as she now said:

"Father told me he was glad his cranberry crop had turned out so well this year, for he didn't feel half so extravagant having Dr. Bowdoin."

"It must be kind of hard for your father to make

both ends meet," now remarked Mrs. Scudder, her purring voice expressing a great appearance of sympathy. "And you not able to earn anything, S'lome."

The girl dropped her eyes suddenly. There was a perceivable space of time before she replied, still with lowered eyes.

" It's a great trial to me that I can't earn anything," she said.

" To be sure," quickly responded Mrs. Sprague, in a hearty voice. " My Lizzie always said she was awful sorry for you. She said you was as ambitious as any girl she knew."

Salome's eyelashes flashed up. She looked at the woman who had spoken thus. She was going to reply, but Mrs. Scudder asked immediately:

" Is it true what Mis' West said 'bout your bein' ordered to Floridy ?"

" It's true that the doctor said he thought it would cure me to go there this fall and stay till June," she answered.

" I don't see how your folks can do it," said Mrs. Scudder. " Be they goin' to try ?"

" I think they will." Here Salome moved her hands with a quick, impatient movement in her lap. She pressed a little ring she wore on her slender third finger up over the knuckle, then back again. " Father and mother both said," she began, " that they'd rather spend all they had than to have me ill. If they could help me they didn't think anything of the money—and then," here she began to speak rapidly and with only a partially subdued eagerness, "and then if I get well I can work and earn money myself, and I could make it all good to them. Not that they'd want me to, but I should like to do it."

Into Mrs. Scudder's large light eyes, fixed intently as they were on the girl, there came a moisture that made them for the instant look larger and bluer than usual. In her own mind she was thinking she was a fool to let herself be touched by Lyman Gerry's daughter. It wasn't any worse for Lyman Gerry's daughter to be threatened with consumption, if that was what it was, than for any other girl. And perhaps there didn't much ail the child, anyway. She certainly didn't look very sick, only not rugged.

"Oh, you'll be gettin' married," Mrs. Scudder responded, as soon as she could speak in her ordinary tone.

Salome only made a slight dissenting and almost contemptuous gesture with one hand in reply to this remark.

Mrs. Lamkin now entered with a very shiny three-pint pail in her hand. She would not offer the pail to the girl, lest the movement might be taken as a hint for her to go; she therefore placed it on the table.

"Do you really think you sh'll go to Floridy?" she asked, with something like awe in her interest.

"Yes; but it's all uncertain yet. Father said he should know in a day or two. He's got some arrangements to make."

The three women sat in profound silence for a few moments. It was impressive to be in the presence of a girl who actually expected to go "down South."

"You ain't goin' alone, I s'pose?" Mrs. Lamkin suggested.

"Oh no; mother'll go if I do. We shall have to go as cheaply as we can, you know. We shall have to manage." Here she smiled, as she added: "But we are Yankees, and we ought to be able to manage."

"Don't you dread it?" inquired one.

Salome rose. She moved to the table and took the tin pail.

"Dread it!" she exclaimed. "No, indeed. I long to go." She turned to her hostess. "I'm afraid you've robbed yourself, Mrs. Lamkin," she said; "this pail is full."

"No, I ain't. But don't you be in a hurry—or are you afraid your beau'll git tired of waiting?"

"My beau?" repeated Salome. "Oh, you mean Dick Chapin. No; he won't get tired. He likes to wait. Mother'll be so glad of this sweet pickle! Good-bye."

Salome walked quickly out of the room.

The three women immediately rose and went to the windows, being careful to stand back a little, so that they would not be seen in case either of the young people outside should glance at the house. But they did not glance that way.

Dick Chapin raised himself from the gate against which he had been resting. He stepped forward and took the tin pail.

"Well, what did the Lamkin woman want?" he asked.

"She wanted to send mother that pickle. But what they wanted most of all was to find out how much Dr. Bowdoin charged for coming here from Boston, and if I'm going to Florida."

Young Chapin gave a disdainful sniff, and he swung the pail in a way dangerous to its contents.

"They?" he asked—"who's they? Did the Lamkin have company?"

"She had callers with go-to-meeting bonnets on—Mrs. Sprague and Mrs. Scudder."

"Mrs. Scudder is an old cat! Did she purr at you or scratch you?"

As the young man put this question he turned and looked solicitously at his companion.

But Salome did not seem to see the look. She was walking with a serious air, with her gaze fixed directly in front of her.

At last Dick turned away, with a disappointed expression growing on his face.

"You don't seem to know I'm with you," he said, sharply.

"I know you're spilling that sweet pickle," she answered, making a spring towards the pail and seizing it.

"Oh, confound the old stuff!" he responded. "You think more of that than you do of me."

"Mother thinks more of it," Salome answered. She glanced into his eyes as she added, "and it's made of Bicknell pears, too."

As he met her glance the young fellow flushed up to his hair. He laughed; he half stopped in his walk and then made a step nearer Salome, who did not pause, but who continued to go straight on.

"Of course I want your mother to like me," he began.

"I should think so," interrupted the girl. "You'd better. Mother can see right through anybody."

Dick gave a half groan. "I wish you could see right through me, S'lome."

He waited a little; then he asked, "Don't you want to know why I wish so?"

Salome shook her head. "No; I never did have much curiosity."

"Curiosity! Oh, S'lome, you're awful hard on a fellow!"

Salome laughed in the most cheerful manner. Her laugh was interrupted by a slight cough.

"I don't know why I'm hard on you just because I don't want to see through you," she remarked.

Dick Chapin's rosy, comfortable face was very melancholy as he kept it turned towards his companion.

"Oh, S'lome!" he cried, "you are just like ice and iron and stones, and all those horrid things. I can't melt you a bit; I can't stand it—I can't! And now you're going down South, and I might just as well go and hang myself first as last."

"It seems to me I wouldn't hang myself, if I were you," responded Salome, maintaining her cheerfulness. "You might be awful sorry if you did."

"Well, if I was sorry I shouldn't know it; there 'd be that comfort in it," said the young man; and then he added, with great unction, "the main thing would be to make you sorry, S'lome."

The girl laughed again, but she made no other reply.

After a long silence, during which the pail of sweet pickle was once more nearly wrecked and once more rescued, Dick Chapin suddenly paused in the middle of the dusty highway. There was so much emphasis in the way he stood still that his companion instantly paused also and turned inquiringly towards him.

The sunlight fell over the girl and full upon her face, intensifying its lovely, youthful tinge, and sharpening the delicate outlines.

"Well?" she said, a little impatiently.

"I can't stand it!" said Dick Chapin, in a tone which was almost ferocious, and which contrasted comically with his round face.

Salome shrugged her shoulders slightly in a way she had, which was not in the least a Yankee way.

"I'm sorry you can't stand it," she said, "but I don't know what's going to be done about it."

"I know what's to be done, S'lome, and you've got to do it."

"Oh?" questioningly from the girl. "Is that so? Why, Dick, I never knew you so mysterious before, nor so interesting."

"I'm glad I'm interesting," said Dick, "and I hope I shall grow more and more so; because you've got to promise to marry me, S'lome."

On the last sentence Dick's voice sank so as to be almost inaudible.

He put forth his disengaged hand and grasped the girl's arm. She stood quite still, not attempting to move from his hold.

She was thinking that it was the first time any man had ever asked to be engaged to her, and that the moment was not thrilling in the least. But perhaps that was because Dick Chapin had a tin pail of sweet pickle in one hand. She wished he had put that pail down; it made him ridiculous.

"You've got to, S'lome," he repeated.

"Oh dear!" she exclaimed, almost involuntarily; "why don't you drop that pail?"

Dick's jaw fell at the irrelevancy of this remark. He knew in an indefinite manner that girls were the strangest things in the world. Just now he felt that it was useless to try to understand any of them, particularly Salome Gerry.

"The pail?" he gasped; "why, I thought you were specially careful about this sweet pickle, 'cause your mother likes it."

"But it makes you ridiculous," she retorted swiftly. "You've no idea how you look, standing there proposing to me with that three-pint bucket of Mrs. Lamkin's, and your face as round and—and rosy as if you were asking me the price of apples."

"Gracious!" gasped Dick. Then he began to explain that he could feel just as much as if his face were a yard long, and he thought she was as cruel as she could be; and he hoped she knew what she meant, for he'd be dumbed if he knew anything about it.

At this stage in his remarks Salome made the assertion that she didn't mean anything.

"Then I wish you wouldn't happen to choose such kind of words, as long as you don't mean 'em," he retorted.

She began to walk rapidly now.

In a few moments they reached a place where there was a gap in the wall from which a much-worn path led across a field.

The two turned towards this gap.

"There's no need of your coming any farther," she said.

"I don't expect there is," he replied, "but I'm coming all the same; and I'm going to set my pail down on that flat stone by the pine-tree. I can set it down, and I guess you can make my face long enough if you go on this way. When we get to that pine-tree, S'lome, I'm going to ask you again to marry me. This is one of the things I know my own mind about, and I'm going to know yours, too."

TWO KINDS OF LOVERS

For the first time in her acquaintance with Dick Chapin, Salome forgot to think that he was not tall enough, and that he looked too much like a girl. She gave him a side glance which was full of curiosity. She walked demurely by his side with her eyes fixed upon the pine-tree as the spot where her companion was again going to propose to her. It was all very funny, but her face was now set in a somewhat puritanical expression, which was often visible upon it.

It had never occurred to her that Dick would want to become engaged to her. Her mind did not go further at present than an engagement. Yes, it certainly was funny.

And here was the pine-tree.

As Dick leaned forward to set his pail down, the girl said, hastily:

"I guess we ought to be going right along."

"And I guess we can stay a minute," he answered, "and p'raps I sha'n't have another chance."

He had carefully placed the sweet pickle on a flat stone, and had assured himself that it would not "joggle," as he said, inwardly. Then he stood up quite straight.

Salome continued to look like a little Puritan, but

2

she felt a distressful inclination to laugh and to ask Dick Chapin if he might not better take ether. This idea of taking ether became so prominent in her mind that she was almost afraid she should grow hysterical if the interview continued many minutes longer. But her aspect revealed nothing of this inclination.

"I want you to be engaged to me."

Young Chapin spoke in a voice which was rather loud, from his desire to make it impressive. Before he could be answered he went on still more loudly:

"Now you're going to Florida you'll be seeing lots of fellows, and I want this thing understood before you start. We can be married when you come back, you know; and we can write to each other. It'll be awful hard on me to have you gone, but we can write. Do you know how long it takes for a letter to go?"

Salome had now almost turned her back upon him.

"No, I don't," she answered.

"Well," he went on, "I should think we might write once a week, shouldn't you?"

Notwithstanding the assurance in the words he used the young man's appearance was anything but assured. His hands, shut tightly, hung down by his side; his eyes were strained, and he bent forward with a piteous air towards the girl, who did not look at him at all now.

"Don't you think we might write once a week?" he repeated, not speaking so loudly, and feeling that there was something not very encouraging in Salome's shoulder and back.

Salome was gradually recovering from that hysterical inclination to laugh.

"I don't see why you want to talk like this," she

said at last, now turning fully towards him. "I'm not going to be engaged to you."

"Why not?" sharply.

"Because—because it wouldn't be right."

She spoke hesitatingly, and looked entreatingly at him as if to ask him not to say any more. She was beginning to be extremely uncomfortable. The only clear idea in her mind now was to do what was exactly right.

"Yes, 'twill, too!" he cried, eagerly. "It'll be just right. Say you'll be engaged to me—do!"

"But I sha'n't."

The reply came with what seemed a cruel abruptness.

The young man shrank back a step.

"Oh, S'lome, you can't mean that," he said; "why won't you?"

"Why do you want to make me tell?" she answered. "Do you think I like to tell?"

She was gazing at him solemnly now. There was no color in her face, save that her lips were so scarlet that the delicate skin seemed too thin to keep the vivid blood within it.

Dick Chapin again nearly groaned. "How do I know what you like?" he cried out. "But I know awful well what I like and what I want."

Salome's face grew even more intensely solemn.

"I wish you'd stop talking that way, Dick Chapin," she said, "for I don't love you the least bit in the world. That's why it would be wrong to be engaged to you. You see you've made me tell you right out."

It was a moment before Dick spoke. Then he asked, in a whisper,

"S'lome, is that a fact?"

"Yes, it is."

The young man turned and took up the tin pail. Then he set it down again on the flat stone. His face showed that the idea which had just come to his mind was quite terrible to him.

"P'raps you're going to be engaged to Walter Redd. Oh, you needn't be mad; and of course you needn't tell if you don't want to. Has he asked you?"

"No; he hasn't. I'm going home now."

Salome moved away with decision. Dick caught up the tin pail again.

"He's sure to ask you," he went on, hurrying to the girl's side. "He's been in love with you ever since he came to the town."

No answer from the girl save her slight shrug of the shoulders.

"I don't blame anybody for being in love with you," he said.

Another shrug, and silence. Salome ran a great risk of falling over the stones of the pasture, she went at such a headlong gait.

"I shall spill this sweet pickle as sure's I'm alive, if you go on like this," at last remarked Dick.

"You're not obliged to go so fast," was the response, without any pause.

"I know it, but I'm going with you."

There was nothing more said until the two came out into the road opposite the Gerry house. Then Salome paused and took the pail.

"I'm ever so much obliged to you."

She spoke so gently that Dick started visibly and looked hopefully at her. But his look instantly sank.

"You're very welcome," he replied. "Good-bye."

"Good-bye," still with the utmost gentleness.

He lingered.

"If you don't mean anything," he said, "I wish you wouldn't speak like that."

"Like what?" in astonishment.

"Why, in that kind of a voice, just as if you—just as if—"

Dick Chapin paused, unable to go on.

"Just as if I what?" persisted Salome.

"Just as if you almost loved me. Oh, S'lome, if you do like me just a little, you know, we can be engaged, and when you are really engaged you'll begin to like me better and better. Don't you think so?"

There was a perceptible hesitation in the girl's manner. She was wondering if that was the way people became engaged, and if then they became more fond of each other. But it did not seem right.

She put her hand unconsciously up to her chest.

"No; I don't think so," she said, decisively.

"Then if you don't think so," returned Dick, speaking with more power than he had yet used, "you must not say anything in that kind of a voice, I tell you. I can't stand it—I can't stand it."

She looked at him in a bewildered way. She had not the least idea what he meant.

Still the young man lingered. Salome wondered how she had had any inclination to laugh. She almost wanted to sob now.

"I've got to go over to the Falls next week," he said, "and it's most likely I sh'll have to stay right along. I can have a steady job there. So I sha'n't see you again."

Salome again put her hand up to her chest.

"I thought you only just liked me," she said, her eyes now fixed on his face.

"Liked you!"

He could not say any more. He gave her one look straight down into her eyes, then he hurried along the road.

Salome hastened across the broad sweep of fading grass up to the house. As she placed her foot on the step the door opened swiftly, and her mother put out her hand and drew her daughter within the house.

"Child," she said, anxiously, "the wind is east; it's been east for more than an hour."

"It's no matter, mother. I haven't felt it at all."

Salome sat down quickly. Her mother snuffed at the sweet pickle, and said she guessed Salome had been to Mrs. Lamkin's. Then she sat down in a chair which she drew close to her daughter. She took off the girl's hat and brushed back the loose locks which fell over the intent face. Salome looked up at the woman. The strong brown eyes which met her gaze seemed to radiate strength and rest into her palpitating frame.

She leaned back in the calico covered rocker, keeping the hard, rough hand in hers.

"Your father's seen Uncle John," said Mrs. Gerry.

Salome suddenly sat upright. But she grasped her mother's hand still more closely.

"Oh, mother!" she exclaimed.

Then it appeared as if she could say nothing more.

Mrs. Gerry smoothed the slender fingers that lay in her palm.

"Uncle John promised that he'd lend four hundred dollars," she said, "but he should want a mortgage on the east wood-lot."

"Then we're going, mother? We are going?"

The young voice was so full of intense hope and joy that Mrs. Gerry smiled as she answered:

"Yes, we're going, and the sooner the better. But Uncle John is a hard man, a hard man."

Salome was too young, too full of the egotism of youth to care much on what conditions the money was obtained, since it was obtained, and she was going to Florida.

She left her chair. She began to walk about the room.

She coughed two or three times, but she did not seem to know that she did so.

"Yes, indeed, the sooner the better!" she exclaimed, her whole face radiant.

All at once it occurred to her that it was selfish to think only of the mere fact of her going. She stopped in front of her mother; she bent over her, putting a hand on each arm of the chair.

"Will it be very bad for father, giving that mortgage?" she asked. "I must be real mean not to think of that the very first thing. But, don't you know, mother, when I get well—" here she began walking again, "when I am well I shall get some kind of a position, and I shall earn money, and then I shall help father. I've always wished I could help him somehow. Here I am almost twenty-three, and except that year I made chain from the jeweller's I've never earned anything. I suppose I ought to have kept on making chain."

"You know it didn't agree with you; you know how it made your side ache," said Mrs. Gerry.

But Salome did not hear her. She had paused by the window, and was looking intently out into a large

oak-tree which stood in the yard, its dry leaves rust-
ling.   The red of the setting sun was upon it.

"To the South !" she cried, suddenly ; "why, it's like
a dream, isn't it, mother?   I know I shall get well."

"I wish you wouldn't talk like that, Salome," said
Mrs. Gerry, sharply.   Then she laughed constrainedly
as she added, "You know it isn't a good sign to say
such things."

"No matter about signs, you old mother !" cried
Salome.   She took two or three sliding, waltzing
steps across the floor.   Her eyes deepened.

> "'Tis the clime of the South, 'tis the land of the sun—
>   Can he smile on such deeds as his children have done?'"

She recited these words in a thin, sweet soprano
voice ; then she turned towards the elder woman and
asked :

"What does that mean, anyway, mother?   It
sounds delightfully wicked, doesn't it ?"

"Salome, nothing is delightfully wicked," returned
Mrs. Gerry, with some anxiety.   "Byron was wicked
enough, but he was very far from being delightful to
himself."

"But he was delightful to other people, wasn't he ?
And that's the thing, you know; to have people love
you."

"No, it's not the thing at all," quickly returned her
mother, with asperity.   "Don't you get such an idea
into your head."

Salome stood in the middle of the room looking down
at her mother.   There was a certain expression on her
face which made it quite impossible to believe that the
same face had ever had anything Puritanical in it.

"The only thing is to be right; it's the only thing in the world."

Mrs. Gerry spoke with an almost passionate emphasis.

Salome came quickly and knelt down by her mother's side, laying her arms across her mother's lap.

"You've certainly brought me up right," she said, warmly.

"Oh, I don't know," answered Mrs. Gerry, again pushing back the hair from the child's forehead; "I hope so. If I've lived as I ought, and you have felt my life, why, then you've been brought up well."

Mrs. Gerry smiled now in a way that changed her worn face back into what might have been its youthful look.

"You've always been such a good girl, Salome. Sometimes I've thought you were too conscientious. So I was startled to have you speak sort of—sort of carelessly just now. You know there is such a thing as having a morbid conscience. I've been afraid you had it."

Salome smiled vividly. She rose to her feet. It seemed impossible now for her to remain any time in one position.

"I've had times of thinking so myself," she exclaimed with a laugh; "thinking I was too good to live, you know, and that I must grow just a little wicked if I wanted to spend much time on this earth. Those old Sunday-school books that Aunt Eudora talks about so much have taught me one thing: if you want to live you mustn't be too good. Now, don't you worry, mother; you know I'm only in fun. The thought of really going to Florida has set me wild."

Again the girl took two or three waltzing steps over the old carpet.

She paused in the middle of the floor.

"We sha'n't need any heavy flannels, shall we, mother?" she asked; "and my old jacket will do, though you've always said it wasn't thick enough. And when shall we actually start?" she asked.

"I've set the time for a week from to-day. I'm in a hurry to get you off. The frosts are so sharp now—"

Salome clasped her hands—

"'Tis the clime of the South, 'tis the land of the sun,'"

she interrupted; "oh, I know I shall get well!"

All day the mother and daughter talked of their journey. They worked about the house, Salome performing the lighter labor; and all day they planned and planned, the girl with an almost ominous exuberance of spirits—at least, Mrs. Gerry was afraid it was ominous.

Neither had been much more than a score of miles from home, except that the mother had once been to Portland by boat, and the sea-sickness she had experienced made her now afraid to go to Florida by steamer, though that way was the cheapest of all the routes she had studied. What if they should both be sick and she not able to take care of Salome?

That was her constant thought—if she should not be able to take care of Salome. As for the girl, she did not care which way she went, and she was again planning how she would earn money when she came back. She said she wished she had some vocation; she didn't know as she could do one thing better than another. If she could only paint, or sing, or make verses.

Thus she prattled on as she went here and there about the house. Her cheeks grew flushed at last and her eyes still more bright.

Mr. Gerry was not to be at home until the next day. He had driven twenty miles to meet " Uncle John " for the final arrangements about the mortgage, and to get the four hundred dollars.

When at last supper was eaten, the dishes washed, and Salome was lying on the lounge in the sitting-room, there came an imperative knock at the front door.

" I do hope we sha'n't have company to-night," exclaimed Mrs. Gerry.

She took the lamp and went into the entry. Salome sat up and passed her hands over her hot face.

The next moment a tall young man followed her mother into the room. He had on a long, rough overcoat, and he looked immense in size as he stood there; it seemed as if he were magnified in the light of the lamp which Mrs. Gerry now replaced on the table.

He held a gray cap in his hand, and this cap he shifted from one hand to the other several times before he sat down.

The chair almost creaked under him, and his coat lay in a long fold on the floor on each side of him. This was Walter Redd. He had a swarthy face, with black eyes and brows. His mouth was small, and there was a slight protruding of the under lip, which gave him the appearance of a person who always had his own way. But perhaps, after all, it was only his great size which produced that impression. We are not yet so enlightened but that bulk of body gives the idea of power.

Mrs. Gerry resumed her seat and the stocking she was mending for her husband. She said it was getting cold, but then one must expect chilly weather the last of October. Then she glanced at the visitor and suggested that he take off his greatcoat; he'd be very uncomfortable if he sat with it on.

Walter Redd rose and divested himself of a garment which must have we'ghed a good many pounds.

When he sat down again he wiped his face with a handkerchief that was yet in its immaculate folds. He remarked that Mr. Barstow had had more than two barrels of cranberries frostbitten because he had been so slack about having them picked. But then Mr. Barstow was slack about everything.

Possibly one might at first have thought that young Redd was diffident, but he was not in the least, even though he might be awkward. And he was not what we used to call "forward," either.

Mrs. Gerry, with the blue woollen sock drawn over one hand, and her darning-needle in the other, looked for one questioning instant at the young man as he spoke. Then she glanced at her daughter.

Salome had moved to the head of the lounge, had pulled the balsam pillow up under one arm, and was leaning heavily upon it. She was not looking at Redd; her eyes were fixed apparently on her red wool slippers, which showed beyond her skirt.

"It seems too bad to lose cranberries," now responded Mrs. Gerry, when she perceived that Salome was not going to reply. "They bring a good price this year."

"First-rate price," said Redd.

He reached forward and put his cap on the table.

His hand showed large and well formed, but rough with out-door work.

"I've made over fifty dollars on that little bog I bought of the Curtis heirs."

"Have you?" said Mrs. Gerry, cordially; "why, Walter, that's doing real well."

"So I thought. I was pleased enough about it."

Thus far the young man had not looked at Salome save with the instantaneous glance which had told him she was in the room when the two had nodded at each other on his entrance.

Now his eyes swept deliberately over her, and were only removed when they had reached the red wool slippers.

At that stage in the gaze his dark face seemed to deepen a very little in color, but it was unmoved otherwise.

"How's your health now, Salome?" he asked.

The girl was very weary of being asked about her health, but she replied, politely,

"Thank you; I think I'm full as well."

"I think she is better, if anything," said her mother, quickly.

Salome's face was quietly set in its most ordinary look, a serious, what one might almost call a conscientious, look, and which aided a certain tendency to coldness in her expression which the sensitive features and eyes could not quite contradict.

"They were telling down to the store this afternoon," said Redd, "that you was both going to Florida. Is that true?"

The young man was carefully trying to speak correctly, and he usually succeeded.

Each of the women waited for the other to reply, so

there was a slight pause before Mrs. Gerry said she supposed it was true. They had had Dr. Bowdoin, and he advised that Salome spend the winter in Florida; he thought she would be completely cured of her weak chest. On the whole, as he seemed so positive, they were going to make a great effort and go.

"I wish father could afford it," exclaimed Salome, with emphasis. She added that when she came back she should earn money herself, so that things would get even after a while. She asked Redd if he didn't think it would be a good plan for her to begin to learn type-writing while she was in Florida, so that she might go right to work when she returned. She wished she knew just what would be best.

She lifted the little fir balsam pillow and put her face in it, inhaling strongly its perfume.

Redd did not look at her. He addressed his reply to her mother.

"Girls seem to do most anything now," he said.

Having made this remark, he lasped into complete silence. He sat with apparent calmness, as if not caring how long the silence lasted. He had the appearance of having the waiting power well developed.

When he did speak it was quite to his purpose, and he again addressed Mrs. Gerry.

"I called here to-night," he said, "because I wanted to see Salome specially. May I see her?"

Mrs. Gerry gathered her scissors and her ball of blue mending yarn from the stand. She refrained from looking at her daughter.

"I'll go right into the kitchen," she responded. "It's warm there."

She walked out of the room. Walter Redd remained sitting almost immovably in his chair. Salome held her pillow again to her face. She was fighting against a strong impulse to follow her mother into the next room. She was afraid Redd was looking at her. She wanted to make some quick, impatient movement. But she was almost as motionless as her companion. Almost—for there was a kind of suggestion of movement in her, while he was as without stir as a log.

Why is it that those who can remain apparently inert have such an advantage over the beings who quiver with evident life? Why should *vis inertiæ* conquer so often in this world?

Salome supposed he was going to ask to be engaged to her. She thought it was rather strange that she, who had never before had a proposal in her life, should now have two in one day.

She wondered what those girls to whom men were constantly proposing did in the circumstances. She wished she knew some one to ask.

But those whom she knew had received proposals had always said "yes." The matter would be perfectly simple, and she would need no advice if she were always going to say "yes."

After a while the silence, the perfect stillness became almost unbearable; Salome glanced quickly at the man who sat there opposite her.

She found that he was gazing openly and unswervingly at her. She wondered irritably how much longer he would do that, and she could not ask him what he wanted, since he must see her "specially," as he had said.

She sat upright now, and put her pillow on the lounge with a decided motion. She told herself that she would not endure this much longer. What did Walter Redd mean by coming here and sitting like that?

If another moment passed in this way she would open the kitchen door and call her mother.

Now Walter spoke.

"I s'pose you know what I've come for, Salome."

"No, I don't know, either," she answered.

"Now, don't say that," he rejoined, "because you ain't stupid one bit, and you know I asked your mother to go out, or just the same as asked her, so I could tell you I wanted to marry you. And that I came over just for that. I've meant to do it for some time, and when I heard them say you were going to Florida I made up my mind I'd—"

"Oh, I wish you'd stop!" interrupted Salome at this stage in Redd's remarks. Then she said, penitently, "I beg your pardon, Walter, but I'm very tired to-night."

"Well, I ain't going to tire you. Just tell me you'll marry me and I'll go right home."

As he said these words the young man leaned forward a little.

At the same time Salome shrank back. If she could only say "yes" how easily she could end the interview, she thought.

"But I can't tell you so," she answered.

"Of course you've known all along that I love you. Ain't you known that, Salome?"

"No; I haven't."

"I s'pose I must believe you, but I don't see how you could help knowing that—no; I don't see how you could help knowing that."

There was a curious weight and strength in the way

the young man spoke. His manner impressed Salome in a way that confused and mystified her. She was conscious of trying to gather herself as if for resistance. At the same time there was something strange and bewildering in her consciousness which pleaded—she did not know for what it pleaded.

She did not think Redd's last remark called for any reply, and she did not attempt to make any.

Redd still maintained the same position, bending forward towards her. He seemed in no hurry to speak again.

Salome sat there in front of him. She heard her mother open the kitchen stove and put in wood. She held herself on the lounge by a distinct and painful effort of her will. She felt the veins in her neck begin to beat painfully, and that constriction which was so much of the time across her chest was greater than ever now.

If Redd should remain many more minutes she could not answer for what she should do.

"I wish you knew how I love you," he finally said. No answer.

"But I can't tell you," he went on. "I haven't got any words. All there is to me loves you. It's all been so strange since the first of my knowing you. I ain't hardly known myself. Salome, I don't see but what I've got to have you. I've got to have you."

He sat perfectly still as he spoke these words. His quietness of body contrasted indescribably with the emotion in his voice.

The girl turned suddenly and bent down to the head of the lounge, hiding her face in the cushion again, and quivering as she did so.

"I wish you'd go," she said, her voice muffled by

her position. "It's dreadful to have you talk like that."

"It's dreadful for me; I'm sure of that," he answered. "Do you really want me to go, Salome?"

"Yes."

Redd rose. He took his overcoat and put it over his arm.

"Don't you think you could bring yourself to marry me?" he asked.

"No," from the lounge.

"You're sure you know your own mind? They say girls are awful strange about knowing their own minds."

"I know mine."

He stood holding his coat and looking down at her; stood quietly and easily.

"Then of course I ought to go."

He did not move.

"But I don't see how I can give you up. Salome, I've got to have you. Don't you see, I've got to have you?"

The girl did not lift her head, did not move.

Redd carefully laid his coat down in the chair whence he had just taken it. He stepped over to the lounge and lifted the girl in his arms. It was useless for her to struggle. She did not. She only averted her face against his shoulder and was still.

"Salome, ain't there any chance that you've made a mistake?"

"No, no."

He held her for an instant. Then he put her carefully back on the couch. He stood looking down at her.

"I won't plague you any more now, Salome," he

said, "but I'm going to hope you'll change your mind.
I don't know anything about women, but everybody
says they are quite likely to change their minds. So
I sha'n't give up. I wouldn't give a cent for my life
if I gave up thinking about you."

He put on his coat, shaking his broad shoulders
into it. He took his cap; he passed it from one
hand to the other as he had done when he came in.

"I'm going in a minute. I wanted to say something about that fifty dollars I made on that cranberry
bog. I sha'n't need it; I'm doing first-rate. I know
your father's got to reckon pretty close to send you
to Florida. You just let me give that money to your
mother. It might make things a little easier for you.
It'll do me a lot of good if you will; more'n you know.
And I sha'n't think you under any obligation. You
can pay it back when you get to earning, you know,
if you want to."

It was a moment before Salome said:

"I know how kind you are, Walter; but we can get
along real well without it."

She sat up now. She put her hands to her cheeks
for an instant. Then she looked up in the young
man's face.

He met the glance, then turned with a quicker
movement than he had yet made.

"Well, good-bye," he said.

III

ANTINOUS

Sitting by the cook-stove, where, like an American
mother, she had retreated that a young man might
have an opportunity to ask her daughter to marry
him, Mrs. Gerry forgot to go on with the mending of
her husband's socks. She sat with one stocking on
her hand with her finger through a large hole. But
the hand lay idly on her lap. Her eyes were fixed
on the blaze of the lamp, and her mouth was shut
tightly.

At last she leaned her head back on the chair, and
took a long breath.

"Salome will do what she thinks is right, anyway,"
she thought. " She always was such a conscientious
little thing, and such a spirited little thing ; only lately her not being well has kept her down, somehow,
and she ain't seemed like herself."

The sound of steps, and then of a door closing,
made her start up quickly. She hurriedly drew off
the stocking from her hand and almost flung it on
the stand. She stood up. Then she waited, fearing
that her daughter might want to be alone; or perhaps
the girl would come to her.

Several moments passed. There was no sound,
and Mrs. Gerry could bear it no longer. She walked
to the door and opened it softly. Salome was lying

on the lounge as if she were asleep. But her eyelashes directly lifted. She sat up, and gave a short,
nervous laugh. The laugh terminated in a cough.

Mrs. Gerry sat down by the girl. Salome leaned
her shoulder against her mother.

"If you want to learn how much folks think of you,
just let them know you're going away," she remarked.

Mrs.Gerry said nothing. Her face showed her anxiety.

"First, 'twas Dick Chapin, and now it's Walter
Redd," went on Salome ; "and, oh, mother, it isn't any
fun at all to be proposed to. Some of the girls talk
as if it were fun, but then they said 'yes,' " returning
in her mind to her former thought on this subject.

"And you didn't say 'yes ?' "

"Oh no, of course not," in surprise ; "why
should I ?"

"I didn't know how you felt, Salome. I've wondered a good deal about it, but I didn't want to ask
you. And you don't care for either of them ?"

"No, indeed ; why should I ?" again. "Besides,"
laughing and coughing, "you know Aunt Endora says
a woman never ought to love any man but her husband, and I haven't got any husband. Mother, I wish
we could start for Florida to-morrow."

Mrs. Gerry wondered if Salome would give any
more particulars concerning the incidents of the day ;
but she did not.

And every hour after seemed to be filled with prep-
arations for their journey, and for the limited house-
keeping they were arranging for.

Every neighbor called with profuse offerings of advice. Not one of them had ever been in Florida, but
all felt competent to give a good deal of instruction.

The advice and the instruction, oddly enough, chiefly hinged upon flannels and overshoes — "rubbers." Everybody was afraid the Gerrys would not take sufficient of these safeguards against the climate and the storms.

Mrs. Lamkin even went so far as to make and bring over, as a token of friendship, a pair of red flannel under - vests, made from something which seemed about a quarter of an inch thick. These were for Salome to wear when she was really settled down for the winter.

During the conversation it transpired that these vests were made from some garments which Mr. Lamkin had been obliged to discard on account of the superlative degree of the power of shrinking inherent in them.

Mrs. Lamkin explained how she herself had washed these "robins," as she called them. She went into the minutest detail as to this process of washing, and she ended by saying that she never took so much pains with anything in her life, and she didn't see how under the sun they managed to shrink so.

"But there's one thing about it, Mis' Gerry, you can be sure they can't shrink any more. 'Tain't possible. And they'll wear forever."

Mrs. Gerry took a fold of the stuff between her thumb and forefinger. She expressed a polite hope that Mrs. Lamkin had not robbed herself.

That lady replied "that she knew they'd jest lay 'n' git all moth-eaten, and so she had made them up for S'lome, S'lome having a weak chest, so."

Salome sat quite still during this call, her thin, earnest face somewhat averted from the woman who had brought this gift.

When Mrs. Lamkin had departed the girl rose, and, lifting one of the made-over robins, she shook it out and dangled it in front of her mother. She did not now smile in the least, but her eyes danced in a sparkling light.

"Put it down, Salome," said her mother, sharply. "Mrs. Lamkin is really fond of you; and she means well; and it must have been a lot of work."

Salome obeyed. While she was folding the garment the door opened again, and Mrs. Scudder came in.

This lady, when seen without her best bonnet and kid gloves, was not nearly so imposing. Even the folds of gray hair on each side of her face seemed to have diminished in size. But her pale eyes stood out just the same, and her voice was so soft that one almost expected to hear her purr.

"Mis' Sprague said you was really goin' to-morrer," she remarked, as she sat down. "Be you?"

"Yes, we expect to," answered Mrs. Gerry.

"Well, I should think you'd want to git off now; you're kind of unsettled, 'n' all tore up in your mind. I've been makin' some fried pies, 'n' I brought some. Mis' Sprague said you was goin' to take the victuals for your trip in a basket. They say it's dreadful expensive buyin' victuals on a journey, 'n' I knew you'd got to save money, of course."

Mrs. Scudder put a good-sized paper bag on the table. It showed some spots of grease, and its odor also revealed that it was the receptacle of the fried pies.

"They're real nourishin', if you can digest um," she said. "They're mince. I knew consumptive folks could eat most anything. It's the mince-meat

I'm going to make my Thanksgiving pies of. I guess
it's kind of decent. How be ye, S'lome? Do ye
perk up any thinkin' of your journey?"

"I believe I perk up a little, thank you," answered
the girl, gravely.

"I s'pose that's excitement," responded Mrs. Scudder. "I hope you won't git so excited that you'll
all cave in when you git there."

"I hope I sha'n't cave in," replied Salome.

Her mother looked at her anxiously, but the girl's
demeanor was irreproachable.

"Dick Chapin's gone over to the Falls," remarked
Mrs. Scudder. "Mrs. West said he was awful down
to the heel. I told her I guessed I knew why."

Mrs. Scudder's eyes roamed over Salome's face, but
Salome, though her face might have a feverish color
in it, rarely blushed.

She did not blush now.

"Do you put lemon-peel in your mince-meat?"

Mrs. Gerry asked this question somewhat hastily,
and she listened with absorbed attention to the reci-
tals of the conditions under which Mrs. Scudder
thought lemon-peel ought to be put into pie-meat.

The conversation was kept strictly within pie-meat
limits until Mrs. Scudder rose to go. Then she said
that she had almost forgotten one of the main things
she had come for, and that was to warn the Gerrys
to look out for snakes when they got to Floridy.
Southern countries were full of snakes, she had understood. She suggested the constant wearing of
rubber boots. She said Mr. Scudder had several
pairs of rubber boots which he had got through with,
they having become leaky. But their leaking didn't
make any difference in their repelling power as re-

garded snakes. Should she send Mr. Scudder over with some of these boots? They, the Gerry's, could have them as well as not.

Seeing her mother hesitate in her first helpless amazement, Salome hastened to say that her father had some old rubber boots which they might use, but that they were just as much obliged to Mrs. Scudder.

And the visitor departed. Salome turned to her mother. She looked intently in her face for an instant, then she dropped on to the lounge and laughed until the laugh was turned into a cough.

It was very early the next morning when they started.

Many of us know how desolate an early start is. Particularly is it so in the fall or winter.

Unable to sleep, Mrs. Gerry rose at four o'clock. She shiveringly dressed by the light of a little kerosene lamp, while Mr. Gerry, by the light of another little lamp, was making a fire in the cook-stove. His face, seen dimly, was set in the most gloomy expression. He hurried out to the barn with the milk-pail. By six o'clock the horse must be harnessed, and they must start for the station so that the travellers could be in Boston in time for the express to New York.

Mr. Gerrry was going to do his own work while his wife and daughter were gone; he could not afford to have a house-keeper. Now, as he pitched the hay into the mangers, he felt that affairs were too bad to be borne. He could do his own work, or leave it undone; but to stay there and worry about Salome—he really did not know what would become of him.

He was a little man, with a narrow face and dreamy-looking eyes; it was a face that showed at the first glance that the owner of it would never be " forehanded," and it was a face that would win love from a strong nature, and it had won—and kept—his wife's love through many trying years.

Very little was said at that morning meal. Mr. Gerry found it difficult to speak. He was continually gazing at Salome. His conversation was mostly confined to urging the girl to drink more milk, and to say that she'd be awful faint travelling if she didn't take all the milk she could.

And Salome tried to drink the milk, though it was very hard to swallow. She was looking at her father and meeting his eyes, then dropping her own. He heaped his plate with food, took up his knife and fork with an air of ferocious appetite, suddenly put them down, pushed back from the table, and said he must go and harness.

When the door closed behind him, Salome clasped her hands together with a gesture that was not like the gesture of a Yankee girl. She turned her face towards her mother.

"Oh, it's awful hard on father!" she exclaimed. "It makes me feel wicked."

Mrs. Gerry was conscientiously and persistently trying to eat her breakfast that she might keep up her strength. Whatever happened, she knew that she must be strong.

"I know it's hard on him," she said, "but it's nobody's fault. Don't feel wicked."

In a moment Mrs. Gerry rose from the table. She went into the "L" and stood an instant at the open door. The stars were glittering in a clear, far, unsympathetic sky; but all over the eastern heavens there was coming the faint, blue light of the morning.

The cocks were crowing in the yards in the neighborhood.   The air was sharp with frost.

Mrs. Gerry loved that cold sky, and she liked the indescribable odor of the frost.

It was heart-breaking to her to leave her home.

She glanced towards the barn.   Through its dingy window she saw the glimmer of a light.   She half suppressed a sob that rose to her throat.

She suddenly lifted the skirt of her gown and flung it over her head and shoulders; then she ran out across the yard and entered the barn.   She ran as lightly as if she were no older than her daughter. Perhaps at that moment she felt no older; and there was a tinge of red on her face and a glow in her eyes as she hurried over the barn floor which was littered with " swale."

Mr. Gerry had been pitching away the horse's bed. His lantern was hung on a peg at the end of the stall. Instead of giving light the lantern seemed only to make deep and grotesque shadows.   The whole place was full of the strong odor of hay.

The man stepped out on to the floor.

"Why, Salome!" he exclaimed.

He dropped his pitchfork and advanced towards his wife.   He put one arm about her.

" Oh, Lyman," she whispered, " it's so hard to go! And how lonesome you'll be!"

He did not speak immediately.   Then he said, with tremulous cheerfulness :

" Don't you worry, Salome.   I don't expect to be real gay, but I've made up my mind to weather it somehow.   If only the child gets well—"

" Yes, yes," interrupted Mrs. Gerry, trying to resume her usual manner.   " But I didn't mean to give way so; I've got to have all my strength. I feel sure," with great cheerfulness, "that the child will be ever so much better. I'll run back now. You'd better harness right away."

Mr. Gerry led out the horse. He flung the breast-plate and traces over the animal's back. Then he could not see. He leaned against the old meal chest, putting both hands over his face with a feminine gesture.

The horse reached down to the floor and began nosing about for a wisp of sweet hay, the long leather straps dragging here and there as it did so. Then it got its forefoot on one of the traces, and its head was held because the breast-plate had fallen to its ears.

Mr. Gerry dashed his hands down. He sprang forward and struck the horse's leg lightly. He went on harnessing with great haste.

As he buckled the last strap he exclaimed, aloud,

" All there is about it is I've just got to stand it; and I'm willing to stand it, too."

It was a cold, early daylight when the two women said an apparently calm good-bye to Mr. Gerry on the platform of the little station. The cars were sweeping around the curve just north of them. The instant they stopped the conductor sprang out and said,

" All aboard !"

The solitary trunk was swung in the baggage-car. Mrs. Gerry and her daughter hurried up the steps with the hand-satchel and with the large basket of lunch, which they hoped would serve them until they reached Jacksonville.

Mr. Gerry, on the platform, caught one more glimpse of them through the window of the car; then the train had glided on inexorably. He stood there alone.

The station-master came up to him, meaning to be friendly.

"Going to bach it, ain't ye, Gerry, now that the women folks are all gone?"

Gerry nodded.

"'Tain't no fun to bach it, now, I tell ye. I tried it when my wife's mother was sick. I'd ruther be whipped than do it agin. Folks goin' to be gone all winter?"

Again Gerry nodded. He began to walk away. This man's voice and words were intolerable to him.

The station-master kept by his side. He was telling himself that he was awful sorry for Gerry, and that he would cheer him up a little.

"S'lome'll come back bright's a button," he said. "Looks pretty bad now, that's a fact, but she'll be all right."

By this time Gerry had reached the place where his horse was hitched. He unfastened the rope eagerly. He felt as if he could not wait until he could get away from the man. As he put his foot on the wagon-step the other said:

"Did you see young Redd git aboard the train?"

He winked as he asked the question.

"No, I didn't." Gerry was now tucking the blanket about his legs.

"Jest as the cars had got under way Redd jumped over the fence the other side the track and swung on to the last car. Odd, how he never seems to hurry, but he's a feller that always gits there, I guess."

Mr. Gerry nodded. His horse started at a brisk pace towards home.

In the cars there were very few people. It was cold and desolate, the heat not having diffused itself.

The men sat with their hats drawn forward over their eyes, the women had a huddled look.

Notwithstanding Salome's longing to go South, she found the starting so melancholy that she would gladly have gone home and given up the journey.

So she felt for half an hour. Then the sun was higher. She ceased to think so poignantly of her father's face as he stood there while the train began to move.

The sun pushed its way through some fleecy clouds and shone out triumphantly in the clear blue of the heavens.

The girl turned to her mother; she was going to tell her that this sunshine was a good sign, but she did not speak. There was something in Mrs. Gerry's attitude that hushed the words on the girl's lips, and yet the woman was sitting up erect, with the large lunch-basket on her lap and her face turned straight ahead, her features calm.

"She is thinking of father," said the girl to herself, and she turned away conscious dimly of a surprised conviction that her father and mother loved each other.

Hitherto she had never thought about that possibility. They were very old in her eyes, too old to love much, anyway; but now a curious light came into her mind. This light made her heart beat more rapidly. With something like shyness she put out her hand and took her mother's hand, pressing it almost with violence for an instant, then dropping it. Her eyes were full of tears as she bent forward and whispered, quickly:

"Oh, mother, I didn't think how you'd hate to leave father! But we can write to him every day, you know. That'll be something to you—and to him, too, won't it?"

These swift words breathed so unexpectedly into her ear made Mrs. Gerry's face break from its set look and become trembling and soft.

She made a movement as if she would lean her head on the young shoulder so close to her. Then she restrained herself and took herself in hand.

She spoke cheerfully :

"Of course it'll be something for him and for me. We'll both write to him. You see, Salome, I never left him before since we were married—only to go over to Aunt Eudora's."

Mrs. Gerry smiled courageously at her daughter. She glanced from the window and said she was glad they had such good weather for the beginning of their journey. She was going to take it as a good sign. Then the eyes of mother and daughter met, and the two smiled at each other. After that smile the girl sank back in her seat in content.

She was starting for Florida. This knowledge made those huckleberry fields have an aspect which they had never had before. She wondered why they looked so strange. It seemed to her that this was the first time she had ever seen them. And the old farm-houses. She was already travelling through unknown countries.

After they had stopped at the first station, Salome felt that it was a very exciting thing to travel. She wondered how those men could sit with their hats over their eyes and never look through the window. And two girls across the aisle were talking incessantly, without apparently knowing they were travelling.

Suddenly those two looked behind them, glanced significantly at each other, and were silent.

Some one was coming along from the far end of the car. It was young Redd. He nodded at the two girls. Would he sit down in front and talk with them?

No; with that almost ponderous slowness of movement which was one of his characteristics, Redd let his tall frame down into the seat behind Salome and her mother.

"Glad you've got such a nice day," he said, leaning towards them.

"Yes," said Mrs. Gerry; "it makes it so much more cheerful."

She could not help looking curiously at the face behind her. She found it so calm, so impassive, that she could have doubted the reality of his love. And she felt a certain irritation against him that he should look so calm, for calmness so often gives the impression of assurance, or of stolidness.

Redd now settled himself comfortably, putting his arm along the back of his seat. He did not speak again for two hours, not until the train was going through some dingy suburbs preparatory to entering Boston. Then he leaned forward once more. He addressed Mrs. Gerry. He had not yet noticed Salome in the least.

"Going to New York by the Shore Line?"

"Yes."

"I wish you'd let me get your tickets and see about your trunks. It's a bother for women," he said.

When they had entered the station, the noise outside, the people going to and fro, so confused Mrs.

Gerry that she was very grateful that Redd happened to be with them. She gladly accepted his offer. She gave him her purse and the check to their one trunk, which Mr. Gerry had tied about with such a profusion of rope.

Then she sat down, and her head began to ache at the sight of the people walking, always walking.

But Salome did not sit down. She could not.

Redd had disappeared. Presently he came back. He gave Mrs. Gerry two long tickets. He put some bills into her hand. He said he had ventured to get a carriage; he explained that he was doing first-rate, and he could afford to spend a dollar once in a while. They would go right over to the other station, and the trunk would go with them. So they would make a sure thing of not having the trunk late.

He took the lunch-bag and the satchel and walked out to the entrance, the two women following.

He had not once looked at Salome.

They had not long to wait before the New York train was ready. How the people streamed in! Mrs. Gerry wondered that she had thought she could know how to travel. She was tormented by a desire to count the people.

Mr. Redd stood in the aisle of the car where he had conducted them.

"I've been looking up the trip," he said. "You know you go over to Jersey City. After that you won't change till you get to Washington. It's easy enough. You can't go wrong."

"Oh no," responded Mrs. Gerry; "of course it's easy. We shall be all right."

She had never felt so bewildered and helpless in her life. She didn't know it would be like this. If

4

she could only get used to the people and the strange noises.

"Perhaps you'd better take a sleeper right through from New York," remarked Redd. "They say folks don't get so tired, nearly."

"Oh no; we expect to get tired, and we can't afford a sleeper anyway. We've calculated on not having one. I'm so much obliged to you, Walter. But ain't you afraid you'll be taken along?" anxiously; "ain't we going to start?"

But Redd did not reply. For the first time he was looking at Salome. He stood solidly in his place, though the people were now crowding hurriedly past him.

A bell sounded. There was the cry of "All aboard!" outside. The cars gave a lurch.

The young man, with no appearance, even now, of haste, bent over Salome.

"Good-bye," he whispered. "I don't give you up. I never shall give you up. Good-bye."

He strode to the door. The cars were now gliding out of the station.

Mrs. Gerry watched him breathlessly. How foolish he had been to stay so long. He would get his neck broken. But no. There he was, safely outside the car, and looking up at her with a smile.

She smiled back at him. And somehow she was aware of a warm feeling in her heart for him, a feeling which she had not known before.

She turned and looked at her daughter. Salome's head was bent to her hand. She was pale; but no paler than was usual with her. As the mother gazed she saw a tremor of eyelid. Then suddenly Salome raised her head and met her mother's gaze.

"Do you know that we are on the way South?" asked the girl, joyously.

And with those words she seemed to fling from her everything but a kind of childish delight in the journey and in the object of it. She gazed at everything. She looked with never-ending interest at every person who entered the car; at the people who swarmed outside in the stations at the larger towns. Her face grew grave as she witnessed partings, or she smiled sympathetically when a friend met a friend.

Sometimes the young men in checked ulsters and brown derby hats, with russet bags hanging from their shoulders, turned to look a second time at the thin, sensitive face at the car window.

They thought that girl didn't know much about the world, and she had rather fine eyes; where was she going, anyway?

And one young man, who had devoted some time and attention to the subject, said that the old woman and that girl in the shabby jacket were going to Jacksonville; he had succeeded in seeing their tickets when the conductor had looked at them.

At this information the two others who formed a group near the door of the smoker laughed boisterously, and one of them exclaimed, as well as he could with a large cigar gripped between his teeth:

"You're going to Jacksonville, too, ain't you, Moore? I tell you," to the other member of the group, "Moore's always in luck."

Moore scowled at this and drew back slightly. There was some savageness in the tone in which he replied that he didn't suppose he was the only fellow on board the train who was going to Jacksonville. The next moment he announced that he was sick of the smell of tobacco, and he walked with rather an emphatic manner into the next car, where he sat down, drew his hat over his eyes, and appeared to be gazing intently at nothing.

He was thinking that he had been a confounded idiot when he had told those fellows that he had found out where that girl was going. She seemed a nice little thing. He did not like to remember how those fellows had laughed. He wondered if he had ever laughed like that. It was a coarse, vulgar thing to do; and it was odd he had never noticed that kind of thing before.

He shook himself impatiently in his place. He glanced down the car. He could see the straw turban with the bunch of black velvet and the blue wing on it. She was sitting in the same place. How tired she must be. He would like to know if she were going to Florida for her health.

He rose and walked through the car in the most hurried manner, as if on an important errand. He turned neither to the right nor to the left. In ten minutes he returned, moving very leisurely. He looked full at Salome and her mother as he did so. Yes, she was tired. As he sat down again he found himself thinking that she never could bear the journey in this car. What had her mother taken her in this car for, he asked himself, angrily. She couldn't endure it. And they were not in New York yet, wouldn't be there for more than two hours. What was her mother thinking about?

At this stage in his musing Moore caught himself up with a smile of amusement.

He drew a magazine from his satchel and settled himself to read.

He was one of those young men who have a complexion like that of a blond woman. Underneath such a skin the blood shows too freely.

Moore's beard was yellow and forked, being carefully combed in that manner. Evidently he paid great attention to his mustache also, for the ends were drawn out and curled up in that fashion which one sees in the portraits of that mythical D'Artagnan. Underneath this mustache, and scarcely hidden by it, Moore's lips showed rather too red and full. His eyes were not blue, but a light, changing hazel, with some tinge of yellow, as if from his beard.

Altogether, Randolph Moore at this time in his life was one of those young men whom it was a distinct pleasure to meet and to look at. Any elderly person would smile involuntarily at sight of him, and would part from him with regret. He might have posed in any tableau as "Youth," there was so little of the past in his aspect, and so much of the future. His beauty was of that exhilarating kind that goes so well with the general idea of the future, which is always to be indescribably lovely.

When he had been in college somebody had called him Antinous, and the name had been immediately hailed as the most appropriate thing that could be thought of. It was rather cruel, however, that his set should have degenerated into the fashion of changing that word to "Tinny." But that is what those college boys—I beg their pardon—those college men did, and never, except on the books of the university and on formal occasions, was he known by any name save Tinny Moore.

And struggle as he might to overcome the feeling, he was never able to hear that word Tinny without a shrinking, as the "skin shrinks from the burr." But he did succeed in concealing that he shrank.

He left college with no love in his heart for the men there and for the place where he had been Antinous, and where he had made no mark at all, but had simply been one of the ruck which had barely captured the B. A. for their names.

Now he was in his twenty-fifth year, and was a "runner" for a boot and shoe firm in a suburb of Boston. But he had an uncle, and prospects.

He had a seat in one of the parlor-cars on the train, but he did not acknowledge to himself why he did not occupy it more. What he did acknowledge was that a fellow saw a great deal more of human nature in a common car. And he had not yet been a travelling salesman long enough to become tired of human nature.

In a few moments the train began slowing up for a large station. Moore, who had not read a whole page in his magazine, put it back in his satchel.

He sauntered out to that door which was nearest to the seat occupied by the Gerrys.

He suddenly made a resolution which he acted upon directly the train came to a full stop.

He stepped to Mrs. Gerry's side and looked down at her.

He lifted his hat.

"We stop here twenty minutes, madam," he said. "Won't you let me bring you a cup of tea or coffee?"

IV

"SLEEPERS AND BUFFETS"

MRS. GERRY started. She had not noticed Moore until he spoke. She was so weary even at this early stage of the journey that she was alarmed lest she should not be able to take care of her daughter. Her head ached blindingly. The luncheon she had eaten from their basket had been tasteless to her.

She looked up and met the young man's eyes. She smiled with pleasure and gratitude.

"Yes," she answered, "I shall be glad if you will bring me a cup of coffee."

Moore lingered.

"And the young lady?" he said. Salome also glanced at him, and she also smiled.

"I should like a glass of milk," she replied. Moore darted from the car, and they saw him run into the restaurant.

"What a pretty boy!" exclaimed Mrs. Gerry, with some animation.

"Yes; but who cares for a pretty man?" said the girl.

"Well, I care for beauty wherever I can find it," was the response, "and I do want some coffee. Get out your purse, Salome, won't you?"

Salome had the shabby little purse extracted from the shabby satchel before Moore appeared from the restaurant door. ·

He was followed by a boy bearing a tray on which were two or three dishes besides the coffee and the milk.

Mrs. Gerry's face clouded over with disapproval; and by the time Moore had reached her she was looking decided reproof at him.

But the young man laughed with a gay disregard of anything she might say to him. And when he laughed one was very likely to laugh with him.

He took the tray from the boy and gently placed it in Mrs. Gerry's lap.

"It is fried chicken," he said; "and I made them swear it had been fried within the week. If they have perjured themselves, is that any fault of mine? Madam, don't scold me, please. You see my mother never scolded me, and at this age I couldn't bear it, anyway. And I thought if you would let me eat a bit of bread and a drumstick with you, you would forgive me and would not think it necessary to feel under any obligation."

Mrs. Gerry was more cheered at hearing his careless, hearty young voice than she had been cheered by anything in many weeks.

She had started from home with the fixed resolve not to speak to any one whom she met. Had she not read how dangerous it was to exchange even common courtesies with strangers on a journey? Did she not fully know that the ravening lions who go up and down the earth in steam-cars and steamboats always wear the most attractive outside appearance?

Yes, she knew all this; she knew it when she looked up in Moore's face and found it so inspiring in its beauty and its unlimited good-will. And she immediately trusted him as if she had known him all his life.

But she would hand him some money, from which he scrupulously selected the price of the coffee and milk he had brought.

He lounged against the seat in front of them and ate his roll and chicken, and they ate also, with a gayety and relish which to Mrs. Gerry, when she thought of the time afterwards, seemed almost miraculous.

During this impromptu repast the two young men who knew Moore came strolling in, each with a toothpick in his mouth. Moore impatiently interposed his shoulder between him and them.

They stared solemnly as they went by. Then they paused and stationed themselves where they could gaze directly into Moore's face. It was in vain that he tried not to see them. He could feel their eyes boring into the back of his head.

He heard the conductor cry outside. He snatched up the tray and ran quickly towards the eating-house with it.

One of those young men was on each side of him.

"Oh my!" cried one.

"I wish I had your cheek!" cried the other.

"Give me the tray and you go back to her," said the first.

"All right," exclaimed Moore, with unexpected acquiescence. "Take it. I'll pay the taxes."

And he thrust the tray at the young man, who mechanically took it, while Moore ran back to the car.

"Sold!" cried the person who didn't have the tray to the one who did have it. The conductor shouted again.

The tray was hustled on to the counter; some

money was flung after it, and the checked ulsters caught on to the last car as it glided by the platform.

The two young men had lost their toothpicks, and they felt like giving Moore a few stinging slaps on the side of his handsome face.

Instead of doing that, however, they agreed to stand round within sight of that lucky fellow every minute of the time until they reached New York. It would do him good.

Moore got very weary of that espionage. He could not look up without meeting those eyes fixed upon him. He wanted to rush out and knock those fellows down and jump on them. He had intended to linger near Mrs. Gerry and speak to her when he had a chance. But in half an hour he gave up that intention. He walked sullenly into the parlor - car and sullenly took out his magazine again. But after a time he became really interested, and he forgot about those two women with whom he had lunched. The lamps in the cars were long ago lighted. Outside, as the train sped on, the fiery dots that showed where were houses and street lamps became more and more numerous. Each spark glowed to Mrs. Gerry and her daughter when the car door was opened like some fantastic and evil spirit. For by this time even Salome was so weary that she had lost all the cheerful hope with which she had started that morning. Was it only that morning? Was it not rather weeks ago since she had seen her father standing there in front of the little station?

The man with the trunk checks jingling from his hand and with his arm thrust through the handle of a lantern had long since gone through the train shouting, "Baggage express! Transfer to Brooklyn and all parts of the city!"

From the time when he had appeared the Gerrys had expected momentarily to arrive in New York. They had listened eagerly when any train official had entered. And still, outside, in the intensity of the darkness, the lights increased, and the tall houses became taller and had now grown into long blocks.

Mrs. Gerry had shown her check to that man who went rattling his bits of brass. Somebody behind her had given up her check and received another.

One of the principles on which this woman had started from home was never to relinquish that little metal square. If she let that out of her possession she virtually threw away her trunk. Everybody had told her that.

She touched the sleeve of the express agent and anxiously showed him her own check, holding on to it tightly, however, lest he might be tempted to snatch it from her.

He bent down and looked at it.

"Oh, you're all right. You've nothing to do till you get to Jacksonville," he said. "You wa'n't going to stop in Ne' York?"

"Oh no."

He hurried on and slammed the door.

Just then the train plunged into the tunnel from which it emerges at the station. Salome put her head for a moment on her mother's shoulder. She coughed.

"How tired you are!" whispered Mrs. Gerry.

The girl laughed slightly. "And this morning I thought I should never be tired," she said. She drew a long breath and added, "Oh, I wish we could be checked through like our trunk, don't you? How are we ever going to get over to Jersey City? Isn't it to Jersey City we have to go?"

Mrs. Gerry stiffened her body and her mind. "I guess we shall get over there easy enough," she answered. "There are plenty of folks to tell us, heaven knows."

"Yes, but if they shouldn't tell us right," responded Salome, despairingly. "You know how much we've read about what dreadful things they do in New York."

Mrs. Gerry tried to smile in a reassuring manner.

She was thinking that she wished she could see that young man again. She could ask him anything, and he would know all about those things of which she was so ignorant. At last she expressed this hope aloud.

"He?" returned Salome, with some petulance. "He has forgotten us long ago."

"Very likely," was the response.

And at this Salome was so surprised that she immediately wished to dispute her mother's assent.

It was true, nevertheless, that Moore had forgotten them.

But when the train was actually under the roof of the Grand Central, and passengers were gathering up bags and putting on wraps, Moore suddenly remembered, and he recalled them with a wish to help.

"They are just like lambs," he said to himself, with a smile of superior knowledge. "They'll think they are going to be devoured."

He flung his coat over his arm and hastened out.

He was obliged to go through two cars, and many

of the passengers had already poured out of the train,
which had now stopped.

Moore's tall figure enabled him in a moment to sat-
isfy himself that the two women had gone.

He sprang off the step. He felt unreasonably disappointed. He walked forward among the crowd,
conscious of something like a desire to hustle them
right and left. Where were those two, anyway?

He was going directly on that night. It was only
common humanity for him to assist them—they would
be so awfully frightened. And how tired that girl
had looked! What was there in her face? She was
a real little Puritan, with a leaven of something else
in her. How on earth did he happen to forget them?
Well, setting his mouth, he was going to find them.
Moore found, at this stage in his thoughts, that he
would rather miss almost anything in his life than to
miss finding those two fellow-travellers.

He tried to reassure himself. If they were going
straight on, as he was, he should come across them
on the train. Then he asked himself if they had a
place in a sleeper. Of course they must not spend
the long night sitting bolt upright somewhere. It
would kill that girl.

Here he hurried on more impetuously than ever.

He did not see them, and he went into the ladies'
waiting-room, carrying a very anxious face.

Just within the door some one touched his
arm.

He turned with unreasoning eagerness, only to see
one of his acquaintances of the journey.

"You're all right," said the wearer of the ulster,
grinning derisively; "she's in here. Ta, ta."

And the young man grinned still more broadly as

he met Moore's ferocious glare. Then he walked out into the street.

Moore stood a moment, trying to detach one figure from another in the moving groups before him.

And all the time they might be going down towards the ferry.

But that confounded fellow was right. There she was. She was half-way down the long room. She seemed to be alone. And she was leaning back in her chair, her face showing very white at this distance.

Moore started forward precipitately. Then he checked himself, and by the time he came near Salome he was strolling with apparent aimlessness, and appeared to see her quite by accident.

But he came forward briskly, with his hat in his hand, a warm, eager smile on his face.

"This is good-luck for me," he said; "now do let me be of service to you. You see, I know all about this route, and I'm going to Jacksonville, too. I told you that, didn't I? We'll take the transfer."

"Oh, thank you so much!" returned Salome, looking at him with delighted relief. "If you can only find mother! She has gone to make some inquiries. You see, we don't know a thing about travelling. It's all so confusing; and one gets tired, you know. But we thought we were very wise, for we had read every particular about each route South. Oh, there's mother!"

Salome rose as she caught sight of Mrs. Gerry hurrying towards them. Moore quickly took the Gerry lunch-basket and bag.

"Reading doesn't tell you much," he remarked, gayly; "you see, there's nothing like experience. Now you follow me, ladies. Just make believe I'm your courier, to whom you are paying a very high price to conduct you to Florida."

Mrs. Gerry's face looked pathetically relieved when she saw this young man. The answers to her questions had confused her. Those answers seemed to suppose that she already knew things of which she was entirely ignorant; and then that constant necessity that she must do everything the cheapest way hampered her. She wanted to have a comfortable carriage for Salome's sake, and thus be carried to that ferry of which every one had spoken. But no; there was a cheap way to go.

Now she hastened forward, and said quickly to Moore: "You must not conduct us in any expensive way, for I can't afford it, and I would not allow you to pay. They just told me how we could — and I suppose there's the elevated road—"

She pronounced those last words as if she were mentioning some ravening monster that was yet understood to be tamed for man's use. Moore nodded.

" I think we'd better take the L road, after all," he said. " It'll save so much time, and it's cheap. You shall pay every cent of your fare, never fear. Here we are. Now don't hurry up these steps."

He glanced back at Salome. He wanted to offer her his arm. He had never realized before how trying those long flights of stairs could be.

The electric lights shone in ghastly whiteness all about them. The outlines of the hurrying figures were accentuated strangely. Human beings seemed to be transformed by that light into a weird combination of the human and the goblin; and surrounding them, like something tangible, was the never-ceasing roar of the city.

Salome felt that she was no more Salome Gerry, the girl who had been ordered to Florida, but she was —in truth, she did not yet know what she was. And that young man whom she and her mother were following—he was something evolved out of this strange order of things.

What if he should not lead them to that ferry, but should take them somewhere and rob them? With this last thought in her mind, as she toiled up the steps, she looked up at Moore. It was at that instant that he was glancing down at her. He smiled with such helpful kindliness that Salome felt guilty that she had allowed such a shadow about him to pass through her mind. In the recoil from that suspicion, which yet was not a suspicion, she might for the moment have trusted him too much.

But of the two women whom young Moore befriended that day, the elder one was by far the more warmly grateful. She had felt the burden and the stress of the journey with an almost prostrating power, and she had borne all the time her anxiety for her daughter, an anxiety which she must conceal. A hundred times she would look furtively at Salome. She saw accurately the increase of weariness. How would she ever get to Florida?

She recalled the gloomy prophecies of those people at home who had insisted that Dr. Bowdoin was wrong, and that the girl ought to stay at home; that she was not "able to be gadding about."

It was as if their conductor had a magic power, Mrs. Gerry thought. It was not of the slightest use to try to distrust him. She could hardly discern how much this magic power might be ascribed to a knowledge of the art of travelling.

Somehow, without any more worrying, the two found themselves across the ferry and aboard the train waiting in Jersey City, and Mrs. Gerry had kept the sharpest watch that there should be no luxury of transportation. She knew precisely what every fare had cost and paid it on the spot; and Moore was too well bred to resist this wish on her part.

All the time, however, until he left them on the train, he was trying to construct some plan by which that girl could have at least what rest a place in a sleeper would afford. His own half section had been secured when he had bought his ticket in Boston.

He went forward into that car now and sat down. He put on his little gray travelling cap mechanically. Then he took it off and returned it to his satchel; then he wondered where his cap was, and wished that he had brought it along.

"She'll be so awfully tired by morning," he was thinking. And he asked himself if that girl were going South for her health. And then he repeated his mental assertion concerning how tired she would be.

It was really not to be borne. She couldn't spend the night in one of those seats. And the filthy air there would be in that car by midnight, when the men would have their boots—with their feet in them—tilted up in the air some way, and their mouths would be open, and—of course something must be done about it. Those women did not know how exhausted they —she—would be by four o'clock.

Moore sat quite still for half an hour with his mind what he called "on the stretch" to think of some plan which would not wound Mrs. Gerry's independence, and yet which would give them half a section in that sleeping-car.

5

During this process of thought Moore did not once ask himself if his pity would be so keen if that girl had happened to have a square face and heavy mouth, instead of the face and mouth she really did have. And yet the owner of a square face and heavy mouth might be able to suffer a great deal if she were in the grasp of incipient phthisis, and need a great deal of pity also.

After a while Moore rose. He found himself obliged to leave his seat even more often than is usually the case with travelling young men.

"There is no use," he had decided; "I shall have to tell a taradiddle or two. But I hope I shall be for-given. I'm going to do evil that good may come."

When he appeared beside Mrs. Gerry and Salome he did not look like a person who could do evil even for the sake of good.

He leaned over Mrs. Gerry. " I thought I'd come and let you know that there's a half section in one of those sleepers that's been unexpectedly given up," he said, and thought, "I haven't told a lie yet. I didn't expect to give it up, that's true enough."

Mrs. Gerry looked questioningly at him. She did not distinctly know what a half section meant. Only it must be a place to sleep. And she could not af-ford it.

"You see," went on Moore, "it's given up, and you and the young lady might just as well have the use of it. It won't cost a cent, and will be there idle."

" But somebody else might hire it," said Mrs. Gerry.

" Oh no ; it was engaged, you understand," was the response, with great glibness; "and since the person who engaged it will not occupy it—that's the way they do in these sleepers."

Moore's words ran along with a quite convincing appearance of truth.

"I happened to think of you and Miss—Miss—"

"Gerry," prompted the elder woman.

"Miss Gerry, and it seemed really too bad that the half section should kind of run to waste, you know, and Miss Gerry could rest; that is, she could come nearer resting than she can here. They don't have any air in sleepers, but what there is is better than there will be in this car. And you know you can put your nose up to the window and think you're breathing. And then you can press that electric button, and row the porter no end, and wake up all the folks if you can't sleep and want some amusement."

Moore talked with the utmost ease, for he thought he saw signs of relenting on Mrs. Gerry's face.

How could she refuse on account of Salome?

"Let me take these," Moore said. And again he picked up the basket and the satchel. And again the two followed him.

Mrs. Gerry was thinking that it was really Providential. And since it was not the custom to sell a section—whatever a section was—to anybody else, after it had been engaged and given up, why it was just a mercy to Salome; so the mother decided not to question their good-fortune any more.

But at the door she did restrain their guide long enough to say that she herself could sit up well enough, but if her daughter could have a chance to rest—

"Oh, there's room for you both," was the response.

Moore stepped across from one car to the other; then he put down his burdens and reached forward his hands, the train surging and lurching on.

Mrs. Gerry could not help clinging fast to him;

but he was disappointed that the girl stepped across with something of the lightness of a cat.

The sleeping-car seemed to the dazed eyes of the two thus entering it like a wonderful palace in which they had no right. The polished woods reflected the lights; the people sitting there were, of course, quite another order of human beings. The beds were not made, but Mrs. Gerry supposed they were to rest on those beautiful seats. And everybody seemed so languid and indifferent.

Salome gave one glance about her, then she looked at no one.

She was conscious of a swift, strong wish that she might dress like a certain girl she passed and who did not seem to know that any one had come in.

But Salome saw that girl shoot one eye-gleam at Moore, who was not conscious of it.

The young man saw his charges seated, then he hurried away to inform the conductor that he had given up his section, and to warn that official not to betray him.

Presently the porter came with solemn respect and suggested that the ladies might just as well have their bed made if they were tired; ladies often had their beds made as soon as they came. And would they be so good as to sit over there?

The intensely respectful black man did not divulge whose silver dollar was now in his pocket, nor who had proposed this course of action to him.

The former owner of that dollar had considered the advisability of proposing that the proper black man also offer supper to the two women as one of the arrangements that were included in the engagement of any part of a section in a sleeping-car, but this thought was discarded as being too broad ; Moore was afraid that, ignorant as she was about travelling, Mrs. Gerry would immediately suspect that it was an impossibility for a railroad company to be so munificent as to "throw in" meals.

But as the two sat across the aisle and saw the porter work that mysterious change which culminates in the production of a bed with sheets and blankets, Mrs. Gerry decided that it would be a good time to partake of a lunch from their basket. While they were thus feasting on viands which had dried a great deal within the twelve hours, Moore came in.

That young man had walked a great deal since he started from Boston.

He was now again smitten with an almost uncontrollable wish to order the most sumptuous banquet that a "buffet-car" can produce, and have it placed before these two. But he held sternly to the resolve he had just made concerning this matter.

He said he only came in to say that, being in a sleeping-car, they wouldn't have to change in Washington. They need not be uneasy about a change anywhere ; just stay where they were. And he hoped they would rest, and he was sure Miss Gerry would be better in the morning, and—and—here he seemed to change his mind as to the propriety of saying something, and finished with, "Good-night."

As Salome responded to this parting salutation, and as Moore stood with his cap lifted, Salome saw that beautifully dressed girl look at him again, and she fancied there was an inquiring scorn in the glance ; and as the young man walked away the scornful eyes were fixed on the country girl, whose own eyes kindled with indignation and flashed out for an instant.

What did it mean, anyway? Was that stranger wondering why a young god should stand solicitously before a shabby little thing like Salome Gerry? For an instant the shabby little thing stared insolently, then the eyelids dropped and the face quivered slightly. Salome found that her insolent stare had exhausted her. She thought that she hated that girl. As soon as she could she looked at her again with a curiosity she could not quite subdue, and now there occurred what seemed like a miracle to Salome.

The perfectly dressed young woman smiled with a beautiful, full brilliance, apparently right into Salome's eyes, and Salome's eyes dilated as if to receive that smile, and she hated the giver of it no more. And when she was lying upon her bed an hour later, and was gazing with half-awake sense out into the dusk of the night through the window, somehow the feminine face and the masculine face were inextricably mixed, and she was dreaming of them even while she thought she was fully awake.

She slept late and soundly, much to her surprise. Her mother, lying patiently by her side, hardly slept at all; but the mere knowledge that her daughter was resting was so refreshing to her mind that she almost fancied that her body partook of that refreshment.

Meanwhile, Moore had ample opportunity to know to the full what a sacrifice he had made, and he was a youth who liked all the luxury he could compass. His presence was so pleasing, his address so attractive, that he had jumped—so his friends said—into an excellent position. He had a good salary and an interest in the business for which he travelled, and he spent his money freely. He would argue that money was of no possible use unless you spent it. He said he didn't want any heirs of his to have the chance of handling his money. And if he followed his present mode of life he would probably succeed, as far as regarded his heirs.

But now he was sitting with his head back on the seat of a common car. It was midnight, and the hours until morning would last a week. And how was it that everybody's boots seemed to smell of stale tallow? And how infernally a man looked asleep with his mouth open. And how could a human being sleep in such a place as this, anyway? Having asked this last question, Moore's own mouth fell apart and he was asleep himself.

Salome was alert and eager and hungry in the morning. Her mother acknowledged that she had "had her worry for nothing" about the child.

The girl sat by the window and watched the country as it swept on by her. It was a charmed day for her. When at last they had gone through Richmond, though clouds had lowered and here and there a large flake of snow came floating indolently down, she was fancying that the air was different: it was milder. She was continually turning to her mother with a soft fire in her aspect and saying: "Do you know, mother, we are really going South? Oh, I am just as happy as I thought I should be! I wish father knew!"

She sent a postal-card to her father from every stopping place. The porter had offered to do anything for her, and it was he who posted her notes. She thought sleeping-car porters were the kindest creatures in the world.

Why should she suspect that another dollar caused

this one to hover respectfully and helpfully about the two women through the entire journey? If this functionary were shocked at the early hour in which his special charges left their couch, he concealed his surprise and hurried to turn their bed back into its daytime form.

Salome had furtively assured herself of the place where that girl would pass the night, and after her own struggle to dress herself on her knees, her first glance saw that the curtains hung undisturbed before the resting-place of the unknown. Indeed, the draperies were motionless all along on each side of the narrow aisle. Their own section was the only one divested of its curtains.

And now, as the two sat there in that apparent forlornness which is so peculiar to the inhabitant of a sleeper in the morning that it might almost be called the sleeping-car despair, the black man came along with even an added obsequiousness and asked what they would please to order for breakfast.

It will be now perceived by the astute reader that young Moore had, in the desperation of his sympathy, reversed his decision concerning supper.

The early morning wisdom had made him decide that Mrs. Gerry could still further be deceived—for her own good. He trusted that he should never attempt to deceive people save for their own good.

"What?" said Mrs. Gerry, somewhat sharply, when the colored gentleman put his question to her.

He repeated his inquiry.

"But we've got our breakfast with us," said Mrs. Gerry.

"We furnishes anything you pleases to order, gratis."

The man made this assertion with such calmness, with such an air of having said the same thing to scores of passengers daily, that he was very deceiving.

"Do you mean that meals go with a sleeping-car?" asked Mrs. Gerry, thinking of a beefsteak for Salome.

"On sleepers and buffets, yes, ma'am," calmly responded the man.

Mrs. Gerry wavered. Her daughter put her lips to her ear and whispered:

"Mother, I don't believe it. Don't let him bring anything. You wait."

Whereupon Mrs. Gerry told the attendant that she wasn't ready yet.

"All right, ma'am; any time." Mrs. Gerry turned upon her companion.

"Why don't you believe it?" she asked. "And what earthly reason should that negro have for telling us such a thing if it isn't so?"

"It isn't reasonable," was the reply.

"Well, that's a fact," returned Mrs. Gerry; "it doesn't seem reasonable. But I thought if you could have a good steak now, and some milk—"

"Never mind. I'm going to find out a few things for myself," said the girl. "Let us eat more of that evaporated chicken from the basket."

"I shall ask that girl a question—that girl who smiled at me last night," Salome was thinking as she put her teeth into the chicken from the basket, and she began to watch for some one to emerge from behind a certain curtain.

MISS NUNALLY

"I BEG your pardon." Salome hesitated, but she repeated her question, now speaking in that rapid way which was quite different from her manner of enunciating at other times.

"I wanted to know," she said, "if it is the custom to furnish meals in these cars—I mean without extra charge. You see," still more quickly, "I never travelled anywhere before, and the porter said—"

Here Salome paused. She was standing by the seat of that "girl who had smiled at her"—for this was the way that person was designated in her mind—and she was looking down at her with the most undisguised admiration.

The stranger had at last risen. She had in some way made her morning toilet with such success that from appearances she might have performed this function in her own dressing-room.

The blond hair lay in lovely half-curled locks on her forehead; her skin was in color and texture like a faintly tinged rose-leaf; her thick, light eyelashes gave a quite enchanting appearance to her eyes; a faint, indistinguishable perfume exhaled from her as if it were a part of her personality; her short upper lip was raised a little now as she threw back her head slightly to look at her interlocutor.

"Yes," said this girl; "and what did the porter say?"

"He said," answered Salome, "'that we furnishes meals on sleepers and buffets to them that wishes.'" Here she paused to laugh slightly. Then she added, "I suppose this is a buffet and a sleeping-car, too, isn't it?"

The blond girl had a little slab fitted in front of her preparatory to having a breakfast placed upon it. She seemed to be travelling entirely alone, and also seemed eminently capable of travelling thus.

"Yes," she said again. Then she moved nearer the window, made a slight motion with her hand which glittered with rings, and said, "Please sit down here." Salome obeyed, taking her place with complete self-possession, but with a kind of shyness withal.

The stranger was carefully pulling out her long gloves, which she would not put on until after her meal.

"Did the porter tell you that?" she asked.

"Certainly."

"Well, the porter lied."

"Oh!"

"Yes. Railroad corporations don't furnish anything gratis."

"But, how strange—I don't understand—" began Salome.

The other girl laughed, and in her laugh was such a curious and full knowledge of the world that Salome felt like shrinking, and inwardly reproved herself for that feeling. She had a consciousness that that laugh revealed something. Oh, what was it?

"Of course you don't understand — how should you?" was the response. Then, with a suddenness which still was not abrupt, she asked, "Will you tell me your name?"

"Salome Gerry."

"And mine is Portia Nunally. I suppose you are going South for your health?"

"Yes. But what made that porter say such a thing to us?"

"Do you really want to know?"

"Indeed I do."

Miss Nunally laughed again, and again Salome had the same desire to shrink away; but this time she was also conscious of some kind of attraction which more than counteracted that other emotion.

"I will tell you. The porter told you that because he was ordered to do so."

"Ordered? Well, but by whom?"

"Oh, you must guess that."

Now Miss Nunally turned and gazed full at the face so near hers. Salome met the gaze with clear, uncomprehending eyes.

"Well, you are innocent!"

"I hope so," was the indignant response.

"But there is a great charm in ignorance and inno-cence," replied Miss Nunally, as if she were in some way apologizing for her companion. "If you want me to explain fully, I will tell you that this black man has probably been hired by that beautiful masculine hu-man being with the golden beard, who looks as if he had stepped out of some old mythology."

"Oh!"

Salome did not blush. Her eyes gave one flash; she pressed her lips together and averted her head, her gaze resting blindly upon the country that stretched barrenly about them.

Miss Nunally looked with calm contemplation at her.

The servant now arrived with the tray bearing her breakfast.

Salome rose.

"Thank you," she said to the girl; "but I can hardly believe it. There is no reason why a stranger should do such a thing. That young man has been very kind to us, but there is no reason—not the least."

Miss Nunally poured the milk into her coffee.

"But don't you know that some young men go about doing good just like that?" she added. "The capacity for indiscriminate philanthropy inherent in some of these handsome gods is perfectly marvellous."

By the time this sentence was finished Salome again felt that she hated that girl.

She went back to her seat. As she sat down she inwardly asserted that what she had just heard could not be possible.

But in the next moment she told herself that it was true; and more than that: it was true that that young man had paid for the section in the sleeping-car which she and her mother were occupying.

She took hold of her mother's arm with a sharp grip. At the same time she bent forward and lifted the lunch-basket.

"Why, what's the matter, Salome?"

"Nothing; only I'm going back into that other car."

The girl rose. Her figure and face were so determined that Mrs. Gerry picked up the bag and rose helplessly. But she could not refrain from saying as she did so:

"But why—what?"

"Oh, don't talk now," whispered the girl, "but come."

As she followed her daughter, Mrs. Gerry could not help wondering fearfully if this sudden whim were some phase of Salome's disease; and the wild hope that there was a doctor on the train went through her mind.

At first they could not find seats in that common car—how odious and how common it seemed now!—but at last they were crowded in with their hand-baggage.

Mrs. Gerry anxiously examined her daughter, but she could only see a hint of her profile.

"I hope you know what you've done this for," she said.

Salome shrugged one shoulder.

"Yes, I know," she answered. "It is because—"

When she had proceeded thus far in the giving of her reason she was struck dumb with a sudden resolution that she would not tell her mother what that young man had done. No, she would not tell; although when she had started to leave the sleeping-car she had thought that she could not wait to talk over the whole affair. But now, no—now she must be silent.

"Well?" said Mrs. Gerry.

"It was because I had a whim that I wanted to get out of that sleeper. I couldn't stay there a minute longer. I thought I should choke."

"I think you'll be much more likely to choke here," said Mrs. Gerry, trying to be resigned to this whim; "the air is horrible."

"Do you think so? Why, it's quite delightful."

Again Mrs. Gerry asked herself if incipient phthisis affected the mind. And she would, if she could do so privately, ask the conductor if there were a doctor in any of the cars.

After a moment of silence Mrs. Gerry remarked that she was afraid that young man would think them very rude.

"It's of no consequence what he thinks," said Salome.

Then she recalled the exact intonation of Portia Nunally's laugh, and shivered a little as she did so.

Mrs. Gerry drew herself up. It would not do to yield in every way just because Salome was not well.

"I think it's of consequence for us to be polite," she said, with some severity; "and that young man—"

Salome shrugged her shoulders again.

"I'm so tired of hearing about that young man," she said.

"You're not tired of hearing me talk about him," sharply replied Mrs. Gerry, who had a fleeting inclination to put her hands on the girl and shake her, "for I've hardly mentioned him. I—"

"Mother," Salome faced round towards her companion, "I don't know what I shall do if you go right on about him. I—" here she laughed—"I don't know but I shall begin to cough. If I cough you'll be obliged to be silent, for I can't hear what you say. Oh, you dear old thing," putting her head on her mother's shoulder, "can't you let me have a few absurd notions? What's the use of being a woman if you can't be unreasonable? Just tell me that, will you?"

Mrs. Gerry breathed a long sigh of relief.

"I must say you are taking full advantage of your being a woman," she remarked. "But it isn't half so comfortable here. I didn't know there was such a difference."

After a while, during which Salome had her face steadily turned towards the window, without seeing anything, she began to repent that she had taken this sudden action. But it was not the kind of repentance which leads to reformation.

Her face gradually took on its most serious expression.

She was going through one of her habitual processes of self-examination, and she was finding herself a very reprehensible creature. She was afraid there was hardly a leaven of good in her. She was quite discouraged /about herself. She had not had what she would have called a "good spell" at self-examination since she had first known she was going to Florida.

She was convinced that self-examination was an extremely wholesome process, because it wilted one so and was so disagreeable. Sometimes it required a full twenty-four hours for her to recover and regain anything like a comfortable view of herself after one of these "spells."

But thus far in her life she had found it an absolute necessity to examine her own soul at frequent intervals, and with a rigidness and relentlessness that would have suggested the probability of her finding some terrible moral canker spot.

At these times it was as if her identity were under a microscope and she had her eye upon it. She found herself under that magnifying power to be quite a monster of sin, and she was ferocious in her judgment of herself.

Was it at such times and for hours after such periods that her face had that austere look which was in such marked contradiction to the face itself?

Mrs. Gerry had had occasion more than once during Salome's childhood to remonstrate with her upon
her tendency to a morbid conscientiousness.

The mother had told her husband that Salome was
growing too fast, that she did not sleep enough, that
she must be out-of-doors more. The woman, watching her child with healthy common-sense as well as
with love, decided, as that cynical Frenchman had
long ago decided, that the conscience of an extremely
healthy human being is usually quiescent, whether
that human being be good or bad. But there was no
cynicism in this New England woman's decision ; and
she would have been inexpressibly shocked had she
ever thought to carry out this kind of reasoning still
further.

Prosper Merimee's recipe for the preservation of
beauty—" a hard heart and a good digestion "—is an
excellent recipe for the procuring of a certain kind of
mental repose ; that is, if a person is willing to de-
generate into a pagan.

Randolph Moore had never in his life had an hour
of serious self-examination.

There wasn't a bit of use in any such kind of thing
as that. He meant to do about the right thing, and
if that wasn't enough, he should like to know what
was enough. He wasn't going in for that kind of rot,
not he. It took all the vim out of a fellow. Why, a
fellow wasn't better than a wet rag if he were continually poking about in his spirituality, and fishing
up this or that dreadful thing and making no end of
a row over it. Why, contradictorily, he knew a man
in his class in college who was always up to that sort
of thing, digging down into himself and analyzing
motives, and that. He was an awfully good fellow,

6

too, smart as a trap; he was a minister now. He, Moore, wouldn't like to be one of his congregation; but there was no milk-sop about that fellow, either—had moral courage, and moral courage was a thing most folks didn't have. It was easy enough to be brave physically, but when—

So Moore used to talk when he was upon the subject of that classmate of his and the more impersonal one of self-examination.

At this moment this young man was in the smoking-car. He did not care much for smoking. He said it was beastly—which it isn't, as beasts have no such human proclivities—and, besides, tobacco left such a taste in one's mouth.

Moore had walked a good deal up and down the train, but so far during the day he had kept himself from entering a particular sleeper. He had made a resolve that he would not be hanging about them all the time. He did not find it necessary to explain who it was he meant by "them." And he didn't know but that they might suspect something when the darky offered them breakfast. Perhaps he had gone too far that time.

He played "railroad whist" with some men, who seemed as if they would go on shuffling and dealing those cards for years, chewing the ends of their big black cigars as they did so, and grunting rather than speaking the few words necessary to be uttered. At last Moore flatly refused to continue. He looked at his watch. He glanced out of the window. There were the Carolina pines, and there were the negroes rolling about the barrels of tar.

"We are really getting down a little," he said.

He strolled outside and stood with his feet well

planted, and his hands thrust into his pockets, his travelling-cap pulled down over his eyes.

He inhaled with a keen delight the pine odor; he was aware of the softening atmosphere; the fluff of white cloud here and there in the blue heavens told him that he was escaping from the winter. Those shambling negro figures leaning up against those barrels were just the figures for the rest of the scene.

Then, with a swift, sweet poignancy, a thought of some one came to him. It was the thought of an ascetic and yet flexible face.

Moore took off his cap. The action was involuntary and almost mechanical. When he replaced it he smiled. Then he turned with the air of a man with a definite purpose, and hurried into that car where he expected to find Salome and her mother.

Miss Portia Nunally, very much bored with her novel and quite weary of the sight of pine-trees and darkys and tar-barrels, saw him coming, and began to read intensely. Still, she knew the precise instant in which to look up, and she could not help smiling derisively when she saw the young man's disappointed face.

Yet, though her smile was derisive, there was that in it which drew Moore's glance to her, and in the moment her eyes met his her smile changed indescribably. But she did not look at him any more at that moment. She returned to her book with a renewal of absorbed interest.

Moore, after staring again at that empty section as if his stare might materialize the forms of the two who had left that place, turned about and strode out of the car.

Miss Nunally dropped her book beside her.

"He is certainly a beautiful youth," she was thinking, disdainfully, "and he is in love with the little Puritan girl; or he is going to be in love with her. There is nothing in the world so uninteresting as the man who is in love—but not with you."

Here Miss Nunally pushed one lock of hair gently back from her right eyebrow; and in its present position it was evident that this lock of hair was superior as an attraction to what it had been before. But you would not have said that its owner knew this fact.

Moore's impatience took him very rapidly. The instant he entered the second car his eye darted intuitively to the seat where the two women sat. The next moment he was standing beside them.

Mrs. Gerry bowed to him cordially; Salome gravely. Salome was still under the dominion of her mood of self-examination. Besides, she knew what this young man had done.

"I'm so sorry," began Moore, eagerly, "but I suppose you have found me out."

Mrs. Gerry looked at him with an amused interrogation in her face. Salome, after her demure greeting, looked out of the window.

"We are usually sorry when we are found out," said Mrs. Gerry; "but I don't know what you mean. How have we found you out?"

"Oh, don't you know?" still more eagerly. "I'm afraid Miss Gerry knows. She isn't approving of me now, and it kills me not to be approved. If I'm not found out I won't confess and repent. But if—Mrs. Gerry, do believe my intentions were good. They were, indeed. There wasn't an ulterior motive in me; that's the simple truth. I do wish you would go back into the sleeper. It is really too bad to make me feel such a wretch; I can't bear it. I saw how weary you ladies were; and I knew so well how you'd feel after sitting up all night that—"

Here Moore paused with his eyes on that averted face by the window. He could not possibly know that at this moment Salome was hearing again Miss Nunally's significant laugh, and that the remembrance hardened her heart.

She did not change her position in the least.

Moore tried not to show his discontent. He made no attempt to finish his sentence.

He moved slightly to let some one pass. Then he bent down still lower, giving his whole attention apparently to Mrs. Gerry.

" Please, please, don't be hard on me!" he exclaimed, in the lowest possible tone. Mrs. Gerry was somewhat bewildered.

" But I don't know what you mean," she said. Here there was a very slight but impatient motion from the girl who was staring through the window.

" It was just my kindness of heart, Mrs. Gerry," Moore said, now beginning to be aware of a genuine sense of embarrassment, and consequently feeling angry with that girl. " I wanted to do you a service, and I knew you wouldn't take my chance in the sleeper if you knew it was mine."

Here Mrs. Gerry drew herself back a little, and Moore stood upright, frowning and twisting his mustache.

He was thinking that he was entirely mistaken when he had fancied himself interested in that girl. She was nothing but a little cold-blooded prude of a Puritan, and he didn't care in the least what she thought of him, or whether she thought anything or not. And evidently she wasn't going to look at him again.

"I'm very sorry," said Mrs. Gerry, with great dignity, "but, of course, we cannot deprive you of your rights any further. And—and—" here she could not help looking up at him with that affectionate admiration with which middle-aged women were often tempted to regard him, "and I am so sorry that you deceived us."

Moore met her look with eyes that, unknown to their owner, were melting with wistful deprecation.

"You can't be half so sorry as I am," he said. "And now you'll be uncomfortable all the rest of the journey, and you won't let me help you; and, worst of all, you will always distrust me. I don't see how I'm going to bear it."

As he said these last words he looked again at Salome, and she now turned suddenly and looked at him.

"Miss Gerry," he said, impulsively, "do intercede for me with your mother. I can see that she is going to be severe."

Salome lowered her eyes. Her countenance did not change from its former expression, and what it was that the lowered lids concealed the young man could not guess.

"It will be as well for you to plead your own cause," she answered. "But I am sorry you deceived us." She could not help adding: "That black man offered us breakfast, too."

Moore drew himself up.

"If you are going to be obdurate—" he bowed stiffly and walked away.

" Really," he was thinking, "if those women choose to take things in that way I've had enough of them."

And he went and took a hand again with those bores who had never stopped playing railroad whist. And he trumped his partner's trick so that his partner swore viciously. But Moore had not even noticed what card had been turned for trumps.

Left by themselves, the two women gazed out at the scenery again. Salome seemed completely absorbed in the interminable flat stretches of country where now and then were lonesome little settlements.

Occasionally she raised her window and put her face to the opening, inhaling deep breaths of the delicious air as she did so.

Nearly an hour passed. All at once, without any preliminary remark, Salome turned to her mother and said, with some sharpness,

" I don't know why you need to have been quite so hard."

Mrs. Gerry jumped out of a partial doze.

" Hard !" she exclaimed ; "what are you talking about ? Oh, you mean that young man ? I thought I was very mild with him. He is one of that kind that wins you in spite of yourself. But we ought not to be won by a mere face and manner," sententiously.

" I don't know as he won anybody," said Salome. " Anyway, I'm weary of hearing about him."

Mrs. Gerry fixed a wondering gaze on her daughter.

" How tired you are !" she exclaimed. " Can't you lean on me and have a nap ? It does seem as if we never should get there now. I suppose the last half of anything is always the most tedious."

The girl did as her mother suggested. She rested her slight form within her mother's arm and closed her eyes.

And at last, three hours behind time, the train drew slowly into Jacksonville, and Mrs. Gerry and her daughter stepped out of their car so begrimed and so bewildered that the younger woman was almost bereft of all care as to what should become of them.

They had not seen Moore since his confession.

Now, as they stood there hesitatingly, and as the people hurried about, and the colored drivers came solicitously among the throng, the young man walked by them and ceremoniously doffed his cap as he did so.

He was not in a good temper. He said it was the last time he would ever notice a girl with that confounded Puritan face. He didn't know that he cared if she were made ill by the journey. It was nothing to him, anyway.

He took a seat in a carriage. He told the driver to take him to just what hotel he pleased.

Where was the girl going? He didn't believe they could afford to stay in Jacksonville. Well, he should probably never see her again. And he didn't care in the least.

After a few moments' hesitation Salome and her mother went into the waiting-room.

Mrs. Gerry felt that she had never before known how irritating it is to be poor. It was dreadful to her to have to pay out her money so fast. She wanted to stop over night in this city, but the expense—Salome must go on, no matter how weary she was. They could not rest until they reached their journey's end. Somebody up at home had known somebody else who had a cousin who was settled near St. Augustine.

It was upon this clew, for economy's sake, that Mrs. Gerry had decided upon St. Augustine.

She would hire a room, a log-house, anything, and she would establish herself and work, no matter how hard, while Salome should benefit by the climate. Florida had a great deal of climate; there was always enough of that.

Mrs. Gerry had in her pocket the most accurate instructions as to how to find the place not far from St. Augustine. Now, as she inquired of the ticket agent, she almost produced these instructions that she might consult with him about them.

But something held her back from doing that.

The train would start in an hour. She turned to inform her daughter of the fact. Salome was sitting by the smouldering fire on the hearth. The girl dared not acknowledge to herself how weary and discouraged she was.

At the other side of the fire a thin, stooped man sat looking dully at the coals. He had just had an attack of coughing and expectoration which had seemed to shake his frame so that he could scarcely breathe. Now he sat there panting and exhausted. He was alone. A large valise, with a cane resting on top of it, was near him on the floor.

Salome was gazing at him with an undefined sensation of horror and premonition in her heart. Presently he took a small flask from the pocket of his overcoat and drank from it. Salome detected the odor of whiskey, and the odor sickened her.

The girl wanted to rise and walk outside in the beautiful sunshine, but the sight of that man sitting there so obviously, so horribly, in the grasp of consumption, held her fast.

He appeared to revive slightly after his draught of whiskey.

He looked uneasily at the clock. What a dreadful thing that he had left his home to come down here hoping—but did he hope? Salome shuddered. She wished that she had not seen him.

Among the people coming and going the girl was now aware of some one, aware without the aid of sight. But she turned that her eyes might assist her.

Miss Nunally had just walked up to the ticket office. She walked erect, and with something like insolence in her gait. But she waited respectfully until Mrs. Gerry should step aside.

Salome rose quickly. She approached the ticket window. She was dominated by a quick coming desire to speak to that other girl, and by a fear lest she might lose sight of her.

She heard her ask for a ticket to St. Augustine, and she was conscious of a sudden relief in the hearing.

Miss Nunally moved away with her eyes fixed upon her open purse. But she had seen Salome, and now glanced at her, smiling.

Salome spoke quickly.

"Oh, I'm so glad you're going to Augustine! Please let us hang on to your skirts. You see, mother and I never went away from home before, and we think the most dreadful things about travelling. If I were strong I shouldn't mind it. Don't tell me I have been too bold," ending her speech with a shy wistfulness.

Salome was thinking that it was not in the least like her to have spoken in that way. She wondered that she had done so. She thought it might have been somebody else. And yet she continued to look with that deprecating pleading at the girl near her.

She could not understand why Miss Nunally should have for her both an attractive and repellent power. At this moment it was the former that was uppermost.

As for the other and more sophisticated girl, she was interested and amused. She had decided that she had never before met any one who impressed her as being shy to a superlative degree, and yet who was perfectly self-possessed, and who never blushed.

"Perhaps I can make her blush," she thought; and then, with compunction, "but she is ill, and that would be cruel."

But Miss Nunally's compunctions never lasted long, if they stood in the way of any preference.

"So far from thinking you are too bold, I am positive you never could be bold at all," she answered. "Yes, by all means, hang on to my skirts. I've been down here half a dozen times. Where are you going?"

Miss Nunally sat down and began to unpin a little veil that had been fastened across her forehead. Even with gloves upon her hands she was successful in the first attempt. She put the pin between her lips and looked up at her companion, who was standing before her.

"I told you, to St. Augustine."

"Oh, but you don't expect to camp out in the Plaza there, do you?"

Salome put her hands together. It was a gesture she would not have allowed herself if she had not been very tired and, as she would have said, "nervous." She always intended to hold her corporeal self in quiet.

"The Plaza?" she repeated. "I did read something about that. We've got to manage, you see, on account of being poor. It's a great deal more hateful to manage when one is travelling than when one is at home ; and it doesn't seem to amount to much, either. We are going to try to hire a room outside the city. There's some one up at home who knew some one who has a cousin here, and we didn't know but it might be cheaper. Since we left the North our whole beings have been absorbed in seeing what was the cheapest way to do things. Why," with a slight grimace, " I've hardly had a chance to think whether my cough is better."

And now she coughed, and involuntarily put her hand to her chest.

Miss Nunally's face changed from its rather cool curiosity to one of soft sympathy.

" I wish I could do something for you," she said ; " but I don't know anybody outside the city, and only Northern people in it, and I'm going to the Ponce."

This she said as if going to the Ponce precluded the possibility of her usefulness towards persons who were obliged to " manage."

" Besides," she added, unexpectedly, " I'm poor as a mouse myself."

Salome could not help exclaiming " Oh !" and glancing at Miss Nunally's gown and wrap and hat and gloves. The glance even included the irreproachable leather satchel she had placed in a chair near her.

" Yes," said the other girl in response to that glance, " I know I'm ragged out very well now. In fact, I will have decent clothes anyway—mamma knows that well enough."

Here Miss Nunally laughed. And Salome again

felt the discordant note, but not so keenly as she had felt it the first time.

"I couldn't stay at the Ponce without a frock or two, of course. My aunt is there; it is she who invites me, and what is more to the purpose, she pays the bills. There's a man there whom she wants me to meet."

Salome made no reply to this remark. But she was thinking that that last sentence was in some unexplainable way in unison with Miss Nunally's laugh. She sat down by the fire in that chair which had been occupied by the consumptive stranger. Then, recalling that fact, she rose quickly and began walking up and down near Miss Nunally. Mrs. Gerry was looking up their trunk, filled with the resolution that she would not relinquish the Jacksonville check until she should hold in her other hand the St. Augustine check. She did not know but that baggage-masters might have a kind of legerdemain at their command by means of which they could spirit away into non-existence any piece of baggage not having attached to it a bit of numbered brass.

Miss Nunally gave her face little dabs with her handkerchief. As Salome drew near her again she said:

"I rather like to talk to you. If you want any advice I can give it to you."

"About what?" eagerly.

"Of course about the only thing in which a girl should be interested—a man. In this case that beautiful creature who gave you his place in the sleeper. I warn you not to think of him; he is fickle. It is impossible for a handsome man not to be fickle."

To herself Miss Nunally was saying. "Some time I will ask that girl why she doesn't blush."

VI

MRS. GERRY felt that she could write a large volume about the way folks lived in Florida. And then the volume would not tell half. Powers of human expression never could tell half. Shiftless!

She wrote home to her husband that the Burgess family, who lived at the foot of Beech Hill, were thrifty in comparison with the people down there.

This was a strong expression. "Up home" a person had only to say, "as shiftless as a Burgess," to express all that could be expressed concerning that bugbear of a New England mind.

And Mrs. Gerry would also have liked to write another volume about the difficulty in finding the residence of Job Maine, for that was the name of the man who had a cousin in Massachusetts who had known some one who knew that the Gerry's were going to Florida and "had got to manage."

Salome had remained in the railroad station at Augustine, while her mother fared forth in quest of knowledge of Job Maine. By this time Salome was in such a state of nervousness and physical fatigue that she was "a trial." But Mrs. Gerry would not acknowledge that fact even in her own mind.

The elder woman longed to go to a hotel, put her daughter in a comfortable room, and when she was rested go on. But she thought of that mortgage to Uncle John, and of that solitary man who was in the lonesome farm-house toiling and saving for them.

So she made Salome lie down on a settee in the station. The girl put her head on her bag, and her mother covered her with her own old blue waterproof.

As Mrs. Gerry was going out at the open door a woman who had been watching the two and whose eyes were red and swollen, came forward and asked, in a whisper,

"Consumptive, ain't she?"

Mrs. Gerry stepped quickly out before she replied,

"I don't think she is, really ; but we were afraid she might be."

The woman followed her. She nodded.

"Yes ; that's just the way. Perhaps she'll be helped—but my boy—"

Here the speaker choked. Mrs. Gerry, with a suffocating pain which was mingled with indignation at this cruel want of consideration, said, tremulously,

"Oh, I'm so sorry," and she gently touched her companion as she spoke.

The woman now put her shabbily gloved hands over her face.

"He died yesterday; I'm taking him home. I'm all alone."

In the shock which came to her as she heard these words, Mrs. Gerry felt as if she could not stand.

But she did stand, straight and strong.

"If I could only do something!" she exclaimed.

"I felt as if I must speak to somebody," said the other.

"Yes, yes," returned Mrs. Gerry, "I know. But don't, don't tell my daughter, will you?"

"No, indeed; of course not." Then, trying to speak cheerfully, "I guess she'll get better; I 'most know she will."

She turned forlornly away. Mrs. Gerry hurried down the street.

She had already made inquiries of the ticket agent as to the whereabouts of Mr. Job Maine. But the man had shaken his head impatiently—"never heard of him."

Mrs. Gerry explained that she believed Mr. Maine raised "truck." She did not quite know what truck was, and felt that it was absurd in any one to raise it; but that was all she knew of Mr. Maine, that and the fact that he lived not far from Augustine.

Now, thinking the matter over as she walked along the street, she decided that the post-office would be the place to go — of course, Job Maine's address was here; this would be the nearest town. And as she walked she recalled that the woman who knew the cousin of Mr. Maine had said she would be sure and have that cousin write; although there was no doubt but that he could be found easily enough.

It seemed to be perfectly understood by the person acquainted with Job's cousin that Job frequently came to Augustine, presumably with his truck.

There was one encouraging fact in the talk which Mrs. Gerry had heard about Mr. Maine, and that was that he had come to Florida a great many years ago on account of his health, and he had entirely recovered from the affliction of the lungs which had threatened to carry him off. Having recovered he did not come home. It was rumored that he had openly declared that he had had enough of New England, that he never wanted to see another flake of snow in his life. And he had married. After his marriage a silence had settled down, broken only by the rumor of truck raising.

For the hundredth time since her journey began Mrs. Gerry recalled minutely everything she had learned about Mr. Maine, and she was obliged to own that her knowledge was extremely meagre.

She hurried on, hardly noticing her surroundings. She saw the Barrier Gate, and paused for an instant in her walk, her pulses stirring with the attractive suggestiveness which the first sight of that gate always causes. Beyond were the towers of the old fort. And everything was modified by the wonderful sweetness of the sky and air.

"How Salome will like this!" softly whispered the woman to herself; "and she will get well—she must get well!"

Then she recalled the face of that woman who had just said "she was all alone."

Mrs. Gerry compressed her lips and turned into St. George Street, asking her way to the post-office; then hurried on, noticing nothing more, only dimly conscious in her preoccupation of a strange loveliness of atmosphere surrounding her.

It seemed to her that she was thinking of nothing but that figure which was lying on the settee in the railway station; that she was caring for nothing but to get Salome where she could rest.

It could hardly be expected that a girl who looked as Miss Nunally looked and who dressed as she dressed would be able to lend a helping hand in a search for Job Maine.

She had bidden Salome a somewhat airy good-bye; she had said she should be sure and look her up;

7

then she had entered her aunt's carriage, which was in waiting for her, and Salome had despondently watched the horses trot sedately away.

At that moment Salome thought she cared only to find a place in which to lie down ; a place where she could lie for days and days, and not smell car smoke, nor see a boy with books or magazines to sell.

Her consciousness at this moment was very circumscribed.

Mrs. Gerry had no difficulty in finding the post-office.

As the mail was in process of distribution she was obliged to wait wearily. She diversified this waiting by selecting different people who came in and asking them if they could tell her where Mr. Job Maine lived.

No, they had never heard of Mr. Maine.

The crowd increased ; but at last, when the little windows were opened, she thrust herself forward. She hardly dared to analyze her emotions at this time for fear she would not know whether she were waking, or whether she were engaged in a nightmare pursuit of a myth which she had chosen to name Job Maine.

The attendant at the window repeated the name. He turned and asked somebody a question. The decision arrived at was that if Job Maine ever came there it was at such rare intervals that no one remembered him.

Taking pity on Mrs. Gerry's worn and harassed face, the clerk examined a pile of letters. There was one for Mr. Job Maine. It was from Massachusetts. Mrs. Gerry felt an immediate conviction that this was the missive that Job's cousin had promised to write concerning the possible arrival of the Gerrys.

She felt hope die within her. There might be a person in St. Augustine who knew of that man, but how could she find that person?

In desperation she asked to be directed to a cheap lodging-house. She must go somewhere. Then she went forth to find Mrs. Marks, on Tolamato Street. It was a shabby enough house, and seemed to smell of something she could not define, and which made her want to cry with a sudden rush of home-sickness; and the rent was five dollars a week.

It was a man with greasy skin and Hebraic nose, with his feet thrust half-way into carpet slippers, who showed her this room, and who assured her it was one of the best locations in the city, and that she was within five minutes of .everything.

But to be within five minutes of everything was not the reason for her coming to Florida. She said she would look farther, whereupon the man came down half a dollar on the rent, and when she was out on the street he had taken off another half-dollar, and asserted that he was now giving her the rent, and that he should be ruined.

She hurried away, now convinced that she should be obliged to stay an indefinite time in the town and spend an indefinite amount of money before she could find Mr. Maine, if she ever found him.

"If I only knew somebody here," she whispered to herself.

The glittering carriages rolled by her; men and women on horseback cantered softly over the sand of the street—oh, every one had money enough. Why did she come to a place like this? And there was her husband at home denying himself that she and Salome might be here.

"Thunder ! Why in time don't ye git, if ye can git ?"

As a drawling, strident voice called this out directly behind her, Mrs. Gerry sprang aside and pressed up against a building.

There was no sidewalk, and the queer little highway seemed at that instant full of vehicles.

Directly behind her was a cart drawn by a mule, or, rather, it was fastened to a mule, which was not drawing anything now, but had stopped apparently from its own volition. This animal wore a few pieces of harness and a few fragments of rope, which seemed to be very insecurely tied upon him, and which connected him to the cart behind him in a mysterious manner.

The cart was broken at the side, and the break was mended by the nailing across it of a couple of barrel staves. But one of these staves had pulled away from its nails, and when the mule moved the barrel stave flopped more or less, in accordance with the motion of its propelling power.

The bottom of the cart was what might be descriptively called " open work," for there appeared to be more apertures than anything else. But these apertures were now concealed by some old cotton bags tacked across. These bags were there temporarily, and to enable a few cabbages and sweet-potatoes to remain in the vehicle until they should be sold.

The driver and owner of this turnout was sitting with great calmness on one front corner of the cart, with his feet braced against a shaft.

He was long and thin and yellow. He had a beard which was also long, and so thin that it allowed the contour of his chin and cheeks to be plainly seen.

I have no wish to keep a reader in suspense, and I will state immediately that this person was Job Maine, and that he believed himself to be now engaged in selling truck.

But Mrs. Gerry did not know that it was Mr. Maine. She believed she was looking at a specimen of a cracker. How could she by any means guess that this was a man New England born and bred?

Mr. Maine, however, had not forgotten the appearance of those people among whom he had grown up. He did not ask his mule to go on immediately. There was always time enough.

He leaned on his elbow and gazed down at Mrs. Gerry, who was only a few feet from him.

Perhaps some unaccustomed pulse was awakening in his heart, but this organ was so unused to such pulses that his face had long ago forgotten how to reveal anything of them.

This face might have been a piece of leather, so far as any expression was concerned.

And yet the owner of that countenance was curious.

"I ruther guess I c'n hold in my mule for a minute or so," remarked Mr. Maine, not glancing at the animal, whose whole attitude might have been taken for an illustration of the verb "to droop."

"I c'n 'most always hold him in," he added, explanatorily, as if his assertion might be doubted.

When this gentleman had said "I ruther guess," there had come to Mrs. Gerry a quick feeling, as of recognition, not of the individual in the least, but of the Yankee in a generic sense. Still, of course, this must be a cracker.

"Jest arrove, I cal'clate?" inquired Mr. Maine.

" But the season ain't to its height till after Christmas. Still, they're droppin' in. Consumption ?"

" I'm well," answered Mrs. Gerry, not knowing why she lingered.

" You don't look consumptive 'n' you don't look like one of them that has money rottin' 'n' has come South to git rid of it."

Mr. Maine apparently had the whole day in which to sit there and converse, and his interest in a Yankee, dull as was that interest, was something like excitement to him. He saw great numbers of Northern people every year, but he rarely saw this kind of a Northern person.

He rolled something that was in his mouth from one side of his face to the other. He passed the back of his hand across his dry, pale lips.

Mrs. Gerry now made the assertion that she had no money rotting. She made a step forward, and said also that she had no time to spare.

" Don't rush round so," said Mr. Maine. " There's all the time thur is, ain't they ? Did ye jest come in ?"

" Yes. And I've got to find a lodging, a cheap lodging. Is there any such thing here ?"

The man slowly shook his head.

" There ain't nothin' cheap in Augustine in this season," he replied. " You're barkin' up the wrong tree—'less you want a cabbage. I'll let ye have one er them cheap."

Mrs. Gerry had never in her life felt such a frantic sense of inability and incompetence. She wanted to wring her hands and cry out.

But instead of doing that she hardened her figure and her face as she remarked, coldly, that she didn't need a cabbage at present.

Then she began to walk on. Mr. Maine reached forth one foot and applied it to the rear of his mule.

The animal shuddered ; but he did nothing else.

"There ain't no hurry," Mr. Maine called out. "I tell ye you've got all the time they is. Can't ye be a darned bit congenial with another Yankee?"

When she heard that last word Mrs. Gerry stopped instantly. She turned back close to the cart.

"'Stonishing," said Mr. Maine, "how hard they take everything. Seems if they wished life was one everlasting tooth-pullin' 'n' they bracin' up aginst it."

"Are you a Yankee?" the woman asked, quickly, with a strong emphasis on the pronoun.

"Certain. And I bet you come from Massachusetts."

Yes, Job Maine was conscious of a something that seemed like interest. He hardly knew what to make of it. He didn't know as he wanted to be interested. It was quite a good deal of trouble to be interested, and it took considerable out of a man, somehow.

Mrs. Gerry was not only surprised, she was becoming excited.

"Yes," she answered. She went on, rapidly, "I did come from Massachusetts. I've brought a daughter down here. She isn't well. I'm trying to find out where Job Maine lives. But I'm about discouraged."

With an involuntary movement, of which he was not conscious, Mr. Maine again reached out his foot and applied it to the mule, who again shuddered, but did not go on.

The man's leather face underwent some kind of a contortion.

"'Tain't no time for ye to be discouraged," he remarked. " If you c'n only stop your hurry I'd like to say sumpthin' to ye. But a man can't talk if he's hurried to death. He can't collect himself, some way."

Mrs. Gerry tried to remain quiet while her companion should collect himself, but she could not refrain from hoping that the process would not be long.

She waited for several minutes while Mr. Maine continued to gaze at her.

" Well ?" she said at last.

Job was leaning forward, with his elbows on his knees.

" I do 'low," he now began, " that you kinder faviour old Lef'tant Bourne 't I used to see when I was a boy. Yes, I certain sure do see the Bourne look."

Mrs. Gerry was so weary and so anxious that she feared she might become hysterical. And there was a confusing air of unreality about this interview.

" Elbridge Bourne was my father," she said. " Who are you ?"

Mr. Maine bent his head over the side of the cart, opened his mouth, and allowed his huge quid of tobacco to drop into the sand ; at the same moment his hand was thrust into the pocket of his trousers in search of the remnant of unchewed " plug " that he hoped was there.

" I'm Job Maine," he answered. " That's about the size of me, ma'am."

Mrs. Gerry walked up to the house near her and leaned against its wall.

She felt ill and weak. She had not guessed this. She thought her last hope was removed. She had a sickening pity and contempt for that man in the mule-cart.

But Mr. Maine became what for him might be called cheerful.

"I'm exactly the 'possum you're after," he said, "'n' here I be. 'N' I ain't the feller ter let a ole neighbor slip. You come down onter the Plaza in an hour or two, or some time ter day, 'n' wait 'n' I'll pick ye up 'n' I'll take ye out to where I live. There's two houses on my place. I'll let one of um on the easiest kind of terms. 'N' I'll throw in the climate. There's jest as much climate out there 's there is here to the Ponce, exactly. Sometimes I think there's more. 'N' there's the ocean. 'N' ozone. One of these hotel fellers was talkin' 'bout ozone the other day. We've got that, lots of it. We've—"

His drawl appeared to be going to continue interminably. And as his voice droned on Mrs. Gerry made up her mind.

She would hire his house. Whatever it was, she would hire it. She already began to picture to herself how cosily and cheaply she and her daughter could live.

"I'll take your house," she said, breaking in upon his words. "Can we ride out with you?"

"That's what I've ben sayin'."

"And when shall we be on the Plaza?—you mean that little park?"

Mr. Maine nodded.

"Some time ter day," he answered.

"Some time to-day? But tell me something more definite than that."

"Can't. Ain't you ruther pertic'lar? I've got to sell my truck. I've got ter flax round for the ole 'oman.

You 'n' the gal be there ter day, ye know. Lor', if you ain't there when I bring round I c'n wait. If we ain't got all the time they is, I sh'd like to know who has got it? That's what I say."

He put his foot against his mule again ; and he now repeated this movement until that creature started into a walk and at last disappeared.

Mrs. Gerry went back quickly to the station. She was elated. She kept saying to herself that if they had a house of their own they should be dependent upon nobody.

An hour later the two women were sitting on the Plaza.

With a well-considered disregard of the expense, they had been to a restaurant and partaken of an excellent meal. And this meal had had its effect upon body and spirit.

Salome sat on the little iron bench with her hands folded upon her lap. Her mother was beside her. The girl's face was haggard with fatigue, but as she sat there it seemed to become in a measure transfigured. It was still worn and thin and pale, however. The sunlight fell full upon her; a faint breeze came from inland. In this breeze was a certain penetrating softness that entered into Salome's blood. It was not like anything she had ever known before. It appealed to something in her which, she thought, wakened for the first time to respond to it.

Even in this first day she was conscious of a mysterious relaxation of nerve and spirit. But she was very weary. She did not want to look at the people who were continually sauntering here and there, and talking and laughing, and not seeming to notice this wonderful air.

Sometimes a dog would come up in a friendly manner to the two strangers, nose about them, then trot off again. There were a great many dogs; sleek, well-kept creatures, who evidently had not come South under any necessity to "manage."

Often Salome would throw back her head that she might the better inhale a long breath. Often her mother would look at her. Once she asked:

"Are you resting, dear?"

And the girl met her mother's glance, smiled, and responded in an ardent voice,

"Oh yes, yes."

So they sat on, mostly in silence.

After an hour the two rose and walked down to the sea-wall. They looked over at Anastasia Island. They gazed at their left upon the gray fort.

Salome suddenly put her hand over her eyes, laughing slightly as she did so.

"I don't want to see anything to-day," she said; "I only want to sit still and let this air and this sunshine have their way with me. Let us go back to the Plaza. How delicious to be where there is a Plaza! And I like to look at the Spanish inscription on that monument."

So they sat down again, and the number of people increased as the afternoon wore on; and more dogs came and welcomed them to the South. The odor from some rose gardens behind tall fences became more and more perceptible. The sky deepened in color. The date-palm in that yard stood out with even a greater distinctness.

Mrs. Gerry began to be uneasy. She was continually looking out upon the streets surrounding the park, hoping to see Job Maine's equipage.

It was in vain that she tried to comfort herself by thinking that they had all the time there was.

Salome did not seem uneasy. When at last the sun was casting longer shadows, the girl pulled a thicker shawl about her shoulders, and continued to wait placidly. Indeed, just then Salome was hardly aware that she was waiting. Afterwards she used to think that some other soul entered her body on that first afternoon when she sat in the Plaza so calmly, not knowing then about this other soul with which she would have to deal.

Fanciful, was she? Yes; but then fancies are sometimes more true and more powerful than facts which may be accurately demonstrated.

Mrs. Gerry rose and walked to the railing of the park. She must see Job Maine somewhere. She wished that she knew which way to go in search of him. And when she did see him she must find out what he would charge for rent. It was an oversight unworthy of a Yankee to engage a house without knowing the expense of it.

And she did not wish Salome to be out in the night air. As she walked restlessly around the park she glanced back at her daughter. The girl was stooping forward to pat the head of an Irish setter who had paused by her side. The slanting sunlight was upon her. The mother suppressed a tremor as she noted the transparent pallor of the face. But it was a happy face, a strangely happy face just now. Mrs. Gerry did not understand. Her own mind was so full of anxieties. But she was grateful. Suddenly she thought:

"It is because we have come to Florida. Well, the air is lovely. But I cannot rest until we can get settled."

And again she tried to see Mr. Maine's turnout among the carriages that were coming down King Street, or turning out towards the barracks. Everybody was gay; everybody was happy.

The military band struck up its inspiring music. A horse bearing a woman on its back, directly opposite Mrs. Gerry, began to curvet by the side of an open carriage.

Mrs. Gerry looked with some bitterness at the rider, and to her great surprise the rider bowed. It was Miss Nunally. She turned the horse's head and rode nearer.

"Beautiful, isn't it?" exclaimed the girl, joyously.

She was looking charming, and she knew it.

"Very beautiful," was the reply.

"Portia!" called a lady from the carriage.

Portia waved her hand at her aunt; but she did not obey until she chose. She never did obey any one until she chose.

"Where is Miss Gerry? I hope you're nicely settled. I shall look you up. Good-bye."

And she cantered off.

The bitterness upon the face of the woman deepened as she watched. The next moment she became aware that Miss Nunally's horse, in its gayety of spirits, was near colliding with a mule that was coming round from the other side of the old market.

The driver of the mule was at that particular time engaged in reaching forth his foot and applying it to his steed—with no effect. But plainly no effect was expected.

The animal continued to walk at the slowest pace at which one foot may be placed before another. He seemed to experience a difficulty in lifting his feet from the ground, as if the earth were a strong magnet which held his hoofs down.

But time accomplishes many things, and time brought Mr. Job Maine at length opposite the woman who was waiting for him.

When he saw her he immediately stopped his mule and leaned forward to support himself with his elbows on his knees.

Just at this moment the sun dropped down below the horizon. There was the sound of the sunset gun. The date-palm was magnified against the red sky. The military band began to play in its softest manner, " Non ti scordar di me."

" Be ye 'bout ready?" asked Mr. Maine. " I 'low I'm a mighty ways toward bein' busted, I've flaxed round so."

He reflectively passed the back of his hand over his mouth. Whether for the purpose of cleaning his mouth or his hand it was impossible to say, for both seemed equally in need of some kind of a cleansing process.

With the going down of the sun Mrs. Gerry's ebbing spirits had sunk to a very low state.

" Yes, I'm ready," she said, " but our trunk must be taken; and it's night now; and I don't know as Salome ought to be out. I don't know what to do," despairingly.

But Mr. Maine was not in the least despairing.

" Now I've ben 'n' got some boards put in the bottom of this thunderin' cart, over them holes, I reckon I'm goin' to have them boards used. You'll git in, that's what you'll do. And the gal—where is the gal? I ain't goin' to flax round 's I've ben doin' sence I seen you, Mis' Gerry, for nothin'. Git in.

But there ain't no hurry. We've got all the time they is."

" But the trunk—"

" A man 'd think you hadn't no confidence in him," remarked Mr. Maine. " I'm reckonin' on gittin' that trunk right soon."

" To-night ?"

" Naw ; course not ter night."

" But what shall we do ?"

" You'll stay with me 'n' my ole 'oman. Don't you count on our havin' no horspitality into us ? And ain't ye ever heard nothin' of Southern horspitality ? That's what gwine to happen to you now—its Southern horspitality."

Sometimes this gentleman said "goin'," and at other times he said " gwine."

Mrs. Gerry tried to discover by Mr. Maine's face whether he was now indulging in sarcasm. But she might as well have endeavored to read some human expression upon a well-baked potato.

" Is the gal fur ?" he now inquired.

" What ?"

" Is the gal fur ?"

Mrs. Gerry turned away. She had resolved to go with him.

She said that her daughter was sitting right here on the Plaza. She would bring her. She would be gone but a few moments. As she walked away she heard Mr. Maine remarking, as if he were saying the words casually to himself, that they " had all the time they is."

Presently the two women appeared. Salome had not been informed of any particulars in regard to Mr. Maine. She only knew that her mother had met him

in what seemed a Providential way, and that a house
had been engaged. To both these strangers a house
meant a house, even though it might be an extremely
humble structure. They rested upon that thought.

Salome came serenely on beside her mother.

When she saw Mr. Maine she involuntarily said
"Oh!" below her breath, and paused for an instant in
her walk.

But she came forward as her mother explained to
the person in the cart that this was "the gal." She
held out her hand. Mr. Maine placed his hand with
such looseness on her palm that it directly dropped out.

He said they might climb in if "they had a mine
ter," which they proceeded to do, he sitting in his
chosen position on a corner of the cart and watching
them, but without any show of interest in the pro-
ceedings.

Once he remarked, what was self-evident, that there
wa'n't no seats, and he added that he had flaxed
round and got some boards laid over the thunderin'
holes.

It was a work of some difficulty to mount over the
edge of the cart, but the feat was accomplished at
last. The mule was kicked into a walk, and the
equipage started out by the barracks. The band was
still playing on the green opposite.

Carriages were standing there that their occupants
might hear the music. Horseback riders were sitting
here and there. Out in the Matanzas a few yachts
were coming slowly in, their sails beginning to flap as
the day breeze died away.

Beyond the island there was the sound of waves
breaking on the long beach. But, more enchanting
than all, there was the Florida air, which smelled of

the sea and of pine-trees and of roses—which, in short, came straight from the plains of Paradise.

Salome did not care if she were sitting on the bottom of that cart. She cared only for one thing, and for that she cared with all her heart: that she was in Florida.

She grasped her mother's hand. She did not look at all like a Puritan maiden.

"'Tis the clime of the South—'" she whispered.

But before she could finish her quotation she happened to see a man on horseback lifting his hat to a girl on horseback.

And the red light from the west showed that the man was that young Moore, and the girl was Miss Nunally.

8

VII

AN AMANUENSIS

"What I really need, you know, is an amanuensis. I always thought I should do better if I dictated."

Miss Nunally, to whom this remark was addressed, turned from the mirror where she was standing; but she only turned a very little, and still remained where she could obliquely see herself in the glass.

"Well," she said, "why don't you get one, then?"

Miss Nunally's aunt, Mrs. Darrah, leaned back with an impatient movement among the cushions of her divan.

"Get one?" she repeated. "Portia, you are certainly a very trying person. One would think that in your position you would offer to write at my dictation."

The girl faced round rather unexpectedly.

"What do you mean by my position?" she asked, with the utmost haughtiness.

"Mean? why, I mean that you are—why," shrinking a little from wounding her niece, "that you are my guest, and that you ought—"

"You needn't go on, Aunt Florence," interrupted Portia, still more haughtily. "I understand you well enough. You mean that I am a poor wretch, and that I ought to creep and crawl so that I may keep you good-natured."

Miss Nunally turned back to the mirror, and carefully selected a red rose from a bowl and held it up to the side of her face. She was trying to demonstrate that blond women may successfully wear red roses. Her upper lip lifted in a slight smile as she saw the effect, and she decided that she would wear an enormous bunch of red roses at her belt that night at dinner. Then she smiled again, and her little teeth, which were more than half gold, seemed to have a malicious gleam to them.

"As for my writing to your dictation," she went on, easily, "you know there isn't a printer in America who could read what I should write. I can't read it myself. I write the English hand."

She laughed.

Mrs. Darrah, a small woman with a doll-like face, and hair brushed up in a high roll from her forehead, somewhat nervously arranged the shawl about her shoulders.

"It's all a notion, your writing that horrid hand," she said. "You know it took you a long time to acquire it."

"I know it did. And now I hope you don't think I'm going to give it up and write for a printer. Besides, I haven't any vocation towards labor of any kind."

"You're an awfully trying girl, Portia!" wearily.

"Oh, I know that," from the person at the mirror. "But you knew all about me before you sent for me to come to Florida."

"But I have forgotten that you— Portia!" with uncontrollable irritation, "won't you stop twiddling those roses and listen to me one moment?"

Miss Nunally walked away from the mirror and sat down in front of her aunt.

"You dear old authoress," she exclaimed, "how am I going to help being what I am? You know you don't believe that people can change. Don't you remember in your last novel you distinctly say that no one ever repents?—that everybody remains essentially the same all their lives?"

At mention of her last novel Mrs. Darrah's face became more amiable. She loved her novels as some mothers loved their children. If other people did not love them, in the secret recesses of her heart Mrs. Darrah knew that it was for the lack of good taste, and she pitied those people.

She smiled involuntarily.

"Yes, I did say so; but I was following out a certain theory. I'm not sure I think like that."

"Oh, but I had quite made up my mind," said Portia, now coming over to the divan and adjusting one of the cushions, "and I was so glad. It's such a comfortable way to believe. You are just what you are, and you needn't take the trouble to be anything different, and that's the end of it. I agree with your last novel, Aunt Florence. Now, please don't go and upset all that, will you?"

Mrs. Darrah looked in a pleased way at the girl, whose air was now anything but irritating.

"But I'm thinking of illustrating the other side of the question," she said. "I—"

Portia made a quick movement.

"Pardon me, Aunt Florence, but do you really want an amanuensis?"

"Certainly. I find that my idea—"

"Oh, do pardon me, but I know precisely the person."

"But couldn't you, Portia? You know I'm used

to you.   A strange presence might interrupt the flow
of—"

"But this one wouldn't—not a bit. She's just made
to order, and she wants to earn money; and you know,
aunt, that I can't be confined to any fixed hours. I
should be wretched; and you know"—here Portia
unpinned one of the red roses from her corsage and
smelled at it daintily—"you expect me to be pleasing
in the sight of men, so that I may make a good marriage. I can't work and I can't beg, and I must have
money; and that's why you invited me down here,
you dear thing, you, so that I might have my innings,
you know."

"Oh, please don't put anything so broadly as that!"
remonstrated Mrs. Darrah.

"Broadly!" repeated Portia, indignantly. "You
know I never put anything broadly in my life."

"We won't discuss that"—from the divan. "Your
father and mother want you married. They say they
shouldn't rest in their graves if you were not married.
They never know exactly what you are going to do—
only that it will be something that they would wish
you wouldn't do. Certainly, Portia Nunally, you are
the kind of girl who ought to marry. And Heaven
have mercy on your husband!"

"Amen! for I wouldn't have any mercy. If you
could not deceive men so easily I should have more
respect for them. It's hardly any fun setting traps
for creatures who fall into them so quickly."

"I won't dispute with you," responded Mrs. Darrah. "I don't want to talk about men; I want to
talk about my amanuensis. Where is she?"

"Out somewhere beyond the Maria Sanchez. Somewhere where they raise truck; somewhere where they

eat cabbage all the time. She said, the last time I saw her, that if she died in Florida, it would not be phthisis which killed her, but it would be cabbage."

Mrs. Darrah shuddered.

"But there isn't any nourishment, to speak of, in that vegetable. I mean to write—"

"So I told her—about the lack of nourishment, you know—and she said she was a living demonstration to the contrary. She does look better."

"What is her name?"

"Salome Gerry."

"Where do you see her?"

"On the Plaza—two or three times. She comes in to sit there. Fancy! She says she makes believe she is over in Spain somewhere."

"Does she know anything?"

"Know anything?" Miss Nunally laughed, and then added, "She comes from Massachusetts."

"Go and bring her to me."

"This moment?"

"Of course. I don't know where the Maria Sauchey is; but you take William to drive, and—"

"No; I will ride; and I don't want anybody with me. I have an idea where she lives, and I've been meaning to go."

Miss Nunally put her finger on the button of the bell; and when her call was answered, she gave her order with a certain cool dominance which characterized her when speaking to a servant, and which must have induced something besides liking in a servant's heart.

When she came to her aunt's room in her riding-habit, a few moments later, that lady said :

"I've been thinking"—pausing.

"Well?"

"If the girl's clothes should smell of cabbage—"

"Oh, they won't. If you had seen her you wouldn't say that."

Miss Nunally stood fitting on her gloves with her whip under her arm.

"Well, if you are sure," returned Mrs. Darrah; "but it occurred to me that cabbage was something that they used to have at home when we were so poor—by the way, why does that vegetable always accompany poverty? That's an interesting question. Please hand me my note-book from that table. Some time I will write an essay. I can see how it might be made very telling. But you are sure that she won't bring any odor?"

"Positive."

"And she isn't a coarse little thing? You know I can't bear anything coarse near me. I never should have invited you, Portia."

"I shall leave you to judge whether she is coarse or not," interrupted Portia, in her usual ruthless manner, which was yet smooth, and which possessed the merit of rarely irritating her aunt.

It was a curious fact that strangers nearly always thought that Miss Nunally was the one possessed of wealth, and that she was hospitable and kind to her aunt Florence, taking her round with her and paying the bills.

This fact greatly amused Mrs. Darrah. She confided to some of her friends that she never could have endured her niece if the girl had acted in the least like a poor relation. It tickled Mrs. Darrah's sense of humor greatly to see Portia domineering in that insolent, polite way, and she gave money quite freely that the girl might know, as she said, "the feel of it in her pocket." Not that it remained long in her pocket. For Miss Nunally was generous with that free-handedness that frequently belongs to people who do not know how difficult it is to earn the money they spend or give out. And this pauper, for Portia sometimes indulged in the ridiculous luxury of calling herself a pauper, was, when she chose, a very fascinating woman. But she was not married. And she was nearer thirty than twenty.

She would sometimes remark, in a confidential manner, that she would say "yes" to the first respectable man with money who should ask her to be his wife, and that not until she was married should she dream of falling in love.

"Of course," a shocked hearer would respond, "you will love your husband."

Whereupon Portia would look full in the face of her companion, and smile in an utterly indescribable manner.

"Really," superciliously, "I didn't know women were in the habit of loving their husbands. But I shall love mine quite distractedly. I shall make him run to heel like a spaniel, and I adore spaniels."

Altogether Miss Nunally was considered by mothers to be a dangerous kind of person to have wandering loose among their innocent young daughters. Not that they could put their finger on anything. And that, they said, in conclave, was the very worst feature about Mrs. Darrah's niece: you could not put your finger on anything. So, and because she was Mrs. Darrah's niece, she was admitted everywhere.

But she was too daring; one never knew when she might do something really to injure her reputation.

Men with wives found her too charming. Men engaged to the nicest girls in the world discovered that
there was something in Portia Nunally's smile, and
something in her voice—it was impossible to tell
what it was; but it was easy enough to decide that it
was potent.

It was, thus far, in vain that Mrs. Darrah warned
the girl that if she went on at this rate the men would
find out that she was not the kind of woman that
would make a good wife.

At this point Portia would laugh. And Mrs. Darrah would sink back in her chair and say she was
sorry she had asked the girl down to Florida.

Then Portia would laugh again, and remark that
she knew very well that she had come there to get a
husband, and that her aunt would not be so cruel as
to send her home without one. For then the whole
thing would have to be done over again. And women
grew old so soon.

Portia had a light contralto voice, and on these occasions she would sometimes stand with great de-
mureness before her aunt and sing with ardor the
following lines:

> " ' A husband, Saint Catharine ;
> A handsome one, Saint Catharine ;
> A rich one, Saint Catharine ;
> A nice one, Saint Catharine ;
> And soon, Saint Catharine.' "

Mrs. Darrah would smile, and then groan.

" But you don't give one the idea that you are—
well—domestic. You know that is what men like,
Portia."

" I certainly never will cook a man's dinner, and I

never will mend his stockings—if that is what you mean, Aunt Florence."

"Oh," in despair from the elder woman, "I don't know what I mean!"

"Write a book about it," was the flippant counsel. "When a person doesn't know exactly what he means, then that person writes a book, and then other persons don't know what he means, either. But you may label me as 'warranted domestic' if you choose, and I will not deny the statement if you think the husband will come any sooner."

It will be seen that there was a degree of frankness between these two concerning the subject of marriage, and that they were not in the least sentimental.

And it was this girl who now rode out of St. Augustine alone on her horse, or rather upon the horse her aunt had provided for her.

But she first cantered around the little Plaza to make sure that Miss Gerry was not there.

Then she struck out at a brisk gait down Marine Street. A number of officers were sauntering about by the band-stand. She saw them all, and, more than that, she knew that they all saw her, and that they would be obliged to say that she rode well.

They did say that. And the oldest among them explained to the others that that girl belonged to the Darrah woman; that the Darrah woman—the one who wrote books, you know—had been trying to marry her off for two or three years now, but somehow the men were shy when you came right down to hardpan, you know. Awfully fetching girl, though. Could look a man's heart right out of him.

"Did you tell your wife that, Major?" asked one.

And the Major winked with one puffy eye and said he always told Mrs. Major everything. Whereat the rest laughed.

And Miss Nunally, well past them long before this time and beyond St. Francis Street, was leaving the bit of a city behind her and making for the Maria Sanchez Creek.

She had never been this way before, and that solitude that is sorrowful and yet winning, and which seems to belong peculiarly to the South, immediately appealed to her.

It was low tide, and groups of little bare-legged negro boys were picking up oysters and pounding them open between water-worn stones, greedily swallowing the morsel, chattering, shrieking, and singing as they did so.

The waters of the Matanzas glittered beneath a clear sky. This was one of the days when a northwest wind blew and rolled up lines of foam the other side of Anastasia; when the ships going up or down out there on the ocean were so clearly defined that they seemed sketched against the sky.

The air was exhilarating without being rasping. The levels stretching away in front of the girl and at her right were brownish green, a deep hue that changed its tints as the wind blew over them.

As Miss Nunally sat on her horse a group of wild marsh ponies came in sight, galloping up from the banks of the Sebastian River. Miss Nunally's own steed suddenly straightened himself and whinnied shrilly.

The little ponies paused in their sweeping gallop, and stood with heads erect and manes flowing back. One gave a snort, then another and another, after which they all turned and galloped back to the Sebastian River again.

"If I were a wild marsh pony," soliloquized Miss Nunally, "I should not be obliged to have so many gloves, and mamma and Aunt Florence would not be trying to find me a suitable husband. And "—she looked up with a sudden change of face—" I should be under such a sky as this all the time."

The girl's horse walked on for half an hour through heavy sand and palmetto scrub. It was along this way that Salome Gerry toiled when she came into town to sit on the Plaza or on the water-battery of the old fort. But she maintained that it paid her. Yes; although her shoes were the receptacles of a great deal of sand, and her skirts were festooned with sandspurs, and red bugs disported themselves upon her.

It was not far beyond the curves of the shore, where the little river emptied itself silently into the ocean inlet that they call the Matanzas, that Mr. Job Maine resided. It would hardly be correct to say that he lived. He did not live anywhere. He resided; he stayed.

And this was where his truck grew; that is, it grew here when it grew anywhere. But if truck is not planted it will not grow, even in Florida.

There was the long trunk of a pine-tree which Mr. Maine had some years before, in one of the times when he "flaxed round," to quote his own words, burned at the roots so that it fell to the ground.

Mr. Maine ever since had "aimed" to cut this tree up for firewood. But thus far he had anticipated that it would be considerable trouble to cut it up, and he had not done so; and he did not always find it quite convenient to plough and put seed into the ground at the proper time. Altogether, things were quite a good deal of trouble to Job Maine. What he really wanted to do was to sit on that pine which he had burnt down and meditatively suck a pipe, or roll tobacco from one side of his mouth to the other. His pigs ran about in the sand. He did not know, or care, what they ate. He only knew that he should eat them when he was ready. And if he had planted kale, he should boil some kale with the pork, or, rather, he should tell his wife to do it.

Mr. Maine, as he sat on his pine-tree, used to say that it was "turrible hard work to git er livin', 'specially if a man had a wife to support. Women were so 'xtravagant."

This gentleman now looked forward to longer periods of sitting on that tree, for he was to be in receipt of a regular income of five dollars a month from Mrs. Gerry as rent for the building which she and her daughter occupied.

It was not worth one dollar a month, but Mrs. Gerry did not know that. She was sure it was the cheapest way she could live.

And the ozone was thrown in. In fact, Mr. Maine said he should not charge a cent for the climate, anyway.

As the house in which the Gerrys lived was built of logs, and as the interstices between the logs were not filled, the two women felt that they had nearly as much climate when they were in the house as when they were out of it.

"And as it is air I want," said Salome, cheerily, "why, I cannot complain."

But everything was bitter as gall to Mrs. Gerry. She hated that wretched, one-roomed hut, with its clay and log chimney, which had great holes in it. There was no window, only the door to let in light. And the door had no hinges, and was to be taken up bodily and set in its place. As this could be done better without the hovel than within it, there was much discussion between the two women as to how they should get in after they had put the door up from the outside.

Mr. Maine, when consulted, said he aimed to fix that door before his tenants went North. And meanwhile he professed entire willingness to come any time when the women were inside and put up the door. He said most likely he should be settin' on that pine-tree restin', or somewhere near, and if they scritched he should hear them and would set the door right up. And he shouldn't charge anything, either.

Being interrogated as to the safety from evil people which this door did not provide, Mr. Maine said he supposed two women wouldn't be safe up North, but here in Florida he was of the opinion that they were safer with a door like that than if it had a burglar-proof lock on it. He argued that no man coming along and seeing that door in that condition would think it worth while to take it down.

"Why, Mis' Gerry, don't you see that a feller would say to himself: 'There ain't nothin' behind that thar do', 'n' I sha'n't tech it.' That's about what a feller 'd say. 'N' he'd go on 'n' break in somewhar whar they was fastened and bolted and chained up. Ain't that reasonable, say? But I don't say but what I aim to fix up that do' 'fore you go North."

Mrs. Gerry would reply, sharply, that she did not reason in that way.

She had gone to St. Augustine and had bought a bed, a table, and two chairs. These articles, together with a lamp-stove, were now standing in the hut. Everything else she had managed to bring in their trunk.

Every time it rained she appealed fiercely to her landlord to do something about stopping the leaks. He said that was another thing he was aiming to do 'fore she went North. As yet there had been only showers in the two weeks since their establishment in the cabin.

At first, Mrs. Gerry was in a panic lest Salome should take cold. But she did not. Nothing seemed to hurt her. She was out-of-doors all day. She laughed at inconveniences which made her mother almost frantic with indignation. "People needn't live so," the Yankee woman said a dozen times a day.

When it did rain they would sit by a fire on the hearth, with the door leaned up in its place. And Mrs. Gerry would say that the only reason the old hut didn't burn down was because it was raining. That was no kind of a chimney.

" And what shall we do in a north-east storm ?"

" Let us wait until the storm comes," recommended Salome.

Her mother turned and looked at her sharply. She hardly felt that she knew the child.

" That's no way," she said, with some edge to her voice.

" What's the use of taking life so hard, mother ? Do you know I sometimes feel as if I wouldn't fight any more ? At home, you know, everybody is fighting something. They fight their own sins a good deal. I am going to take things easy."

"Perhaps you'd like to take things as easy as Job Maine?"

"I've found out how delightful it is just to sit in the sunlight," answered the girl, earnestly. "And I'm tired of resisting, resisting. That's all life seems to be, in the North. And here it's yielding, yielding. It's a great deal more comfortable. I don't think I understand myself any more, mother," with increasing earnestness. "I seem to be somebody else. It's just as if there were something in me that I didn't know about, and that coming here had called into life. I have a great deal more physical energy than I had, but I have thought that in some pre-existence I was something or other that just loved to live in warm air and sunshine, and that didn't care much for anything else. Or that I am not the kind of girl I thought I was. I don't think so much as to whether a thing is right or wrong any more. And, worse than that, I'm glad I don't. It was so very trying to be always asking myself that, you know. I used to feel sometimes as if I was like that story about the sharp blade wearing through the scabbard. You see I'm different, somehow. Do you think I'm going to be very wicked? But if I am, I don't believe I shall repent one bit."

Mrs. Gerry, who was tacking up some cotton cloth against the walls, hoping it would keep out wind and rain, got down from her chair that she might the better look at the girl, who was leaning in the doorway and gazing out into the sunshine.

But, after all, as the woman told herself, it was not so much what Salome said as the tone in which she said it.

There was something in that voice that frightened Mrs. Gerry. If the voice had not been in such close sympathy with the words—why, what had come over the child?

"I can explain the mystery," Mrs. Gerry said, with more assurance than she felt.

Salome turned her glance to her mother. There was so little of anything austere in the young face now, that it was difficult to think there ever had been any such quality there.

As the mother met the daughter's eyes she repressed an exclamation of anxious surprise. She restrained herself from shrinking back a step. For one painful instant she felt as if it were the glance of a stranger. Then that feeling passed.

She rarely caressed Salome. But now she suddenly dropped the hammer she had been using and put her arms about the girl.

Salome smiled, and responded warmly to the caress.

"But you have not explained," she said.

"Oh, that is easy," responded the woman, now holding the other away from her and gazing at her.

Then she forgot for the moment what she had been going to say. A sense of bewilderment was upon her. Her clear mind seemed to be groping helplessly.

"Well?" said Salome, still smiling.

"When you were at home you were ill, more or less, and your body reacted on your mind and made you morbid. You certainly were morbidly conscientious. It used to worry me that you would think you were so liable to commit so much sin. You were always such a good girl, Salome. You were so anxious to do right."

"And I don't care a bit now whether I do right or not."

"Of course you can't be always thinking of that.

9

If the attitude of your mind is right you will involuntarily take the right path. We needn't be examining ourselves all the time."

Mrs. Gerry became more and more earnest in spite of the fact that she was telling herself that the girl had taken a whim—it could be but a whim.

"But I don't think the attitude of my mind is right any more. That's what I'm trying to tell you, mother."

Salome disengaged herself from her mother's arm. She walked about the cabin touching absently this and that. The sunshine, warm and penetrating as sunshine is in Florida in November, came through the doorway and seemed to fill the place.

Salome came back and stood in the sunlight again.

"You know," she said, "when we experience religion they say we are born again, and are really different."

"Yes," was the response.

"Well, that's the way I feel—as if I had been born again, only not into any spiritual life, but into the richness, the opulence, of this earthly life. Perhaps," speaking less earnestly, "perhaps I am drunk with this sunlight. I know I feel as I fancy the old pagans must have felt—that I will make the most of this life. This we have, this we are sure of while it lasts."

"Oh, Salome!" exclaimed her mother. "That's only a vagary. You are getting well, and because your bodily strength is so much greater you are having these notions. You are—"

A voice outside interrupted Mrs. Gerry's words.

"Hello! Hello the house!" said the voice.

And at the same time a horse's head came into sight from the other side of the cabin.

And presently it was seen that there was a girl upon the horse.

Salome sprang out from the hut with an eager exclamation.

" I came for an amanuensis," said Miss Nunally.

VIII

"MATERIAL"

SALOME walked up to the horse and leaned upon its shoulder, hardly greeting the horse's rider in her interest in what that rider had just said.

"Really?" she asked; "oh, please don't joke about such an important subject as my earning money. But what can you want of an amanuensis?"

"I didn't say I wanted one. I said I came for one, and I have. I'm going to dismount. Give me your hand. There. Oh, how do you live here? I have no vocation for roughing it. I was made to be rich; but I am poor. It's horrible to miss one's destiny, and to be conscious of it."

Miss Nunally had stepped within the cabin and was looking about her. But there was no insolence in her manner now, and Mrs. Gerry, who had been sure she should heartily dislike this girl of whom her daughter had spoken, was surprised that she should be drawn towards her in some way.

It was true, however, that when Miss Nunally chose there was a certain delicate, almost admiring defer-ence in her manner which few resisted—until they came to think the matter over and to decide that they ought to resist.

Now when Mrs. Gerry looked at the elegant figure sitting upon one of the straight wooden chairs she told herself that this was not at all the kind of girl of whom she approved ; why, then, did she like her? For Mrs. Gerry was quite decided in her own mind that she should never be drawn to anything of which she did not approve.

Salome stood in the doorway, her eyes fixed on her guest.

“ But we cannot miss our destiny,” she said. “ Our destiny will come to us.”

“ You think so, do you? Then if I am destined to marry a rich man, Aunt Florence need not have been to the trouble of having me down here.”

And Miss Nunally gave that short, character-revealing laugh from which Salome involuntarily shrank. But now the tone and the laugh seemed to contain a bitter self-mockery.

“ You said you wanted to earn money,” she went on, immediately. “ Come and write for Mrs. Darrah.”

Salome could hardly believe what she heard. Then her face fell.

“ But I am not a type-writer or a stenographer. Oh, it is too bad ! But I will learn ; yes, I will learn directly.”

She turned with a fiery impulsiveness towards her mother.

There was a sharp envy in Miss Nunally’s heart as she looked at her. She rose quickly. Had she ever been as young, as unsullied as this girl ?

“ I can’t wait,” she said ; “ I must go back immediately. Come this afternoon, before my aunt changes her mind. She writes books, and my advice to you is, don’t rely upon people who write books.”

“ But I will go now.” Salome stepped forward. There was a touching enthusiasm and hope in her slightest movement. She was thinking of her father, and that now she could, perhaps, be a help.

"If there is any danger that she will change her mind, do let me go now."

"Very well. But you will walk and I shall ride, and thus you will make me feel mean all the way. And I don't enjoy feeling mean. But I will sacrifice myself."

The two girls started back. Mrs. Gerry warned her daughter not to expect anything. It was wisest never to expect anything in this world.

When at last they came to Marine Street on their return Miss Nunally, who had been unusally silent, suddenly stopped her horse, which had walked all the way while Salome had plodded on behind, hardly conscious of the deep sand or of anything save the deliciousness of the air and a general and wonderful sense of well-being and elation.

When Miss Nunally spoke to her she was composing the letter to her father which should accompany the first money she would send him.

She could see the look in her father's eyes when he read what she would write. She was not going to be a useless creature any more.

She came up beside Miss Nunally and looked inquiringly at her.

As for Miss Nunally, she gazed so steadily at her companion for a moment that Salome's eyes fell, and she unconsciously moved a step away. She wished to put up her hands before her face, but she restrained herself from doing that.

"Come; come here, closer," at last said Miss Nunally.

Salome's first impulse was to say "No; no—I will

not.” But instead of yielding to that impulse she slowly obeyed and came close to Portia, who leaned forward and put her hand on Salome’s shoulder, pressing somewhat heavily upon it.

“ What is it ?” asked Miss Nunally, in an absorbed manner.

“ I don’t understand you,” was the reply, given in a somewhat cold voice.

“ What has happened to you ?”

“ To me ? Nothing. Only I’m getting well.”

“ You are really getting well ?”

“ Yes, certainly. Can you not see it ?”

“ Then it must be the reassertion of the body and its predilections—and the effect of climate. I don’t think people half understand the effect of climate on the moral creature that is supposed to be in each one of us. Of course I don’t mind such things ; they don’t have any effect on me—I’m not good, anyway. But you, Miss Gerry, do you mind my telling you that when I saw you on the train a few weeks ago you looked like—now you can’t possibly guess what you looked like, can you ?”

“ No.”

“ Of course not. The idea positively haunted me afterwards. You were precisely a visible New England conscience. It was just as if I had met a conscience, you know—a stringent, rigid conscience that brought its owner up in the shortest kind of way, and tormented no end. Now, wasn’t that odd — for me, Portia Nunally, to meet a naked conscience, if you will allow me the term ? Wasn’t it odd ?”

“ Very,” still more coldly from Salome.

“ You need not be offended. I have something more just as strange to tell you. It is more than a week since I saw you; and when I did meet you last I fancied you were changed. Now I'm sure of it. You don't look that way any more. Do forgive me for being so personal."

"What way?" asked Salome, ignoring the last remark, but looking very much as if she would not forgive.

"Why, like a conscience, you know. Positively, I would not think now that you had any more of it than I have. And those who know me best say I haven't any—that is, not any that stops me from doing anything I want to do. Are you offended, Miss Gerry?" with some show of solicitude.

"Yes, I am."

Salome did not know why she felt such a strong emotion of terror. Had she not told her mother that very morning that she was glad that she was not now so constantly asking concerning the right and wrong of a thing? She looked about her as if she would escape from something, she knew not what. Then, with a swift grasp at self-control and reason, she came again near Miss Nunally. She even smiled as she said:

"It is silly to be so very fanciful. You have been saying absurd things."

Portia gathered up the bridle that had fallen forward on the horse's neck.

"Yes, I know it; but absurd things are sometimes true things," she answered. "Besides, I am not alone in this fancy about you."

Salome said nothing. She was fast becoming composed again.

"Why don't you ask me who else has had these absurd ideas concerning you?"

"Well, who has?"

"The young man who was so kind to you on the journey down here," said Miss Nunally.

"Indeed!"

"Yes," looking at Salome. "He has since confided these fancies to me. Miss Gerry"—Portia reached forth and laid her finger lightly on Salome's cheek—"Miss Gerry, I have long wanted to ask you a question."

"Ask it."

"Will you answer me truly?"

"If I answer at all."

"Of course that; but will you tell me why you never blush?"

Having put this interrogation, Miss Nunally dropped all seriousness of demeanor, and she waited for no reply. But she did not immediately go on; her horse still remained quiet.

"My aunt, Mrs. Darrah, requires only one recommendation as regards you, Miss Gerry, and that is negative. There must be no odor of cabbage about you. I have been your guarantee on that head."

The two girls laughed.

In half an hour Salome was sitting in Mrs. Darrah's room. That lady was among shawls and pillows, as usual.

Salome was trying not to be overcome by the magnificence of the hotel, and was at the same time feeling a sort of longing kinship with it. Mrs. Darrah, after the first glance at her visitor, sat upright and looked again at the girl. Salome waited for the other to speak. She had been ushered in by Miss Nunally, who had immediately left them.

Mrs. Darrah had times of rather priding herself

upon her frankness. She now said that her niece
had given her reason to believe that the girl she had
spoken of was not coarse, and that she, Mrs. Darrah,
could not endure anything coarse near her. She explained that she had been obliged to endure a great
deal when she was young and poor, but now that she
was old and rich she did not propose to bear anything
disagreeable.

Salome could think of no suitable reply to make to
this statement, so she remained silent.

"You don't look coarse," now frankly remarked
Mrs. Darrah. She followed this up by asking abruptly if Miss Gerry had read any of her books.

"No."

"I am glad of that. I shall like the judgment of a
young, unsullied mind. It is the judgment of such
minds that I want. The critics don't think much of
me; but, then, I make things even by not thinking
much of them. You remember what D'Israeli says of
critics, Miss Gerry?"

"I don't think I have ever known what he said,"
replied Salome.

"Really? Well, he said that they were those who
had failed in literature and art. And I agree with
D'Israeli. We might begin work directly. I believe
that I feel the coming on of the divine afflatus. I like
to call it that. It pleases me, though it probably is
no more a divine afflatus than is that peculiar aura
which precedes an attack of epilepsy. I don't cherish
any delusions—about myself or any one else. I know
precisely how my work ranks. Please sit down at that
desk: you will find pen and paper there. Yes. Perhaps you use a stylo. No? Choose your pen, please.
Dip it in the ink. It annoys me to have a person dip

a pen for the first time after I begin to dictate. Are
you ready?"

Salome had obeyed. She now wheeled round in
her chair and explained hurriedly that she could not
write shorthand, and, perhaps, after all, she ought not
try to fill this position. And she could not help adding earnestly that if Mrs. Darrah would only have pa-
tience with her she would immediately begin the study
of shorthand.

Mrs. Darrah had now leaned her head back and
seemed about to close her eyes; but she kept her
eyelids raised until she had assured Salome that she
did not insist upon stenography; that she should
probably dictate very slowly, but the young lady might
learn it at her leisure.

"Are you ready now?"

Salome, with an ungovernable sense of the ludicrous
upon her, dipped her pen again, and said, "Yes."

She held her hand suspended for a moment and
gazed intently at the blank sheet of paper before her.

In spite of the fact that Mrs. Darrah was not in the
least awe-inspiring, the knowledge that she had written things which had actually been printed impressed
the girl a great deal. She could not help wondering
as to what were the sensations of a person who had
seen her name in print. Such a woman, she fancied,
could never again be entirely unhappy.

With these things in mind she continued to hold
the pen over the paper.

And the silence also continued.

At last she gave a furtive glance towards the woman
in the lounging-chair; but she withdrew her eyes suddenly, for they encountered Mrs. Darrah's gaze fixed
upon her.

That lady was gazing at her as if she were something which interested her, and which could not be aware of her rather impersonal inspection.

"I am not accustomed to dictation," said Mrs. Darrah; "besides, I never compose rapidly. Let me see your handwriting, please. Show me what you have written."

"But I haven't written anything."

"Oh yes, that is true. I cannot decide how to begin. This is the first chapter, you know. So much depends upon the first chapter. You see, I have written a novel of philosophy, a novel of passion, and now I am going to begin a novel of sentiment; and sentiment gives one quite a scope. Don't you think so, Miss Gerry?"

Salome did not dare to lay down her pen; so she dipped it again in the ink.

"Don't you think so?" repeated Mrs. Darrah.

The girl turned towards her companion.

"I'm afraid I don't know what sentiment is," she replied, deprecatingly.

The woman's face brightened. She sat upright again.

"Oh, that is delightful!" she exclaimed. "Oblige me by handing my note-book—the one bound in blue. Thanks. And my stylo. Thanks again. The idea! a young girl not to know what sentiment is! But I thought your face was unusual. You are probably an embodiment of sentiment, only you can't define the word. How suggestive! And with your face! If I can only work this out! But, then, no wonder you can't define the word—nobody can. It means everything. It is the atmosphere of life. Without it everything would be but an arid desert. It is—"

Mrs. Darrah had been writing rapidly all the time she had been talking. She now ceased speaking, but continued to write for a moment.

Then she shut the little book, and pressed the top of her pen thoughtfully against her chin.

Salome's face was set in the utmost solemnity; and this solemnity was becoming quite real. Whether this woman were deep or shallow was not, perhaps, absolutely apparent; but the girl felt that she was sincere. She made up her mind to ask Miss Nunally for one of her aunt's books. In her ignorance she felt that one of these books would give the key to the writer's character. She was asking herself whether she should first choose the novel of philosophy or the novel of passion, when Mrs. Darrah broke the silence by saying:

"You are so suggestive, Miss Gerry. Did any one ever tell you that before?"

"Oh, no, no!"

Salome hardly knew whether to resent this remark or to be amused by it; but she made no other response.

She dipped her pen in the ink. She was afraid that Mrs. Darrah might suddenly begin to dictate, and that she would be obliged to put her pen in the inkstand after the first sentence was spoken.

Mrs. Darrah again leaned back and again closed her eyes. The girl suspected that this was the attitude in which the authoress would eventually compose; and by this time Salome was longing to know what the dictation would be.

But the lady immediately opened her eyes; those eyes, though small, were very bright, in that kind of way in which a bird's eyes are bright.

"I find I am changing my mind about this novel," she explained. "I'm not sure that I shall begin it to-day. Let us converse for a while. You understand, Miss Gerry, that I shall pay you just the same whether you write or not. It is your time, of course, which is valuable. Let us settle the terms. I want you to get here at nine every morning except Wednesday and Saturday. On those days I give myself to society— that's what I call it; but I hate society, really. I want you to stay until after lunch. You will lunch with me in my own rooms here. I don't go down for that meal — it worries me. I will pay you ten dollars a week. Does that suit you?"

Salome laid her pen down. She was going to clasp her hands, but it occurred to her that that gesture might seem theatrical.

She turned towards Mrs. Darrah, who could not help murmuring:

"Certainly you are suggestive. I have never seen a girl like you. And I thought I had seen them all."

"Will it suit me?" exclaimed the girl. "It is too much. I'm afraid I shall not earn it. But I will learn shorthand as soon as possible."

"Very well. But it is not business-like to say that any sum is too much. Write a few sentences and let me see your handwriting."

Salome eagerly obeyed. Then she carried the sheet of paper to Mrs. Darrah. The girl wrote an upright, clear hand, with no flourish.

"I have one accomplishment," she said, shyly, "or, rather, it is almost a gift. I can imitate any hand with very little effort."

"Ah," indifferently.

Mrs. Darrah absently put her pen to the paper and

wrote one of her favorite quotations. It was that sentence in which St. Augustine says to God :

“ Thou hast counselled a better course than Thou hast permitted.”

Salome’s eyes kindled. She bent forward.

“ Who said that?” she asked, quickly. “ That is true. I have felt that; yes, I have felt that. But I did not know any one else was so wicked as to feel it about God. Who was it, Mrs. Darrah?”

“ It was St. Augustine,” with amused regard upon the girl.

“ And I know that St. Augustine was so good,” sighing as she spoke.

“ Yes, certainly. You see you are not alone in your wickedness, Miss Gerry. However wicked you are, or however good you are, you will find that somebody else has been just as good and just as wicked. There is no originality left; sin is no longer original.”

Salome listened. Then she took the sheet of paper to her desk, and in a moment she carried it again to Mrs. Darrah. Under that lady’s writing she had placed a copy.

“ In my next attempt you could not tell which was your own,” she said. “ And I’m often tempted to copy hands. It’s no good, though. Only it sometimes amuses me. I often write to father so that he doesn’t know whether the letter is from mother or me. Oh,” forgetting her resolve to be very proper, “how glad father will be that you let me work for you. But, Mrs. Darrah, really you must see that I earn my money.”

“ You are earning it now.”

“ Now? I am only talking now.”

"Miss Gerry, do you object to being used as material?"

Plainly the girl did not understand the question. But Mrs. Darrah would not explain. Instead, she leaned back and closed her eyes again. She wished to shut in an idea that had just come to her. She would have explained that ideas were so rare that one was justified in doing almost anything for the sake of capturing one.

Salome sat in her chair by the desk.

She sat in perfect quiet lest she might disturb her employer. She had never, to her knowledge, seen an authoress before, and she hardly knew what to expect of one.

She silently examined the specimen of author-craft before her now. Did they all have such little dried-up faces, with such lines about the mouth and eyes? And did their eyes have a way of diving into one? And what was it to be " material?"

Could it be possible—here Salome started somewhat; no, of course it could not be possible—that Mrs. Darrah had meant that she wished to make use of her, Salome Gerry, in a novel? That would be quite ridiculous.

The silence and the quiet lasted so long that the girl suspected that Mrs. Darrah had gone to sleep, and she was becoming sleepy herself, when the lady, without the slightest warning, opened her eyes as if they had only been closed for an instant, and said,

"We will begin now, if you please."

And again Salome put her pen in the ink, and this time the dictation really began.

To the girl's great surprise she found she was interested in the words she was writing. She felt sure that it was the beginning of a novel, and it must be here in St. Augustine. And she wondered if she were going to care for that man who was described as having a face which seemed to be all profile.

She hurried on and on. Her pen flew over the paper. And underneath all her thoughts was the resolve that she would begin that very day to study shorthand. All that was said besides the dictation were the words·

"Have you that?"

"Yes."

Two hours later, Salome, having lunched alone with Mrs. Darrah on viands whose names she did not know, but whose substance she enjoyed, was going along one of the galleries of the hotel preparatory to descending to the main entrance.

She thought she had never felt so exhilarated and happy in her life. And this building, with its Spanish suggestiveness and rich decorations — how she could enjoy a life which gave her such things. She was dimly conscious of something awakening in her which called for these surroundings—something more than the mere superficial liking of a girl who for the first time becomes acquainted with the sumptuous in this world.

Life should not be bare and rigid and austere. Life should be full of color and enjoyment. What was that mysterious and elusive thing called happiness? Pleasure, at least, might be attainable.

She was feeling this rather than thinking it, aware of many hitherto undreamed-of possibilities that might enter into the experience of human beings, when some one touched her softly on the shoulder.

10

It was Portia Nunally, who was now just going down to her lunch.

"Well," she said, "and what do you think of the authoress?"

Salome hesitated. "She has been very kind."

"That, of course, since you are what you are. But tell me," drawing still nearer, "does she think you are material?"

Salome's eyes drooped quickly.

"She said she thought she could use me," she answered, in a very low tone.

Miss Nunally clapped her hands gently. Salome moved a step away and averted her face.

"I predicted to Mr. Moore just now that she would use you, and what do you think he said?"

"I'm sure I don't know," indifferently.

"He said that he thought you must have a dual nature. Now that was a foolish thing to say, since we all have that; a good and a bad nature. And they fight incessantly if you don't, in the very first place, narcotize the good-nature. Then life is endurable, and you stand a chance of having a good time."

Salome looked up quickly.

"That must be so!" she exclaimed, with startling earnestness.

"Oh yes; I've known that for a good many years. If you wish to be comfortable, it is the first lesson to learn. So I told Mr. Moore. He said he didn't believe it. He's quite strong on the necessity of a high spiritual life. Fancy! And he's the man, you know, who told you such lies—for your good—on the train. Did you know his name is Randolph Moore?"

"No."

"It is."

Miss Nunally moved on a few steps with Salome beside her. They descended the stairs together. Then, as they were about to part, Portia turned, and said :

"When will you tell me why you never blush ? You see you certainly are good material for my aunt. She says that it is not people whom we understand who stimulate us ; it is people who seem contradictory, and whom we are obliged to study as if they were puzzles. She knows me so well that she has no use in the world for me. Ah, here is Mr. Moore now, and I have promised to present him to you, Miss Gerry."

The young man came forward with unmistakable eagerness. Salome looked at him with an earnestness which she never thought of trying to conceal. She was thinking of what Miss Nunally had just told her : that this person was " quite strong on the necessity of a high spiritual life."

She wondered if that were true. Mr. Moore began immediately upon a subject which had evidently been occupying his mind.

" I've wanted to meet you so much, Miss Gerry, and be introduced properly, you know. Are you going ? Do let me walk with you a little way."

Miss Nunally hurried on down the stairs. She waved her hand at them, and turned into the dining-room.

The two went on along King Street.

Although Moore had so much to say, he did not speak until they reached the Plaza. Then he looked at his companion. His face was full of a softened light.

He was thinking that he had hardly known that he

had longed so strongly to see this girl. He had been occupied with business and pleasure. He had been down to Tampa and up the St. Johns, and now it seemed to him that he had been thinking of Salome Gerry every moment since he had seen her.

He had come to St. Augustine with a letter to Mrs. Darrah, and that lady had made much of him, as nearly every one did. And Miss Nunally had been uncommonly interesting. Indeed, he had come back now to this little city for the second time because he should see Miss Nunally. He lived up quite fully to the conviction that a man should never avoid an attractive woman.

But just at present he was sure that in the last few weeks he had thought of nothing but Salome Gerry.

"Oh, I hope you have forgiven me!" he exclaimed at last, his voice thrilling on the words.

"Forgiven you?" questioned Salome.

"Yes; don't you remember? For deceiving you about the sleeper and all that. I can't forget how you looked when you knew I hadn't been quite— quite on the square, you know. But do believe me when I tell you I'm truthful. You've no idea how tired you looked. It seemed to me that I couldn't endure to think of you as sitting up all night in that hideous car. Now, won't you forgive me?"

The two had stopped as by a common impulse when they had entered the park.

Salome said now that she would forgive Mr. Moore; that it was not a matter of any importance; and that he had been very kind.

Then she began to walk towards Marine Street. She was impatient to tell her mother about her engagement to write for Mrs. Darrah.

The young man kept beside her.

" Don't send me away, then," he urged, keeping step with her. " Let me go with you for a little, and let me call on you. Surely your mother would receive me."

Salome laughed. She was thinking of the house on Mr. Job Maine's truck farm.

" But you wouldn't care to have me call, Miss Gerry?" asked Moore, hardly knowing how to interpret the girl's laugh, and feeling somehow repulsed by it.

" No," she answered; " I shouldn't like to have you come."

Then, seeing the expression of pain which came to the young man's face, she hastened to say :

" You've no idea how we are living. It's a wretched place, but being in Florida we are going to put up with it. Anything for the sake of being here, on account of my health."

Moore's face lightened with boyish happiness.

" And is that all the reason ?"

" Yes."

" Then I'm going to walk out with you now and see your mother. She was kinder to me than you were, Miss Gerry. And how much better you look. You have no idea how glad I am to find you."

Moore's eyes shone. His whole face was radiant. His glance was constantly seeking his companion's. He was telling himself over and over that this girl was charming—charming.

She did not look precisely as she had done on the train. That was because she seemed now so much stronger in health, he supposed.

The two talked of a thousand things. Moore had

never felt himself so brilliant. Everything he said had an air of cleverness, he thought. He had hardly known before that he was such a clever youth; that his ideas were so lucid, and that he could express himself so much to the point.

Not that he really thought of himself at all. He did not think of anything. He was like one floating in some atmosphere which both exhilarated and soothed.

But he was not in the least surprised. Nothing in the way of good-fortune could surprise Moore. Thus far he had had most things he wanted.

He did not fail to learn the days when Salome would be with Mrs. Darrah and when she left the hotel. He said business would keep him in the vicinity a week or two. He wasn't staying at the Ponce; oh no, poor people didn't go there. He felt quite overwhelmed at venturing even to call there. He laughed much as he talked. This laugh seemed to be a sort of escape for the abounding spirits that bubbled up in him. He felt half drunk with something, he knew not what. In his own mind he said it was the climate; but he must own that the climate had never affected him in this way before.

So two weeks passed. He had only missed three days in that time when he had not walked out the two miles through the sand and the dwarf palmetto with Salome.

It was the last day of the second week, when Salome, coming into the city in the morning, went to the post-office as usual. She found a letter from her father. It was addressed to her mother, but she always opened her father's letters. She opened this one, leaning against the wall of the office as she did so. It was not long. It began abruptly:

"I haven't let you know that I couldn't keep up my interest on the mortgage on the farm. I haven't paid it for three years, and now you know I've borrowed $400 more on the east wood-lot. I could have staggered along if it hadn't been for Salome's sickness. But I don't begrudge all that has cost. No matter what comes if she gets well. But it's tough. Uncle John is going to foreclose. He says he can't afford not to. We are under his thumb. If I had $800 within a week I could weather it—for now. The old place 'll be sold. It's belonged to the Gerry's for one hundred and fifty years. I'd rather die—well, I ain't lucky. Don't wish you hadn't married me, Salome. And don't come home. That would only make things worse. Keep this from the child. She needn't know it till she comes—home I was going to say—till she comes North again—unless some devilish meddler writes it to her. You needn't worry about me. Only let the child get well."

Salome leaned yet more heavily against the wall. She read the letter a second time. She wished people would not walk in and out of the place as they did. It confused her. And she must think. It was because of her. Eight hundred dollars. Within a week.

She folded the sheet of paper and carefully put it in its envelope. She walked quickly to the Ponce.

Mrs. Darrah had a headache, but she told the girl to sit down at the desk and wait a half-hour, when she might join her.

So Salome sat down alone in the sitting-room.

Mrs. Darrah's note-books and her check-book were lying there with sheets of MS. and blank paper.

Salome immediately took up the check-book. She turned its leaves swiftly through her fingers.

Then, without the least hesitation, she filled in a check for $800, and signed Florence Darrah to it, apparently in Florence Darrah's own hand.

She went to the door of the lady's bedroom and said that she would go the post-office, but would return directly.

She stepped back to the desk and wrote a note to her father, saying:

"It happens that a friend who is rich will loan us this money. So it will be all right, and the farm need not be sold. There'll be no hurry about the pay. But I think I shall be able to attend to that. Dear father, I am getting so well, and I am earning. Don't tell mother this, and I shall not show her your letter. I read it first."

In five minutes the letter with the check was posted, and Salome sat waiting at the desk.

She was telling herself that she was very glad she had sent that check.

IX

GEORGE ELIOT somewhere says that it is the habitual restraint or indulgence of years that determines what one will do in some sudden stress of temptation. And so indeed it is ordinarily. But there are some natures in which there is a lurking power that has slept, but that awakens with an unexpected puissance that seems to make an entirely different person of one whom we have thought we knew perfectly. Some phases of character lie dormant for years. There are those whose consciences are long keyed up to such painful activity, such morbid sensitiveness, that the reaction is inevitable, and sometimes deeply disastrous. For a reaction often brings more or less of recklessness of mood if not of deed. If highly strung natures reach heights, they sometimes reach depths also of which the commonplace soul has positively no conception.

When Salome returned from posting that note and its enclosure to her father, she sat for half an hour in Mrs. Darrah's sitting-room awaiting that lady's pleasure.

She had forged that name with as complete suddenness and absence of calculation as she would have snatched her father's hand from burning coals if her father had been powerless to do it for himself.

And now as the moments went by she was aware only of a thankfulness that she had done so. She was not conscious of any clearness of thought as yet. In fact, she was hardly thinking at all. She was vaguely picturing to herself her father's gratitude and joy when he should receive that letter.

It had seemed to her that the thing must be done instantly. She had no time to arrange to ask anything of anybody. And, besides, it was not in her nature to ask favors.

She hardly knew how cold her hands were or how her eyes stung with an unaccustomed heat. She was absently writing meaningless words on a sheet of paper before her. Her mind seemed entirely filled with wondering whether Mrs. Darrah would care to dictate this morning. On several days the whole of the time had been taken up in conversation—that is, Mrs. Darrah would lounge among her pillows and ask questions of the girl who sat in front of her. At some of the replies she would seize her note-book with an exclamation of delight and make an entry in it.

"It is not so much that I must get on with my novel as that I must study you," she once remarked. "You needn't shrink," as Salome made a slight move-ment; "you must be studied. It is the penalty you pay for having that kind of a face."

"But what kind of a face do you mean?" asked Salome, with some distress in her tone. She felt a little as if a process of vivisection were going on and that she was the subject.

"That's just it," replied Mrs. Darrah, with apparent satisfaction. "I can't tell you in the least what kind it is; it is several kinds of a face. Severe and indulgent, reckless and discreet. You see I have no idea how to classify you.”

“’Then please don’t try to classify me, Mrs. Darrah. I’m just a common sort of a girl. I used to have times of rigid self-examination, but I’ve given that all up since I got well. I suppose that goes with illness, don’t you?” looking with some eagerness at her companion, who was watching her intently.

“You mean,” said Mrs. Darrah, “that

> “ ‘When the devil was ill,
> The devil a monk would be ;
> When the devil was well,
> The devil a monk was he.’ ”

Salome laughed. She began to be aware now that she was greatly excited.

“ Yes, that must be what I mean, though I hate to think so. Now as I look back upon my life I think I was very good. But I didn’t think so then. I thought I was a vile, sinful creature. I used to find such wicked thoughts when I groped round in my mind. I did really and truly want to be a high spiritual being, and I was always what they called ‘ rather feeble.’ I wasn’t well. Now I am well I don’t think at all about being a high spiritual being.”

Salome’s eyes deepened as she went on. She was very earnest, for her lips were slightly tremulous, and there was a white light all over her pale face.

Suddenly she rose from her chair and took a step towards Mrs. Darrah. She pressed the palms of her hands softly together after a manner which she had.

The small and sparkling eyes of the elder woman were watching her keenly. Mrs. Darrah’s pulses quickened a little as she met the girl’s gaze.

But as suddenly as she had started Salome turned away. She walked back to the desk and mechanically took up her pen.

With her face thus averted she said that if Mrs. Darrah did not wish to dictate, perhaps she would let her go home.

"Certainly," said the lady. "But come here."

Salome came to Mrs. Darrah's couch. Her hands were taken a moment, then dropped.

"Ah, I knew they were cold. I should like to be very kind to you, Miss Gerry. I am a lonely woman, and I have a great deal of money. You don't look as if you were mercenary. If I ever get Portia married —well, well, run along now. Come to-morrow. And don't work too hard at the shorthand. We do very well as we are, eh ?"

Salome left the room. She forgot that she had said she must go home. As she went down the stairs she heard Miss Nunally's voice, and then a man's laugh and quick rejoinder. The sounds grated on her. She hurried down across the Plaza and did not stop until she had reached the fort. She sat there on the water battery. She hardly noticed whether others were there or not.

The air blew softly from the south. The island opposite looked asleep. The small craft in the Matanzas glided silently back and forth almost at the girl's feet.

"I'm so glad I did it," she whispered at last. " Something had to be done immediately. Miss Nunally says that Mrs. Darrah is generous, but that she thinks a great deal of her money. I am very glad I did it. When I tell Mrs. Darrah—for of course I shall tell her—"

She did not finish her sentence. The air was so

lovely, the environment was so beautiful and still, so novel to her; she had been so starved for just such an atmosphere for body and soul that she forgot to try to finish her sentence. To certain kinds of sensitive natures there is an opiate as well as an invigoration in surroundings.

But at last the girl rose. As she paced slowly along by the fort walls, turning her face more fully to the breeze, she glanced about her as one glances who is thinking of some one. She gained the sea-wall and walked upon it, now moving absently, her eyes cast down.

But she had seen that some one. Up there, among the saddle-horses standing for hire, was a figure she was not likely to mistake.

But Moore probably would not see her. This was earlier than she generally left the Ponce, and he would not be looking for her now.

She went on more and more swiftly. If she passed on beyond the park he would have no more chance to see her, and she would not look; she would hurry that that moment of uncertainty might the sooner be over. She would walk out alone this morning.

Now she had almost reached the barracks. No, he had not noticed her. He would presently go up to the hotel and lounge about until the usual time for her to leave Mrs. Darrah. Then would he be disappointed? What would he do? Would he come out to the little log-hut? Would he?

"Ah, Miss Gerry, are you trying to run away from me?" cried a voice close behind her.

Moore ranged up by her side, and bent down to give one eager look into her face.

"Don't—oh, don't—tell me you were wishing to escape me! But then, if that is the truth, you must tell me so, and I shall have to bear it. But I could bear anything better than that—anything in this world, Miss Gerry. Do you know that? Tell me, do you know it?"

There was an intensity in the young man's voice and face which heretofore he had succeeded in repressing, in great measure. But suddenly, at sight of Salome now, he had felt it to be a sheer impossibility to repress it any longer.

He glanced about him impatiently.

It would be some moments before they were out of the city and in the deep solitude of the palmetto scrub. It seemed to him that the restraint he had kept over himself in the past could not be maintained for another instant.

"Tell me!" he repeated, imperatively.

She did not glance at him. She looked out seaward; and it was what appeared to her companion a long time before she said:

"Tell you what?"

And still she did not look at him.

He hardly knew how to answer her, for he had forgotten precisely what he had said. How could he remember what words he had used? Words were nothing. There was nothing in the world of any importance now save to be with this girl, and to have her turn to him and look as such a face as hers must be able to look.

Moore quickened his pace. "Do let us walk faster!" he exclaimed. "Let us get away from these streets! I hate these streets!"

Salome obeyed. The two hurried on. The man concentrated all his thoughts apparently upon putting the settlement behind them.

Presently they were out in the waste with only the stretch of sand and of water ahead of them, and safely behind the towers of the hotels and the gray walls of the old houses.

Moore turned impetuously. He put his hand on Salome's arm.

"Oh, don't go on so fast!" he pleaded.

She smiled, still without looking at him.

"You are very hard to please," she responded; and she spoke almost in a flippant tone, as if such a tone might be a kind of defence to her. "You wanted to walk fast, and I hurried. And now —"

"Now," interrupted Moore "now we are away from all those people, I want to keep away from them. I want to be with you, Salome Gerry. I want to be with you all my life. All my life."

His warm, ardent voice repeated those words as if he could not put sufficient meaning into them.

There was no reply. Salome was still hurrying as well as she could through the sand.

The crows, in a large flock, were flying between her and the sun.

Suddenly she became aware of those birds. She thought it was they who cast a shadow upon her heart. What was it? Surely they could not do that.

She gave him a lustrous look, in which there was something of fright.

"Did you see them?" she asked.

"See what?"

"The crows. They went right over us."

At this instant she thought of the check that must have started two hours ago on its journey North to her father. She was very glad she had sent it. She would tell Mrs. Darrah by-and-by. Not because she was sorry, or repented, but because she did not know exactly when it would be found out that Mrs. Darrah had not herself signed it. It would not be found out directly; she was quite sure of that. And perhaps it would never be discovered. Anyway, she would have time enough to consult with Mrs. Darrah, and her father would pay his Uncle John. She could arrange somehow. It would not take her two years to pay for it, if there was any disturbance. Of course, she knew vaguely about forgers. But other forgers did not have the incentive which had inspired her to do the deed. Her conscience did not trouble her in the least. But she supposed there would be some arrangement. She would speak, perhaps to-morrow, to Mrs. Darrah.

But she wished those crows had not sailed over just then.

Moore glanced up at the sky. To him the sky seemed to be blessing them. He did not see the crows. They had flown out across the river, and were preparing to settle down on the beach.

"I did not know you were superstitious," he said, trying to speak calmly.

A tremor passed through the girl's frame.

"I did not know it, either. I don't think I am."

Impelled by the power of his presence, she turned slowly towards Moore and looked at him.

The two had paused in their walk. They were standing and gazing into each other's eyes.

All at once a strong vibration shook the young man. He bent towards Salome, but he did not touch her. He had imagined love like this. He had known that a great love like this would some day overwhelm him in unspeakable rapture.

There was not the slightest egotism in his mind or in his voice as he whispered, in a breathless way:

"Oh, I know you love me! I know you love me—as I love you!"

And the girl whispered in return:

"Yes—yes—yes."

He took her hands and put them palms together, and then pressed his own over them, still keeping his eyes on hers.

Did several moments pass thus?—or only one breath of time?

There was a hoarse, multitudinous cry in the air above them.

It was the crows coming back to the main-land.

Again Salome trembled. She tried to draw away from the grasp which held her.

"There they are!" she exclaimed, still in a whisper.

He smiled happily.

"But I thought you were not superstitious?"

And again she answered:

"I don't think I am."

She glanced at the stretch of blue ocean beyond the island. But it was not blue now; there was a haze like a silver veil spreading from it inland. The air was warm and sweet.

The crows had gone out of sight.

"We must go on," she said.

"No matter; since I go with you," was the response.

The two walked in silence. Moore could not look at anything but the figure by his side. But Salome did not now look at him. She was gazing straight ahead of her. There was a white splendor on her face.

"Are you happy?"

She heard Moore's voice. She stopped walking, turning towards him and clasping her hands.

Instead of waiting then for her reply Moore said, immediately :

"Do you know how happy I am ?"

"You look happy," she answered, in an almost inaudible tone.

"If I were happier I could not breathe—I could not live," he said, with the extravagance of a lover who believes what he says and who knows that no man or woman before him has ever fully known happiness.

After another short silence Salome said, now speaking with great rapidity :

"I have thought of something which makes me wretched."

"No, no !" he exclaimed. "But tell me what it is. I can drive it away."

"It is something Miss Nunally said."

"Miss Nunally ?" he smiled, incredulously. "What was it ?"

"It was something like this : that you had great ideas of a high spiritual life. Now, have you ?" with intense earnestness.

"Yes, I hope I have. I mean to have," he answered. "I do try to live—that is, I have times of trying—as if I had such an ideal. But, you see, a man is so subject to moods and temptations. But now that you let me love you, Salome, I feel as if, indeed, I might be a far better man—as if my striving might amount to something. Oh, you cannot conceive what you are to me ! You—"

"Don't !" she cried, with some sharpness. "You needn't feel that way."

"Need not ?" in a wondering question.

“ No, no !”

“ But why ?”

“ Because—you see it would not be fair.”

“ Not fair ?” he asked.

She appeared to find some difficulty in going on.

“ No.   Because I—I myself don’t care for a high spiritual life.”

“ Not care for it ?”

Moore was so perplexed that he could only repeat her words.

“ No.   I used to care, above everything.   I used to be striving for it all the time.   But now I don’t think anything at all about it.   Now—” she hesitated ; then she smiled in a way that made a most fitting accompaniment to her words—“ now I want to have a good time ; I’m tired of being conscientious.   Conscience doesn’t go with this air and sky.   As Job Maine says : ‘ It’s quite a good deal of trouble ’ to be conscientious ; and you are not half as happy, either. Did you ever think the doctrine of the first Epicureans had some reason in it, Mr. Moore ?”

When she ceased speaking, now, Salome laughed a perfectly care-free and infectious laugh.

Moore joined her.   He did not in the least believe what she had just been saying.   And he did not believe that she believed it.   And yet—why should her face have just that expression, if she were merely talking “ for fun,” as he would have said.

As for himself, Moore was extremely well aware that a “ high spiritual life ” was still a great way from him.   But he had told the simple truth when he had said he had seasons of longing for it and striving for it.   He could not imagine that any one could deliberately and truthfully say that he did not care for it.

It was one of Moore's favorite subjects. He liked to talk about it; it always made him feel better. To talk earnestly on this topic had somewhat of the effect of having made a notable attempt towards something better. He was not aware that, while words are a great deal cheaper than deeds, they yet bring, oftentimes, more self-complacency than the deeds themselves.

Moore was not given to the examination of his own soul, as has been stated previously in these chronicles; but it was a truth that he did have a high standard of manly living. Not that he always lived by that standard, by any means: who does? But he could not have dreamed of denying that standard.

And he thought Salome now was jesting when she said she did not care for these things. Of course she cared.

The young man was not likely to spend much thought, however, on such subjects just now. He could hardly be said to think upon anything as he walked by the girl's side.

It was now noon: one of those noons when Florida, in the fall or early winter, forgets that she is not really a tropical country, and takes to herself the heats and the odors of those Caribbee isles which lie not so many miles to the south.

The air glimmered hotly over the sand. There was very little wind. In some pools of water, that shone in the sun, frogs were piping monotonously. Salome liked the frog cries. It was a sound that told her, day after day and night after night, that there was no real winter in that land where she had come.

When a mocker flew past her, and, alighting on a tree, sang to her, her heart beat with a kind of suffocating joy and pride in this world and in mere animal life.

The mocking-bird clung to the branch of the wild orange, and gave out his sensuous and yet spirit-moving song.

Salome turned to Moore and found his eyes on her absorbedly. That gaze made her stammer slightly at first, but she said, with sufficient clearness, speaking out her thought :

“ We are given mere animal life here ; and it is so lovely—so lovely! Now I don't feel ill I seem to know for the first time that just the breath of our nostrils may be exquisite joy. Don't you think so, Mr. Moore ?”

“ Think so? I don't know. I'm not capable of thinking to-day. I'm only living.”

“ Yes, yes ; that's it. To be only living,” she returned. “ I hoped you would understand me. If I say anything like this to mother she has such a grieved, anxious look come over her face that I cannot go on. And then I've been brought up so well ” —smiling joyously—“ that she thinks I am changed. And I am—I am.”

The girl again stopped in her walk. She stretched out her arms with a gesture of happiness and abandonment to the delight of the atmosphere and the sunlight, and the mood that was upon her.

Moore, gazing at her, wished that her arms had been extended towards him. But something held him back from touching her.

“ Florida has come into my heart,” she said, fervently.

Her arms dropped to her side, and she began to walk on again.

Moore took her hand and held it closely, keeping step with her. Many warm words came to his lips to be spoken, but he did not utter them. It was enough to be walking thus with her. Why should he want to speak?

Once she turned towards him her pale face, which wore its look of exalted enthusiasm.

Then he put his quick question again:

"Are you happy?"

"How stupid you are!" she cried, speaking lightly, lest she might reveal too much.

"But tell me!" he urged.

"Well, then, if you will have it: I am wretched; I am miserable."

"I don't believe it," quickly, and pressing nearer her.

She smiled at him.

"Then if you do not credit what I say, you will not believe me when I tell you I am happy."

"Try me and see."

Now she laughed.

"No, no; I will not risk it. Let us hurry. I must tell my mother. She likes you, Mr. Moore; you are one whom everybody likes. How strange that must be. And I—Mr. Moore, I wish to say something to you."

The girl stopped again in her walk. She had withdrawn her hand from her companion.

"I am listening," he said, "and I wish to suggest to you that you might call me something besides Mr. Moore."

She made no reply to this remark. He immediately asked:

"What do you wish to say to me?"

He was wondering how he could ever have thought himself interested really in anything else in the world.

“ If you will promise to stand perfectly quiet, and not to come near me—”

“ Yes, I promise,” he said. There was a soft sparkle in her eyes ; and there was a tremble upon her smiling lips.

She clasped her hands with a movement full of indescribable fervor.

She looked up at him, and then her eyes instantly drooped below his gaze. She was silent.

“ Oh, what is it ?” he asked.

“ I thought I could say it to you,” she answered, after a pause. “ But I’m afraid I cannot.”

“ You must ! You must !” not moving from his position a few feet from her.

Her eyes were turned downward. She put her clasped hands suddenly up to her heart.

“ I love you so—I love you so !” she said.

“ Oh, Salome !”

Moore made one uncontrollable step forward ; at the same time the girl stepped back.

“ Remember your promise,” she whispered. “ You are not to come near me.”

“ Oh, Salome !” he said again ; and he added, passionately, under his breath, “ My darling ! my love !”

She made no response. After an instant she began to walk on so rapidly that she had the appearance of running away. Moore kept beside her. He perceived that she did not wish him to speak, so, though it was very difficult for him, he remained silent.

After a while they came within sight of Job Maine’s estate. There were the two miserable hovels. There was the stretch of sand where Mr. Maine ploughed, and where he raised his truck. There were a few cabbages standing desolately on their stalks and trying feebly to "head up," and some sweet-potato vines straggled about discouraged. Mr. Maine had been aiming to do some hoeing for more than two weeks, and he was still aiming.

His figure was visible sitting on the tree trunk. A puff of smoke sometimes passed from his dry, white lips. He saw the two coming along the path. He took the trouble to move a very little, so that he might have a better opportunity to gaze at them. In thus gazing he let the fire in his pipe go out. He sucked strongly at the blackened clay tube for a moment, his thin cheeks hollowing, and his whole face contorted. Then he removed the article from his mouth.

"Durn!" he said, sullenly and slowly. "I ain't had half my smoke out."

He looked towards his cabin, thinking to call his wife to bring him a coal from the hearth : but no one was visible. He put the pipe in his pocket.

The path, such as it was, wound among the stumps of pine-trees directly by where he sat.

Mr. Job Maine did not seem to be in a good-humor to-day. In the morning he had asked Mrs. Gerry to advance him another month's rent. As she had already paid ahead for two months, she had refused to grant her landlord this favor.

He was thinking now that he should like to go and tell that Yankee woman to pack up her duds and tramp. Still, Mr. Maine had sense enough to know that she probably would neither pack nor tramp at present ; and it was considerable trouble to tell her.

He had already brought in a bill of three dollars for the night and day in which Mrs. Gerry and her daughter had remained under Mr. Maine's own roof, receiving what he had at their first meeting called "Southern horspitality." At the end of that time Mrs. Gerry had absolutely driven him forth to Augustine for her trunk. She had said that another twenty-four hours spent with Mr. Maine and his wife would kill her, even if her daughter survived.

And Mr. Maine had charged one dollar for getting the trunk, and one dollar for allowing Mrs. Gerry to sit in the cart with him while the mule took them by imperceptible degrees into the city and back again.

The gentleman explained that it was not so much the mere act of driving Mrs. Gerry into town and getting her trunk that was worth money, as that his time was valuable. It was a day's job, he said ; and that day, he asserted, he had aimed at doing a number of things. He remarked that at this season of the year he was " jes' 's hurried 's he could be ;" whereat Salome laughed in as care-free a manner as if she were at a play, and this speaker were one of the actors.

But Mrs. Gerry was not care - free, and she had a wild wish at the moment to be a man, and to have a stout whip in her hand, and to lay that whip with the utmost violence over this creature's shoulders.

What she had first thought was a lazy good-nature in Mr. Maine she soon discovered to be only the inertia that would not rise to active anger or to activity of any kind.

Mrs. Maine began immediately to tell languidly all she had endured since her marriage. She never spoke on any other subject but this endurance, and the difference there was in her present condition and her condition when she was a young girl.

Salome would look at her with incredulous wonder. In her heart she did not believe that Mrs. Maine had ever been a young girl.

The woman would sit at one side of the fireplace— for she seemed to want a fire whether the day was hot or cool—and tell what luxuries had been hers when she was young—"befo' thur wah."

She never failed to assert that her family was one of the "fust fam'lies down in Alabawm."

And, furthermore, she always said that her parents had opposed her marriage, but that she had married "fur love."

Salome would look at the speaker, and then out to the pine log at the speaker's husband, who had been married "fur love."

Then the girl would shudder. One day she asked her mother if it were possible that Mrs. Maine could ever have loved, or if Mr. Maine could ever have inspired that sentiment.

"Because," she said, emphatically, "if that has been possible, it would be a good thing to die before that kind of a disillusionment comes."

Mrs. Gerry laughed, and replied that she felt positive that Mrs. Maine had never belonged to a first family in Alabama or anywhere else; but as for love, why, that was too mysterious a subject to discuss.

"There was Caliban," said Salome, meditatively.

Now, as she was walking along the path with some one quite different from Caliban, the sight of Job Maine on that log gave her a shock.

She stopped, and laughed somewhat nervously.

"What is it?" asked Moore.

"You see that man?"

"Maine? Yes."

"Well," laughing again and shuddering also, "his wife has told me a score of times that she married that man 'fur love.'"

X

A LITTLE TENNIS

THE man who had been married for love continued to gaze with a stolid persistence at the two young people coming towards him through the thick sand. They came on with comparative lightness, considering that the sand pulled at them as if it had been alive and wished to draw them under.

Job felt a dull envy of them. He had always been phlegmatic, but now, seeing these two, he assumed in his own mind that he should have been "jest as peart 'n' go ahead" if he had not been threatened with consumption and been obliged to come South, and if he hadn't married such a kind of woman. He knew of plenty of reasons, besides the reason inherent in his own character, why he was what he called an "onlucky man."

His pipe having gone out, he had fallen back on his "chaw," which he retained in his mouth even while he smoked.

He was crouching forward, with his elbows on his knees, in his usual position.

A black and white hound, which was just terminating an often-renewed battle with the fleas which infested him, rose from the shade of a banana shrub. This banana had once been planted by Mrs. Maine, and it had lived as well as it could in spite of the frosts which nipped it every winter.

The dog shook its flapping ears and walked slowly towards the new-comers.

Salome stooped to pat the animal as it stood patiently beside her. She was glad to see the hound. The abounding, exuberant happiness in her heart made her hand linger with even more than its ordinary gentleness upon the dog's head.

"Good-morning, Mr. Maine," said Moore, with some effusion, and to be effusive with the man before him was an act of singularly poor judgment.

"Mornin'," responded Job.

"How's your wife to-day?" inquired the young man, his good-will including everybody.

"Wall," said Mr. Maine, slowly, "it's her day for them shakes, 'n' she's got um bad. Sometimes I think them first fam'lies in Alabaum has shakes wuss 'n' common folks."

There was not a hint of a smile on the man's face.

Moore laughed, and responded that he supposed there were drawbacks even to the joy of belonging to the Alabama first families.

"You bet," was the response. "Mis' Maine," went on Job, "needs whiskey; she needs it bad. If I had half a dollar I should hitch urp 'n' go in 'n' git it fur her. But when a man has a wife to s'port he can't always hev money in his pocket."

Moore put his hand in his own pocket. His fingers touched a silver dollar.

He did not believe in the man before him, and he had a sincere contempt for him. But to-day he would have given money to any one.

He extended the silver piece to Job Maine, who held out his dingy yellow palm for it.

"I'll borry it," he remarked. "I ain't no objeck of

charity. I'm—" Here he paused as if he could hardly find words to describe himself. He finished by saying, " I'm a Massachusetts man."

Moore laughed again.

" I wish I could say the same," he said, " but I'm only a New-Yorker."

" Sorry to hear it," said Mr. Maine; " but then you ain't to blame. 'Tain't fair to blame er feller fur what he can't help."

He lifted himself slowly from the log.

" Thar's my ole 'oman. That's her scritch you hear. I s'pose she wants some blamed thing or other."

" Whiskey, perhaps," said Moore.

Each member of the group gazed up towards the residence of Mr. Maine. A woman had appeared in the always open doorway.

" Job! Job, I say! There ain't er stick er firewood hyar! You go 'n' curt some! Do it right soon !"

" Yes," said Mr. Maine, " that's her scritch. Them fust fam'lies of Alabaum hev right pow'ful scritches. They do that."

The man turned towards Moore.

" You ought er take warnin' by me, you young feller, 'n' look out 'bout gittin' into thur noose. It's a turrible strain on a man to hev to s'port a wife. I should hev had prop'ty if I hedn't hed to s'port a wife. Women are so thunderin' 'xtravagant."

" I say, Job, you !" came from the hut.

" Yes," remarked Mr. Maine, " it's her scritch. I reckon I sh'll hev to be gwine."

But he made no further movement for some time.

Moore and his companion walked on. The hound

followed them with drooped head and languidly waving tail. What with the fleas and the extreme uncertainty of his meals, the dog was not as happy as a dog should be.

Upon occasion he made long trips, lasting several days, into the barrens towards the south. At those times he hunted on his own account and he ate what he caught. He would come back comparatively sleek. But since the arrival of the Gerrys he had remained at home, and he had chosen their cabin as his home. There he shared a great many Indian-meal "fire-cakes" and swallowed many chicken bones. His poor, despondent-looking tail became less and less despondent. Something like animation was now and then visible in his eyes.

What did he care that his master called him a "durned ole houn' that didn't know whur he belonged?"

This dog now managed to trot on ahead a few yards towards Mrs. Gerry, who was sitting out-of-doors in the shade cast by her cabin.

Moore hurried forward, his face and eyes glowing. He went straight up to Salome's mother. He bent down on one knee by her side, and put his arm over her shoulders.

His action was so genuinely spontaneous, so evidently from his overflowing heart, that it made him more winning to Mrs. Gerry than she had ever known him. Of course she knew what was coming. She flushed and grew pale.

She glanced at her daughter, but she could not see Salome's face.

Yielding to the impulse upon her, and to the bright attraction of youth and ardor and truth in the young man's handsome face, the woman kissed him on each cheek. He had flung off his hat. She passed her hand over the thick light hair which was now closely cropped.

Tears came into her eyes and fell upon that hair, glittering keenly for a moment.

Moore's own eyes were blurred. He thought that he had never before had any sense of what he had missed in not having known his mother.

"Dear Mrs. Gerry," he whispered, "I cannot tell you how I love her. Do you think I love her enough? She has all my heart. She shall have all my life. But what can any man's heart or life be in comparison with the happiness of knowing that she—"

Moore hardly knew how he had put the sentence together. It seemed lumbering and stupid, and he did not care to finish it.

He lifted his head and turned to look at Salome. But she had gone within the cabin. She was sitting by the bed with her face pressed into the pillow.

She wondered why at that moment she should think of Walter Redd, and should for the first time ask herself if he had really suffered. She wondered why, though the reason was plain enough. She heard indistinctly the voices of her mother and her lover outside. She wished that she might go away and be alone for a few moments. She did not wish to see any one—not any one.

She rose; she shook back the hair impatiently from her face; with her hat in her hand she went out and walked away in the direction of some pines which Mr. Maine had not yet burned down.

The place was a rolling rise of land. From its summit one might see the Island of Anastasia, with its light-house, and could catch a sight of the long, glittering line of blue ocean beyond. Everywhere hereabouts one was likely at any time to see that blue stretch of the Atlantic.

The hound, who had been sitting on his haunches by the group in the shade of the hut, instantly suspected that Salome had left the place. He rose and solemnly followed her, keeping one pace behind her until she paused on top of the little hill.

She stood very quietly, looking off seaward. The dog sat down, and was ready to wait any length of time until it should please his companion to start.

At the left, two or three miles away, were visible the church spires and the hotel towers of St. Augustine. But Salome did not see them. She was gazing with vague intentness towards the ocean. The mist which had been gathering there was spreading more and more thickly from the sea inland.

But through the mist the sun still shone with a subdued and dreamy luminousness. It was so warm that the mocker which had come and preened himself upon a stiff stalk of golden-rod now stood indolently, with his wings lifted. The frogs, which day and night kept up their pipings, were now voiceless, save that once in a while one would give a shrill, wavering call, and that was the only sound, save the undertone of the waves on the farther side of Anastasia, and the kindred undertone of the air in the tops of the tall Southern pines.

As Salome stood there, with the hound sitting close behind her, a little flock of mourning doves came running along through the rank, coarse grass. The dog turned his head gravely towards them, and they rose and flew away.

Salome saw the sober, small birds; she watched

their flight, but she did not know that she did so. She turned apparently scrutinizing eyes upon everything about her, but chiefly she kept her gaze on the ocean. Still she was thinking of nothing which her eyes saw. She was really aware of nothing but a penetrating and piercing happiness.

But all at once a shadow came across her rapt face. She was wishing that those crows had not flown over her, over her and Randolph Moore. She made a quick and uncontrollable movement forward. The hound rose and stood ready.

She glanced down at him.

"Dear old Jack!" she said. And Jack licked the hand which hung by her side. His yellow-brown eyes were upturned in pathetic question and confidence.

Salome spoke aloud, but what she said had no reference to her lover.

"By the day after to-morrow father will have the money." And she added, below her breath, "I'm glad I did it. I should not have thought of doing it for myself, but I'm glad I did it for father."

A joyous voice from the direction of the cabin called:

"Salome! Salome!"

She turned to see Moore coming with long strides across the sand, pushing aside the scrub-oak limbs impatiently, his face showing eager and ardent.

Salome was suddenly beset by an inexplicable instinct, which imperatively suggested flight.

But she knew she could not fly; the sand would make her feet like lead.

She put out her hands with a quick gesture of denial. The gesture was so decided that Moore paused.

"Let me come," he said.

"No, no! Go back to Augustine."

"But when shall I see you? Don't be cruel to me, Salome."

She did not answer his last remark.

"I don't know. To-morrow, perhaps. Go, please; I want to be alone—with Jack," glancing at the dog with a slight smile.

"Do you mean it? What a hard-hearted girl you are! And your mother has been so kind to me."

"Yes, I mean it. But my mother is always kind."

Salome moved away from the young man who stood looking at her. He lingered a moment, his eyes upon her receding figure. He was acutely disappointed. He thought, with a sigh, that girls were scarcely like human beings. How could she go away from him thus if she loved him? He could hardly give up the joy of a few more words with her, of a moment of silence.

But she was walking resolutely. Then she meant what she said. Girls so often did not mean what they said. He supposed he must obey her. It required a good deal of resolution to enable him to set his face unflinchingly to walk back to Augustine, and it would be so long before the next day.

But he began his return, and he did not pause until he had reached the Plaza. Here he sat down. He was still confused with his happiness. It was with difficulty that he could return the greetings of acquaintances who sometimes sauntered by. He was glad there were not many out now. It was not two hours after noon. Of the people who believed that they constituted society, no one was visible.

There was a suffocating odor from the sulphur water that bubbled in the old market from the artesian pipe. There were times when this odor overpowered everything else in the vicinity. But then every one said it was "so healthful," and a great many Northern visitors absorbed immense quantities of that water, that certainly smells and tastes unutterably nasty. There ought to be some compensation for drinking it. Robust health would not be too great a reward for the violation of one's tastes which it is necessary to suffer in swallowing this liquid, which seems to lie under the whole State of Florida, waiting for the boring process to release it.

After Moore had sat a while, the sight of a man going into the post-office aroused his business instincts. When he had first come to the town he had come with the intention of selling that retail dealer "a bill of goods." He had not yet succeeded.

He walked rapidly across the street, revolving what he would say. He thrust every other thought into the background, and by the time he had joined that man the "drummer" was completely to the fore.

But the girl out there in the barrens had no goods to sell, and nothing with which to occupy her mind, save the remembrance of the young man who had pleaded with her not to send him away. He had called her cruel. She now began to fear that she had been cruel. She thought of him as suffering and disconsolate. She did not think of him as selling "a bill of goods" with eagerness and a dash of shrewd satisfaction. He made a memorandum of the articles and the amount, and then, as he strolled off with a satisfied look on his face, he began to think of Salome again, and he began to arrange in his own mind how he could plan his business so that he might stop in Florida the longest possible time. He did not like to think of the day when he should be obliged to go North.

He took out his memorandum-book and studied it, with a view to having entirely to himself that hour on the following day when Salome would leave Mrs. Darrah. Having done this, he decided to practise at tennis an hour or two with Miss Nunally. He found, however, that Miss Nunally was already practising tennis with a big man who had a military air and a voice which sounded as if it were quite used to the utterance of big oaths.

Portia greeted Moore with one of her best smiles as she nodded to him. But she did not ask him to join the game and make an awkward third.

The young man felt irritated. Miss Nunally was extremely fetching this afternoon. It was a real pleasure to watch her as she played, she was so agile, so alert, and so graceful. She was one of those women who never do anything which they cannot do gracefully.

As Moore stood watching the game, thinking every moment he would go away, but not going, he felt more and more aggrieved and injured that that big, bass-voiced Major should be there. That man was too fat to play tennis. It made him puff, and his face was almost purple. And a man like that was absolutely absurd in flannels. How on earth could Miss Nunally look at him when he spoke to her? Moore declared to himself that it made him sick to see such fat cheeks as the Major had.

He did not care particularly for Miss Nunally, but she was very jolly, and had a way of understanding a fellow, and she was never stupid.

If he could not be with Salome he much preferred

to be with a girl like Miss Nunally rather than with any man.

At last the game ended. The Major ogled Miss Nunally as he told her it was better to be beaten by her than it was to beat any one else.

Miss Nunally smiled at him, and replied that she thought he could have the pleasure of being beaten by her for a good many times if he didn't go somewhere and practise more.

"Go somewhere?" he said, ogling again; "I want to come here."

"Jove!" was Moore's thought, as he leaned against a tent - pole. "How can she bear it? And he's fifty, sure."

But Miss Nunally seemed so well able to bear it that she smiled again, even more alluringly than before.

"Very well; come here, then. But you are an awful bore."

These last words were spoken in such a way that the Major felt complimented. He straightened himself. He put one pudgy hand on his hip.

"I'm bound to come, anyway. I wish I hadn't got to go now. I promised Lucas I'd be with him at tiffin. I shall see you again to-night; so it isn't good-bye."

He took off his cap, showing his bald head as he did so. He bobbed his head slightly at Moore, who bobbed his still more slightly in return. Then he walked away.

"What in the name of common-sense does he say 'tiffin' for?" inquired Moore, when the Major was beyond hearing. "Isn't lunch a good enough word?"

"Not for the likes of him," answered Portia, with a

laugh. "I think he was in India for a week or two once—and habits cling to one."

"Jove !" said Moore, this time aloud, curling his lip.

"You needn't say 'Jove' about Major Root," returned Miss Nunally.

"Why not ?"

"Because I'm going to marry him if he will kindly ask me, and I think he will."

Moore started into an erect attitude.

"Oh, Jupiter !" he cried. "That is too much, Miss Nunally. You don't mean that. I shall forbid the banns."

"Oh no, you won't. It will be an eminently suitable marriage. He wants to buy a young wife, and I want to sell myself to a rich husband. You see, upon occasion, I can use very unequivocal words."

"But—but—" stammered Moore.

The two looked full at each other for an instant.

It was Moore who turned away with a resentful sparkle in his eyes and a flush on his face.

He had become, in a way, quite intimate with Miss Nunally and her aunt during the past two or three weeks. Moore was the kind of a man in whom women quickly and naturally confide, and they never repented this confidence, for, as yet, he had never taken advantage of any such manner from women. There was a frankness and a simplicity and a comparative purity in this young man's character ; and perhaps I ought to add, so much winning beauty in his face that feminine human nature was almost invariably drawn to him.

Mrs. Darrah used occasionally to ask her niece :

"Where is that young fellow whom I like ?"

"Is the world so poor in young fellows that there is only one whom you like?" Portia would question in return.

"I have lived a good many years, and I have seen but few radiant young gods like this Moore," returned Mrs. Darrah. "Why, one may really sun one's self in his presence."

"I'll tell him so," said Portia. "No doubt he will be gratified."

"If I could only put him in a book and have him really alive, all the women in the civilized world would buy that book, and I should be, for a week at least, the most prominent author in America. The critics would forget what they have been saying of me. I wish you would hand me my note-book, Portia; not the blue one, the green one; I put the masculine traits in the green one. Now, why isn't Mr. Moore just as natural a character as those myriads of uninteresting, neutral creatures that swarm in the novels in these days?"

Mrs. Darrah paused to write a few lines. Without looking up, she said:

"I shall not be surprised if you leave a note, some day, Portia, pinned on to your toilet cushion, saying you have found that you cannot endure life save as you can live it with Moore; that you hope to be forgiven, and so forth; and would I still let that legacy stand in my will? I should not blame you overmuch."

Mrs. Darrah wrote in silence for a moment.

"I shall certainly put him in my novel of sentiment," she said, "and I think I could make it interesting if he should be in love with a girl like my amanuensis. I don't quite know whether I should like to be in love with her myself or not. She is more than one girl."

"That might give a variety, then," said Portia, who was turning over a pile of laces. "When her husband that is to be gets tired of one of her, he can amuse himself with another of her. Miss Gerry ought to be congratulated."

Instead of replying, Mrs. Darrah repeated :

"I shall certainly use him," and continued to write in her note-book.

It was this conversation with her aunt that for some reason came to Portia's mind now, as she stood in the tent on the tennis-ground with Moore.

Perhaps something in the young man's face made her recall it. Her own face wore a look of gay reck-lessness. She swung her racket back and forth, and smiled as she did so.

"If Major Root's first wife were living," she re-marked, "she could probably tell me how the Major looked when he was young, and not so—well, not so fat as he is now. Don't you think he must weigh a great many pounds, Mr. Moore?"

"Disgusting!" cried that young man. "Oh, Miss Nunally, are you really going to marry that—that—"

"Gallant soldier," finished Portia. "I told you yes, if he asks me."

As she pronounced the last words she glanced up at Moore, and Moore made an impetuous step tow-ards her.

"If you were my sister now I would shut you up in a dungeon until Major Root had married some one else."

"But I am not your sister; and if I were, you would be so eager to have me 'provided for,' that you would be contriving ways so that the Major and I might meet."

"Never!" cried Moore, violently. "I respect women too much."

Portia laughed.

"It always amuses me when I hear a man say he respects women," she said.

"Good heavens!" The young man was quite excited. "Don't you think that I, for one, respect women?"

"You?" The girl gazed at him contemplatively. After a pause she continued: "Yes, I think you do. But you are different. And you are young."

"I am not precisely an infant," said Moore, dryly.

Portia walked across the tennis-ground. Then she came back and said, abruptly:

"Why don't you tell me? Do you think your face has not revealed it long ago?"

Moore suddenly seized the girl's hand. But she withdrew it instantly.

"I did want to tell you," said he, eagerly. "It seemed to me that I must tell somebody, and I don't care about being confidential with a man. Men are so kind of hard and—crude, but—oh, Miss Nunally, you can have no idea how happy I am!"

"Can I not?" smiling sympathetically.

"And when you talked in that dreadful way about marrying old Root, why, really, it was very hard to bear. If you wait you may see some one whom you will love, and then—"

"Oh, as to that, I've been in love two or three times," she interrupted.

"Really?"

"I thought so. It is so difficult to tell when you

have the genuine article, you know, Mr. Moore, that I think I am very sensible when I make up my mind to do without it entirely. Then I shall have no disillusion to suffer. If Major Root gives me some diamonds, and makes a good settlement, I know exactly what I've got. But you—"

The girl's eyes were caught for an instant in those of her companion.

"You make me so sorry—so sorry, Miss Nunally."

Moore spoke out from his heart, and his voice was unsteady from the excess of his sympathy.

"I am not bidding for your pity," she answered, quickly. "Of course she loves you."

"Not of course," withdrawing a little as he replied, "I can hardly believe in such a—"

"Such a miracle, perhaps you would say," supplemented Portia. "I can't stay here any longer now. It is very fatiguing to play tennis with Major Root, and I must have a long rest before dinner. Do you want to see my aunt? I think she is composing— one never knows accurately when she is going to compose—but she seems always ready to see you."

"No; I will take a boat and go across to the North Beach. Since I can't see you, I will see no one."

"Oh, thanks! I will tell Miss Gerry," laughing.

"I didn't mean it that way."

"I know that. Good-bye!"

Moore had gone but a few steps when he heard Miss Nunally's voice pronouncing his name. He went back to her. She held out her hand. With frank interest, she said :

"Mr. Moore, I wish you every happiness."

She did not wait for any response. She walked

into the hotel. The young man stood watching her until she had disappeared among the shining-leaved shrubs.

Then he retraced his steps along the path. He shook his head as he said that it would be a good thing if somebody would shoot that heavy Major. Women were very strange. A man might think they were all refinement and delicacy, when, presto! they were the most indelicate and unrefined creatures in God's world. He did not understand it.

But there was one woman whom evil of any kind could not approach; one feminine nature which could not contemplate anything that was really sin.

With this thought in his mind, Moore went to the wharf and stepped into a boat, rowing rather indolently out across the river.

That night he was summoned up to Jacksonville on business. He found it peculiarly hard to go. Even the prospect of selling an unusually large "bill of goods" did not reconcile him. He had no time in which to see Salome. He left a note in the postoffice for her. He promised himself to be back the next day.

Meanwhile, the next day Salome did not appear at Mrs. Darrah's. But at the usual time a rather prim and exceedingly neat middle-aged woman was ushered into the presence of the authoress, who sat waiting rather impatiently, her ideas being brilliant and flowing this morning.

"Oh," said Mrs. Darrah, without any preface, "you are her mother."

"Yes. I came to explain that I didn't wish her to come to-day. She seems to have a cold. I thought she was almost well."

Mrs. Gerry paused.

"Don't be worried about that," responded Mrs. Darrah, briskly, "she'll get strong. By spring she'll be all right."

"Do you really think so?" with an uncontrollable quaver in her voice.

"I'm sure of it. She isn't ill; only delicate. Sit down. I'm greatly interested in your daughter, Mrs. Gerry."

The worn face lightened. It did not surprise Mrs. Gerry in the least that any one should be greatly interested in Salome.

But she would not stop. She had left the girl lying wrapped in shawls out-of-doors. This cold, however, was not like the same thing in the North. In two days Salome seemed as well as ever. She went back on the third day to Mrs. Darrah. She found a letter from Moore, saying he had gone to Tampa, and bewailing his fate.

"Come here and let me kiss you," said Mrs. Darrah, when Salome entered. "If you had not come to-day, I was going to send Portia out there beyond the Maria Sanchez."

The speaker drew the girl down and kissed her cheek.

"Let us talk a little first," she said.

"I have something to tell you," Salome responded.

XI

CONFESSION

The girl had placed herself in her chair by the desk. She had taken off her broad hat and turned her face fully towards her employer, who was looking at her with a mild interrogation in her glance.

"But I ought not to take up your time," said Salome, hesitatingly. "Perhaps I will wait until the dictation is over."

"Oh no," was the return; "I said we would talk a little first. You are looking very well this morning, Miss Gerry. You seem not to have a care in the world."

Salome smiled happily.

"That's what my mother said when I left her, and it seemed to be such a comfort to her."

"I should think so, indeed. And you are really getting well?"

"Thank you, yes. I am well; my cough is gone. I am just living now, for the first time."

Mrs. Darrah contemplated her companion in sympathetic silence.

"It is not life at all—the life of an invalid," went on Salome, speaking with unusual freedom. "I don't see how I endured it up home. It was always that I must not do this, for it might overtax me; I must not do the other thing, for fear that—oh dear! And I was always wondering if my cough would be better at night, or would the early morning air be too bracing? And I must eat things that would make blood. And my view of the world was so narrow, and I was so given to self-examination. Oh, I was a miserable, narrow little thing! But that girl is buried somewhere up in New England, where she lived. Do you think she will ever come to life again, Mrs. Darrah?"

Instead of replying, Mrs. Darrah remarked:

"You interest me so much! And I thought I knew all the girls and young men long ago."

Salome went on in the same tone she had been using, and with much the same expression of face.

"But I mustn't talk about myself so much. I'm sure to be a bore if I do that; because, as Miss Nunally says, then other people can't talk about themselves. She says that's what everybody wants to do. I was going to tell you that I put your name to one of your blank checks in your check-book a few days ago."

Salome gazed calmly but with undisguised interest at her employer.

Mrs. Darrah suddenly left her cushions and sat upright. Then she sank back upon them and responded:

"I suppose you wanted to see how well you could do it. Let me look at it."

"But I have sent it to my father. He needed the money."

"What?"

Mrs. Darrah sat upright again.

"He needed the money," repeated Salome.

Mrs. Darrah gazed a moment in silence; then she said:

"Hand me my note-book, please—the blue one."

But Mrs. Darrah did not immediately write in the book; she held it in her hand while she gazed at the girl, who returned her gaze in a shy but self-possessed manner.

"Does your mother know?" at length asked the woman.

"Oh no!"

"Why didn't you tell her?"

"Because I knew she would be unhappy about it. She would think I had done wrong."

Here Mrs. Darrah fell to writing rapidly a few lines.

Presently she looked up. "And what do you think about it yourself?" she asked.

"Well," reflectively, "intellectually I know it is wrong, but somehow I don't have any feeling about it."

"Oh, you don't have any feeling about it?"

Mrs. Darrah wrote again. Her keen, small eyes were like sparks of light now.

"Does your father know?"

Salome rose impulsively. Her eyes flashed, but she resumed her seat directly.

"No—do you think I should let him know? I had to—to prevaricate. I wrote that a rich friend would lend the sum. And you know I was sure you would let me work out the amount."

"Oh, you were sure of that?"

"Yes. And there was no time. You had a headache that morning. I thought I would talk with you about it. I can work out the amount; and father, nor mother either, need never know anything concerning the affair."

"May I ask what the sum is?"

As she put this question Mrs. Darrah had in her mind fifty or a hundred dollars.

" Eight hundred dollars," was the answer.

"Good heavens!" Mrs. Darrah's face darkened somewhat. As Portia had once explained, this woman, while she was generous, was yet fond of her money.

"It was a mortgage on the farm," calmly went on Salome, "and father would have kept up the interest, only I've been such an expense to him. I felt as if I were responsible, you see. And I will work it out. I'm perfectly willing to work it out—I've meant to do that. I shall be able to use shorthand in a month or two, and I do hope, Mrs. Darrah, I can be very useful to you. I'm sure I can be."

An enthusiasm began to shine in the girl's face.

Mrs. Darrah made an effort to retain the calmness which had threatened to leave her; but she could not yet lean back on her cushions.

" Have you an idea how long it will take you to pay me at your present salary?" she inquired.

"Oh yes," cheerfully; "I've reckoned it precisely."

"You have?" Mrs. Darrah spoke rather helplessly.

"Certainly."

"But I may not want you all the time. Do you think I write every week in the year? And perhaps I shall decide not to have you work for me."

"If you do that I can still work somewhere," with gay courage came the answer.

Mrs. Darrah now gave up trying to be calm. She had never been so surprised in her life. She began walking about the room.

"I suppose you know what you are, Miss Gerry?" she said, after a moment, stopping before the girl.

"What I am?" inquiringly.

"Yes; that you are a forger—neither more nor less."

Salome was silent for a space. She lowered her eyes.

"Yes," she said, raising her glance as she spoke; "I suppose that is the name of it. But it was for father, and I was sure you would allow me to make up the sum to you."

"But the sin of it!"

"Yes," repeated Salome, "of course, there is the sin of it. I knew that, as I said, intellectually; but I did not care, in my heart, for that. You had plenty of money. I was sure you would not suffer until I could pay you."

Mrs. Darrah paused by her couch, where she had dropped her note-book. She snatched it up and wrote in it, as if she must in some way relieve her excitement.

She turned to the girl. "But your conscience? Where is your conscience, Miss Gerry?"

"That is what I ask myself," was the reply. "I think I must have left it in New England."

"You used to have one?"

"Oh yes; and it was a very good one, too, for it was continually troubling me."

Mrs. Darrah now threw her note-book on the couch, apparently that she might clasp her hands.

"Oh, if I could only work this out!" she exclaimed. "I would astound the critics."

Salome looked at her companion wonderingly.

"Do you mean anything about me?" she asked.

"I mean everything about you," was the answer.

The girl seemed puzzled. She remained silent, watching her employer as she moved about the room. After a while Mrs. Darrah paused in front of Salome.

"Have you anything more to say?" she asked.

"I don't know that I have. Yes; I suppose I ought to tell you that I am sorry."

" Not unless you are sorry," said the elder woman, who now returned to her couch, and who arranged the cushions there with a great appearance of interest. But she kept up her watch of the girl.

Salome began to speak slowly, but soon was enunciating rapidly, as was her habit, as if the words came too fast to be spoken.

" You remember," she said, "that I said—or did I only think it?—that, intellectually, I knew it was wrong. I know that just as well as you can tell me. But then, suddenly, I knew how my father was suffering, and I knew he never could pay the money himself; and there was your check-book; and I could write your name, and you were rich; I had not the least feeling that held me back, and I haven't now, and I don't think I ever shall have."

"The sin of it doesn't trouble you ?"

" No."

" Even Portia wouldn't have done that," remarked Mrs. Darrah, suddenly.

Salome made no reply. She was absorbedly engaged in considering herself as a third person, and in trying to decide what she should think of that third person. But she gave up the attempt without having come to any decision.

" And Portia would do some strange things for money and what money brings," went on Mrs. Darrah, following out her thought. "For instance, she would legally sell herself to a man whom she dislikes. But, then, she is not peculiar in that."

Salome, hearing this, could not restrain a gesture of disgust.

Mrs. Darrah was watching her. She again wrote in her note-book, the blue one, which contained the hints concerning feminine nature.

"I see you still retain the fine 'Daphnean instinct,'" she said. "But who can tell how soon you may drop that?"

"Oh, Mrs. Darrah!" cried Salome, with keenest remonstrance; and now she blushed, which was a rare occurrence for her. As she felt the blood rush to her face she thought of Miss Nunally's question, "Why do you never blush?" and the blood came up more hotly than ever as she recalled those words.

"I hope you will allow me to pay that money," said the girl, after a pause. "It is much more reasonable that I should work and earn money now than that father should have to do it. I am young. And, somehow, father never could get money together like some men. I shall be so glad to help him. You will be sure to see that father nor mother never finds this out, won't you, Mrs. Darrah?"

This question was put with a confiding earnestness that acted like a sudden clutch upon Mrs. Darrah's well-worn heart.

She did not reply immediately. When she did speak, it was to put another question.

"Have you reflected that an act of this kind, that any crime, makes falsehood necessary?"

"No—that is, I had not thought much about it."

"Do you care whether you lie or not, Miss Gerry?"

"How can I say? Of course I know it was a lie to put your name to that check."

"Certainly."

"Well, I don't care about that; only I care intensely that father and mother should not know it. They would feel so much, you see."

"Naturally."

By this time Mrs. Darrah had made her decision concerning the money. She was very wealthy; still, even wealthy people do not enjoy having a sum stolen from them. But in this woman the author in search of material was very strong, and she was vitally interested as to how this would "turn out." She felt that it was better than any novel she had ever read; far better than any she should ever write. Would this prove only one instance of curious moral aberration, or was it the first in the process of moral deterioration? And all this talk of the girl about her conscience? Of course, her conscience had never been a healthy one. It must have been deeply unhealthy, as were the consciences of some invalids, particularly if they were women who had been brought up with an eye specially to the conscience.

And what had there been in the history of Salome's immediate ancestors? And what prenatal influences? Was Mrs. Darrah about to come upon something that should explain what she called the different faces of the girl?

With these thoughts in her mind Mrs. Darrah now spoke:

"I should like to see your mother."

Salome became very pale. But she said, steadily, "You do not mean to tell her?"

"No."

"What shall be the arrangement?"

"This: I shall allow you to borrow that money. But your mother must know why you seem to receive no salary from me. Tell her the whole story, except that you used my name. Show her your father's letter, for, of course, you have not shown it to her. Tell her I lend you the sum, and you repay me as you can. I will see that the check is not disputed."

"Oh, how good you are!" cried the girl.

"Very," was the satirical response. "Don't be grateful."

"But I feel so grateful, Mrs. Darrah."

"I suppose so. Now, I want to see your mother. We will not write to-day. Go out there where you live—ask your mother to call upon me this afternoon about five. I will send a carriage for her if she cannot walk."

"She will gladly walk," was the reply. "And I will tell her what you said about the money?"

"Yes. Now, good-bye until to-morrow at nine."

Salome left the room. As she emerged from the hotel she stopped by one of the fountains. A rush of sweet air came from a garden of roses.

The girl lifted her head and inhaled the perfume. She stood by the fountain and smiled to herself.

The woman whom she had just left remained on her couch a moment. Then she rose and pressed the button of the bell. She requested the servant to ask Miss Nunally to come to her.

When she had done so she said to herself that she felt as if she should go wild if she stayed there alone and thought another moment.

Portia came in, not in the most perfect good-nature.

"Do you want anything particularly, Aunt Florence?" she inquired. "I was reading one of your novels."

"Novels are very insignificant things when compared to real life," was the rather startling response.

"Not your novels, aunt, dear," replied Portia, "and, besides, I was just getting sleepy, and I must restore myself somehow if I am to see Major Root this evening."

"You are always talking about yourself, Portia," fretfully.

"No; but sometimes I do like to speak of a subject of real interest to me. What's the matter, anyway? And where is Salome Gerry? You actually look excited, Aunt Florence."

"Do I? I'm thinking about a new novel."

Portia yawned.

"I have almost made up my mind not to go on with the novel of sentiment, but to begin one about—"

Portia yawned again.

"I wish you'd stop doing that, Portia. It is very annoying when I am talking. Did you see Miss Gerry when she left?"

"No. Why?"

"I was going to ask how she looked."

"Why, how should she look?" in surprise.

"That's what I don't know in the least. That's what I should like to find out," said Mrs. Darrah.

Portia now showed some interest.

"Aunt, it is too much for you to write novels. Can't you stop it?"

"Stop it!—with material thrust into my hand?"

"I know it is asking a great deal; but you certainly do give me the idea this morning that novel-writing is too much for you."

Portia gave a scrutinizing gaze about the room. In spite of her yawning, and the sound of her words as they are set down on paper, she did not have the appearance of being impolite, and she rarely did have that appearance. She possessed the power, in remarkable degree, of being insolent under the garb of politeness. Not that her aunt cared whether she were insolent or not. There was a certain aroma of personal presence about Portia Nunally that made one forgive a vast deal in her which would have been unforgivable in another. And when Portia chose to be deferential and winning, when she felt like letting her eyes dwell on you in a way her eyes had, then you could hardly be blamed if you lost your head a little.

When you came fully to understand that she was conscious of this way her eyes had, then possibly you began to regain your head a little; but there had been cases when it required a long time for this last desirable consummation to be reached. Men and women alike were her victims. The way she put it, however, was that she was the victim of men and women alike. "On the whole, though," she said once when in a mood of confession, "I like women better. Women know things. You can absolutely rely upon scores of women to know instantly why you talk one way only for the reason that you feel the opposite. There's a great comfort in that. And then the extreme surprise that comes to a well-regulated, properly brought up young woman when she finds that she is in love with another woman—me, for instance. Of course, if she doesn't know it isn't really love, and often she doesn't, there will be plenty to tell her. Sometimes it requires quite a good deal of argument to convince her that if she were in love with a man it would be the real thing. For, don't you see, between men and women 'love for an hour is invariably love forever;' but in all other cases it is an ephemeral, spurious, abnormal article." Here Portia's eyes would dilate, and she would laugh in a way that might possibly make her hearer shiver slightly. Or she would not laugh, but would lean towards you and smile right into your eyes, in such a manner that you felt imperatively moved to find out what kind of a girl she was.

But when a woman is nearly thirty, when she has eyes with a dash of green in them, with thick light lashes, when she is a yellow blonde with very scarlet lips—why, then, it is next to impossible for a man or woman to find out, unscathed, what sort of a person she is. One unfortunate result of a study of character under these circumstances is that presently you do not care in the least whether you are scathed or unscathed ; and you are never precisely the same after such a process of education.

This girl was superlatively sensitive and intuitive. It was not necessary to be that in such a degree for her to perceive that something unusual had happened in this room. The longer she sat there the more interested she became, and the less she felt like yawning.

She moved uneasily. She noted Mrs. Darrah's rather set face.

"I feel my hair beginning to rise on my head," she remarked, at last. "I am almost sure there is a spook in this room somewhere."

"Don't be silly," said her aunt.

Portia was silent a moment. Then she started in a dramatic manner she had.

"There is something materializing in Miss Gerry's chair!" she exclaimed. "Really, Aunt Florence, if you don't tell me why you sent for me, I may go into a state of self-imposed hypnotism in spite of myself."

" I sent for you, Portia, because I have had such a shock that I wanted to divert my mind," was the answer; "and sometimes you can be very diverting."

"Oh, thank you. Did Miss Gerry give you material in a very unexpected manner, or did she have hemorrhage of the lungs?"

Portia glanced about her as if she might see some token of that hemorrhage.

" Portia," said Mrs. Darrah, with solemnity, " what is your idea of conscience?"

The girl sat upright with a quick movement.

" Aunt Florence," she answered, " I haven't an idea of conscience."

She asked, almost immediately, "Have you got into trouble with Miss Gerry's conscience?"

" Don't ask irrelevant questions," was the response. " I suppose, Portia, you have an idea that some things you would do, and some things you would not do?"

" Certainly; when you put it in that way, aunt, I find you quite lucid, and I can answer you," replied the girl; "but, first, don't you want your note-book— the blue one?"

" No, I don't."

" It is rather irritating that I am never material to you, aunt."

"I've known you too long. Now, what would you do and what wouldn't you do?"

Portia considered; at last she answered:

" The things I would do are so very many that I can't begin to tell. But there are a few things I would not do."

" Well, what are they?" with interest.

"The first that occurs to me is that I would not, for the world, wear my hair in that abominable Greek way which that Stacy girl thinks so fine. And I wouldn't have those ugly gathers in the skirt of my frock—not though they were ten times the fashion. If you will give me half an hour in which to collect my thoughts, *ma tante*, I will tell you more things that I would not do."

Portia's face was full of mischief; but it was full of interest also.

Mrs. Darrah was now gazing coldly and concentratedly at her niece, but she was thinking of the face of the other girl who had so lately left her.

"You would steal from a wife her husband's love?" she questioned.

"Yes," promptly; "but that kind which could be stolen would not be very precious—and it would be quite fun to steal hers."

"You would steal her purse or her necklace, or forge her name?"

"Oh, dear, no, indeed!" Portia did not try to conceal her amazement. Then she endeavored to smile as she once more offered to get the blue note-book. She said it seemed to her that it was surely a fitting time for the blue note-book. Then she shrugged her shoulders and remarked that there were occasions when she could wish that she were not the niece of an authoress. After this she inquired if Aunt Florence were rehearsing a plot, or trying on a chapter, and could she assist her in any other way? Should she put on her new evening dress and pose?

"The amount of it all is," exclaimed Mrs. Darrah, without noticing the girl's words, "that we do not in the least know what we are, nor what we would do."

"Now I agree with you ; now you speak truth," responded Portia ; and she could not help adding, "won't you write a novel about that, Aunt Florence ?"

"I wish you would go away," said Mrs. Darrah; "I want to think."

Without speaking again Portia obeyed. She strolled out into the court, and she also stood by a fountain amid the luxuriance of Southern shrubbery, as Salome had done a half-hour before. But Portia's face was not as care-free as Salome's face had been. There were some lines on it now which, in spite of the great beauty and fairness of its skin, made the girl look more than her years.

Presently she walked into that portion of the grounds which Miss Gerry would be likely to pass through. She had a wish to meet Miss Gerry and to ask her a few questions.

But she did not find her; Salome had not lingered long. She had walked out through the sand in a state of calm and content. She was in haste to see her mother and to explain, as Mrs. Darrah had suggested.

It was time now to hear from her father. He would be sure to write as soon as he had received her letter. By to-morrow morning, when the Northern mail came in, she would hear.

Though she was in haste, yet the girl did not hurry. It was not easy to hurry. She was even sometimes tempted to linger, but she kept on, the air coming balmily to her lips and to her lungs, which expanded now with an unconsidered ease. She had been as ready to forget that she had ever been ill, as we all are ready to do that when health comes back to us.

She saw her mother sitting sewing in the doorway with the hound lying at her feet. The door was not yet hung, but was leaning against the wall of the hut. The long leaves of the banana swayed gently near the pine log upon which Mr. Maine was not at this moment resting.

The hound, hearing the slight sounds of her footsteps in the sand, lifted his head. His face brightened, and he rose with the solemn deliberation that is characteristic of a hound who is no longer young. He paced slowly towards the girl, who came forward with that lightness which is a part of youth.

The mother, looking at her, was immediately aware of a joyousness of aspect which differed from the happy expression which had belonged to her daughter for a few weeks now.

Mrs. Gerry smiled in response to the warm, eager smile on the young face.

"Well?" she said.

Salome came and took the work from her mother's hands. Then she sat down on her mother's lap and clasped her arms about her neck. She was smiling all the time.

"Now, at last, I am of some importance," she said.

"Not until now, then?" was the questioning response.

"Of course you and father have loved me, and so I have been of importance that way," replied Salome; "and I have been rather an important burden, haven't I?"

"Yes," drawing the slight form closer, "you have."

"But now I have arranged to help pay off the mortgage. I did not allow you to see father's last letter; I didn't think it was best. There it is. He was in trouble.   Mrs. Darrah has lent the money. Father must have it by this time.   That horrid Uncle John will get it all right; and I'm going to pay it. You see, I'm working.   Work is a great thing.   But I won't bother you; read the letter in peace."   For Mrs. Gerry had seized the envelope eagerly.

"Lyman in trouble!" she said, in a whisper.

Her eyes ran over the lines.   Her hand trembled a little, but she steadied it.

When at last she looked up she could not see her daughter, who still sat on her lap, save in a misty and magnified fashion.

"It's a great deal better to owe Mrs. Darrah than to owe Uncle John, isn't it?" quickly asked Salome.

"Yes; that is, I can't tell.   I must think," was the answer.

"Oh yes, it is.   And it gives me such a chance."

Mrs. Gerry wiped her eyes.   Then she fixed them on the girl.

"This letter is more than a week old.   And Lyman had to have the money directly," she said.   "When did you arrange this?"

"Oh, immediately! Almost the moment I read it."

Mrs. Gerry, even in her surprise and anxiety, could not restrain an expression of something like admiration.

"I did not know you were such a business woman," she said.

"But something had to be done.   And did you think I would not be a business woman, or something worse, so that I might help father?   You see it has all come out right, hasn't it?   We would rather owe Mrs. Darrah than Uncle John; and it won't seem so very long before I can pay it off."

Salome's face was radiant.   She flung herself again upon her mother's neck.

"Now don't say a single 'prudent' thing to me. Just be glad it is arranged.   I am responsible for this. It's the first really responsible thing I ever did, isn't it?   I don't think you quite realize that I am grown up, and that I am an individual."

"I think I shall realize it after this.   I must go and see Mrs. Darrah."

"Yes, but not now," as Mrs. Gerry made a movement to rise.   "You are to go at five this afternoon. She sent for you."

And at precisely five Mrs. Gerry was shown into Mrs. Darrah's sitting-room.   She found that lady alone, and she was greeted by the following remark :

"Sit down, please.   I am going to ask you a great many questions.   I am laying out a new novel."

This was so very much different from what she had expected to hear that Mrs. Gerry was not able to say anything at first in response.   She sat down in silence.

"Yes," said Mrs. Darrah, "I am planning a new novel.   I shall drop my story of sentiment for the present, or I may possibly work the two together."

"And what is the new one to be?"

Mrs. Gerry found it an effort to put this question. Could it be possible that she had been sent for to listen to this kind of talk?

She did not quite know what to decide concerning the woman before her.   But she knew that she herself must say a few things.   She began instantly :

"My daughter says you have been so kind as to—"

"Yes, certainly.   I've lent her eight hundred dollars," interrupted Mrs. Darrah ; "she will work it out —or part of it."

"My husband and I will give our note for the amount," said Mrs. Gerry, with firmness, "and we will have the mortgage transferred to you. Then, in any event, you will not lose. It will be a great relief to us. I must say that my daughter should not have done this without consulting with her parents."

"Done what?" with a sharp look.

"Borrowed this money. I will attend to the mortgage."

"Very well, as you please. I have not the slightest doubt of your honesty."

"Thank you," stiffly.

"But I want to ask you some questions, Mrs. Gerry. Let us call it part of the bargain, if you please, that I ask you some questions. Shall we?"

"I see no objections; though I can't imagine what you will want to know. And, of course, I must use my own judgment about answering."

"Of course," was the response; "and I can see your judgment is excellent. But I am the most harmless creature in the world, Mrs. Gerry. Still, I have my hobbies. Let me get my note-books. I may need both the green and the blue one. I am immensely interested in your daughter. I want to make some inquiries about your father and mother, and about your husband's father and mother. I may even go so far back as another generation. Now, please don't think me demented, will you? No, you won't. Thank you so much for that. Were Miss Gerry's parents and grandparents and great-grandparents all New England people? That's a very general question to begin with, isn't it?"

XII

THE MOTHER

WHEN Mrs. Gerry heard these interrogations she did not reply immediately, and her face changed indescribably. She glanced at her companion, and met Mrs. Darrah's eyes fixed upon her. Had those eyes been merely probing and inquisitive she could have braced herself coldly, and have put on an armor which might have essentially aided her in this interview. But unexpectedly she encountered an expression of sympathy and gentleness, and the mother's whole attitude changed from that of defence to something quite different. As for Mrs. Darrah, she could not explain to herself why this woman's strong, controlled face should so modify what she might have called her professional curiosity into something human, something which had little to do with the novel which was forming itself in her mind, though she still felt indefinitely that she might probably come upon some rather rich " material :"

As the silence continued, Mrs. Darrah said, in a voice not much above a murmur:

" I am always so deeply interested in grandparents. Once in a while a person runs upon such strange things in grandparents."

Mrs. Gerry did not speak. That she was thinking deeply and painfully was apparent. When she had met that look of sympathy from her hostess the New England woman felt it a distinct relief to cease from holding herself in such a stiff mental attitude.

It seemed to her that she was aware of a reaction from the alertness and the care that she had constantly exercised since she had left her home with her daughter. And, curiously, at the same time also she was conscious that she feared the approach of some new and as yet entirely unformed care. She was not in the least given to vagaries or superstitions, however. She could have smiled at herself that Mrs. Darrah's sympathy should so quickly seem to weaken her.

She sat upright in her chair, in strong contrast to the lounging figure opposite her.

" Before I reply to you, Mrs. Darrah," she said, " I want you to tell me what has suggested such questions to you."

" Why, your daughter, of course ; who else ?" was the prompt response. " Don't you know that she is not a usual kind of a girl ?"

Mrs. Gerry could not help an uneasy movement.

" I see that you don't like that," went on Mrs. Darrah. " Like all upright, conventional natures, you distrust the unusual."

" Yes, I do !" emphatically.

" And yet," reflectively, " it is to the being out of the ordinary that the world owes its greatest debts."

No response to this remark. Mrs. Darrah opened one of her note-books, saying, as she did so,

" But we are straying from the subject of grand-parents."

" They were not all New England people," said Mrs. Gerry, with abrupt precision. " There was one

14

exception. That was my grandfather, my mother's father. Of the rest there is absolutely nothing to say, for they were the common country folks in one of our villages up home."

Mrs. Gerry pressed her hands together quietly but closely upon her lap.

Mrs. Darrah took a position removed from her cushions. Her eyes sparkled with interest. But there was a marked expression of kindness upon her face.

"Please don't think me hard and disagreeable," she said; "but you can't imagine how interesting this is. I quite reckoned upon the unusual one in your daughter's ancestry. Miss Gerry is so contradictory."

Mrs. Gerry's hands griped each other more closely than before.

" Have you noticed it, too?" she asked. "Then it certainly must be true. I have continually told myself that it was my fancy. What do you think it is, Mrs. Darrah? Perhaps it will be a relief to talk to you. Has Salome said anything very strange? Oh, tell me what is in your mind! The child has such a —such an expression sometimes comes to her face. I can't describe it."

" Try to describe it," said Mrs. Darrah, eagerly.

A sombre kind of smile passed over Mrs. Gerry's lips as she met her companion's glance. But she felt that it was safe to go on. The genuineness in the writer's character had decidedly risen to the surface to meet the same quality in this woman. Besides, it was not until this moment that Mrs. Gerry had what she would have called a "realizing sense" of the strain and the anxiety in every way which had been upon her since she had left her home. Almost the only human beings with whom she could speak, save Salome, were Job Maine and his wife. And she did not write of any anxieties to her husband. She had never put any burdens on him which she could bear alone. Though she had not really spoken it in words to herself, yet none the less she had all her married life acted upon the knowledge that she must bear trials by herself all that she could; that she was better fitted to bear trials than Lyman was. And now as she sat in this richly appointed room, and was dimly conscious of the approach of a trouble in some strange new guise, with a thrill of faithful and protecting love she thought:

"I must keep it from Lyman; I must bear it myself."

"Tell me about it," repeated Mrs. Darrah. "I know I make novels, and I like to get odd facts; but, Mrs. Gerry, I do believe it will do you good to talk freely with me."

"I believe it will," said Mrs. Gerry.

She drew a long breath. She was thinking that she had not known she was so tired. And then she had a vivid sensation of thankfulness that her daughter was better. Whatever happened, Salome was better. At this she grew more cheerful.

"It's all done with long ago," she said, "and it's only because you have been kind that I'm willing to tell you. My mother's father was not an American; he was what we used to call an 'outlandish man.' He was born in Martinique, but his parents were Spanish. I saw him only a few times; he died when I was a child. I remember well his large eyes and his curious, dark skin. My mother was the only child, and she did not resemble him in the least—everybody said so—she was clear Ware, like her mother. She was a real Puritan girl. Salome used to look just like her grandmother, and she had that kind of a conscience that is always fretting and wondering, and making the owner of it afraid that he or she doesn't do just right. That was my mother. Salome has her features now. But somehow she doesn't look like her any more. I don't quite understand it. But then, perhaps, Mrs. Darrah, it is not necessary that we should understand everything."

Mrs. Gerry paused. She smiled rather sorrowfully and wistfully. She was wondering if this woman, who must be wise, since she wrote books which were printed, could not say something to help her.

When Salome had had what the doctors called incipient phthisis, her mother had not felt nearly so helpless as she did now when there seemed to be nothing the matter with the girl, and she was happy.

"Whether it be necessary or not, we can't understand everything," responded Mrs. Darrah, quickly. "But we can try. What kind of a person was this Martinique gentleman?"

"I don't think he was a gentleman at all," was the answer; "at least, he was not what I call a gentleman. I think of him now as I thought of him as I used to see him when I was a little thing. I loved him with a kind of ardent fondness, though he was a withered old man; that is, he seemed very old to me. I could have believed he was a hundred—any age. I used to plead to sit on his knee. I would stare into his eyes, which were so soft and so dark. They were as different from any eyes I knew anything about as if they were not human eyes. He was only an animal. But no "—Mrs. Gerry paused here so long that she apparently forgot that she had been talking, and that some one was listening. But Mrs. Darrah was patient. She sat with a note-book in her lap and a pencil in her hand. But she had at this moment no thought of writing.

The warm air blew in through the open windows and stirred the drapery of the room. Somewhere in the court a woman was singing something of which only the piercing high note was audible. More and more Mrs. Gerry felt that it was a relief to her to speak. It often happens that to a stranger one may unseal what to one's kin would remain forever closed.

"How strange children are!" she now suddenly exclaimed. "I remember one day the minister called. I was a small thing in a long 'tire' to cover my new pink calico frock. I was picking over blackberries, and was sitting on a stool in the kitchen with a dish on each side of me, one for the good berries and one for the poor. It was hot, so hot that the perspiration kept gathering on my face, and I kept putting up the back of my hand to wipe it off. We were going to have bread and milk for supper, for mother said she would not make a fire for fear there would be a thunder tempest. There were thunder-heads rolling up all the time in the west.

"Grandfather was lying on the grass. He was perfectly happy. He said it was an awful climate, and it was only on such days as these that he thought it was warm enough. He would lie in the sun for hours and hours. If I came near him he would fondle me. I used to know even then that he did not always tell the truth. I had discovered that about him. I hardly knew what to think of it. You know, Mrs. Darrah, that to the old-fashioned, average child such as I was, to tell the bald truth was as necessary to life as it was to breathe."

Mrs. Gerry looked at her companion, who nodded quickly.

"My mother was like an incarnation of truth," went on Mrs. Gerry. "I told you she was a real Ware. And she was conscientious to a painful degree. But she loved her father, I really think, better than anything else in the world. And he was so lovable— so lovable. Everybody, everything loved him, Mrs. Darrah. But you couldn't trust him; he had no principle; he wasn't upright. And he was so kind; his heart was so gentle; he had such a way with him; and he loved so, Mrs. Darrah—" here Mrs. Gerry suddenly left her chair and stood upright. But she made no gesture. Her eyes burned in her controlled face. "How do you account for such things?"

"My dear Mrs. Gerry," was the response, "we don't account for them."

"But we ought — we ought," replied the other. "You know it isn't right to love a man or woman of that kind."

"They talk about loving the sinner but hating the sin," remarked Mrs. Darrah, with an incredulous smile.

"I know that. But we can't do it. We can't do it. The minister spoke about that on that afternoon. He spoke in the most general way, as ministers often do. But he liked my grandfather; I really think he loved him. I know he broke down and cried, and couldn't go on with his remarks when he tried to attend grandfather's funeral."

Here Mrs. Gerry ceased speaking and resumed her seat.

Mrs. Darrah quoted in a half whisper those lines:

 " ' There's many a purer and many a better,
  But more loved, oh, how few, love!'"

"It is really astonishing and depressing that we should be able to explain so little," she went on. "It isn't goodness; in short, we have no more idea now what makes a person inspire so much love than they had in pre-Adamite days, when I imagine they never asked, and never cared. I wish we did not ask and did not care—since there is no answer—absolutely no answer."

The woman spoke with an intensity of emphasis that showed that she was thinking of something in her own past.

After a moment she glanced at Mrs. Gerry, who was sitting with one hand over her eyes.

"I suppose your grandmother loved that man?" she said.

Mrs. Gerry looked up.

"Yes, yes. You can imagine. And, Mrs. Darrah, it must be a horrible, horrible thing to love what we don't approve. But she loved him from the first. We never knew how he happened to stray into our village. It was hay-making time. They were short of hands. This fellow came walking along one hot day with a violin under his arm. He said he would like to work. They took him, just for the hay-making. I don't think he would have stayed any longer, only he saw her, you know. She was a fair, prim little thing, with blue eyes and ash-colored hair. They say he was wild with love for her. And she? No one could reason with her in the least from the very first.   She had a will.   She said she should run away and marry him if they opposed her.   They knew she would do it ; so they gave up opposition.   And he won upon them all, too.   But how could they approve of him ?   And they never knew anything about him—what he was, or where he came from—only what he told ; and he did not always tell precisely the same stories.   And how he would play on the fiddle !   Strange tunes that made your heart beat and melt, and that took your breath away from you."

Mrs. Gerry paused again.   She spoke in a kind of spasmodic way as the memories came to her.

"Oh, how you interest me !" murmured Mrs. Darrah.

But Mrs. Gerry did not appear to hear her.   Her mind was in the past.

" How did it come out ?" inquired Mrs. Darrah.

"Come out?   Oh, she married him.   But how was she going to live with a love so at odds with her nature and her upbringing?   She could not stop loving him, and she could not approve of him.   When my mother was born she gave up the fight and died— and she died in her husband's arms.   And she died telling him that no woman ever loved a man as she loved him."

" But he lived—he lived," said Mrs. Darrah, bitterly. "Yes ; life wasn't over for him."

" They thought it was over for a long time.   But, as you say, he lived.   And he loved his little daughter in a way that made some of the people wonder.   He was still a young man.   You .might have thought he would have grown to have other interests.   But he never looked at another woman.   He came to be one of the regular objects of the village, he and his child, for he always had her with him. She grew up just like her mother. She never told a lie, or prevaricated. But she knew that he did both; he couldn't be trusted. I'm sure he would have stolen, or forged, or embezzled, only he was indolent; he embarked in no schemes, and his wife's father let him and his child live with his family. All summer he basked out-of-doors. He said we didn't know how to live. It was life to let the sun soak through and through you, and not to care so about right and wrong. Things would take care of themselves.

"How many times I have heard him say, with his sweet smile: 'Things will take care of themselves.' I didn't know what he meant then. I know well enough now."

Mrs. Gerry came to another pause.

She turned to the woman opposite her. The reticent, solitary mother seemed impelled to speak out.

"Can you imagine how I have watched my daughter?" she exclaimed. "And, more than that, how I have tried to conceal that I watched her? Not even my husband has ever suspected that I did so, and I would hardly acknowledge it to myself.

"But she was always such a good child! I thought she was too conscientious. I almost distrusted that part of her as morbid. She was morbid. She was never a strong child. She seems well now, really well. You can have no idea how I used to watch her. When I grew older I understood what the minister said that hot day to my mother. He said something about heredity. I wondered what that word meant. And he hoped that only the gentle traits would be transmitted. My mother almost groaned as she replied that she hoped so; that it would kill her, it would kill my father, if any child of his should inherit—there I lost what she said. I know well enough now what it was. And I know that I did not inherit.

"Sometimes, in the midst of that sickly kind of regard for conscience, Salome would say a word or two that would make a shudder go over me. That word or two made me fear that her conscience was morbidly, not healthily, alive. But she is such a good girl! and she has such a tender heart! And she is so well now—and so happy!

"Mrs. Darrah, I insist upon your telling me why you wanted to ask me these questions about grandparents." Here the speaker smiled slightly. "What has the child been saying?"

Mrs. Gerry's face was set in a determination to be answered.

Mrs. Darrah took up a note-book and began turning its leaves. The simply bred countrywoman would be no match for the woman of the world in any demand like that.

"Well," replied the other, easily, "she hasn't said much. A few things about the folly of being in a state of resistance all the time—things which my niece might have proclaimed a dozen times and I should hardly have listened. But you are aware that Miss Gerry is a different person from my niece. She is excessively interesting, as all contradictory natures are. And her face—really, if I were a young man I should be in love with her: and, being in love, I should be driven into a score of desperate moods every twenty-four hours, because her face would tell me—good heavens!—what wouldn't her face tell me?"

Mrs. Darrah ended in a voice of undisguised enthusiasm. But the mother's features grew almost rigid.

"Is that the way she affects you?" she asked.

"That is the way she affects me," was the answer.

"And I have always distrusted everything that was not easily read," responded the other. "I distrust such things now." And silently Mrs. Gerry cried out: "Oh, what is best for my child?"

Perhaps Mrs. Darrah had never been more deeply moved to pity than by this woman, who would never have asked for pity from any one; this woman who had always been the one upon whom people leaned, who helped people.

If the mother knew what her daughter had done—worse than that, if the mother knew the serenity of her daughter's mind concerning what she had done; these were the words which were going through Mrs. Darrah's consciousness as she looked up at the figure before her.

The trained observation of the author took in every detail of that figure, which, in its unadorned outline, was like a visible symbol of absolute, transparent integrity.

"She would grieve to death," was Mrs. Darrah's conclusion; and in her thought she added: "If it were twenty times the sum I would shield the child."

Aloud she said, in answer to the mother's remark:

"There's where we make a mistake—in distrusting what we don't understand. If people couldn't understand us, we would not wish to be condemned, perhaps, by reason of their stupidity."

Mrs. Gerry looked relieved.

"That is true; that is Christian," she said.

"Certainly it is," lightly; "and now it strikes me

that we are two old wiseacres who are doubting the
ways of Providence. Let us talk of something cheerful
—love, for instance. That beautiful youth whom they
called Antinous—he has been discriminating enough
to fall in love with your daughter instead of with my
niece. Tell me about it. It is quite appropriate. Of
course she loves him ?"

"Yes."   As Mrs. Gerry replied her face lightened,
as faces were likely to do when their owners thought
of young Moore.

"Now that is pleasant to think of; therefore let us
think of it."

But Mrs. Gerry made no response. She could not
keep her mind upon Moore.

She turned and picked up the black straw bonnet
with its black ribbon bow upon it. She held it
thoughtfully in her hands a moment, her worn, anxious face softening. She looked up. Then she advanced and held out her hand, which Mrs. Darrah
took and cordially retained.

"It's curious how I have talked to you," Mrs.
Gerry said, after a short silence, during which the two
women gazed at each other. "I don't think I've
talked so to anybody else in the world. Any of my
folks would have been frightened. They'd have thought
Salome was—why, some kind of a criminal, I suppose.
But you—you haven't been shocked. You have done
me a great deal of good."

There came a very lovely light into the woman's
eyes as she went on :

"I didn't know before how—how good it might be
to speak out so. I never do speak out. It isn't my
way. I can't seem to do it. But it does relieve one,
doesn't it ?—if it is to the right person."

There was a naivete in the woman's voice and manner which appealed to her hostess, and made her grasp the hard, brown hand still more closely as she rose from among her cushions.

"You self-contained creatures," she said, "always take life in such a hard way. You lock things up in your own souls. Now my advice to you is: never have a thing locked up in your own soul. Tell everything. Talk of everything. You have no idea what an airy, light, care-free kind of a sensation will be yours. It's like letting breeze and sunlight into a close room. Try it, you close, reticent, Yankee woman."

Mrs. Gerry smiled.

"I have tried it, and I am better already," she said.

"And don't worry because your daughter is a mixed creature—a Yankee and a heat-loving creole, and what not. She must live out her life, as we must live ours. If ours goes in a straight line—well, how much thanks to us for that?"

"But I want Salome to be good!" cried her mother, out of a full heart.

"And happy," supplemented the other.

"And happy," repeated Mrs. Gerry. "And now I must go. How strangely I have talked to you," she repeated. "Good-bye."

"Good-bye, and be sure you don't try to understand everything."

"I shall be sure I can't understand, anyway, try or not." And Mrs. Gerry walked away from the hotel, beginning her journey back to the truck farm without even glancing out across the water, or at the old fort, or up at the sky, which was now bending at its very loveliest over the old city.

She trudged along, her parasol held at exactly the right angle, her face straight forward, and gradually growing red with the heat.

Half-way through the palmetto she saw some one sitting at the root of a pine with head thrown back, hat off, and rings of hair blowing about her forehead. It was Salome. She did not rise as she saw her mother; she smiled and waved her hand. And when her mother had come still nearer, she reached forward and grasped a fold of her skirt, saying:

"Sit down here with me. You look so tired, and I am so rested; come. There, that is right. Now you are obeying me as you ought. Put your head on my shoulder for a moment. You are always resting me some way; now let us turn about."

Yielding to the gently compelling gesture, Mrs. Gerry leaned her head on the girl's shoulder, and the girl looked down at her with a smile that was so intensely happy that it almost alarmed the woman who saw it, for she felt that, as she would have phrased it, "it was not natural to be so happy as that."

"I thought it was time for you," said Salome, speaking in a kind of murmur. " I've been sitting here a long time; not that it seemed long, you know. I'm not sure that I should ever want to leave here. Don't you think, mother, that there is any kind of animal that lives entirely on Southern air and Southern sunshine?"

" I never heard of such a creature," was the reply.

" But there must be, don't you think?" went on the girl. " And that's what I should be if the talk about reincarnation were true and I could have my choice. When I die I should like to come back as some live thing that could always be in tropical sunlight; could always hear the hot wind in the tops of trees and the warm ocean coming against heated sands."

Salome's eyes met her mother's as she ceased speaking. Mrs. Gerry had raised her head. She was startled and terrified at the look of languor and of fire in the child's glance. And then she asked herself why she should be terrified? Was it abnormal that the young, susceptible nature should be so moved by its environment, by the flow of renewed life?

Solome threw her arm over her mother's neck.

"Don't look so frightened," she said; "I don't believe in reincarnation. I'm perfectly orthodox, I suppose. But really, mother, shouldn't you think a tiger, for instance, 'burning bright,' would be very happy?"

"No, I shouldn't!" with great decision.

Salome laughed gently. She kissed her mother's cheek.

"Oh, what a Northern woman you are!" she exclaimed. And then, after a pause, "But I shall never be a Northern woman again."

"What do you mean?" sharply.

"I mean that I would not live North; I couldn't," shuddering. "Do you think I would go back there after having been under such a sky as this? Look up into the heavens, mother. Oh, life is worth living here. Only I'm afraid I shall love life too well. Do you think I shall? Tell me, do you think I shall?"

"It is natural and proper to love life," Mrs. Gerry replied, somewhat primly. She felt that her child was getting away from her in some way. She wanted to reach out frantically after her, but she could not.

"Natural and proper!" repeated the girl. "I begin to think that I am unnatural and improper. But I can't be really wrong, since you are my mother," with another caress. "Only, you see, I can't even imagine that I could live North again. I did not live there; I hated it."

"But in the summer," began Mrs. Gerry—"think how it would be here in the summer."

"Yes; I have thought," replied the girl. "It would be hot—hot. It would be delightful. And I suppose I should never cough again. I should always be as well as I am now. I was never well before in my life. I was only a 'little more comfortable,' or 'not quite so comfortable.' You and father will have to move down here. Father might have an orange grove on the Indian River, or he might learn of Mr. Maine how to raise truck."

Salome laughed again at this last thought, and her mother smiled faintly.

"And what about Mr. Moore?" asked the elder woman. "Have you told him?"

"Not yet. But I shall tell him. He must arrange some way. I've been thinking that we must all live on the Gulf coast. They say it is cold here sometimes, after Christmas. And I will never, never endure the cold again. It is like death to be cold."

Salome was now leaning back against the tree. The two did not speak for a long time. Mrs. Gerry was trying to rest, and at the same time she was trying to cast out of her mind the formless fears which invaded it. She was continually telling herself that she need not be anxious about the fancies of an imaginative girl. But the fact which griped her hard and relentlessly was the fact that she herself had never been in the least as Salome was now. She had never had that nature; she could not understand it; she had to own, with a sick feeling which was worst of all, that

she was repelled by it. However sympathetic we
may be, what we have not felt, what we cannot feel,
remains forever beyond the pale of our sympathy;
beyond our judgment. And then love becomes a
torture. It was a torture at this moment to Mrs.
Gerry. She could not understand; but her love for
her child was so keen and so strong that it seemed
to her that God would not be so cruel as not to give
her understanding of her daughter's heart. She felt
as if she were thrust out, not by Salome's will, but by
a bitter and inexorable something for which no one
was responsible.

These events, these combinations for which no one
is responsible, how unbearable they seem sometimes!

After a few moments Mrs. Gerry began to tell how
kind Mrs. Darrah had been, and how relieved they
would all be that Uncle John could be paid.

Salome, with her head against the tree, watched her
mother with interest. She was thinking all the time
of the check she had signed, and she was telling herself that she was perfectly positive that it was wrong
for her to have done that. Yes, she knew it was
wrong; but she wondered why she did not feel that it
was an evil thing to do. She had no feeling whatever
in that direction. But she knew. She knew how the
wind blew over the snow-banks at home in midwinter;
but she did not feel it, and she meant never again to
feel it. What was the use?"

An impulse to explain to her mother came to her.
It was difficult to think that Mrs. Gerry could feel
differently from what she herself felt.

"Of course I shall tell her some time," she thought.
"But I will wait. She will be grieved; and why
should I grieve her? But how lovely everything has

15

come out!   If I had waited I might not have been in time with that money.   I wonder what Portia would say to what I have done?   Portia is not so particular about her conscience as mother is, or as mother used to teach me to be.   I must tell Portia."

The day was already ended when the two women left their place by the tree.   The sun had gone down in a red sky; the flat stretch of country lay in a warm calm under the rapidly growing moonlight.   The birds were flying in the long, blue spaces towards the west.   The frogs were croaking.

The two walked on hand in hand.

"There is only one thing about living here," Salome was saying—"one thing which is not so pleasant, I mean."

She swung her mother's hand back and forth as she spoke.   She was smiling, but her eyes were slightly anxious.

"Two things, I should say," responded Mrs. Gerry, who had now fully resumed her cheerfulness; "and they are Mr. Job Maine and Mrs. Job Maine."

"But they are one," was the retort, "don't you know.   And she married him for love.   I don't mean them; I mean the crows, mother."

Mrs. Gerry turned and looked full in the girl's face.

"The crows?"

"Yes; they will sometimes fly over my head, and between me and the lovely blue sky.   I wish they wouldn't."

XIII

MRS. GERRY was conscious of a very helpless feeling when she heard her daughter make that remark about the crows. She replied that she supposed that the crows must fly somewhere.

"Oh yes, mother," said Salome, earnestly; "but not between me and the sunlight, and when I am with—" she hesitated; then she went on, "when I am with Randolph Moore."

Having said this, Salome lapsed into silence.

The wind seemed to be rising from the east. The waves began to pound on the farther side of Anastasia. The light from the large moon made the sand glisten sharply. The stiff spikes of a Spanish bayonet-tree shone with a hostile aspect. But the air was sweet with an intoxicating mingling of odors.

Mrs. Gerry was becoming more and more depressed.

Suddenly from the direction of the truck farm which they were now approaching they heard the drawling, nasal tones of their landlord:

"I've ben aimin' to hang that thur do' for some weeks now," Mr. Maine said, "but I'm so kinder crowded with work, 'n' my wife she's continually needin' wood cut, or sumpthin'. A man can't 'complish nothin', if he has er wife. Women ain't no consideration. Course, you c'n hang them do' if you want er. I sha'n't put nothin' in thur way of yer hangin' them do'. I ain't thur man to put nothin' in no other man's way, I ain't."

"All right," responded a clear, energetic voice. "Then I'll do it. I've been aiming to hang it, too. Only I never could think of the confounded screws and things. But I've got them this time. Come, Maine, hold up the door, can't you, while I measure about these hinges?"

The two women had paused involuntarily at sound of that voice, for both recognized it as belonging to Moore.

Salome's grasp tightened on her mother's hand. Into the girl's eyes there sprang a new light.

"It is Mr. Moore," said Mrs. Gerry's calm tones. "So he has come back."

The elder woman walked forward, but Salome lingered for a moment under the banana shrub. She saw Moore drop his tools and turn eagerly. She saw that, while he greeted her mother, his glance sprang to her.

She came forward demurely now, and held out her hand.

She said she hoped he had had a successful trip. Had he sold many goods?

Moore held her hand. She repeated her question about the goods.

"I don't know," he answered. "I believe so; that is, I forget. I'm sure I don't care."

Salome tried to withdraw her hand, but could not.

"Not care?" she exclaimed; "aren't you afraid that those people who employ you will turn you off?"

"No; I am only afraid that you are not sufficiently

glad to see me. I have been gone for months—years."

"You have been gone five days and about three-quarters of a day."

"Then the time has seemed as short as that to you?" in a melancholy tone.

"Time has literally flown with me."

"Salome !"

"Mr. Moore !"

"Oh, how inconsiderate you are !"

"Inconsiderate because time has flown ? Would you have had it drag ? Would you have had me suffer —hanging my head and weeping because you were travelling about and enjoying yourself ? Tell me that !"

The girl laughed gently. Her eyes shone humidly. She was afraid; her happiness made her tremble and draw aloof.

"I don't want you to suffer," said Moore, gazing at her wistfully. He thought he had not half known how attractive she was to him; and that moonlight— or was it the moonlight ?

The black and white hound came from within the hut and stood by the two, looking up and wagging his tail.

Salome bent down to stroke his head. But Moore did not notice the animal; he did not know the dog had come.

"Thank you for not wanting me to suffer," was the somewhat airy response.

The young man stood in silence. He was puzzled and grieved. But he would not relinquish the girl's hand.

He had lived their meeting over and over, and his

imagination had not once made it in the least like this.

He drew his companion away among the pine-trees, Jack following with his head hanging.

Moore thought he would try a more matter-of-fact kind of conversation. He put Salome's hand through his arm. He endeavored not to look at her for a moment, but he found his eyes constantly returning to her face.

He was telling himself that he loved her a thousandfold more than when he had seen her last.

But he began bravely on his matter-of-fact topic.

"I had a disagreeable kind of a piece of work down in Tampa," he said. "There's a fellow there who has been using our firm's name. He has done it twice. But the last time was once too many. Our Mr. Donaldson wired me to act my own judgment—said he wouldn't overlook it again, even though the man had a wife who would be likely to die of shame. He couldn't help that. I had to do the whole thing. It was of no use to deny—so the wretch confessed. He cried and sobbed. I should have let him off, but I knew Donaldson too well to do that."

"Do you mean that the man had forged?" asked the girl.

"Yes. He was in an awfully tight place. But of course he is a scamp."

"A scamp?"

"Yes, certainly. It's no good to be weak about those things. But I tell you I don't want to be the one to get an officer to nab a poor wretch again, and I won't, either. I felt as if I were a criminal myself. It was heart-breaking, and then his wife—no, I swear I'll never be mixed up in such an affair again! You see, I'm too soft. I can't see people suffer—and I thought of you, Salome. But I'm thinking of you always. I thought of how your kind heart would grieve for that woman—and for the man, too; and I hated myself—and yet I was doing right. Why do you sometimes hate yourself when you are doing right?"

' Salome did not answer. She had clasped her other hand over her companion's arm, and was now really leaning upon him.

Moore looked down at her. He forgot what he had been talking about. Why should he remember, when at last she glanced up at him?

But she did not let the subject drop.

"You said he forged?" she asked. She hung upon his arm.

" Yes; but don't let us talk about him any more. You see, I was driven to saying something because—because you didn't seem glad to see me."

" Not glad to see you?"

She touched her cheek for an instant against the sleeve of his coat. But when he bent eagerly over her she withdrew a little and said :

" But I want to talk more about that man."

" What man?"

" Why, the forger. I suppose it is a crime?"

" Well, I should think so! And a particularly mean, underhanded crime, too—to use another person's name."

" Yes, I suppose it is," said the girl ; " but somehow it doesn't shock me as it ought. But, of course, I know—I know."

Moore stopped in their slow walk. He looked surprised.

" Why on earth should we talk about forgers when

we haven't seen each other for—for months?" he asked.

"For five and three-quarter days," was the reply; and she smiled at him. While she still smiled she continued, "But I have a special interest in forgers."

"Why?"

"You will be extremely shocked if I tell you."

Moore's surprise increased. "What a curious girl you are."

"Yes, I think I must be." She gazed up at him now with a deep seriousness. "Still," she went on, "you think you—you think you care for me?"

"Think? I am sure. It seems to me there is nothing else I care for in the world."

He spoke with impetuous quickness.

"Oh yes, there is something else," lightly, though with the serious look still in her eyes.

"What is that? But you are mistaken, Salome," earnestly.

"Am I? But don't you care to sell a large bill of goods? Isn't that what you call it?"

Moore laughed joyfully. He pressed his hand over her clasped hands on his arm.

"Who told you that?" he asked. "I believe I am a tolerably good drummer-boy. That's why I get a good salary. That's why I shall be able to take care of you, Salome; why, I am able now; we might be married directly. I will ask your mother. Let us ask her now; there is not the slightest use in waiting."

He spoke hurriedly. He had that fear so common to lovers that something dreadful would immediately happen to separate him from the woman he loved.

"How foolish you are!" exclaimed the girl, in response. "Do you think I am going to be hustled from one hand to another like—well, like a bill of goods? No, indeed. I can't be married for a long time to come."

"Why not?"

"There are a thousand reasons."

"Give me one of them."

"I'm going to be Mrs. Darrah's amanuensis for a number of years. I'm learning shorthand and type-writing; I intend to be very useful to her."

Moore looked about him in the moonlight as if hopelessly trying to find some answer to Salome's words. But he found none.

"About how many years, if I may ask, do you expect to work for Mrs. Darrah?"

He put this inquiry with a great appearance of calmness.

"I haven't quite decided. Several," was the reply.

"Have you signed a contract—have you sold yourself, as they used to sell themselves to Satan?" with an increase of vehemence.

"Who used to sell themselves to Satan, Mr. Moore? And Mrs. Darrah is very far from being like Satan."

"If she keeps you from me she is worse than Satan," said Moore, with more sharpness in his tone than the girl had ever heard before. He made an uncontrollable gesture of anger as he continued, "But what can you expect of an authoress? Women have no business to—"

"Don't say ridiculous things, Mr. Moore," interrupted Salome; "I would write books myself if I could."

"But you can't—thank fortune!"

"I'm not so sure of that. Sometimes I feel as if I could," was the reply.

Moore tried to regain his temper. He could hardly tell why he felt so deeply irritated.

"You know what Alphonse Karr says?" he remarked, with some lightness.

"No; I don't know what any one says—least of all Alphonse Karr."

"He says that a woman who writes a book is guilty of two crimes: she increases the number of books and decreases the number of women."

"Then I hate Alphonse Karr!"

After this from Salome there was silence. The two continued to walk on between the trees where the moonlight fell in broad patches on the wiry grass.

The hound paced on behind them.

Salome had now withdrawn her hand from her companion's arm. She looked removed from him.

Moore's nature was too essentially sweet for him to remain long in anger. But this meeting was so different from what he had anticipated. He could hardly tell why he felt so heart-sore.

How coolly Salome had spoken of remaining a number of years with Mrs. Darrah! Of course she did not care for him at all as he cared for her. He did not suppose that women knew much about how to love. Women were so cold, and—and mysterious.

At this point in his thoughts Moore took the girl's hand and kissed it with the utmost gentleness.

"I suppose I've been wrong some way," he said. "Men are so stupid—that is, we are called stupid."

"But you don't feel stupid?" asked Salome.

"Don't let's speak in that way any more. Salome, you don't know how I love you," with kindling eyes, "and I thought, I hoped— Dearest, do you think you do care for me so that in time you will care a great deal?"

Salome drew back. She pressed her hands together while she looked at her lover.

"Don't you know how that will end?" she asked. "Don't you know? It will end in my loving you infinitely more than you love me. I have read that—and now I am sure of it. Yes, now I am sure of it."

"That is impossible! Impossible!" cried Moore. "I want to tell you that I—"

Salome drew away with a decided movement.

"You know I told you I wanted to talk more about that forger," she said.

Moore stared. His face fell. He had poignant sense of being baffled. He almost felt that he was being trifled with. But when he saw the girl's face he was more puzzled than ever.

The young man made a great effort and took himself in hand.

"Well," he responded, "I am ready to listen to all you have to say about the forger."

Salome now came a little nearer.

"Did he feel very badly?" she asked, with great interest.

"Yes; he did."

Moore was deciding in his own mind that he was entirely helpless in her hands. And he was remembering with a kind of despairing thrill that moment some days ago when she had voluntarily told him that she loved him. It seemed to him that he had thought of nothing but her words, her tone, and her face when she had spoken thus.

And now here she was insisting upon talking of

that miserable incident. He was very sorry he had mentioned that man.

"I suppose," said the girl, "that was because somebody was going to suffer for what he had done —his wife, for instance."

"Perhaps," was the answer, "and perhaps he was repenting."

"Oh, do you think so? It wasn't so very bad; I suppose your firm are able to bear the loss without much inconvenience?"

This time Moore stared harder than ever.

"It will not inconvenience us very much," he answered.

"Then why do you make such a fuss over it?" inquired Salome.

"I didn't know I had made a fuss." Moore hoped that he should not become any more confused than he was now. Of course she was playing upon him. It was all very strange.

"You said that it was a mean, underhanded kind of a crime," now remarked the girl.

"So it is."

"I must say that I have a great sympathy for that man," said Salome.

Moore caught eagerly at this.

"That is because you have such a kind heart!" he exclaimed.

"No, it isn't that," she said.

"Isn't that?"

"No. But I shall shock you if I tell you why."

"Don't mind about shocking me," he replied, with a hint of bitterness, "but tell me."

She came nearer to him, she put her hand on his breast.

"Well, it is this," she said : "it is because I don't care about right and wrong."

His arm had gone round her quickly when she had approached him.

She leaned against him with a movement full of tenderness and trust.

"No; I don't," she went on. "Now, are you sure you care for me?"

Before he could give the ardent answer which rose to his lips, she continued :

"You remember I told you that I didn't care for the higher spiritual life either."

"Salome—" he began, but she would not let him go on.

"I know what it will be when you get away from me; you will begin to think of what I have told you—and it's the truth—and you will wonder about me, and ask yourself if you ought to love me; and, by-and-by, sometimes, when you ask yourself this question, you will answer: 'I almost wish I had loved some one else; perhaps some one else would have made me happier.' That's what you will think. No, no, don't interrupt me! And if you should come to that conclusion after we are married — do you know what a dreadful thing that would be? I could not bear that. I certainly could not bear that."

As she ceased speaking Salome laid her head on Moore's shoulder. She sobbed. But she controlled herself immediately and was perfectly quiet, while her companion held her closely and poured out tenderly emphatic assurances, the words coming from a full and sincere heart.

At last Salome lifted her face and spoke. But her

words did not seem to have any reference to what Moore had just been saying.

"I have been thinking that I don't seem to have any conscience. If I'm not going to have enough to make me good I would rather not have any. It wouldn't be agreeable to have just enough conscience to torment one, but not enough to keep one right."

Moore held the girl at arm's-length for an instant. His face was radiant with happiness. Of course these were the vagaries of a too sensitive spirit.

"I'm not afraid," he said, with the sublime confidence of youth and love. "I can face any destiny except the destiny which takes you from me."

"Do you really feel sure of that?" she whispered.

"Yes, absolutely sure."

"And I need not worry any more about it?"

"No, no. Why, Salome, I don't understand you. You are morbid."

There was that in Moore's tone and face which could not fail to comfort the girl.

"No, I am not morbid now," she responded. "I used to be, up North, before I was really alive. But now—"

She bent her head to his shoulder again.

"Now?" he repeated, bending over her.

She pressed her face still closer against him.

"Now," she answered, in a muffled voice, "I am trying to endure your presence, Mr. Moore."

"I am glad you are beginning so early," he said, "for you will be obliged to endure my presence for years and years—as long as we both live."

"I hope so," from his shoulder.

Then Salome suddenly raised her face and quickly passed her hand across her eyes.

"What discipline it will be!" she exclaimed. "And I am afraid I have been a little — a very little sentimental, Mr. Moore."

"You certainly have, Miss Gerry."

"I take it all back."

"No; you shall not take a word back," firmly.

"I didn't know you were such a tyrant," standing away from him.

"I am. It is well for you to learn that fact early. Oh," with a quick break in his voice, "how happy I am!"

Salome was a few paces from him, her hands hanging by her side. She stood in a space of moonlight. Was it that light which made her have at that moment a certain intangible appearance—as if she were more spirit than flesh?

"And you don't care to talk about the forger any more?" Moore inquired.

"I never want to think of him again," with a swift gesture of her left hand. "But," she added, as if under a strong impulse," I don't blame him. Perhaps—"

Moore waited in silence. He was not now thinking of the forger, though he had mentioned him again.

"Perhaps," went on Salome, "it was a kind of reaction some way, and he may have done it for some one he loved. No: I don't blame him in the least. Are they going to put him in prison, Mr. Moore?"

"I suppose so. But are we going to keep right on conversing on this topic?"

"Oh no. Let us walk down to the Sebastian; or, rather, let us go back, and you may finish hanging our door, and then you will be making yourself useful, while we may enjoy the pleasures of conversation."

"But I would rather go to the Sebastian. Even that stream will be beautiful in this moonlight, and we may enjoy being romantic."

"No; we have had that kind of thing sufficient for to-night. Think how this light will serve for putting on those hinges."

"Hear her talk of that kind of thing! Of hinges!" cried Moore, looking round him as if for an audience.

His spirits were so high that if he had been in the least superstitious he would have felt some fear mingled with his exaltation.

"Don't speak disrespectfully of the very light of life, Salome, even in jest. But I will make a bargain with you. I will go back and hang that door if you will take my arm as we walk; and if you will not hurry me, and if you will allow me to be as—we will say as romantic—as I please; and if you will not snub me, no matter what I say."

Salome looked at him with a great appearance of admiration.

"I don't wonder they took you into the firm almost immediately," she said; "for you do know how to make a bargain. Give me your arm and let us start. I aim to have that door hung this evening."

Later, when Moore had left the little log-hut and was walking slowly towards Augustine, into his rapturous mood there came one question, or rather one remark:

"How oddly she talked about that poor wretch of a forger!"

But the thought left him immediately. It did not return until late in the night—or, rather, early in the morning—when he wakened suddenly in his room at the San Marco.

Almost before his senses had fully thrown off sleep his mind formed these words :

" How strangely she looked when she talked about that poor fellow down in Tampa !"

And again the thought left him immediately and he slept again, thinking of other words she had spoken.

He had not gone directly to his hotel. He was convinced that he should not sleep at all. Why should he sleep when his waking was so happy ?

He strolled slowly into the town. The clocks struck ten. For " society " the evening had but just begun.

He heard the sound of band music, of waltzes, from the Ponce. That building was brilliant. He stopped in front of it ; then he sauntered into the grounds. A few people were walking here and there. The plashing of water, the peculiar rustle of the thick leaves of orange-trees, the odors from the cape jasmines, the low laugh of women—Moore paused with his hands thrust into the pockets of his morning-coat. This was no place for him among these people in evening-dress. But still he lingered, taking in the beauty of his surroundings with a keen delight. Everything that was beautiful was now a thousand times more beautiful to him—for did he not love ?

Presently from an avenue there came two figures. Moore soon knew them to be Major Root, resplendent in a vast, stiff expanse of shirt-bosom whereon a diamond glittered, and on his arm a slender figure holding itself with a peculiar air of grace and independence. Of course the latter was Portia Nunally.

Moore had hardly decided as to the identity of the two when the woman paused and withdrew her hand from its support. She said something rapidly.

16

The man seemed to demur, but his companion insisted. He took her hand, kissed it with an elaborate air, and then walked away.

Miss Nunally now came quickly forward in a manner that showed that she had previously seen and recognized Moore. She did not pause until she was close to him.

"Congratulate me," she said. Her face was flushed; her eyes sparkled. But there was a certain constriction across her brows which a woman would have noticed.

Moore drew himself up. "No; I swear I won't congratulate you," he said, roughly.

"Then congratulate Major Root, if you think that would be more appropriate."

"No," repeated Moore; and he added: "I feel more like strangling him."

Portia advanced still nearer. She extended her much-ringed hand and put a finger on Moore's sleeve.

"Don't strangle him till the wedding-day," she said, with so much expression that the young man involuntarily stepped back.

The girl also moved away quickly. Then, in that mocking but somehow seductive little contralto of hers, she sung in a half-voice:

> "'She has kilted her skirts of green satin,
>   She has kilted them up to her knee;
>   And she's aff with Lord Ronald McDonald,
>   His bride and his darling to be.'"

"Only for green satin read white surah, and for Ronald McDonald read Major Micah Root. With these slight alterations I think the song must have been composed for me.   What do you say, Mr. Moore?"

"You know very well what I think of — of this cursed kind of a bargain.   It isn't safe for me to say anything about it; oaths are the only words that I want to use."

"And oaths are not fit to be spoken before a refined woman like me, Mr. Moore," responded Portia.

She was standing very quietly.   Her white dress and her jewels gleamed.   She was opening and shutting her fan, and gazing over it at her companion. There was something in her eyes which appealed very strongly to the young man.

"You call me a refined woman, don't you, Mr. Moore?" she asked.

He was obliged to rouse himself somewhat that he might reply.

"I had that impression.   You seemed to me to be exquisitely refined and fastidious."

"Yes; odd, isn't it, that people generally think that of me?   I had such a fancy about myself.   But, you see, I'm not.   I am coarse and vulgar.   I am going to marry Major Root.   It makes me ill to look at him. How red his face is!   How heavily his under lip hangs!   But I'm going to be his wife.   There are three other girls whom I know here in Augustine who would have jumped if he had beckoned to them.   But I've won him.   I shall marry him just as soon as he says; only hanging back enough to be womanly, you know!   And I have to beg for your congratulations, Mr. Moore!"

Moore did not attempt any reply.   He stood gazing at the girl, a deep frown on his face.

She drew up the light scarf that had fallen from her shoulders.

"He just asked me," she went on; " I knew he would do it to-night. I hesitated, and was properly surprised, and I let him plead a little. Then I said 'yes.' But after I had said that word I felt that I could not possibly endure him in my presence for another instant. I saw you here, Mr. Moore. I sent him away. I shall not see him again until to-morrow. Then he will call on my Aunt Florence. My Aunt Florence will feel like thanking him for taking me off her hands. Everybody will envy me, and say how well that Darrah woman's niece has done, after all. The three other girls who wanted to marry Major Micah Root will be green. And I, why I shall

> " ' Be aff with Lord Ronald McDonald,
>   His bride and his darling to be !' "

Moore sprang forward a step. He grasped Portia's hand which held the fan. The fragile thing fell broken to the ground.

"It is atrocious!" he cried, savagely. " I—I won't allow it! No decent man should allow such a thing. A man should remember that a woman is to be loved —to be respected—above all things, to be respected. You don't know how vile a thing a male human being may be and still be received. You don't know what an animal that Root is. I've heard him say things that—that—oh, I can't tell you! I'll go out and kill him. Somebody's got to kill him !"

Miss Nunally was looking intently at the young man's face. She was standing very near him. That constriction across her forehead deepened.

"Please remember, Mr. Moore, that I've led him on. I've intended to make him propose to me. And, in a way, I have enjoyed it—on account of those other girls who will be green with envy, you know. But—" here Portia suddenly spread out her hands as if thrusting something away; her voice broke into a hoarse and not easily distinguishable murmur—"how am I going to endure my life? What is to become of me?"

Before Moore could in any way gather himself for a reply the girl had turned away with a slight laugh and the remark:

"You did not guess that I had such melodramatic possibilities in me, did you? Well, I at least have the merit of not indulging them often. Will you take me back to the ball-room, Mr. Moore?"

The young man offered his arm. The two walked on in silence.

Soon they came among groups of people. Some of them glanced rather superciliously at Moore.

At last, near the veranda, he paused.

"You see, I am not fit to come among these fine birds," he said. "I will say good-night now. I suppose it is useless to remonstrate with you?"

"Quite."

Miss Nunally hesitated after she had spoken that word. Her manner was such that her companion could not immediately leave, as he had intended doing.

"Let us go to that shrubbery," she said; "I have something to ask you."

They walked to the shrubbery, which was odorous with clusters of yellow flowers.

Portia absently plucked a few of these.

" Perfumes are very strange," she said ; "they ap-
peal both to the sense and the spirit."

She extended the flowers to Moore.　He took them.

" Only in these days there is no longer any spirit ;
it is all sense—all material.　I wanted to ask you if
you are sure of being happy with Miss Gerry ?"

" Sure?　Oh yes !　I wish the future were as bright
to you, Miss Nunally."

There was a deep and tender earnestness in the
young man's voice and his face.

Portia looked up at him.

" I knew you felt so," she returned.　" I hope you
will not be disappointed.　I dread telling Miss Gerry
about my engagement.　She is not the kind of a girl
who could do such a thing."

" No !　No !"　With some violence.

" Well, good-night, Mr. Moore.　Stay "—she looked
at him again ; " you may give those flowers to Miss
Gerry with my—with my sincerest good wishes."

She walked away.　Her white dress gleamed in and
out among the trees, then was gone.

XIV

WHEN Moore had left the log-house where he had hung the door, Salome had stood outside in the moonlight for a long time, with the hound sitting near her. She could hardly be said to be thinking of her lover. She was merely not thinking at all. The Florida night was all about her. The monotonous level was never monotonous to her—least of all, now. She liked to hear the movements of unseen birds in the trees. She liked to take in, with all its inexpressible, serious beauty, the very spirit of this bewitching land, this land which had healed her body.

Mrs. Gerry sat in the doorway. She could hardly restrain herself from telling her daughter that she must not stay out in the night air. But she remembered that the night air no longer harmed the girl. Nothing harmed her. There was not an hour that had passed since her coming here that had not been full of healing and beneficence to Salome. For the first time she was in a climate so thoroughly congenial that merely to live was a blessing. She was well. She had thrown off the alarming symptoms with that rapidity of which youth is sometimes capable when influences are accurately adjusted.

Now her mother could not remove her gaze from that slight figure that was alert with life and with that happy prescience which in itself is an elixir. But Mrs. Gerry did not like Florida. If she had been given to expressing herself with great strength she would have said that she hated it. Everything, in her eyes, was wrong ; for was not everything different from New England ? And to be compelled daily to see such people as Job Maine and his wife—that experience alone would have made her miserable. And these were almost the only people she saw. She had to buy chickens of them at exorbitant rates. If Mr. Maine did an errand for her he charged her well for it. Of late Salome had insisted upon bringing out parcels from Augustine when she returned from her work with Mrs. Darrah. And it was only of late that Mrs. Gerry had really decided that Salome was amply able to do this. It was so strange not to be continually shielding the child and taking care of her. At first the mother would demur, and the girl would say : "But you know, mother, I haven't incipient phthisis any more," and she gayly did as she pleased.

Now, as Mrs. Gerry, with relaxed mind and body, sat in the hard, straight chair in the entrance to their hut, Salome suddenly left her musings by moonlight and walked straight up to her mother. She leaned against her in silence for a moment. After a while she asked :

"Do I look like any of my relations, mother ?"

Mrs. Gerry was accustomed to abrupt remarks from her daughter, so she only smiled slightly as she answered · "You always used to look like my mother, and at times like her father. Now you grow every day to have his expression. You are so mixed, but then we are all that way."

"Like her father ? He would be my great-grandfather then, wouldn't he? What kind of a man was he? You never talk about him."

"Perhaps I haven't. But then one doesn't give much talk to grandfathers; and I have had other things to think about—you, for instance."

Mrs. Gerry was instinctively bracing herself. She hardly knew why. Salome was liable to take up a whim and follow it. And she had always been pertinacious in the most unexpected directions.

"Yes, I know I've been a great anxiety to you. But what kind of a man was your mother's father?" repeated Salome.

Still she was not thinking very strongly, even then, of what she was saying. While she had been standing out there in the moonlight it had occurred quite powerfully to her that she was not at all what she would have called a New England girl. Such girls were proper and narrow and rigidly upright; they never had an "accidental thought" whose "possible pulses" were not immediately stifled. They were, above all things, "reliable." They were reliable because they could not help being so.

This was the way Salome Gerry inwardly described the typical Yankee girl. If she did not choose her adjectives correctly she none the less thought that she so chose them. And she would have described herself before she left home in those words. Particularly would she have warned herself against the possible pulses of those accidental thoughts. It was the irregular things which must be avoided. It was the irregular, exceptional things which had such astonishing power; and astonishing power, in the creed of the common-place, must of course make for evil—until it should be labelled and arranged. Anything which had been labelled and arranged, however, could no longer be considered abnormal or exceptional.

As Salome stood leaning by her mother's chair these thoughts went confusedly through her mind. She was often confused in these days. Everything outside was so different, and all her inward life was still more different, if that were possible.

There were brief snatches of time when Salome would feel an acute wonder as to why she felt no repentance for the crime she had committed. It was a crime. There could be no doubt of that. And Moore had spoken very severely of such a crime. Though, perhaps, that man down in Tampa had done it for his wife. It was rather curious that Salome came to assert to herself that the man in Tampa had done this deed for his wife.

Now she recalled her somewhat wandering thoughts, and asked once more what kind of a man her great-grandfather had been.

This time Mrs. Gerry replied, promptly,

" Everybody loved him."

The girl fixed her eyes on her mother's face.

" But was he good ?" she inquired.

" He was not what we call conscientious," was the answer.

Mrs. Gerry made a quick resolve. She took Salome's hands and gently drew the girl into her arms.

" He was not a Northern man. He was born down here in the West Indies. He was—well—I know what you are thinking. You are like him in many ways ; but I did not know it. I only suspected it before we came South. Now I know you belong in the South ; it is in your blood—this feeling you have since you came here."

Salome did not seem particularly impressed with this information. She lay with her head quietly on her mother's shoulder and her arm around her mother's neck. Her eyes were intently fixed upon the banana leaves which were slowly waving back and forth in the soft wind.

At last she said :

" Miss Nunally and I were talking about heredity the other day. She thinks that if we really believe in that we need not feel to blame about anything."

Mrs. Gerry's arm tightened around her burden. She wished to exclaim sharply, but she did not. She said, with calm emphasis :

" She is wrong. She is utterly wrong. Such a belief would undermine all desire to be good—all principle."

" What is principle ?" inquired the girl.

" Salome !"

Salome pressed her lips softly to her mother's cheek before she said :

" Of course I know. Am I not your daughter, you principled creature, you? And didn't I go to Sunday-school when the weather was good and you thought I should not take cold? The other day— now listen to me, and don't be shocked—I told a lie."

" Salome !"

An expression of intense pain crossed Mrs. Gerry's face. But she said no more then. The girl went on.

" It was about that venison, mother. I knew you had set your heart on it for me. I told you what I did because I thought it would make your mind easier. And it was of no earthly good to tell you that you could not have it at all. You would soon make arrangements for something else. And it was that poor boy's fault, and I hated to have you blame him."

Again the girl gently kissed her mother's cheek. And her mother said nothing.

"When I was at home and half ill, you know," continued Salome, "I never said the least thing that wasn't true. I'm almost sure I did not. But I did not really care anything about the truth for its own sake, mother. Somehow it seems as if people ought to care involuntarily for the truth's sake, just as they would care for a friend, because they can't help it. I never cared that way. Walter Redd cares that way. I was ill and afraid I was going to die, and full of notions, and I did not dare not to be truthful. And I made a great talk about my conscience. I was just awfully good, wasn't I, mother? But I was afraid; I was afraid of death, and of God. Now I'm not afraid of death at all; it seems so very far off that I can't be afraid of it. And God—well, He doesn't seem terrible to me any more. And when things look as if they would be easier and more comfortable all round if I didn't tell the exact truth, why I'm not afraid any more, you see."

Salome lifted her head and looked into her companion's face. Then she uttered an exclamation of pain.

"Oh, mother, do you feel so badly as that? Is it so very dreadful? Do you give me up? I wanted to tell you!"

Mrs. Gerry's arms clasped the girl with painful closeness.

"Give you up!" she said, sharply. "Oh no! no!

Nothing could make me do that, child. I love you, and I am your mother."

But Mrs. Gerry could not keep the agony out of her face. She bent her forehead to her daughter's shoulder for a moment.

She felt Salome's hand tenderly smoothing her hair.

Truth was the foundation of everything. That was the dominant thought in the woman's mind. There could be nothing without truth. What were all the graces. all the amiability in the world without that one attribute? What would Salome do? When should she believe Salome?

Do you wonder that the woman should suffer thus? This woman, to whom simple uprightness, absolute integrity were as the breath of her nostrils, and to whom they were as natural as that breath? The person of merely acquired virtues receives no such shock from any dereliction.

Mrs. Gerry was born with uprightness in her soul, and she had nourished that gift all her life.

She had a feeling that her daughter was wondering that she should be so much moved. Salome had expected her mother to be grieved and displeased, but she had hardly anticipated anything like this.

The girl put a hand each side of her mother's face, and lifted it so that she could look into it.

Mrs. Gerry thus gazed into the clear, loving sweetness of the girl's eyes. The knife-like question, " How much is she really responsible?" flashed through the woman's mind. But she had always held that people were responsible, directly so. Responsible or not, a person must meet the consequences of his thoughts and his deeds.

Mrs. Gerry tried to regain her self-control. She

tried to speak in her usual calm manner when she said :

"Salome, when you tell me anything, must I ask myself whether it is true or not? To know that you have said it ought to be just the same as knowing it is the truth."

"Yes," said Salome, still looking into her mother's eyes.

"Why do you say yes?" questioned Mrs. Gerry.

"I say it because I know one ought to tell the truth, since that is what you have taught me."

"But don't you know it for yourself if no one had taught you?"

Salome shook her head. "I can't tell about that," she answered. "I suppose I know it; but I'm not quite certain, somehow. I think my moral vision must be kind of blurred, don't you, mother? But please, please don't feel so badly! and let us talk of something else—the night, for instance. And let us imagine how cold and snowy it is at home where father is."

Mrs. Gerry knew perfectly well that it would do no good for her to pursue the subject further now. Perhaps it might never do any good. She had an intolerable sense of helplessness.

"It was time several days ago to hear from your father," she said. "I have been trying not to be anxious. We have not heard since you sent that money to him."

The two talked a few moments about paying Uncle John, and about affairs at home. Then Salome said good-night, and laid herself down on the bed. She was soon asleep. But the mother, though she took her place beside the girl, did not sleep. She lay watching the moonlight through the interstices between the logs, and thinking, thinking.

The fragrant air from the ocean and from the pines blew into the room.

Mrs. Gerry was very quiet. But she did not close her eyes. When the mocking-birds gave out their first flutings to the new day she heard them.

It was quite early on that day, even before Salome was ready to go into the town to her daily appointment, that a figure appeared in the path that led to Augustine.

Salome was washing the breakfast dishes in rather a desultory fashion, stopping every now and then to stroll for a moment out-of-doors. It was upon one of these strolls, with a tin dish in her hand, that she saw this figure. She recognized it, and hurried out to meet Miss Nunally.

"What has happened? And why are you not on horseback?" asked Salome.

"Nothing has happened. And I am not on horseback because I prefer to be on my feet," was the answer. "And I thought we might walk back together."

"So we will. But you must have risen at an unconscionable hour—for you."

"I did. I have been rehearsing all night one of Lady Macbeth's speeches, and consequently I did not sleep."

Salome thought Miss Nunally looked haggard.

"Why did you choose one of Lady Macbeth's speeches," she inquired, "when there are so many other people who have said more agreeable things?"

"Because it was so appropriate," was the answer.

"Don't you think you are very odd this morning?"

asked Salome, with some concern. "And do you mind telling me what speech it was?"

"Yes, I am odd, and I don't mind telling you. It is 'Out, damned spot!' Isn't that deliciously tragic? You see, there isn't any blood on my hand. But Major Root kissed it last night, which is worse than blood."

Salome gazed at the new-comer while she continued to pass the towel round and round the tin dish.

Mrs. Gerry now came from the hut, and in the greetings that passed Portia resumed her usual expression, which seemed to be a mingling of pride and courtesy.

When the two girls were on their way to the town, both under Salome's large umbrella, they kept silent for so long a time that it seemed as if Miss Nunally had, after all, nothing to say. It was Salome who broke this silence.

"Is Major Root a big man with a red face and a loose-looking mouth?"

"Yes."

"I've seen him in the Ponce grounds with you, and I've wondered—"

A pause.

"Well," Portia turned quickly, "what have you wondered?"

"Why, how you could endure to have him near you; and how you could smile at him as you did. If you should smile at me that way, Miss Nunally, I should certainly kiss your hand—unless you forbade me."

"You shouldn't wait until I forbade you."

The two paused as if the interest of their conversation, mild as it looks when written down, was still so great that they could not continue their walk. Portia was looking with winning eyes at her companion, who had always held for her something quite out of the ordinary. She had once confided to her Aunt Florence that if she had not come down to Augustine for the express purpose of getting a husband, and if all her family would not be so disappointed if she did not get one, she should have liked, above all things, to study that amanuensis.

"Let the child alone!" Mrs. Darrah had said, peremptorily. "You would bewitch her."

Portia opened her eyes at this.

"You credit me with—" she began; but Mrs. Darrah ruthlessly interrupted her.

"You know you bewitch people, Portia," she said. "You are one of those things they used to call sirens; and you really ought to be chained to a rock somewhere."

Here Portia lifted her upper lip in that way which showed the tips of her teeth—a way which was not a smile.

"It will be quite sufficient if I am chained to a husband, I think," she answered; and Mrs. Darrah had replied. with a laugh, that she fancied it would also be quite sufficient for the husband.

Now, as she stood with Salome, this little conversation returned to her.

Salome's face was still pale, but it had not now the pallor of ill-health; it was of that peculiar hue which denotes extreme sensitiveness, and the dilating and contracting pupils of the eyes conveyed the same impression. She looked, however, more able to bear this continual play of feeling across her consciousness. She had not now the aspect of an invalid.

17

"I wanted to tell you something," said Miss Nunally, at last, "but you are so very frank about that big man with the red face and the loose-looking mouth that you make it almost impossible."

Salome let her umbrella suddenly swing over her back and drop onto the sand. She seized her companion by the wrist.

"You are not going to marry that man!" she cried.

"Yes, I am."

"But—but—"

Salome found a difficulty in going on. She turned away, picked up her umbrella, and stood a little apart with it over her head. Her shining, distressed eyes were fixed upon Portia. She was thinking of Moore, and of how she loved him. Could it be possible that any woman, least of all the woman before her, could love Major Root? Salome was ignorant of many things. She could never quite bring herself to believe that a woman could decide to marry a man whom she did not love. She was a very simple-minded girl, notwithstanding the complexity of her character.

"But what?" coolly asked Miss Nunally.

There was, however, a flush on the speaker's face, and that same aspect of the brows which had been apparent the evening before.

"I was going to ask," said Salome, with some stiffness, "if you love Major Root. But it is not necessary to ask that. If you think of marrying him, of course you love him."

Miss Nunally made no attempt at a response for some moments.

She stepped within the shade of Salome's umbrella and put her arm about Salome's waist. Her face was so grave, so troubled, that it hardly seemed to be her face. The diablery which was often so pronounced and so charming was all gone. She almost looked old. And it is not years merely which age women. Portia Nunally had lived five years in one all her life. She had never economized in sensation, emotion. She was a spendthrift in every way. That old motto, "Dum vivimus, vivamus," had always been hers. But her rose-leaf skin was not injured, nor the lustre of her eyes dimmed. She possessed that rare gift of the gods which enables one to sleep like an infant the moment one's head is placed on the pillow.

If cares vexed and wearied her, she could throw herself on her bed and fall into that calm and beautiful repose which is represented as coming only to the people with burdenless consciences. She had come to reckon with a dangerous assurance upon this power of recuperation. She had hardly yet learned that the body, even though long suffering, never forgets its revenges. And the preceding night she had not slept as well as usual.

"I told Mr. Moore last evening," she now began abruptly, "that I dreaded telling you of my engagement; that you were not the kind of girl to—to— It is surprising that it should be so difficult to finish some sentences, Miss Gerry. And, then, it is not in the least necessary that I tell you I am going to marry Major Root. And yet I have had for some hours a morbid desire to tell you with my own lips, and receive—your congratulations!"

Portia smiled as she ceased speaking.

Salome withdrew herself from Miss Nunally's arm with an involuntary movement of which she seemed unconscious; but she immediately placed herself again close beside her as she said :

"I can't conceive that a woman can do such a thing. But, then, perhaps I can do things which would be impossible to you."

Something in the girl's manner made Portia forget her own affairs for an instant.

"What things, for instance?" she inquired, quickly.

Salome hesitated.

"I do not always tell the exact truth," answered Salome.

Portia gazed at her.

"With your face, too!" she exclaimed. "But then I don't always tell the exact truth, either."

"I mean," said the other, "that I don't have that regard for truth that I ought to have, and what is far worse, I don't suffer because of it."

"Oh!"

Portia's eyes sparkled with delight. She said she wished she had a blue note-book such as Aunt Florence used. Then, seeing Salome's annoyed expression, she begged her pardon.

Salome did not know why she had such a strong impulse to tell Miss Nunally about that forged check. To her mind it was not nearly so bad as Portia's engagement to Major Root. When she had begun to speak just now she had fully intended to tell of that. She did not know what kept her from speaking those words. It must be, she thought, because she feared that her mother would not like to have her do so. Her mother did not know; but her ideas were very strict.

"I knew you would not approve of my engagement," now remarked Miss Nunally. "I don't know why I should care so greatly whether you approve or not. I don't intend to care the least in the world what any one thinks. Most persons will say I'm a very lucky girl. I'm getting a trifle *passé*, you know. People have begun to ask, 'What! isn't that Nunally girl married yet?'"

"Why should you marry at all?" innocently questioned Salome. "Surely a woman need not think that she must marry."

"It is astonishing how many things you don't know!" cried Portia.

"Yes, that is true," was the modest reply.

Miss Nunally took her companion's hand and held it closely.

"I suppose you think you are in love," she remarked.

"I know I am."

"You have not a shadow of doubt?"

"Not a shadow."

Portia flung rather than dropped the hand.

"Mr. Moore hasn't a doubt, either," she said. "But, for all that, Salome Gerry, you two may be deadly tired of each other before two years are gone."

Salome clasped hard the handle of her umbrella.

"You make me feel as those crows did when they flew over us the other day;" and she shrank slightly as she spoke.

"How was that?"

"Oh, horribly!"

Having said this, Salome gathered herself to go on.

"Of course, a marriage for what seems to be love may turn out badly; but any other kind of a marriage must surely turn out so—is so from the beginning. Miss Nunally, do please tell Major Root that you have changed your mind!"

Portia seemed to set her teeth together.

"There's only one thing in all this world that could make me tell him so," she answered.

"What is that?" quickly.

"Oh, I shall not reveal that. Do you know," taking Salome's hand again, "it is quite on the cards that I should hate you?"

"No! no!" cried Salome. "Tell me why!"

"But I don't hate you. I can't seem to do that. You have such a face; such a lovely spirit. Yes, it must be your lovely spirit."

Salome thought of the check she had sent to her father. She remembered that she had not a strict regard for the truth, and, having remembered these things, she wondered somewhat painfully what it was that this girl could mean by speaking of her "lovely spirit." And she also asked herself how people could be so very much mistaken in her. There was Randolph Moore—with a quickening of the pulses as that name came to her mind—she was quite sure he believed that she had a lovely spirit. It seemed quite impossible to understand herself. Only, she was afraid she was not like what people thought her to be. So she supposed she was deceiving every one all the time.

In the confusion of mind which accompanied these thoughts she turned to Portia as if that girl might be able to help her in some way. She found that Miss Nunally was watching her with the utmost interest. She could not resist an increasing confusion, which showed itself in her eyes and in the curves of her lips. She wished to say something, but she could not speak. A feeling of resentment towards this emotion was growing within her. Apparently nothing had happened to cause this.

As the two stood there Mr. Job Maine, his mule, and his cart came slowly along from the direction of Augustine. He had been into the town; he had made what his wife called a "soon start" in the morning, and he was now on his way back.

Although it was not yet nine o'clock he had had a little whiskey, and this whiskey had made him very amiable. He informed Salome that he had brought a letter from Massachusetts for her mother, and he added the information that Massachusetts was a mighty good State. Then he gave his mule that succession of kicks which resulted, at last, in the animal's moving forward.

This incident appeared to change the current of conversation between the two girls. They now walked on quickly, Salome having come to a sense that it was time she hurried to her appointment. And they talked only in the most indifferent way.

It was hardly more than an hour later, and while Mrs. Darrah was in the full tide of successful dictation in the novel of sentiment, that the door of the room opened unceremoniously, but very quietly, and Mrs. Gerry appeared.

Her face was pale and set. She was dressed in her best black wool dress and her black bonnet. She held a bag in her hand.

Salome glanced at her. Then she dropped her pen and ran to her side. She seized her mother's disengaged hand and held it tight.

"Mother!" she cried, "what has happened?"

XV

"HOW SHOULD YOU THINK OF YOURSELF?"

Mrs. Gerry looked at her daughter with an agony of anxiety in her face. But it was an anxiety to which she must not yet yield; which she felt it wrong even to express in the slightest degree.

She summoned all her strength to her aid. She spoke with a courage which she could not feel.

"I had news this morning that your father is sick," she said, "and I thought it best to go home."

Salome stood as quietly as her mother. But she clung painfully to the hand she had grasped.

"You take the next train North?" she asked, unconsciously speaking in a whisper, as if her father were present and she might disturb him. Before her mother could do more than bend her head in assent Salome added, eagerly:

"I needn't get ready. I can go just as I am. And I can help take care of father."

"No," said Mrs. Gerry. Then she looked over at Mrs. Darrah, who was watching the two with surprise in her face. But Mrs. Gerry had no time to hesitate. She walked straight to that lady, who was lounging among her cushions.

"I have a great favor to ask of you," she said.

"Yes?" was the interrogative response. "Won't you sit down?"

"Oh no! My husband is ill; I must go to him. I can't let Salome go. It is winter up there; she would lose all she has gained. Oh, Mrs. Darrah, how shall I leave her? I know no one but those two miserable creatures out there where we have been living. She can't stay there. I haven't time to get her a place to live in, and we have so little money. But she must stay in Florida, and I must leave in half an hour. Would you help her about a boarding-place? Would you have a little oversight in regard to her, Mrs. Darrah?"

Mrs. Gerry paused. She had been going to say, "It is dreadful for me to leave her," but she was afraid that would sound weak. And she must not only be strong now, she must also seem strong.

Salome stood gazing at her mother.

"Don't be uneasy," said Mrs. Darrah, with the ease which plenty of money sometimes gives. "She can stay here with me. There's not the least reason why she should not. And if I feel like dictating in the afternoon, why, here she will be."

"But the expense—" began Mrs. Gerry.

"It is no matter about that. It will be all right."

"I can't thank you enough; I shall have time to arrange later," began Mrs. Gerry. She glanced at the clock. She turned to her daughter, the tense expression deepening upon her face.

Without speaking Salome ran across the room, snatched up her hat, and was again by her mother's side.

The two went out, holding each other's hands. After a moment Mrs. Darrah passed her handkerchief across her eyes.

The two sped along the narrow streets towards the

railway station. As they went on Salome panted forth the question, " What is the matter with him ?"

"Typhoid fever, your Uncle Lemuel wrote."

Then nothing more was said until they came in sight of the station. They had still ten minutes. But not until the ticket was bought did they speak again.

Then Salome threw her arms over her mother and demanded rather than asked,

" Mother, let me go with you !"

" No, no.   Remember, it is winter."

" You will not let me go ?"

" No!   It is for your good to stay."

" My good !   Oh, what of that ?"

" Salome !   Do you know how dear you are to me ? And, Salome—"

Mrs. Gerry led the girl out upon the platform. For an instant she held her as we poor human beings hold that which is unutterably precious, and from which we must part.

" Salome, will you tell the truth always — always? Salome, you must !"

" Yes, mother "—clinging to her—" yes."

The train bell rang like the signal of an inexorable fate.

Mrs. Gerry stepped into a car. She was borne off with her white face turned towards the white face of the girl standing on the platform.

Salome stood there for several moments. She was dimly aware that there were people chatting near her and sauntering about—people who had come down to see friends off. She even heard the stamping of horses on the other side of the station and the jangle of the harness they wore. She wondered afterwards how she could have noticed such things.

Presently some one left a group of ladies and gentlemen, and came quickly to Salome's side. It was Portia. She passed her hand through the girl's arm with a touch that was so sympathetic that Salome turned towards her with a choked exclamation. But she drew herself up instantly.

"I am very foolish," she said, brokenly.

"But what is it? I have just come here to meet the Jacksonville train," returned Portia.

Salome stood up straight. She brought her face immediately under control.

"Do present me, Miss Nunally; you know you promised to present me to Miss Gerry," said a voice behind Portia, who turned with an abruptness that had something almost savage in it.

"Go away, Major Root," she said, imperiously, "and drive back alone, for I shall walk with Miss Gerry."

The Major stood in annoyed indecision for a little time. But he had confided to some brother officers that one reason why the Nunally was so dashed attractive was that she never toadied to a fellow. She was as dashed independent as if she had a million dollars to her name; and be dashed if he didn't like that kind of thing; it was so dashed different from the rest of the girls. He said "gals" when in conversation with those brother officers.

Now he walked away with that small strut which is often apparent in a man who is not very tall, yet who is conscious of being an army officer.

But by the time he had mounted his dog-cart and was driving away, he thought he was very angry. He had been going to do that Miss Gerry an honor by being presented to her. And there was something interesting about her. Perhaps the Nunally didn't want him to know too many "other gals." He chuckled slightly at this thought, and this chuckle helped to restore him to a better humor. Portia wouldn't tell him to go away when she was his wife. He chuckled again at this idea. He glanced back. There the two were coming along the road arm in arm. They were talking earnestly; or, rather, Portia was talking. It was all make believe, of course, this appearance of interest. Women really disliked each other. Of course, it was dashed natural that they should dislike each other; and it was still more dashed natural that they should pretend to care. And the Major chuckled again.

Behind him Miss Nunally had just shrugged her shoulders, looking towards his broad back, and had said that she wished old Root would drive on out of sight. She was likely to see enough of him in the years to come, but now—another shrug finished the sentence. She turned to her companion, who was by this time perfectly composed, apparently. She spoke in her sweetest manner, and Portia's sweetest manner was seldom resisted. She assured Salome that a journey North was nothing; that Mrs. Gerry would soon send a telegram. And Portia felt sure that it would be good news that would come.

"Why not look forward to good news?" she said. "And meanwhile we must find a home for you in town. You can't stay there in that place my aunt calls so definitely 'beyond the Maria Sanchez.'"

"Oh," said Salome, "Mrs. Darrah has been so kind. I am to stay with her."

"At the Ponce?"

Miss Nunally halted as she asked this.

"Yes. But I hope it will only be for a week or two. Mother will write to me what to do. And she will come back, I suppose, if father—"

She stopped abruptly, unable to go on. She felt that she could not endure the suspense of the next few days. No, she simply could not endure it. But hour after hour must go on, and she must live through those hours as best she could.

"Don't worry," said Portia, gently. "Don't let us run to meet the future, whatever it is to be. And you are to be at the Ponce?"

She seemed to dwell in a peculiar manner upon this fact.

"I shall be a little graybird among all the fine feathers," was the response. "But I shall not be seen. I don't care for all the gayety there; and it cannot be for long."

"No," repeated Portia, "it cannot be for long. But are you going to shut yourself up and brood over the bad news?"

"I can't help brooding over it," was the reply. "And then it would seem disloyal, some way, if I were able to forget it."

"You mean you think your father and mother would be happier if they knew you were miserable?" said Portia.

Salome smiled. She was greatly comforted by her companion's presence. She had never seen Portia in precisely this mood before. She knew that Miss Nunally was many-sided, but the exquisite tenderness of her face and manner now were something she had not previously experienced. She could not help feeling it keenly even in the midst of her anxiety.

When they reached the old coquina gate Miss Nunally paused and held Salome back. A group of horseback riders was just trotting briskly into the city from that long stretch of road where later the sweetness of the yellow jasmine would be filling the air everywhere.

Now every rider wore a small knot of violets, which had been picked among the thickets of jasmine and glossy leaved greenery which rioted in rich life beyond the city.

At sight of Miss Nunally the hats of the young men came off, and their somewhat jaded faces showed the interest her presence was almost sure to waken. Some of them turned to look again at that girl who stood quietly beside Portia, gazing with melancholy, absent glance at the cavalcade.

One or two were able to tell the others that she was the little type-writer, or something of that sort, whom the Darrah woman employed, don't you know. They had seen her going swiftly along some gallery or balcony of the Ponce de Leon. If she were only dressed like the Nunally, don't you see she would be—well, it was really impossible to tell exactly what she would be. As it was, she was kind of an interesting little thing, eh?

Then they had all trotted and cantered by and were talking of the engagement, suspected, but not yet announced, of Major Root and Miss Nunally. The men didn't know how that filly would behave in harness, and the women wondered that a man like the Major should think of marrying again.

The girls remained standing. Salome appeared to have forgotten that there was any reason why she should go on. Portia was studying her with undisguised interest, and she was pitying her also, with a kind of pity that would not have angered the receiver of it.

"Do not let us go to the hotel now," she said, at last. "Let us take a boat. It is soothing to be on the water. One begins to feel better without knowing why."

Salome followed the guidance of the other. They went down to the wharves. Portia chose a trim row-boat, and ordered about the owner of it as she ordered every one whose business at the moment was to serve her.

The man was about to step into the craft when he was told that he was not wanted.

"But you, lady, can't manage a bo't yourself?"

"Can I not?" was the response. "But we are going without you. Come," extending both hands to Salome.

The boat went slowly out among the yachts that swung at anchor all along the coast of the town.

Portia rowed well, as she did everything. She took off her gloves and pulled her hat forward over her eyes. Occasionally she would look at the girl who sat almost motionless in front of her. She saw the strained expression give way somewhat.

Half-way over towards the island Salome started forward.

"I had forgotten Mrs. Darrah!" she exclaimed. "She was dictating when mother came. And she has been so kind. I must go back."

"But you cannot swim, and I am going to the North Beach," returned Portia.

"She has been so kind," repeated Salome, leaning forward. "You don't know how kind she has been about the—"

She paused just as she was about to utter the word "check." It seemed to her that it was not she herself who refrained from speaking that word. She herself would have been willing to pronounce it. She did not know what it was which held her back.

She felt a strong desire to tell Miss Nunally about that check. It was just possible that Miss Nunally would understand and would not be so shocked. She had not told any one save Mrs. Darrah, because she was quite sure everybody would be so shocked. And she remembered very well what Moore had said about forgery. She supposed that was the general feeling. Of course, it was wrong ; but then there were a great many things wrong about which there was no such feeling as that.

"Yes, yes," said Portia, calmly. "I know my aunt has been kind. She has done a great deal for me. But she will forgive you ; and I will explain that it was my fault. It puts one in such a generous attitude to say 'it was my fault.' Do let me have the pleasure of putting myself in that light. Just give yourself up to the influence of this air and water. Was there ever anything more beautiful? Let us drift away out into the Gulf Stream and be carried down to those islands of the blest."

A quick light came over Salome's face. She pressed her hands together.

"To the West Indies?" she asked, eagerly.

"Yes," smiling.

"Yes, yes ; let us go !" went on Salome, still more eagerly. "If we only might sail right down there ! But no—" the light dying out and leaving her more pallid than before. "Of course we cannot go. How foolish I am !"

Portia, who had spoken in jest, was for the moment alarmed.

"You are certainly a very strange Yankee girl," she said, after a silence.

"I am not a Yankee girl at all," Salome answered, with some pride.

Portia was alarmed again.

"Surely," she began ; then she stopped. She drew in her oars quickly and reached forward to her companion, taking both her hands in a firm clasp.

The boat rocked gently. The sands of Anastasia Beach glittered before them. Behind them, quaint, shabby, sumptuous St. Augustine lay in the brilliant sunshine.

"Miss Gerry—Salome !" exclaimed Miss Nunally. Then she tried to speak in her ordinary tone: "What are you, then ?" she asked.

Salome gazed about her. An expression of exalted passion came to her face.

"I am Southern—Southern to the core of my heart !" she exclaimed. "I hope I shall never see New England again. I was dead—dead—there. You don't believe me. I have kept myself calm, as if I were cold. I hate coldness. I am West Indian. The sun—oh, Miss Nunally, do you know what it is to love the sun and warmth and richness, and to hate clouds and cold and meagreness? And to have to be self-controlled and calm all the time? And to keep thinking whether a thing is right or not ?"

Here the girl paused to glance attentively at Portia, who was still holding her hands and looking at her with the alarm she could not quite subdue.

"You think I have suddenly gone insane, Miss Nunally," she said, "but I haven't. I'm perfectly sane.

18

Only a little "—she laughed—"just a very little drunk with being in Florida, and, really, I am a West Indian. That accounts, doesn't it?" She now spoke with the greatest rapidity. " I only knew just a short time ago that my mother's grandfather was born here on one of these islands. You see nobody has inherited from him but me. I am sure of that—sure of that. All the fire and ardor in his blood have come to me—to me. It skipped those between me and him. Oh, he would have understood me. He would not have wondered at me. And when those surges of glorious feeling which go over my soul—when they come, if I could have told him he would not have looked as you do now, Miss Nunally ; he would have understood. And he was never obliged to be cold and self-constrained be-cause he was born in Massachusetts and brought up to think that—that ice was the only respectable thing in the world."

Salome nearly stammered in her hurry to speak.

She came to a pause now. Her face was shining, with no color in it save in the lips. It was so re-splendent that the girl opposite, who was staring fix-edly at her, felt a quick start of pulses in vague but powerful sympathy.

" But—but—" began Portia, hurriedly. Then she gave her laugh. It echoed softly about them.

" I am not precisely the person to preach," she con-tinued, " but self-control is certainly something to strive for. We are very little save animals if we have not that virtue. We want a mask ready to put on, to keep on most of the time. A heart on one's sleeve—"

" Pshaw !" interrupted Salome. " You don't know what I mean. Oh, do pardon me ; I did not intend to be disrespectful. I don't think I want to say any more. Are we going to the North Beach? You know we cannot get into the Gulf Stream unless we go outside. And we can't go outside in this boat. We are always hampered, are we not?"

Miss Nunally did not reply. She felt that her own shallow disregard of the conventions was very shallow indeed when compared with the underlying something in her companion's character. She was deeply interested. She took up the oars and rowed for some time in silence. She was thinking that this girl had only been veneered by her Northern birth and upbringing, and that the superficial covering was revealing what was underneath.

Salome was now sitting in an attitude of perfect calm. Only upon her face there still remained the glow, fading somewhat, of a few moments since.

"I have almost a mind to tell you something," now remarked Salome.

"I am listening," was the response.

"Are you easily shocked?" asked Salome.

"I could almost say that it is impossible to shock me," answered Miss Nunally.

Salome was wondering why she felt so impelled to tell about that check to which she had put Mrs. Darrah's name.

"I thought, since you are going to marry Major Root, that of course you would not be shocked by— by trifles," said Salome. "But that is a rude speech, isn't it?"

"Rather, I should say." Portia had colored with anger. "But go on. We may be shocked by very different things."

"Yes; that is true. Now, I cannot imagine a woman doing as you intend to do. While, perhaps, you

cannot imagine doing what I am going to tell you.
And perhaps you will know whether I ought to inform Mr. Moore."

"I can advise you on that subject directly. Make
no confessions to him. Men never confess anything.
They don't think it worth while, and why should we?
I suppose you have loved somebody else—are still
engaged to him. Nothing is more common."

"No, no. It is about a—well, it is about—"

"Boat ahoy!"

As this call came from the direction of the town,
Miss Nunally uttered an impatient exclamation. The
two looked back. They both felt that it was they who
had been hailed, although there were many other
craft on the river.

There was a small sailboat coming directly towards
them. The sail caught the wind and was distended
stiffly. In the bows there stood a man with his hat
off. He was waving that hat towards them. The light
struck his white forehead, his tanned face, and yellow
beard.

"Boat ahoy!" he shouted again. "Where are you
bound?"

Salome did not speak. But she had instantly recognized Moore.

"What shall I say to him?" asked Miss Nunally,
quickly.

"Anything you please."

"He will ask to take us into his boat," said Miss
Nunally. "You know such an arrangement will make
our trip a very different thing. But if you want him,
Miss Gerry—"

"Where are you bound?" now shouted Moore again.
He was bearing down rapidly upon them.

"No, no," said Salome. "Answer what you please."

"For the North Beach." Miss Nunally had again drawn in her oars. She put a hand on each side of her mouth as she called back.

"So am I," said Moore. Portia looked at her companion as she said, interrogatively,

"We can't forbid him the North Beach, I suppose?"

Salome shook her head. "No; but tell him we want to go by ourselves."

Portia resumed her oars. "You may give him that terrible information," she said. "He may cast himself into the sea and drown himself. I'm not going to be responsible."

Salome now turned, and for the first time really looked at the occupant of the sailboat, which was skimming along with the somewhat leisurely but sure motion of a water-fowl.

Moore bent forward as she turned; he flung up his hat again. He was now so near that she could see the expression of his face. Seeing him thus she recalled his frequent use of the word "cruel" in regard to her. She knew that she was never cruel, and she knew also that he did not really think that she was.

It was very difficult, however, at this moment to say as she did :

"We want to go to the North Beach — by ourselves."

She saw the cloud come over the young man's countenance. But he would not yield before Miss Nunally to that sentimental mood.

"Won't the prayers—the tears—of a poor wretch move you?"

"Not in the least," with gay decision.

"Very well." The sailboat was now alongside.

"I shall take my revenge by hanging round and picking you two out of the water after you have capsized this mere eggshell, as you surely will do."

"We give you full permission to save us from a watery grave."

Miss Nunally glanced in some surprise at Salome, who, it seemed, was at times quite capable of not wearing her heart on her sleeve.

"And when you are saved, how bitterly you will wish you had been kind to me now."

Moore avoided looking at Salome as he spoke. He was holding the gunwale of the row-boat, and his eyes were turned everywhere but in her direction. But in reality he saw nothing save that figure, with its pale face looking towards him with what seemed to him a very reprehensible self-possession. He almost wished that he might have the chance of saving her from drowning. If he did, she would, perhaps, have that expression which he so well remembered. He thought it a distinct wrong to him that she was able to be so thoroughly calm. He quite forgot for the time that he was giving nearly his whole attention to the effort towards being calm and conventional himself. But when were lovers reasonable?

He still held the gunwale. He knew that Miss Nunally was gazing at him with a smile on her face. He knew very well that he ought not to remain a moment longer. And still he did not go.

This meant, then, not only that he could not go with Salome now, but that he should miss walking out to the truck farm with her. This thought made him frown, and it also made him say to himself that she cared very little about seeing him. Every moment since he left her he had been looking forward to that walk. And now how coolly she had made it impossible!

His bright face clouded perceptibly. If she did not care, he would also try not to care. Certainly she was indifferent. Did she not look so? And why need she have deliberately come out on the river with Miss Nunally? There was really no reason.

Having in about three minutes' time wrought himself into an acute state of indignant anguish, Moore now relinquished his hold upon the row-boat. He raised his hat with frigid ceremony, and his boat slid off over the ruffled surface of the water.

Salome carefully refrained from glancing towards that boat. But Miss Nunally looked at it, and at its occupant, who did not turn his head from its straightforward position.

"What curious animals lovers are!" she exclaimed, as she began to row.

There was no reply to this remark. Presently she continued:

"Mr. Moore wanted to pitch me over into the water, and then have it out with you because you had been guilty of not knowing that he also would be boating this morning."

Still no response.

"Perhaps you want to pitch me over the boat's side, Miss Gerry?"

"No."

"It is not too late to call Mr. Moore back. If you quite grovel in your apology to him he may forgive you for not knowing that you might have spent this time with him. Shall I call him?"

"No."

Silence, during which Miss Nunally rowed with great vigor.

"May I give you a piece of advice, Miss Gerry?" she asked.

"I should be glad if you would."

"Well, then, it is this: if there is anything that you think you ought to tell Mr. Moore, don't tell him."

Salome's face changed to a look of intense interest, and was there also a hint of relief in it?

"Oh, why do you think so?" she asked.

"I think so on general principles. And particularly about him. He is intolerant in regard to women, I am sure. He thinks he respects women. Now, beware of the man who thinks he respects women—that is, if you have to sue for his forgiveness."

Salome did not change her position, but she seemed to become rigid as she sat there. Her mind was in a pitiable state of confusion.

"Do you feel sure about this?" she asked.

"I am sure that is the way I should do."

Salome had a feeling that Miss Nunally and she might view things very differently. But then it was not probable that Miss Nunally had committed a crime. That word "crime" always had a strange effect upon Salome's consciousness. She both defied it and shrank from it. And she did not feel at all like a criminal. She wondered if all criminals had this absence of any conviction of sin. She was glad her father had the money, doubly glad now that he was ill. All the feeling she had was that she hated to have people shocked when they knew what she had done. And yet something, she had not the least idea what it was, but something, was often urging her to tell.

There were brief periods when she was almost afraid that she was not entirely rid of that conscience which had so goaded and tormented her when she was an invalid at home. But these periods were very brief, and were becoming more and more rare.

Salome felt moments of acute curiosity as to what Miss Nunally would think did she know of the forgery. This curiosity gained in morbid strength as the two girls strolled over the wide, solitary expanse of the North Beach.

They had tied their boat to the little wharf on the Matanzas side, and walked across to the ocean shore. It had taken them a long time to come across the water, and Portia was weary. She was annoyed, too. That scene with Moore, short as it had been, had irritated her, and her annoyance did not lessen. But Salome felt her spirits rising ; only they were held down by the always present thought of her mother travelling on towards the North. She was never out-of-doors long in this climate and among these surroundings without growing to think of herself as something like a soulless barbarian, whose only life was this life — beautiful, full of enchantment. If only those whom she loved would not be ill. If only she might not love too well. She was beginning to have a suspicion that it might be better not to love anything. In that case she could disport herself in this sunshine without any of that vague but intensely delightful unrest which now so often oppressed her. But love — could she really give that up?

She stood with her hands full of those shining shells and pebbles which people cannot help gathering when they walk on these Florida beaches. Her hat was pushed back ; her hair was flying about her face.

Miss Nunally, walking towards her, told herself that really Salome Gerry had the pose at this moment of some kind of a sublimated human being. Were there ever eyes so full of heaven—and of earth also?

"If I loved that woman," thought Miss Nunally, smiling quietly as she quoted, "I should love but her, and her forever."

Salome heard the approaching footsteps. But she did not turn her head. She continued to gaze out seaward. The ocean, at its lowest ebb, was faintly sliding up the shore.

"I wanted to ask you something," said Salome.

"Well?" said Miss Nunally.

"If you had committed a forgery, how should you think of yourself?"

XVI

QUESTIONING

PORTIA did not reply directly. The question put to her had something of the suddenness and the force of a blow. As soon as she could speak she said:

"If I had done that, and if I were engaged to marry Randolph Moore, I should take great precautions lest he should know of it."

Salome could not imagine why these words should make her immediately think more seriously than ever that she would tell Moore.

She dropped the shells and the pebbles she had been gathering. She thought that Miss Nunally had never before said anything which really repelled her.

"Let us go up there and sit down on that piece of driftwood," she proposed, after an interval of silence. "I am tired."

As the two walked slowly through the heavy sand, Salome asked when was the very earliest that her mother could reach home.

After a little calculation Portia replied. She spoke somewhat coldly. She had a suspicion that her companion was trying to play upon her credulity.

The two sat down on the old timber.

"I really did do it," said Salome, after another silence. She was sure that Miss Nunally had not believed her, and she was now fully resolved to try the effect of a confession on this girl who, Salome believed, was going to do a far worse thing than she had done.

The kind of sin to which we have no inclination, which does not hold for us the least temptation, is the kind of sin which shocks us greatly.

Miss Nunally was leaning forward on one elbow, her face turned so that she might gaze fully at the girl beside her. At last she laughed, and said :

" I don't believe it." Then she laughed again, and continued, " When you go back to the hotel, look in a mirror and tell me if you believe it yourself."

"I don't know anything about that," responded Salome, " but it is true."

"Good heavens !" cried Portia. She lifted her head and looked about her. She turned to Salome, and said, kindly,

" I'm afraid you are worrying too much about your father's illness."

"And so am not quite right in my mind. Is that what you mean ?"

" Yes."

" Then you are entirely mistaken," with great dignity. " I'm perfectly right in my mind. And I have forged."

Miss Nunally's effort to be calm and judicial was evident.

" Perhaps," she said, "if you give me particulars I shall be able to understand. Particulars are sometimes very convincing when a broad, general statement has no effect."

"Yes," promptly answered Salome, " I see that. It was Mrs. Darrah's name I put on a check for my father. He needed money immediately. It was for eight hundred dollars. I'm going to pay it back."

Portia was still trying to be calm, and not "let her feelings run away with her."

" Now do you believe me ?" asked Salome.

" Yes ; I believe you. I wish you hadn't told me."

" Why do you wish that ?"

" Because I don't like to be so confused as I am now."

" Confused ? Oh, I suppose you did not expect me to be a forger ?"

" No, I didn't. Really, Miss Gerry, you make my head go round so that I can't think."

" I will not speak for a few minutes ; then your head may stop going round," was the reply.

In the silence that followed, the two figures sat almost motionless, with faces turned towards the ocean.

It was Salome who spoke first.

" It was for father," she said. " But I don't mean that for an excuse. I'm not excusing myself."

" Does my aunt know ?"

" Yes."

" How did she discover it ?"

" Why," in surprise, " I told her !"

Portia leaned her head on her hand again.

" Your character is just as puzzling as your face," she said. " I suppose, after you had done this thing, what you call your conscience stepped in and made you confess it."

" I don't know," said Salome.

" Do you know why you tell me ?" was the next in-quiry.

Salome hesitated.

" I wanted to know how it would strike you," she at last answered.

" Well, how does it strike me ?"

" Oh, you are greatly shocked and repelled."

Salome gave this reply in tones so sorrowful that Miss Nunally's face softened perceptibly. But she did not give way to this feeling in words.

" May I ask why you did not request Aunt Florence to lend you the money ?"

" It was so sudden, you know. And I had heard you say she thought a good deal of her money. And father must have it directly. And there was her check-book, and I could imitate her hand. And, really, it did not seem so dreadful."

" There was nothing in you that held you back ?"

" No ; there didn't seem to be. Something sprang right up in me that said, ' Do it,' just as if it had been waiting, you see, to spring up when the right time came. I suppose I ought to have shrunk ; but I didn't."

" But where was your conscience ?"

" Oh, I don't know," with some weariness.

Portia was looking with the keenest interest at her companion.

" Then it wasn't what as children we would have called a real, truly conscience, after all, that you used to have ?" she inquired.

" I don't know," Salome said, again. " I suppose it was only my bringing up ; and bringing up sometimes drops away from one. Mine has, I think."

" And it is now that you are the real Salome Gerry ?"

" I believe so ; I'm almost sure of it."

" Don't tell Mr. Moore," Portia said, sharply. " Don't try any of these effects on him."

Salome said nothing. When they were in the boat and Portia was rowing steadily back, Salome asked the question which had been in her mind all the time.

" Miss Nunally, could you have done it ?"

" No !"

Salome shrank a little. It was some moments before she said :

" And yet—"

" And yet"—Portia took up the words—" I am going to marry Major Root. It seems to me I wrong myself most of all. But you, when you forged—"

Salome interrupted in her turn :

" When we sin it is always ourselves we wrong most of all, isn't it ?"

Miss Nunally made a false stroke with one oar and the boat veered almost into another craft. When she was going on steadily again she said that it was of no use talking; one might talk forever and come right back to the same place again. There were some things one felt.

Salome leaned forward timidly. There was a quiver on her mouth as she asked :

" Now I have told you that, do you feel repelled by me ?"

Portia held her oars poised in the air. The two girls gazed at each other. Portia's face softened still more.

" I ought to feel repelled," she said.

" But do you ?" persisted the other.

Miss Nunally's eyes suddenly filled. She could not see the face before her, with its piercing pathos of expression. She drew in an oar and held out her hand, grasping tightly the hand given in response.

" No ; you don't repel me in the least," she replied,

with strong emphasis. "More than that, I cannot imagine being repelled by you, whatever you had done."

Salome's look grew brighter. She would not release the hand she held. But immediately a cloud came over her.

"Still, that may be a mere matter of personal presence or influence," she said. "That has nothing to do with morals, after all."

"No, indeed," was the response; "not anything to do with morals."

Salome let go her companion's hand. Her whole figure seemed to droop for a moment.

"I cannot understand things," she exclaimed at last. "I try to reason. When I recall the old teaching I received, I try to repent. But I don't repent in the least."

"But don't you feel sorry that you did that?" asked Miss Nunally.

"No; I only feel sorry if those I love are going to be grieved when they know it."

"Then don't tell them. I judge that my aunt has condoned the offence. It all rests with you whether it be known or not."

"Yes," said Salome; "it all rests with me."

After this nothing more was said on the subject. Indeed, hardly anything was said on any subject. The two girls landed at the wharf and walked up to the Ponce de Leon. Salome went directly to Mrs. Darrah, feeling that she had been very remiss. But that lady was not disposed towards reproof of any kind. She had been dozing among her cushions, but she thought she had been thinking over her novel. This thought gave her a sense of having been attending to duty, and consequently made her good-natured. Besides, she never saw Salome without an awakening of keenest interest in her as a specimen of the human race. As a specimen, Mrs. Darrah often told herself, Miss Gerry exceeded anything she had ever had occasion to study. The elder woman was always thinking of the forgery, and trying to see some indications in the girl's face or manner that she had done such a thing.

While she thus furtively watched her, the authoress made a great many notes in that book devoted to feminine traits. But when she looked over those notes she found them particularly inane and pointless. Once she dashed her pen through a page of them, thinking, as she did so, that she had never before found words so inefficient.

"And yet," she said, aloud, "there is the girl with that baffling face that yet seems as clear as a lake, and here am I with nothing to do but to study her. I wonder what Portia thinks of her. Portia is a sharp kind of a girl. I will ask her."

And she did ask her niece that very night, after Salome had gone to bed in the room provided for her near Mrs. Darrah.

"I suppose you feel acquainted with Miss Gerry, don't you?" was the inquiry.

"Are you asking that question for the sake of material, Aunt Florence," was Miss Nunally's response, "or just in a human kind of way?"

Mrs. Darrah flushed with anger.

"We will call it a human kind of way," she answered. "What do you think of Miss Gerry?"

Mrs. Darrah thought there was some agitation in her niece's manner. The girl rose and walked to the desk; she began lifting some leaves of manu-

19

script which Salome had written. The clear handwriting flashed up at her somehow like a glance from Salome herself. She stepped away; but still her eyes remained on that writing, and it influenced her something as the presence of the writer influenced her.

"I could be very fond of her," she said, at last.

"So could I," returned Mrs. Darrah, quickly. "But that isn't of any consequence."

"Pardon me, Aunt Florence," said Portia, with her touch of insolence, "but it is of the greatest consequence to me whether I can be fond of any one or not. For instance, think of the difference it would make if I could be fond of Major Root."

"Pshaw! That isn't necessary. You will be fond of the diamonds he gives you."

"Yes; and so, perhaps, I shall spare his life—for a time."

Portia turned again and walked about the room. It seemed impossible for her to keep quiet.

"What do you think of Miss Gerry?" persisted Mrs. Darrah.

Miss Nunally paused with her hands clasped behind her. She did not smile in the least as she replied:

"Think of Miss Gerry? I think a thousand things; and five hundred of those things contradict the other five hundred."

Mrs. Darrah sat upright, as she did when particularly interested.

"That is exactly as it is with me!" she cried. "How strange! But, Portia, I'm sure I know the secret of it all."

"Do you? Then I wish you would tell me; for I don't know it," was the response.

"It is this—do hand me that blue note-book. Are you listening?"

"I am certainly listening; don't put me off like one of your continued stories."

Mrs. Darrah did not notice this remark. She held her pencil poised over her book.

"Miss Gerry is a New England girl."

Portia nodded impatiently.

"She was brought up by a typical New England woman."

Another impatient nod.

"But," said Mrs. Darrah, with great impressiveness, "Miss Gerry had a great-grandfather who was anything but a New England man."

Portia began walking again.

"That is very convenient," she said. "When I do anything evil I shall ascribe the tendency to some grandparent; but when I do anything good, which rarely happens to me, I will say the deed comes from my own individual self. I suppose we have individual selves, Aunt Florence, as well as inherited proclivities, haven't we?"

"I don't know," replied Mrs. Darrah, blankly.

"Then write a book about it," said Portia, flippantly repeating the advice she liked to give her aunt. She turned towards the door. She paused with her face averted. There was a decided look of pain on that face, but her tone was still flippant as she said:

"I could sometimes wish most earnestly that I had had a great-grandfather; and that people would remember him when they judge me. Good-night, Aunt Florence."

Mrs. Darrah gazed at the drapery that had fallen over the door by which her niece had left her.

She was thinking that it would be a great deal better if Portia did care a little for Major Root, since she was going to marry him. But she concluded her thought by saying to herself:

"It is her own choice, however." And then she added, "It was Miss Gerry's choice to forge."

And by this time she had fully decided not to make any entry in her note-book. When the mind travels in a "vicious circle" the mind is not in a condition to make clear notes upon a topic.

Meanwhile the subject of this conversation was lying with enforced stillness upon her bed.

She had been sure that she could not sleep, but she knew that she must assume the position for sleep. She held herself almost rigid until the noises in the hotel had gradually subsided, and she could hear distinctly the swelling of the tide on the outside of the island opposite the city.

When she had been awake in the cabin where she had been living, she had always listened for the sound of the tide. She liked to hear it. In the midst of her happiness it had made her still happier. Now she wondered that, in her wretchedness, this roar of the waves should make her still more wretched.

Her thoughts followed her mother through every mile of the desolate journey. Her thoughts leaped constantly to the end of that journey; to the dreary farm-house where her father was lying ill; or perhaps he was lying dead. Dead! That word came to her incessantly, until at last it was like the toll of a bell in her ears. She felt that she could not wait and live until she could hear. But she must live.

When her mother had left her, Salome had longed

for the presence of Moore as for something that should partially assuage the agony she felt at parting, and at parting for such a cause.

She had never been separated from her mother a week in her life. Constant familiarity and intercourse had knit their love into something stronger even than such love usually is. It was not merely a parting; Salome felt that it was a rending. She stretched out her arms in the darkness.

" I cannot bear it!" she whispered.

Oh, happy is that human being who has never yet had occasion to cry, " I cannot bear it!"

But we bear things. Somehow we bear them; though that endurance leaves us forever after with a mark upon us.

So Salome lay there. She thought many thoughts, but she seemed to herself to be thinking only of her father and mother. She remembered how her mother had told her to be truthful. The girl prayed fervidly that it might be given to her to speak the truth. Unconsciously she used the old phraseology that she had heard in the pulpit at home : " that it might be given to her." She believed that the prayer brought her spirit yet nearer her mother.

It was very dark. But under the door of the room leading into Mrs. Darrah's chamber there was a faint bar of light.

Once the girl heard a swift dash of rain on the little balcony outside of her window. The sound made her want to get up and go out and stand in that balcony so that the rain might fall upon her. The window was widely open, and it let in the sweetness of the Florida night. Salome heard a bird nestle among the leaves of a magnolia that now and then, in the breeze, touched the sash. She heard the bird's indistinct murmur, as if it were dreaming of its daylight song.

Being young and well, Salome, after midnight, fell asleep. But she slept lightly, and did not when she wakened think she had slept at all.

The door under which there had been a bar of light was now open, and a soft brilliance filled her room.

Mrs. Darrah was standing in her wrapper near the girl's bed.

"I could not sleep," she said, gently, "and I was sure you were awake and suffering."

Salome sat up quickly. She pushed her hair back from her face. She could not help holding out her hands, which were instantly taken.

"You are so kind," murmured Salome. She tried not to sob; and the effort seemed to hurt her more than the sob itself would have done.

Looking at the figure sitting there in its white gown, being aware of the struggle Salome was making that she might be calm, Mrs. Darrah for the next few moments entirely forgot that she was an authoress with an inexhaustible craving for "material." She was only a woman whose kind heart was deeply touched. Still it could not be expected that she should become unconscious of the absorbing curiosity which this girl roused in her.

"You are worrying, you are grieving," she said.

As she spoke she sat down on the bedside. "If we could only attain to a philosophy whereby our intensity of feeling might come only upon joyous occasions." She spoke as if to herself. Salome did not attempt a reply. She sat there, trembling both from chilliness and from excitement. She was glad Mrs. Darrah had come in. The voice and the touch of a sympathetic human being were much to her just now. She wanted to speak, to give words to the dreadful anxiety upon her; but she remained silent. It did not appear to her that she had any right to afflict this woman who was so kind to her.

Finally, however, she asked, in a whisper :

" Mrs. Darrah, do you think I can bear it ?"

" Certainly you can. When you are older you will be astonished at the number of things you have borne, and that you can still be happy."

" Is that true ?" piteously. " But you know my mother will be suffering, and I not near to comfort her. I can always comfort my mother."

The last sentence was broken by a heavy sob. Salome withdrew her hands and pressed them upon her chest as she used to do when her breath came painfully from another cause.

" And if I should never see my father again !—"

Here the agony in the young face showed so plainly, even in that light, that Mrs. Darrah said, with some sternness :

" It is wicked of you to yield like this. You will presently be wrought almost into an irresponsible state."

Salome made a great effort. She even smiled as she said :

" Mother says we are always responsible, and that we can bear anything ; and that really God loves us, only it doesn't always seem as if He did. My mother is so strong, Mrs. Darrah."

Salome turned towards her pillow and put her head down upon it.

"I beg your pardon," she went on in a moment, " but I have been lying awake, and I 'got all worked up,' as they say at home. I am going to behave better now."

" That's right. Let me give you something to quiet you. You can't hear from home for two days at least ; and you must rest."

But Salome would have no sleeping draught. She had something of her mother's horror of opiates. She thanked Mrs. Darrow fervently. That lady bent down and kissed the girl's cheek, and then she walked out of the room.

An hour later, being wakeful and uneasy, she softly stepped back to that bed. The girl lying upon it was sleeping.

The next day Portia came for Salome to go driving with her, but Mrs. Darrah announced that she intended to dictate a great deal.

"Work is the best thing for Miss Gerry now," she said.

Salome looked gratefully at her employer. Miss Nunally went her ways, and Salome sat at the desk hour after hour while Mrs. Darrah dictated in the most copious manner.

The amanuensis was not in a condition to take in the meaning of the words she wrote, or she would have known there was very little meaning in them, and she would have suspected that her companion was only spinning sentences to keep her busy.

At last Mrs. Darrah looked at her watch. She suddenly remembered that her niece had once told her that Mr. Moore was in the habit of walking home with Miss Gerry after her work.

But since Miss Gerry did not now go out beyond

the Maria Sanchez—at this point in her thoughts Mrs. Darrah asked abruptly:

"Do you expect to see that young man to-day?"

"You mean Mr. Moore?"

"Certainly. There is no other young man in the world, is there?" smiling slightly.

"Perhaps he is waiting for me," was the reply. "He doesn't know that my mother has gone."

"Does not?" in surprise. "Well, go to the post-office for me. He is no doubt lurking somewhere. Tell him to call here after this. Now go."

But Moore was not lurking anywhere near.

Salome walked swiftly to the post - office. She would not acknowledge to herself how her heart sank as she went on. And she would not look either to the right or left.

She was surprised to find a note from Moore, telling her that business had called him to Palatka again; that he might be gone a few days. The note was rather cold; only a last sentence contained a passionate regret that he must go without seeing her. And he knew nothing of her father's illness.

Salome hurried on to the Plaza and sat down upon one of the benches, holding this note in her clasped hands. Her heart was so heavy that she could hardly think. She was duly thankful that she was, in a way, stupefied. She did not want to think.

She did not know when she should see Moore. A few days he might be gone. A few days sounded like a few years. And she needed him so. That strong, robust cheerfulness of his; that protecting and sustaining tenderness — and he was to be gone a few days. Everything might happen in that time.

Yes, she was truly grateful that she was partially stupefied.

She saw vaguely the people passing in front of her. She heard vaguely their voices.

She began to make an accurate calculation of the number of hours that surely must pass before she could receive that telegram from her mother.

Still absorbed in this calculation, she walked back to the hotel and to her own room.

It seemed to her that she kept up this study all the next day when she wrote almost incessantly for Mrs. Darrah.

At last the telegram arrived. Salome was surprised at her own strength when it was put in her hand, and she opened the envelope.

"Better than I expected. Will write."

Those were the words she read. She turned with a little cry towards Portia, who had brought the message, and who was standing watchfully near. Salome thrust the paper towards Miss Nunally, and then ran to her own room.

When at last she came back her face had such an expression of thankfulness and hope that Portia could not bear it, and walked away.

"Why should we all suffer with that girl in this way, and rejoice too?" impatiently asked Miss Nunally of herself. "There is no reason in it. And she no better than she should be. No; there is no reason in it."

Mrs. Gerry's promised letter came at the earliest possible moment. It was concise. It said that Mr. Gerry did not seem dangerously ill, and that Salome need not worry. It bade the girl find a cheap but comfortable lodging. for they could not accept so much from Mrs. Darrah. Mr. Gerry might need his wife's care for some weeks, and it would not do for Salome to remain at the Ponce de Leon. Still, Mrs. Gerry might be able to return in a couple of weeks. It was too soon yet for her to be able to judge. She was glad that she had not allowed her daughter to come home with her. It was very cold; it was sleighing. There was so much snow that the roads had been " broken out."

Salome shivered as she read ; but she laughed also. She was sure now that her father would soon be better, and her mother would come back to her, perhaps in two weeks. Even when Mrs. Darrah tried to remind her that often typhoid fever was of long duration, Salome could not be depressed. She said she felt almost certain that her mother would be with her in two weeks ; and when she had this feeling about anything it was nearly sure to come to pass.

In two days Salome had another letter ; this time it was only a note. It prayed the child to take care of herself, and it commanded her not to worry.

Salome read this in her room at the back of a house on Bravo Street, for she had lost no time in leaving the Ponce de Leon, as her mother had directed.

This room was small, and the one window looked on nothing in particular. But nothing mattered so long as her mother was away.

The girl read this note so many times that the words lost all meaning. But they had left a deep gloom upon her. She did not know why they had done so.

She put on her hat and hurried out-of-doors. When she was in trouble or when she was in joy, Salome wanted to be under the sky. She could not bear a roof above her.

She walked quickly among the little highways until Artillery Street had led her to George Street. Then, without any intention, she sped along in the direction of the railway station.

Moore had not returned. He had written every day, however, and she had replied briefly. But she had told him nothing of her loneliness or anxiety. It seemed to her it would be like pleading for her to do so.

As she walked, the thought of her lover came to her with a sudden sharpness of longing. She heard the train from Jacksonville coming in. She was now within a few rods of the station. What if he were upon that train?

She hesitated an instant. Then she hastened forward. She was on the platform as the train slowed up. She stood back a little now, fully expecting to see Moore alight. She was already aware of the expression that would come to his face when he saw her. Yet she shrank a little, asking herself if she were bold. Would he think she was bold?

He had written that he might come at any time now.

It was not Moore whom Salome saw stepping from the car nearest her. It was Walter Redd who put foot on the platform. He held a satchel, which the girl, with a thrill, recognized as her mother's satchel. She saw him turn and help a woman behind him. Then she saw that the woman was her mother, pale, worn, exhausted.

In an instant the girl had glided among the people. She reached her mother and took her arm, pressing it to her side.

XVII

TIRED

FOR the first moment Mrs. Gerry seemed unable to look at her daughter or to speak.

Instead, she turned towards Walter Redd and asked, in a high, hard voice:

"Haven't you the check for the trunk, Walter?"

The young man nodded. He walked away immediately. He had made no attempt towards any kind of a greeting to Salome.

The two women stood on the platform, the girl still having her mother's arm. People hustled by them. Two or three glanced at them with keen, sympathetic eyes. At last Salome whispered:

"Mother!"

Mrs. Gerry's tense figure became more rigid.

Her daughter clung more closely to her.

After another silence, the girl said:

"Let us go to my room."

The two walked quickly away. But they had not gone far when Mrs. Gerry stopped. She must still have the care of things.

"Where is your room? We must tell Walter. He will want to see us after a while, and the trunk must be sent, too. I will tell him. Is it Bravo Street? And the number?"

Salome thought her mother looked ready to fall to

the ground.   Only the girl knew that she would not fall ; that she would never fall while she lived.

"I will tell him," Salome said.

She ran back to where Redd stood at the end of the station.   She held out her hand to him.   His swarthy face flushed as he took the hand.

" I wanted to tell you where we are, and where you may send the trunk," she said, hurriedly.   She hesitated.   Then she added, tremulously: "I know you have been so kind."

"No, no !" he returned, with some roughness.

She hastened back to the figure which stood patiently awaiting her.

When the two women were in the chamber on Bravo Street, Salome turned the key in the door as if it were necessary to do so to keep out intruders.

She led her mother to a chair.   She took off the dusty black bonnet and black mantle.   But she could not keep her hands from trembling as she did so. Mrs. Gerry did not tremble.   She watched her daughter intently.

Salome knelt down on the floor and put her arms about her mothers's waist.

" Mother !" she said.

Mrs. Gerry looked down at the young face.

"Yes," she said, "it is true.   Lyman is dead !"

She did not say " your father."   She was thinking of the man who had been her lover and her husband. At that moment she was not so much a mother as a widow.

Salome shuddered.   She had known as soon as she saw her mother on the steps of the car.   But to hear those words, " He is dead !"   That is driving the knife into the wound.   And this, too, must be borne.

The girl did not speak. She pressed her arms yet closer about the form they held. In that first instant she wondered why people sobbed and wept when they knew of the death of one beloved.

Then in another moment she had fallen to weeping in the most violent manner, clinging to her mother all the time, and asking, convulsively:

"Shall I never see him again? Shall I never see him again?"

At first Mrs. Gerry said nothing. But soon she repeated the word "Hush! hush!" in the tone she had used when her daughter was a child.

She bent over the slender form and enfolded it strongly. After a little the girl sobbed less tumultuously, and still later she raised her head and looked into her mother's face. She gently put the palm of her hand against one thin white cheek of the elder face.

"Oh," she said, "how weak I am! And to think what you must have borne!"

Mrs. Gerry pressed her lips together. There were no tears in her eyes. The sweet strength of those eyes shone full upon her daughter.

"And I told Mrs. Darrah," began Salome —here she stopped as if she could not speak again; but presently she went on—"and I told Mrs. Darrah that I could always comfort my mother. Oh, if I could only comfort you!"

Mrs. Gerry's controlled countenance suddenly became suffused with red. Her mouth yielded; her eyes overflowed. In a voice that was strangely like her daughter's she exclaimed:

"Oh, you do comfort me! You do comfort me! It is our little girl, Lyman! Our little girl!"

Her head dropped to Salome's shoulder. For the first time since she had started North she gave way to the suffering in her heart.

And as the young arms held her, as the young voice murmured brokenly to her, she was comforted greatly.

Later the two sat close together talking in half tones, with long pauses, until the sad story was told.

Mrs. Gerry did not dwell upon its details. She could not do that now.

Mr. Gerry had made his will. His debts would almost, if not quite, cover his property, but his widow did not speak of that. She knew that her husband had left all to her, so that she might settle affairs with no hinderance. He had advised her to sell everything, and then she would "know where she stood." That was her judgment also. Lyman had never known exactly where he stood.

Holding his wife's hand, in those few moments when he could talk, he had confessed that he wasn't one of the kind that could get property together. He wasn't thrifty. He didn't know why. He said he had never cared as he cared now. He wished he could leave his wife and child "well off." And he had always worked hard, too. He didn't understand it.

And his wife had upheld and sustained him in his dying, as she had done so many years in his living. He had sent his love to his little girl. Still holding that helping hand, still leaning upon it, he had gone into the other world.

"I cannot tell you how kind Walter Redd has been all the time," said Mrs. Gerry, now speaking in her usual calm way. "I can't think what I should have done without him. He is one to lean upon. And I am to leave the selling of the farm and the wood-lots to him. He will attend to everything. And in the best way, too. He is shrewd and honest, and he insisted upon coming South with me now. I could have come alone very well. But he was a great help. He would have a sleeping-car, too. And I slept each night. It seems strange, but I slept."

"Is he going to stay long?" Salome put the question with but little interest. Yet she listened for the reply.

"A few weeks. He said he meant to come down this winter anyway. He says if he gets back in time for the spring work it will be all right. He wants to look round. Yes, he was a great help. Be as kind as you can to him, Salome. He is a good friend."

"Oh yes, I am sure of that," was the response. "Does he" — hesitatingly — "does he know about Mr. Moore?"

"I told him on the journey. He isn't a man to appear sentimental, you know. You need not fear that from him."

Mrs. Gerry's words seemed strictly true. When Walter Redd called a few moments in the evening, he was so solidly cordial and matter-of-fact in his appearance that his presence produced a decidedly comfortable effect upon the two women. It was like an assurance that the foundations of the earth still remained.

And he did not stay until they were tired of him. When he had gone, Mrs. Gerry repeated earnestly what she had said before:

"Walter Redd has been such a help."

As Salome heard her she was conscious of a decided feeling of rebellion that it was Walter instead of Moore who had been such a help. Then she reproved

20

herself for such an emotion. But she did not quite subdue it.

When the two were left alone, Mrs. Gerry turned suddenly to her daughter. She looked at her more closely than she had yet done. Then she said :

"After all, it is only a very little while I have been gone. But some way you look as if it were a long time."

"Yes, yes. Mother, you forget how I have suffered thinking of you and—and father !"

"Yes, you must have suffered," kissing Salome's cheek repeatedly. "And you have not slept?"

"No, I have not slept."

Mrs. Gerry waited a little before she asked :

"Have you anything to tell me ?"

"To tell you ?" in surprise. "No ; what should I have to tell? Mrs. Darrah has been so kind ; and she has kept me at work closely. I was so glad of that."

"And how is Mr. Moore ?"

"I have missed him so much," replied Salome, quickly. "Just as I needed him—you see, mother, I really did need him in my trouble — he had to go down to Palatka and along the river there. And he doesn't even know you went North."

"Oh, he doesn't know ?"

"I thought I wouldn't tell him," went on the girl, somewhat eagerly, "for I knew he would want to leave everything and come back. It seemed weak to tell him. And I am trying to be strong."

Salome's voice nearly failed her as she made this announcement. She looked at her mother for approval.

"That's right," responded Mrs. Gerry. "It never

hurts us to try to be strong. But I am sorry Mr. Moore happened to be gone. I was thinking all the time I was away from you that he would help you."

Salome hung about her mother.

" You like him, don't you?" she asked.

" Like him?" Mrs. Gerry smiled sadly, and yet with a kind of cheerfulness. " More than that; I love him. How could I help it?"

Salome flung herself at her companion, grasping her impulsively.

" Oh, how lovely that is of you!" she cried, her eyes shining through tears; " but of course you couldn't help it, since he is what he is. But what shall I do if I go on loving him more and more? Tell me, mother; that is what frightens me — to love him so much. Don't you think it would be a great deal safer and more reasonable to have a moderate sort of an affection?"

" First, then," replied Mrs. Gerry, " make yourself over into a safe and moderate kind of a girl."

" But how can I?"

" Perhaps it can be done. A good many things can be done. There was a man who was able to stand on a pillar for a good many years."

" I remember him. But what did it amount to?"

Mrs. Gerry gazed at her child with an inscrutable smile. She was thinking that if Salome could see her own face she would never ask such questions concerning herself.

" It amounted to proving that a man may stand on a pillar day after day and week after week and year after year."

Salome felt that she did not quite understand. But she dropped the subject.

That night the girl really slept for the first time since her mother had left her. She had no cause to worry now. She knew the certainty.

When she woke, her mother was not beside her. She rose and went to the window. The sunshine was streaming into the back yards of the houses opposite. By craning her neck a great deal she could almost see that famous leaning date‑palm which grows near one of the oldest houses. Wherever she was, Salome always wished that she could see that tree. She felt that the sight of a date‑palm assured her beyond a doubt that she was far away from any place where snow could come. In New England there were no palms standing against blue skies.

As she stood there she began to cry, softly and copiously, as the young do often weep when they feel grief, but when happiness stands side by side with grief.

Her mother opened the door.

"I wouldn't wake you," she said, "but it is nine o'clock, and you should be at Mrs. Darrah's. While you are there I will go out to our hut on the truck farm."

When the girl was ready the two walked towards the Ponce de Leon. They met Walter Redd, who had taken a room near. But he did not try to detain them. He looked heavy and sombre to the girl, who was thinking of a face quite different. And suddenly that face appeared.

Hurrying around a corner, eager, his eyes instantly finding the two women, stepping with easy, alert strength, aglow with happiness, Moore hastened to them.

He was just from the station. He had heard

nothing. He was ready to reproach Salome for what he inwardly called her "stingy notes."

But while he grasped Mrs. Gerry's hand his face changed. A warm sympathy and solicitude took the place of every other expression. Another person might have felt sympathy as keenly, but another person might not have been able to show it with such winning sincerity. He shook hands with Salome; but he turned again immediately to her mother.

"What is it?" he asked, in that tone which is hardly above a whisper, and which sometimes expresses so much. "Something has happened to you. Salome, haven't I a right to know when you are troubled?"

But the girl could not speak. It was the mother who must find strength for a reply. In half a dozen words she made answer.

Moore was gazing fixedly at Mrs. Gerry as she spoke. He seemed to divine directly how much deeper was her wound than any that had come to her daughter.

With an involuntary movement, of which he was quite unconscious, he took the woman's hand and drew it closely within his arm, walking on with her silently, not looking at any one.

When the three had reached the hotel he asked if he might wait for them. He said he was sure Mrs. Darrah would not dictate this morning. Would they let him stay with them that morning? Would they please not send him away?

Mrs. Gerry smiled as she nodded yes to his requests. Again she wondered why it should be so easy to smile at this young man. The smile helped her. The very sight of him helped her. There was a glow in her heavy heart as she walked up the stairs by her daughter's side. She was feeling so exquisitely thankful that Salome's future promised so well. Nothing mattered to herself now. She had lived her life. But for the child—for her everything lovely might happen. The elder woman told herself that she must henceforth look at the world and at life through her daughter's eyes. Indeed, there was no other way. To her now life and the world meant merely what happened to Salome. She continued to think of Moore as she entered the hotel and left him. She had no doubt about the essential sweetness and honesty of his nature; and she was not one who judged by externals. She had not seen the young man very much, but she had watched his face and listened to his tones with that keenness which belongs to some women when they know a chlid's happiness depends upon a certain face and voice. A hundred times she had thanked God that Moore was what he was. She was sure his faults were not vital faults, nor ruinous faults. It was better than as if Salome had loved Redd. Redd would have been faithful; he would have taken good care of the child, but he would never have understood her.

As she reached this point in her thoughts, Mrs. Gerry felt a quick start as of alarm.

Understood the child! Who could understand her? "The elements were so mixed" in her that she seemed sometimes a human puzzle, impossible to solve. But why solve everything? Mrs. Gerry's mind ran on with that lightning rapidity which is occasionally one of the clearest processes of which the mind is capable. And all this as she was walking by the girl's side along the space that separated the entrance from Mrs. Darrah's room.

This morning Mrs. Darrah was entirely merged in the authoress ; and the authoress had been reading over her last chapter before she had left her bed. It was not the chapter she had just dictated; she knew that was nothing ; but the one previous ; and, until this morning, she had not known that this also was nothing.

When, in the ardor of inspiration, an authoress believes she is quite firing the world, and when she finds later that what she thought were burning words are only the deadest kind of cinders, then that authoress is not in a good-humor. Do not go into her den at such a time.

Mrs. Gerry, however, knew nothing of some things that were liable to happen to authoresses. So she entered with that reserved self-possession that was characteristic of her.

Salome took off her hat as if she were going to stay to write ; then feeling the atmosphere, she held her hat uncertainly, waiting.

Mrs. Darrah nodded at the two. She forgot for the moment for what purpose Mrs. Gerry had been North, or that she had been North at all.

" I wish you would both sit down," she said, brusquely. " I want to read you something. I've been reading it to myself ; now I want to try it on somebody else. I want somebody else to writhe and twist under it. Now listen to this."

The two had seated themselves. Mrs. Darrah put on her eye-glasses. She glanced over them at Salome as she said :

" Listen, will you ? This stuff doesn't belong in a novel of sentiment at all. It belongs somewhere else. I shall have to start another novel just to get this in."

There was no answer to this remark. Mrs. Darrah smiled in a whimsical way as she began reading.

After a few paragraphs she looked at Salome again.

"Did I really dictate that to you?" she asked.

"You must have done so," was the reply.

"Pshaw! Why don't you say it is your own, that I never could have composed such trash?"

Salome hesitated. In her own mind she knew that she would have been willing to say that if she had only thought of it. But her mother would not approve. What was the harm in speaking things which made life a little smoother, or which opened a way in an easier manner?

But she immediately dropped these questionings in her impatience at this interview. If she were not to work she could hardly force herself to stay in the room. Was not Moore waiting for her? In spite of her resolve not to betray any feeling, she could not restrain a movement which made her mother look at her in reproof. Her mother had always at her command a calm, if somewhat cold, politeness. Her mother sat there now as quietly as if she never had an emotion—as if she were able to listen indefinitely to the reading of that stuff which did not belong in a novel of sentiment.

"What do you think of that?" suddenly asked Mrs. Darrah, looking up sharply. She caught Salome's look of weariness and dislike. Now an author—that is, a woman author, for it is to be supposed that men authors are different—does not relish the perception that she is boring some one with reading her own composition, even though she has first announced that the composition is trash. Of course she has a right to call it trash. But she does not expect to be believed. She knows very well that it is better than any one else would be likely to write.

"But I see what you think of it!" she exclaimed, in a voice of such annoyance that Salome, in the utmost confusion, tried to answer and could not.

Mrs. Darrah had not slept well the night before. Portia, who had been summoned at an earlier hour, had, after a five minutes' tarry, utterly refused to remain. She told her aunt that she knew that she had given her a great many gowns. and that board at the Ponce was rather high; still she was not going to stay in the room just for her aunt to fling knives at her.

"I don't suppose you are out of temper," said Miss Nunally, with that peculiar curl of the upper lip, "but this is one of the times 'when the world is not equal to the demands of your fine organism.'"

"Don't quote George Eliot to me!" returned Mrs. Darrah, furiously.

And here Portia had walked out of the room with her head in the air.

But the Gerrys could not walk out of the room in that way. They must remain, and Salome felt that she was extremely guilty. She might, at least, have pretended an interest. She began to stammer something, she hardly knew what.

"Don't try to explain," said Mrs. Darrah, frigidly, "and don't pretend that you were interested. I shouldn't believe you. You know very well why I might take the liberty sometimes of doubting you. I wish you would press that bell. My coffee was only hot water this morning. I need toning up — in short—"

Here, as Salome walked across the room to touch

the button of the bell, Mrs. Darrah seemed to see Mrs. Gerry for the first time, and to rouse to a consciousness of something besides her manuscript and her ill-humor.

"Oh, dear!" she said, still crossly, "I didn't notice you; I'm sure I beg your pardon, Mrs. Gerry." And then the kind impulses of her heart began to come uppermost. She rose and went to Mrs. Gerry. She held out her hand. "Do forgive me," she said again. "I had forgotten; I am inexcusable. You have come back—and the worst has happened. Oh, what a brute you must think me!"

Mrs. Gerry made some concise response. She was thinking of nothing save the few words this woman had just dropped in her irritation—words addressed to Salome: "You know very well why I might take the liberty sometimes of doubting you." Had Salome been saying something which was not strictly, accurately true? Was Salome forming that habit? But the girl had said "yes" when her mother had strenuously insisted on the simple truth always. She had said "yes," but perhaps all the time she had not meant yes.

Mrs. Gerry felt like reaching out her hands in the darkness. She must clutch at something. But she simply stood there and gazed at her hostess, saying nothing after she had signified her acceptance of the apology. Still it did seem to her as if she could not remain in the room. She really cared nothing for Mrs. Darrah's ill-temper; she did not think of it. Plainly that lady had discovered that Salome was not truthful. Salome was not truthful!

A film came over the mother's eyes. She could for the moment see nothing. But she still stood there with her face turned towards Mrs. Darrah.

The latter said gently that she would not keep Miss Gerry; that she should not work this morning.

Then the two left the room. For once the girl was so absorbed that she did not notice her mother's face or manner; and, indeed, there was little to notice. Mrs. Gerry was only very calm and quiet as they went down the steps.

Moore came quickly forward and joined them. But there was a noticeable shrinking on the part of the elder woman. She summoned her voice, and said, bravely:

"Go on to the truck farm, you two young people. It is better for Salome there; she can be out-of-doors more. I will go back to Bravo Street and give up that room."

The two intense young faces turned simultaneously towards Mrs. Gerry in a gratitude that was unmistakable. But the girl made an attempt to remonstrate; she tried to say that she also would go to Bravo Street; that they would all go out to the truck farm together.

But her mother only shook her head and smiled. She hurried them away. She stood in front of the hotel and saw them walk off. She noted that they were looking persistently ahead with an air meant to indicate that they were never going to glance at each other

When they were out of sight Mrs. Gerry went deliberately and, as she would have said, "did her errands." She paid for the room her daughter had occupied for a few days. She ordered her trunk sent out to the farm. She left word for Walter Redd to be directed to that farm.

Having done this, she stood for many minutes opposite the barracks, with her face turned towards the sea. She had started to walk out to the log-cabin, where she now expected to live for an indefinite time. She had been planning how to make the cabin more comfortable. She and Salome would live there now until the girl should marry, probably. They need not think of going North. Taste and life-long prejudices made Mrs. Gerry contemplate life in the South as a kind of martyrdom—certainly the life that poverty obliged her to live here. But she could live it; it mattered very little. The only way to endure things was the way into which she had been born and to which she had always schooled herself—the way which looked at this earthly pilgrimage as merely a probationary state. What mattered it if she passed it in Job Maine's hut or up in thrifty New England? It would pass. It would pass.

The spare, erect woman, in her homely clothes, stood gazing out upon the glittering water. The ardent sunlight beat down upon her, but she did not feel it. She was thinking of the grave at home, the grave which had been covered with snow the day she left.

"Give my love to my little girl."

Lyman's hollow voice was in her ears. She was continually hearing him tell her to give his love to his little girl.

Mrs. Gerry stood perfectly still. She did not even clasp her hands under the black shawl she wore. The stress of feeling upon her did not manifest itself by any movement of her body.

While she had been taking care of her husband, in the intensity of that time, it was natural that everything else should have been somewhat in the background. She had never forgotten Salome; but the thought of the girl and of her peculiarities had become faint by comparison with the dreadful present. Now it did not seem to the woman that it was simply because of what Mrs. Darrah had just said; it was only a thorough awakening to a knowledge of what her daughter really was.

Mrs. Gerry turned at this stage of her thought and walked quickly, not out of the city, but towards the old fort. She could not yet go in the direction which would bring the possibility of meeting Moore and Salome. And she felt as if she must sit down somewhere; and she must be by herself. Thus far it had not seemed to her that she was tired. The neighbors had all agreed that " Mis' Gerry was real tough; she had held out wonderful."

And she had held out wonderfully. But now, like an overwhelming wave, with the real belief that Salome was not " reliable," the mother was conscious that she was weary, deathly weary. She dared not look forward to the battle of the years.

She sat down on the water-battery where Salome so often sat. But, unlike Salome, the elder woman was conscious of no soothing or relaxing influences from her surroundings. She sat bent forward, with her hands clasped over her drawn-up knees. It was an attitude she had never assumed before—a sort of aboriginal attitude which, in one like Mrs. Gerry, was more eloquent than anything she could have done.

She had never been one who had given up to idle musings or reveries. Now her thoughts went on one after the other, like troops marching in a clear light. They defiled and turned and deployed, distinct in the white light. But they seemed to mean nothing. They were only marching. And the light was so clear on them. She wished the light had been less clear. She was mistaken. They did mean something. Mrs. Gerry moved uneasily. They meant something about Salome's lying. That was the dreadful part of it. There was something which Mrs. Gerry could not understand, though she tried her utmost.

Then her good sense came to her aid and told her that she was so tired ; she had had such a strain upon her that she was now feeling the consequences. She must rest.

She made a slight motion as if she would rise. But she did not rise. Then a fleeting question came through her mind. She asked herself how it would seem if some one should take care of her. She had never been taken care of in her life. She had always been the stronger. She had been glad to be able to have the care.

She bent forward still more as she clasped her knees. She wished Salome had the right idea about truth.

There were footsteps approaching rapidly ; not the footsteps of saunterers, but of one with a purpose. They paused close to her, and a hand was held out. She looked up into Moore's happy eyes.

"We have been waiting for you in the palmetto scrub," he said, "until at last we were anxious. Come, now."

Mrs. Gerry took his hand, which folded round her tired fingers. She tried to smile.

"You remembered me ?" she asked.

And when she had said such words she knew that she must be more tired than ever before in her life, or surely she would not have been so weak as to speak like that.

XVIII

"AND NOW THERE IS NOTHING BETWEEN US"

MOORE stood for a moment silently beside Mrs.
Gerry. He had helped her to her feet, and now had
her hand drawn through his arm.

" I should think we did remember you," he said at
last. "We would not go any farther than the scrub. We
waited for you there. Salome was continually saying
we ought not to have left you. Finally she declared
we must come back and find you—and here I am."

" But where is the child?" Mrs. Gerry was again
reproving herself that she should be so weakly grateful
for this attention. She found it difficult to refrain
from tears. She held herself stiff that she might not
lean on Moore's arm as she listened to the young
man's reply.

" We met Miss Nunally by the old market. She
wanted to say something to Salome. Just then we
saw you, and I came right on. Shall we sit down
here a while, Mrs. Gerry?"

Though she appeared so well able to stand, Moore
had a sense that the woman on his arm was ready to
drop.

" Oh no; I have been sitting here and resting,"
was the reply. " We will go."

She faced about with her prim, concise movement,
her hand still within Moore's arm.

He turned also. Then, with an inarticulate exclamation, he bent over her, literally lifting her in his arms. She had strength to say:

"I can walk well enough," before she lost power to say anything.

While the young man knelt there on the stones of the battery supporting his burden, he saw Salome hurrying towards him. It was she who insisted that her mother should be taken to the cabin. She said she knew her mother would be more contented there than in any hotel or lodging-house in the city.

So the three were driven out in a carriage. Job Maine, at sight of that carriage with its two horses, began to consider whether he could not charge something in the way of a toll for its passage over his land. It took a great deal of tobacco to enable him to carry on this process of thought, and it was also such a work of time that the carriage had gone back to the city, its driver taking a message to a physician, before Mr. Maine had come to any conclusion.

Mrs. Gerry had recovered consciousness almost immediately. She had protested against having a carriage. She said she could walk perfectly well. It was a ridiculous extravagance in Moore, and she herself could not afford it.

Moore laughed in that infectious way of his. He said he was a rising young business man, and that Mrs. Gerry had no idea of the amount of money he made.

But Salome did not laugh. She sat by her mother with her arm about her, watching her face with dilated, anxious eyes. It did occur to the girl that she ought not to let her anxiety display itself with such emphasis, and she tried to conceal it, without the least success.

She was continually glancing at Moore and saying, in an eager, explanatory way :

"You know she is very tired. It is only because she is so very tired."

And Moore would answer that he knew that very well. When she had rested a day or two things would be all right again.

Then Salome would ask, piteously :

"You are sure of that? You are sure of that ?"

And Moore would declare that he was as sure as of his own existence.

Mrs. Gerry was really obliged to lean back on the cushioned seat. And she could only try to smile in reassurance at her daughter.

She laid herself down on the bed in the cabin. She said she would lie for an hour or two and rest.

Mrs. Job Maine, who had not walked a quarter of a mile for years, and who had often announced that she had never been used to walking when she resided with that first family of Alabama, of which she was an adorning member — this lady was now so moved by curiosity that she traversed on foot the distance between her hut and the hut occupied by the Gerrys.

She arrived in a panting state, and sank down immediately in a chair by the door. She had not known why these two women had been away for a time, and she did not know why they had come back. Her husband had wondered if he could not charge more for the cabin if his tenants allowed it to be empty. He said a house "kinder run down when it was left empty."

Mrs. Maine sat in her chair while these thoughts

21

went dully through her mind, and while she watched the three people before her.

Moore had made a fire in the fireplace under the impression that a fire must be necessary. He was still crouching there and coaxing the slow blaze with bits of fat pine.

Salome had found the bottle of whiskey which had been brought South for her use. She had brought some, weakened with water, and was now sitting on the side of the bed watching her mother as she sipped the liquid.

Mrs. Maine sniffed audibly. The odor of whiskey had power to bring a faint hint of an expression to her flat, straw-colored face.

She shuffled her bare feet on the floor.

"I thought I'd curm over 'n' inquire how yo' was," she said, "though it's my day fur thur shakes, 'n' I'm jist drained er whiskey, I be. Job thought las' night he was gwine ter have thur shakes, 'n' her swallered thur whiskey—every durned drap he swallered."

The woman sighed so heavily and so ostentatiously that Mrs Gerry said, in a whisper, to her daughter:

"Give her a cup of whiskey."

The girl obeyed. But she did not try to conceal the disgust the woman excited in her. She turned away her head that she might not see the liquor swallowed. But she heard it as it went rapidly down the woman's throat.

Mrs. Maine did not find it convenient to leave. Having come and having seated herself, she felt that she was rather more comfortable than if she were at home. She drew out a snuff-stick, which, being half chewed, was now in an ideal state for chewing. She moistened it in her mouth, and then skilfully inserted it in a little paper bag of snuff, which never was allowed to leave her person. With a grunt of satisfaction she now put the prepared stick back in her mouth.

"I mout's well be right hyar, if you should need a 'oman's help," she said, glancing at Salome.

Moore now stood up in front of the fire. He was staring at Mrs. Maine. There was a laugh in his eyes but a frown on his brow. Mrs. Gerry's strict sense of hospitality made it impossible for her to ask the woman to go, and, weak as she was and overcome by all she had recently suffered, she was conscious of an hysterical and growing sense of the ludicrousness of this visit.

She turned her head on the pillow. She could shut out the sight of the guest, but she could not shut out the sound of the enjoyment of that snuff-stick, and the sound made her ill.

Moore suddenly started forward from his position by the chimney. He offered his arm to Mrs. Maine, and begged her to show him that big pine her husband had mentioned.

Before she had time to consider she had taken Moore's arm, and he had pulled her up from her chair and walked her out-of-doors. With a laugh that was half a sob Salome put her head down on the pillow by her mother.

Half an hour later, when Moore had left Mrs. Maine safely in her own cabin with a gratuitous half a dollar for future whiskey, he came back and looked in at the open door. He came softly, and took off his hat as he glanced.

Salome was lying beside Mrs. Gerry. The girl's arm was thrown protectively over her companion.

They were perfectly quiet. Evidently they were asleep.

The young man turned away. He had noted how thin and white Mrs. Gerry's face was.

With his hat still in his hand he walked to that fallen pine-tree near the banana where Job Maine so frequently reposed in the midst of the toils of life. He sat down and gazed steadfastly before him. His face was good to look at as he sat there. He was thinking how, henceforward, he would take care of those two women. He was feeling grateful that Salome had such a mother. He reverenced that unbending integrity, that rigid adherence under all circumstances to the bald truth. He had felt that from Mrs. Gerry from the first. Indeed, the person must be very dull who had no sense of this part of the woman's character.

From her Moore's thoughts turned to Salome. The girl was infinitely more charming to him because she puzzled him somewhat. Her "two kinds of faces," as Miss Nunally had once said, would hold his interest vivid for years to come, he believed. Two kinds? She had a dozen. How could custom ever make dull "her infinite variety?"

To Moore it seemed a special gift of Providence that he should love a girl whose nature was so complex. He told himself that Salome inherited perfect integrity from her mother, and from somebody else a richness of life which made her more enchanting than anything he could have dreamed. Yes, he was certainly a very fortunate young man.

He resolved fervently to be worthy of this good-fortune; to live more and more up to that higher life which was always beckoning him. Of late it had seemed quite easy to keep the higher life well in view. Love was a great elevator and purifier.

He had forgotten at this moment what Salome had said about not caring for truth and for the higher life. Her words had not made much impression upon him. He had considered them piquant and unlike what other girls would have said. Other girls would have made a great pretence of love for all exalted states of being.

So Moore mused happily while he waited for the arrival of the doctor from Augustine, or for some sign from the cabin.

As he sat there the black and white hound Jack, who had been thrown into despair by the absence of Mrs. Gerry and her daughter, came despondently loping from a distance among the pines.

The dog was returning from a three days' trip into the barrens. He looked weary and depressed. He had not seen Moore when he sat down on his haunches and gave himself up for a few moments to a battle with fleas. Then he stretched up his neck and howled long and dolefully. He evidently believed his new friends had gone forever, and he was in despair.

At the second howl Moore sprang to his feet. There is hardly a more desolate and depressing sound than a dog's howl.

"Is that Jack?" asked a quick voice from the hut. It was Salome. Her face was whiter than usual and her voice almost sharp. She had always been inclined to superstition, but of late the weakness had grown upon her, as the practical, good-sense vein had seemed to retreat in her.

Moore whistled. The dog came eagerly forward; but he did not notice Moore in the least. He sprang upon Salome, and began that process of devouring which is so pathetic in its intensity of emotion. He had fully concluded that he should never see this friend again; and here she was, miraculously returned.

Salome withdrew with him from the hut lest his demonstrations might waken her mother, who was still sleeping heavily.

Moore instantly joined her. She looked at him reproachfully.

"Why did you let him howl?" she asked. Her voice trembled as she put the question.

"But I couldn't help it. Besides, it is nothing for a dog to howl," was the reply.

"If you had only cared you might have prevented it," insisted Salome, whose face was deeply clouded, and who was not in the least inclined to be reasonable.

Moore smiled with a gentle, but still a masculine, superiority. His spirits were too high for him to be affected by any such trifle as the howling of a dog.

"You needn't laugh," said the girl, and turned from him, with her hand on the dog's head.

Moore protested that he had never felt less like laughing in his life; but that Salome was really foolish if she thought a second time of Jack's howling. It was the fleas.

"The fleas!" exclaimed Salome; and then she asked her companion if he thought men could know any more if they tried. But before he could answer she inquired if he remembered those crows.

Moore looked bewildered. "Those crows?" he repeated.

Then Salome's aspect changed instantly. She went to Moore and put her hand through his arm. She looked up at him.

"Oh," she breathed, " I am so thankful that men are not as silly as women!"

Having said this, she would not linger a moment. She hurried back to the hut, to find her mother still sleeping.

When at last the doctor came he found Mrs. Gerry awake and sitting propped up in bed. She said that she could just as well get up; but still she did not get up.

The decision the physician gave was that the woman was nearly worn out; that she must lie there where she was and be taken care of. He brusquely ordered her to stop thinking, and when she remonstrated he said she could make her mind a blank if she chose, and her mind must be a blank before she gained much strength. He remarked that one woman could not carry the universe, even with the best intentions.

Moore went back to the city with him to get his prescription filled.

And so began those days which, sad as they were, were yet brightened for Salome by Moore's tender and untiring devotion.

The girl seemed to be nothing now but her mother's nurse. She watched and waited, and would not sleep.

It was as if she could not give herself enough that her mother might recover. It was in vain that Mrs. Gerry would say again and again :

" Salome, you must spare yourself. You won't hold out."

Salome would only smile and say nothing ; or she would exclaim passionately that surely God would give her strength now.

Her mother was too weak to contend or to command.   She lay there and submitted for the first time since her childhood to being cared for.

The days passed with strange quickness; and all the days seemed alike to the girl, who sat by the bed or who sometimes placed her chair outside the door, always keeping within reach of her mother's voice.

Mrs. Gerry felt her child's tenderness and care with a poignancy that was painful at first.   But when she would ask Salome what the doctor said about his patient she never knew whether Salome told her the truth or not.

Sometimes Mrs. Gerry would open her eyes to find her daughter looking at her fixedly, as if there were a weight on her mind.   Mrs. Gerry would think she would ask what it was, but she was too weak to do it.

The woman's thoughts partook something of the weakness of her body.   She was dimly thankful that she could not suffer acutely.   It was a dulness that brought at last certain healing with it.

But when the healing began Mrs. Gerry seemed to her daughter more ill than ever.

Walter Redd made two solemn, brief calls at the cabin before he departed on a journey of exploration through the State.   He said he was going to find out if there was any more money to be made in orange groves than in apple orchards.   He talked ponderously on this subject with Salome, and he never looked at her while he spoke.   He did not seem inclined to speak of anything but orange raising.   He went to the bed and shook hands with Mrs. Gerry.   He told her he knew she was pretty sick, but he believed she would come out all right.

It was after that that Mrs. Gerry appeared to grow more ill; at least, Salome thought so.

It was one night, two weeks from her seizure. It was a densely dark time, and a violent south wind was blowing. The trees and shrubs thrashed about; the banana leaves were torn to ribbons.

The frogs piped shrilly.

Salome hardly knew whether it was the night which made her so uneasy. She usually liked a south wind.

Mrs. Gerry had been sleeping fitfully, but when Salome came back from one of her visits to the open door she saw her mother's eyes fixed upon her.

"Child," exclaimed Mrs. Gerry, anxiously, "you must sleep more!"

"Oh, I've been sleeping all the time," came the answer, directly.

Mrs. Gerry's eyes closed again. She was sure that Salome had not slept. She tried to tell herself that this was an amiable falsehood. And she knew that it was only one of many which the girl had told her of late. As she lay there she almost believed that a lie came as readily as the truth to Salome's lips—a plausible, agreeable lie.

Then the woman tried to ask herself if a lie were any worse than covetousness. Was it worse to break one commandment than another? But she was too weak and weary to argue any point now. She only groaned. And to groan was a luxury that she would not think of permitting herself if she were ordinarily strong.

Salome sprang to the side of the bed with her rapid and yet gentle motion. She knelt down with her arm under her mother's neck.

The lamplight fell on the girl's face, and showed it with an uncontrollable terror upon it.

"I have been thinking," she said, in a voice barely

audible—" I have been thinking one thing ever since you've been ill."

" Hush !" said Mrs. Gerry, in her old way of trying to soothe her child.

" No ; I can't hush.   I can't keep silent any longer. For if you should die—"

Here the voice ceased entirely.

Evidently Salome was fighting quietly with herself.

Mrs. Gerry tried to rally, and to say some calm, reasonable words to her daughter.   But the words would not come.   She was too weak.   She lay there motionless, her heart beating painfully.

Finally she whispered, " Raise my head a little higher."

The girl eagerly obeyed her.

In the silence that now followed, the sound of the wind grew louder.   The cabin rocked.   It was sultry. Jack, the hound, lying across the open doorway, rose and sat uneasily on his haunches, yawning audibly.

" Salome," said Mrs. Gerry, who had at last gained a little strength, " does the doctor say I am going to die now ?"

" He said he thought you would get over this," was the answer.

" Is that the truth ?"

These words were spoken with painful emphasis.

" Yes, mother."

Another silence, which at last was broken by the girl.

" But I can't bear this any longer, mother.   What should I do if you should die ?—and then you would, perhaps, know everything.   I am not talking about my grief ; I am talking about something else now. Do you think the dead know everything ?"

“ Salome, why are you saying this ?”

Mrs. Gerry’s heart beat still more painfully.

“Oh, I must say it !” went on the girl. “ I have been trying to speak all the time. But it seemed cruel to distress you. It is cruel.”

Mrs. Gerry could not speak. She was motionless. She was only faintly conscious of a curiosity concerning what the child had to say. Her one absorbing but fruitless wish was to help the child, and help her as she had always done.

“ If you should die,” began Salome again, “and should then find that I had not told you, perhaps you would blame me even more than you will now, and then I could not comfort you. I could not put my arms about you and tell you I am not really wicked at heart—not at heart ; at least, I don’t feel so. But it may be that nobody really feels wicked. Oh, mother—”

Salome’s heavy, persistent voice paused for an instant.

Keenest emotion had now penetrated through all the stupor in which prostration had enveloped Mrs. Gerry.

She raised her head that she might look more fully at her daughter.

When her head sank back again she exclaimed, in a strong tone :

“ Salome, what have you done ? Tell the truth !”

“ Yes, I will tell the truth now, certainly,” was the reply. “ But you need never have known. Only, if it did happen that you knew, and that I was separated from you because I was alive and you were dead—”

“ Salome !” sharply.

“ About the check, mother,” said the girl, quickly.

"What check?" in the same thin, high voice. Mrs. Gerry had never associated any event with a check.

"The eight hundred dollars," said Salome; "the money for father. It was sent by a check, you know."

"You mean the sum Mrs. Darrah loaned?"

"Yes; only she did not loan it at first."

No response from Mrs. Gerry. But she felt herself growing stronger to meet this something that was coming. If it might be a strength that would stay with her!

"At first," said Salome, visibly bracing herself, "it was I who sent the check. I—I put Mrs. Darrah's name to it and sent it directly, because I knew my father must have it. I knew he could not wait. It did not seem much to do."

Still no response from the woman lying there.

"Did you hear?" whispered Salome.

A slight movement seemed to signify assent.

Salome remained quiet as long as she could.

"Mother!" shrilly, and after she could not bear the silence another instant.

"Yes, child."

"Mother, don't you love me any more?"

The agony in the young tone pierced the woman's soul.

Mrs. Gerry's voice might have been mistaken for that of her daughter as she said:

"Love you! I love you more than ever, if that were possible. But—"

Here the voice failed utterly.

"But what? You shall tell me, mother. But what?"

And now Mrs. Gerry's strength began to flag. It had only come under the whip of intense excitement. If it had not flagged, if she had been herself, she would not have obeyed this demand, imperative though it was. She would have realized too keenly how her reply might wound.

Salome was now standing over the bed. The impulse which had been urging her for many days to speak was still strong upon her. She was glad she had spoken. It was done now. There was no secret between her and her mother.

"Why did you say 'but' in that way?" she repeated, with the fierceness of unrestrained anxiety. "You still love me?"

"Yes, yes. But, Salome, don't you think I want to respect you also?"

"Oh!"

When she had uttered this exclamation the girl wavered as she stood there. Then she suddenly knelt down by the bed and pressed her face among the clothes.

As for Mrs. Gerry, she had borne all she could bear at that moment. She shut her eyes and dimly thanked herself that she could not feel anything more. She did not faint, but her mind lapsed into a state as limp and strengthless as her body.

She knew that her daughter was giving her a stimulating medicine, and she tried to make some response. But she could only feebly swallow the liquid and then sink back on the pillow.

In the hour which followed she hardly knew that Salome was all the time kneeling close to her. The girl was perfectly quiet. She often raised her head and looked at her mother. There was nothing for her to do. She must wait now for the shock to have spent itself.

In the midst of the girl's anguish there was a faint

fire of resentment that the knowledge of that forgery should have such an effect. She asked herself if it would not have been better if she had heeded Portia Nunally's advice and kept this secret. Why should she tell? But no. She would not keep anything from her mother. Her mother must know the very worst of her in every way. And that forgery was of course the worst.

The night wore on slowly. Towards morning the wind subsided, and it began to rain in heavy dashes, as it sometimes rained in the summer at home. Salome was obliged to shut the door. The hound begged so to remain inside that she let him stay.

She put on more wood and sat by the fire, feeling very thankful that the dog had stopped with her. She could look at him and think that it would not make the slightest difference to him if she had been guilty of a thousand crimes. It was very uncomfortable that she should have this desire to tell what she had done— she did not understand. Of course it was natural that she should wish to tell her mother. But this strange desire to know what people would think. If some one would only take the affair calmly, as she herself was moved to take it. She tried to consider herself wicked. As she sat there with the hound in those hours before the dawn she quite longed to have what she would have called a realizing sense of her sin.

The dawn was very long in coming. In all the nights when she had taken care of her mother the morning had never lagged so.

But she was glad that no one was with her. Moore had tried to persuade her to allow him to get a nurse. She had refused with something like anger. She said that she should do everything for her mother. She was able. She appealed to the doctor. He looked at her for an instant, and then gave a decided assent.

Privately he informed Moore that it would hurt the girl much more to take the care from her than to let her have it. Only keep watch of her; if she showed any signs of breaking down, why, then it would be time enough to get help.

Salome, however, showed no signs of breaking down.

She was pathetically thankful that she could do this.

Moore came out from the city every day. And almost as often Miss Nunally came, and sometimes the two walked back together. Often also she insisted upon sitting a while with Mrs. Gerry while Salome strolled among the pines with her lover. She would always keep within sight and hearing, however. She was something of a trial to Moore in these days, for she appeared absent and absorbed. It was easy to forgive her that, since her mother's illness explained this mood. It was only at rare intervals that she was what Moore called "like herself." But those intervals atoned for all, and Moore called himself quite a god. He explained this opinion of himself to himself by saying that since this girl loved him he must be a god.

Miss Nunally, as the two walked leisurely back to St. Augustine, used to look at him with questioning and amused eyes. She was very agreeable in those walks. Major Root was never mentioned, and might not have been in existence; although a diamond of his buying flashed upon Miss Nunally's hand.

If she wore no glove, Portia had a way of turning that stone inward so that only the hoop of gold was visible.

Her aunt noticed that her niece was in excellent spirits; and in her own mind she remarked that Portia was just the kind of girl to be made happy by "that sort of thing," meaning an engagement to a rich man —and the authoress added that women were little better than mere animals, after all; it gave them no uneasiness to sell themselves. She was glad Portia was in good spirits, but she could not help despising her a little on account of that fact. One was never quite sure about Portia, anyway. Mrs. Darrah felt that she should not be entirely easy until the girl was Major Root's wife. And then she meant to forget her. She did not think that Major Root was in a position to be congratulated. But that was his business. Meanwhile Mrs. Darrah was obliged to proceed with the novel of sentiment without an amanuensis, and Salome was now doing nothing to help pay the debt she had contracted, or, rather, that which her employer had allowed to be considered as a debt.

The day following that night when Salome had made her confession to her mother was one of those sweet and perfect days which often come to Florida.

Before daybreak the girl had placed herself softly beside her mother on the bed. She had put out her hand and touched her mother's hand. The fingers had closed feebly on her palm. Then Salome had breathed a deep sigh, and had gone to sleep. When she wakened the sun was shining in between the logs.

The girl knew it was late. She sprang up quickly. She had not slept so soundly since her mother was ill.

"It is because I told her," she said to herself; "and now there is nothing between us."

She went joyfully about the work of preparing her mother's breakfast.

As she did so a clear voice called her from the path among the pines.

22

XIX

"AS FOR ME, I LOVE HIM NOT"

IT was Moore's voice that called. Salome, standing by the kerosene lamp-stove, watching the heating of some broth, heard it. She did not move, save that her hand trembled slightly as she took the spoon from the liquid.

"Salome," said Mrs. Gerry from the bed.

She turned quickly. It was the first time her mother had spoken since she had said that she wished to respect her daughter. Mrs. Gerry's intent gaze was on the girl. She beckoned feebly.

In an instant Salome was bending over her.

"Wasn't that Mr. Moore?" she whispered.

"Yes."

"Was that true that you told me?"

"It was true."

"You are sure I didn't dream it," with an anguished wistfulness that was hard for the girl to hear and see.

"I told you," she answered, bearing up bravely.

"Does Mr. Moore know?"

"Oh no, no!"

Salome knew what was coming now.

"You must tell him."

Salome held up her head as she answered:

"Very well."

"Do you mean that you will tell him? Remember,

it will not be fair to let him marry you—to let him think you are very different from what you really are."

As they talked the young man's voice could be heard outside. He was speaking with Mr. Maine.

"I understand," said Salome, still with her head flung up. "But what am I, really?"

Mrs. Gerry could not answer. She moved her head wearily from side to side on the pillow.

"Is the broth ready?" she asked.

Salome brought the broth and gave it with the utmost tenderness, as she did everything for her charge.

Still there was some bitterness in her eyes, and her lips were pressed together. That fire of resentment that she should be considered so wicked was still smouldering in her consciousness.

Yes, certainly, Moore ought to know what a wretch he wished to marry. It had all the time been in the bottom of her mind that she would tell him. Still, with a closer compression of the lips, Miss Nunally was probably right when she advised silence. Of course it was great folly that one, after committing a crime, should wish to proclaim it. Such a thing should be kept securely locked. Somehow it seemed to Salome that she ought to be able to find some one who would not be shocked; some one who, on being informed of this deed, should smile and remark that it was not worth being troubled about. For that was the way the girl regarded what she had done.

The hot drink stimulated Mrs. Gerry. When she had drunk it she held out her arms to the girl, smiling hopefully at her. The mother could not bear to see her child suffering.

"We have each other, you know," said the elder,

with something of her old courage. "And I am sure
I am better."

Salome kept her head down beside her mother.

"You don't respect me," she said, her voice muffled
by the pillow.

Mrs. Gerry winced. She did not reply.

Moore now appeared in the open doorway. The
sight of him had always been something like a tonic
to Mrs. Gerry, but she could not look at him now.
His voice was cheery and hopeful as he made his
usual inquiries. But by the time he had finished
speaking his mood had changed. He stepped quickly
to the bedside. He raised Salome until she rested
on his arm, but he looked only at Mrs. Gerry as he
asked :

"Has anything happened? Are you worse?"

"I am better," was the reply.

Then Mrs. Gerry acted upon a sudden impulse.
She did not quite trust Salome's resolution ; and she
was not even sure that the girl had made a resolution.

"Salome has something to tell you," she said.

The girl withdrew herself from Moore and stood
apart.

The young man was actualy alarmed.

"It is something about that big, black-looking
fellow who came down with Mrs. Gerry," was what
he thought.

He had known, by intuition rather than by perception, that Redd loved Salome. Was she entangled
with that man? Moore braced himself as if against
an onslaught of physical pain. He thrust his hands
into his pockets and shut them there.

Salome went to the foot of the bed and grasped the
cross-piece.

She was thinking that if her mother heard her, she would believe. And already Salome had experienced a little of that emotion which comes when one's word is not fully taken. It is probable that even a hardened liar wishes to be believed when speaking the truth.

Moore looked at her. The sight of her face was like the cut of a knife to him. His whole nature rose up to protect her.

He took a step towards her. A slight gesture from her kept him from advancing.

"Never mind," he said, hurriedly. "Don't tell me anything."

Salome hesitated. She glanced at her mother. But her mother's eyes did not release—they upheld and stimulated her.

"I tell you it is not of the least consequence," cried Moore, unable to prevent himself from reiterating his assurance. "Let us wait. Any other time will do. Why should you suffer so, Salome?"

His voice had a remonstrating tenderness that was very harrowing for the girl to hear.

A rush of feeling came over her. Why reveal anything? Was not the idea absurd? Why try to be so ridiculously honorable?

And yet—

She turned more fully towards Moore. No; she would not retreat. There was something in her that would now have made her go forward, even without her mother's influence.

She kept her eyes on Moore's face. It seemed an impossible thing to do, but it was still more impossible not to watch for every expression that should come to that countenance. If he tried to deceive her by his words, she knew that he could not deceive her with his face. He would want to be kind. She was sure of that.

She clung to the cross-piece at the foot of the bed.

"You know I always told you I didn't care about right and wrong," she began.

Moore nodded. He was too bewildered. There must be something really the matter, however. He could feel something dreadful in the air.

Salome's voice went on now quickly. And she never once took her eyes from his face.

She told her story in the fewest possible words.

She saw everything that came into the man's countenance. When she had said the last word she walked up to Moore and caught sharp hold of his arm, still looking at him. But she did not speak. She laughed lightly.

She went to the door, while he gazed at her.

She stopped in the doorway a moment. As she stood there the hound came and placed himself beside her, licking her hand. She did not notice him. She noticed nothing but the man's face.

Presently she laughed again. As Mrs. Gerry heard the desolation in that laugh she started up quickly and tried to leave the bed. But she fell back.

"You are like my mother, Mr. Moore," said the girl. "You cannot respect me."

And now she walked away.

Moore seemed to need that she should go in order that he might be roused.

He sprang out from the door with a movement that brought him swiftly to the girl's side. He took both her hands, drawing her back into the cabin with him.

"I see you are sorry for me," she said, in the same strained tone she had been using.

"Sorry for you!" he cried. "Good God! Don't you see that I love you?"

There was a very passion of love and pity in his face. But Salome would not allow him to draw her near to him.

She removed herself from his hold and sat down quickly.

"You are like my mother," she repeated, with a painstaking accuracy, as if she feared that she should miss a word. "You cannot respect me."

Moore stood still. He had a frantic sense of helplessness. And into his tumultuous distress there came a remembrance of what this girl had said to him more than once of how he would perhaps some time say to himself that he wished that he had loved some one else.

He could not think clearly. The overmastering impulse upon him was that he must take Salome in his arms; that he must be more gentle, more tender than he had ever been.

He was gazing at her with eager entreaty.

He did not know that Mrs. Gerry had not ceased to look at him since Salome began to speak.

He stepped to the girl's side and put his hand on the back of her chair, bending over her.

She rose immediately.

"I want to be out-of-doors," she said. "I want to be under the sky."

He moved away and let her go.

He sat down in the chair she had left and covered his face with his hands.

He was not thinking anything about whether he respected her or not. His whole consciousness was full of tenderness and of longing to help. He wondered why she would not let him come near her.

Then, like the uncoiling of a snake, came the question: Did he respect her?

He started up in the unbearable agony of that inquiry.

"Mr. Moore," said Mrs. Gerry's voice from the bed, "will you go away now?"

Moore went mechanically to the bed. He stood there, hesitating an instant in a bewildered manner. But it was not in a mechanical way that he stooped and kissed Mrs. Gerry's cheek.

"I shall come back," he said; "I shall come back in an hour or two. Perhaps we have dreamed this."

He tried to smile as he spoke. Then he walked quickly away. He saw standing by the banana-tree the figure of Salome, with the hound just at her hand.

She saw him, but she made no sign.

As Moore walked on he recalled some of the remarks he had made when talking about that man in Tampa who had forged his friend's signature.

At this memory Moore shook himself fiercely as if he might awaken.

But he could not awaken. He went on thinking steadily of that man. He would, no doubt, be sentenced for a term of years. Yes, for a term of years. What kind of a nature was it which could do such a thing?

Moore's mind floundered on among horrible questions, his love making each question a separate, stinging wound.

He had seen people suffer in his life. He had imagined, as the hitherto unhurt will imagine, that he knew what suffering was. But this hour told him that he had not known.

And most of all, he thought, was the sense of confusion, of groping in the dark.

Salome must be very different from what he had believed her to be—very different; or she could never, under any stress, have forged a name. How was he to adjust himself to this new Salome who had within her the capability of doing a mean crime? He must not shirk the words: a mean crime. Didn't she have any moral sense? Had she really meant all she had told him about not caring?

Moore stumbled on through the sand. How curiously she had talked about that man in Tampa! And he had believed all the time that she spoke so because of her kind heart.

The young man paused when he was at some distance from the cabin. He threw back his shoulders, inhaling a deep breath. He could not yet rid himself of the idea that this was something which would presently vanish. It is so difficult for us to believe that a terrible trouble may come to us. To others it may come naturally, but not to us.

Having stood for a moment with that vague air that is so often indicative of suffering, Moore began to walk on again.

His whole mind was now engaged in an attempt at a readjustment of his ideas concerning Salome. He felt that his heart was the same. The complexity of the girl's character had given a keen zest to his acquaintance with her always. He had known that he did not understand her. It was going to be one of the delights of his life to learn to understand her. But that talk of hers which was piquant, which had a flavor so unlike that of any other woman whom he had known, was this possibility in her one of the causes of such words? And her face? The enchanting, un-guessable possibilities of her face? No, no; it could not be.

To be able to do what she confessed, that must require a kind of person quite different from the person whom he loved.

But he loved her. Oh yes, he loved her. He turned and looked back at the cabin. He saw her still standing by the banana, with the hound by her side. It required all his self-restraint to enable him to remain away from her. He was, however, quite sure that she did not wish him to return now.

She had looked at him so strangely. Could she possibly doubt his love? He had never loved her so strongly as now. And now there was an almost intolerable element of pity, a pity which seemed, indeed, to be made up of tenderness.

He was not thinking these things, apparently; he was feeling them.

And all at once it was simply impossible for him to resist the desire to hasten back to her. But he had not gone a dozen steps before she turned and glanced towards him. She waved him back with her hand.

Still he went on. He was telling himself that nothing should keep him from her now.

Just at that moment Miss Nunally came walking along the cart-path from the city. She was but a short distance away. He paused in his walk, staring rather than glancing at her.

She also paused instantly. A flash of something passed over her face.

"Mrs. Gerry—" she began. Moore made one fruitless attempt to speak before he was able to say:

"She is no worse."

"Oh!" whispered Portia, in thankfulness.

Then she came nearer.

"You know about it, then?" she said.

Moore, groping for some foothold, turned towards her eagerly.

"Yes," he answered.

There was so much sympathy and kindness on Miss Nunally's face that the young man extended his hand, moved by that spontaneous wish for contact with a kindly human being which is so natural to us.

The girl put her hand in his, but instantly withdrew it.

"Did she tell you?" she asked.

And again Moore said "yes."

Miss Nunally stood silent. But there was a distinctly felt consolation to Moore in the presence of one who was so plainly *en rapport* with him.

It has been said of him that he was one who asked and found help from feminine nature. It was not like him to suffer or enjoy in silence and alone.

"She was wrong," at last said Miss Nunally.

She had closed her sunshade, and was leaning somewhat heavily upon it. The light was falling full upon her face.

"Don't say she was wrong!" he exclaimed, harshly.

"I mean wrong to tell you," went on Miss Nunally. "But it was noble of her."

"Yes, yes; so it was," was the response, with some eagerness. "Oh, Miss Nunally, I don't understand."

Portia half turned away. She appeared to grow pale as she said, with a touch of impatience:

"There are so many things we cannot understand.

I think it a mistake for us to try to understand as we do."

"But it is impossible not to try when one's whole happiness is at stake," answered Moore, quickly. "You don't know what this is to me. You cannot imagine. You—"

"Yes, talk to me like that," interrupted Miss Nunally, angrily. "Assume that I know nothing, since it pleases you to do so. At least, I know one thing, Mr. Moore."

For an instant Moore's eyes were turned with a personal interest upon his companion.

"What do you mean?" he asked.

"I mean that I am not as good as Miss Gerry."

"You? But you have not—you have not—" Here the young man found that he could not go on.

"I have not committed a forgery," said Portia. "I meant that I would not have risked telling you. I told her not to do so. No; I would not have risked so much as that. Good-bye, Mr. Moore."

Miss Nunally walked back along the path by which she had come. She hesitated, as if she would go to Salome; but she went on.

Moore gazed after her, not seeing her in the least. He did not think of the words she had just spoken. But he thought of them later, when they flashed over his mind with that sudden illuminating power which lightning has.

Now he walked towards Salome with an air which showed plainly that he would not obey any command to leave her.

She shrank away a step, without looking at him. She had an appearance of standing at bay, like some weak animal which, by stress of despair, finally turns and takes a last position.

Moore thought that nothing she could have done could so touch him. But he had no opportunity to speak. Before he could choose among the words that came tumultuously to him, Salome said:

"I am sure my mother needs me."

Having said this, she hurried into the cabin, and Moore could not follow her.

His first impulse was to go back to Augustine. He could see now, at some distance among the pines, the figure of Miss Nunally. No, he would not go. He could not speak to any one; and he felt, after all, that he could not leave Salome.

He sat down on that log so much frequented by Mr. Maine, and presently that gentleman came slouching along from his residence.

This was a presence utterly unendurable. Moore sprang up and darted off into the woods. Mr. Maine cursed lazily as he seated himself. He had intended, when he saw the young man, to borrow fifty cents of him. He had already borrowed that amount a great many times, but that fact was no reason why he should not continue to borrow indefinitely.

Mrs. Gerry had been lying in entire quiet since she had been left alone. To have the body absolutely still sometimes makes one able to believe the agreeable falsehood that one is calm.

But Mrs. Gerry never meant to believe a falsehood, and she knew that she was not calm, though her form might have been a symbol for repose when her daughter stepped within the room and looked at her.

Mrs. Gerry opened her eyes; but she closed them

immediately, unable for the moment to bear the sight of the girl's face.

Directly, however, she said : " It was right to tell him."

Salome said nothing.

Mrs. Gerry moved.

" Do you not think it was right to tell him ?" she asked.

" Very likely," was the answer.

" Then that was the thing to do," from Mrs. Gerry, with an air of finality. She must adhere to that decision, whatever came of it. It was impossible for her to do otherwise. Life, or death, or happiness, or misery were of no consequence to her compared with the things which that decision stood for in her mind.

As she lay there looking at the girl she felt how easily she could give up life and happiness for her. But it was not a question of giving up ; it was something far less simple.

" Do you not think so ?" repeated Mrs. Gerry.

She must persist in this question.

Salome had an expression of deadly weariness in her eyes.

" Oh," said Salome, " you know I don't care about such things."

" What things ?" fearfully.

" Oh, right and wrong. I try to care, because you have taught me. But that isn't really caring. Please don't let us talk any more about it. I'm so tired ! and I want to keep my strength. I want to take care of you, mother."

As she finished speaking Salome bent over her mother, her face suddenly filling with intense and tender affection.

"Lie down here beside me," Mrs. Gerry said.

The girl obeyed her. She placed herself by her mother and took her in her arms. She also became perfectly quiet, but her eyes were widely open all the time.

Half an hour later Salome rose to get some medicine. When she had given it she said:

"There was something in me that would finally have made me tell him."

"I'm glad of that," returned Mrs. Gerry.

"Are you? I am sorry."

"Oh, Salome!"

"Yes, I am sorry. It is that something which will take away all my happiness from me—all my happiness."

She sat down on the bed and looked fixedly but blankly at the face on the pillow.

"Dear child!"

Again there was in the woman's voice a cadence that made it like her daughter's.

"Yes; and I think I have a right to be happy."

"But Mr. Moore loves you," said Mrs. Gerry, longing to comfort the girl.

There was no reply to this remark.

In a moment Salome rose and busied herself about some household duty.

When, a little later, Moore came to the door, she told him, with gentle decision that was quite infuriating to him, that she could not see him again that day.

And he was obliged to abide by that decision. He did allow himself to say that it seemed to him that she was torturing him unnecessarily, and that she appeared to forget that he loved her. "Didn't she care for his love?"

She looked up at him.

"Yes," she said, "I care for your love."

And with that Moore had to leave her.

This time he could not saunter back to the Ponce de Leon, as he had done formerly. He could not go where he would see any one. To make it nearly sure that he should be alone, he hurried to cross the river to that beach which is so broad and long and silent, save for the wave sounds, that it but accentuates loneliness.

But Portia Nunally did not go to any beach. She went directly to her room and sat down there. When her aunt sent for her, she returned word that she would visit Mrs. Darrah by-and-by.

When she did rise from her seat, however, she dressed for a drive with Major Root, and was punctual to the moment when he had said he would call.

Two hours later, when the two returned, the Major was so purple in the face that he was almost black.

He climbed down from his dog-cart and held up his pudgy hand to assist his companion, who availed herself demurely of that assistance.

She was very far from being black in the face; she was quite radiant. She turned to the Major and thanked him very sweetly for the pleasure he had given her by taking her to drive.

The Major took off his hat and glowered. Miss Nunally smiled at him, and then she walked up the entrance to the hotel.

At the top of the steps she turned to look at the gallant soldier, who had climbed back into his dog-cart. At that moment the gallant soldier was lifting his whip for a vicious cut at his horse.

Miss Nunally was still smiling. She shrugged her shoulders as the horse made a leap forward.

"That man will certainly have apoplexy," she said to herself.

She went directly to Mrs. Darrah's room.

"You sent for me, Aunt Florence," she said.

"Yes; but that was hours ago. I don't want you now," was the response.

"That makes no difference; I will stay a few moments. I have such a light heart, my dear relative!"

Portia sat down opposite the divan and began to remove her gloves.

"Have you, indeed?" asked Mrs. Darrah. "I hope Major Root has a light heart also."

Portia laughed.

"Oh, I don't know about that. But I do know that at this moment he has an atrociously bad temper."

"Because of you, of course," said Mrs. Darrah.

"You say that as if people were often having bad tempers because of me."

Mrs. Darrah did not reply. She had a book in her hand, and she evidently wished that her niece would leave her.

But her niece was not going immediately.

"Why don't you ask me why I have such a light heart, aunt?" the girl inquired.

"Well," said Mrs. Darrah, "why have you such a light heart?"

"Because I have got rid of Major Root," was the answer.

"For to-day?"

"Yes; and for all time."

"What?"

"Don't be so shocked. I haven't killed him; he is

23

alive; that is, he is alive if he hasn't died of apoplexy. But he is no longer mine. Think of it! He is no longer mine!"

The girl's eyes sparkled.

"Portia!" cried Mrs. Darrah. She shut her book with a movement that was too forcible to be ladylike.

"Aunt Florence!" was the response.

"Do you know what you are doing?" sternly.

"Certainly. I am taking off my gloves. And, by-the-way, this is the last pair of that last half-dozen you gave me. Really, I am hard on gloves."

"Do you know," went on Mrs. Darrah, sitting severely straight, her face becoming harsh—"have you any idea what you are doing, I say? You are throwing away one of the best chances in Augustine this season. And you haven't a cent of money; and you are getting old—"

"Oh, thank you, aunt, dear."

"Yes; you are getting old," remorsely repeated Mrs. Darrah, "and every year your opportunities will lessen. And an affair like this, and other affairs you have had—they all injure your reputation. And —and—good heavens!—what are you thinking about, Portia Nunally?"

"I am thinking about Micah Root, and that I was a coarse, vulgar little wretch ever to have thought I could marry him."

This answer was given with such a calm assurance of former sin and present repentance that Mrs. Darrah felt helpless and speechless for the moment.

Here was her niece on her hands again. She was no nearer marriage, apparently, than before her engagement to Major Root. What was to be done?

"Can't you write a note to him?" asked Mrs. Darrah, rather weakly.

"A note to whom?" was the candid counter inquiry, given in Portia's most amiable manner.

Mrs. Darrah felt her wrath rising with great rapidity.

"To Major Root, of course," she said.

"Oh, to him?" lightly, " telling him, I suppose, that I found, after all, that I could not endure the idea of life without him, and would he please take me back? Is that what you mean, Aunt Florence?"

"Yes; anything, so that he takes you back."

Miss Nunally rose and walked about the room with her hands clasped behind her. She was so white that the vivid scarlet of her lips seemed brighter in hue than ever. She looked excitedly happy also.

After a moment she paused in front of her aunt.

"I won't be taken back," she said; "not if the Major crept on his knees from the barracks, and had apoplexy at my very feet; and all for love." Here the girl laughed. "Why, for the last half hour I have quite respected myself; and I find it a delicious sensation. Major Root's ring and his little gifts are all in my room in a package, directed to him. I tied the package before I went to drive with him. It was great fun tying that package. Look at my hand"— she extended the slender, sensitive left hand—"it is free; it is not polluted any longer. Oh!" with a grimace of disgust, " how ill it has made me to think of myself!"

Mrs. Darrah sat silent. After looking at her for an instant, Portia asked:

"Why don't you congratulate me?"

Instead of replying, Mrs. Darrah put this question:

" How are you going to be supported ?"

" Perhaps my parents can give me bread."

" Possibly. But the gowns and the gloves? You know you are the most extravagant creature in the world."

Portia glanced down at her irreproachable attire.

" Yes, I know," she answered. " I certainly am not going to wear ugly frocks. Somebody must clothe me."

" And you can't work."

" Impossible! But don't you think the conversation is drifting into a disagreeable channel ?" asked Portia.

" Yes, quite disagreeable," was the response ; " and I insist on your writing a note to Major Root."

Portia stood haughtily erect.

" You know very well, aunt," she said, " that people do not insist with me."

" But you are mad. The season is more than half over, and if you don't settle this season I really will do nothing more for you."

Portia drew near her aunt. She put one knee on a footstool close to Mrs. Darrah, and leaned against her.

" Now," she said, " you are not going to be a wicked, hard-hearted woman, are you?"

" Yes; I am."

Miss Nunally smiled. It was a curious fact that though the elder woman knew she was being cajoled, and knew it perfectly well, she did not resent the fact. More than that, there was something about her niece's personality that made her rather enjoy having her near her in that way, and looking at her with the saucy, attractive face.

" If, after all, Aunt Florence, I am an old maid—a poor, wrinkled old maid who has missed the one destiny for which a woman is fitted—will you not give me, now and then, money enough so I needn't dress like a fright? Only think! Wouldn't you try to soften the fate of a woman who is denied the privilege of being the wife of some man, and of sitting in that sweet, safe corner by the household fire, behind the heads of children, and—and mending his stockings? When you see me growing old, and without any man's stockings to mend, won't you do something for me?"

Portia rose suddenly, and began prancing about the room and singing in a sentimental voice :

> " I have written the letter
> Which will tell him he is free."

At this point she paused in her prancing and her song to say :

" Now, you see, one of those other girls who wanted Major Root may have him; and joy go with her. As for me, I love him not."

" Portia," said Mrs. Darrah, smiling a little.

" Ma'am ?" said Portia, promptly.

" Hand me my blue note-book. At last you have given me a scrap of material."

" Dear aunt," remarked the girl as she brought the book, " I am glad to have furnished you material, even though in furnishing it I have lost a husband."

She went out at the door. But she returned immediately to say " Adieu," with the exaggerated tone and accent of an actress who comes back to the stage to bid farewell again to her lover, who has waited in position near the right centre for that farewell.

XX

"HE WILL COME BACK?"

MRS. GERRY began to mend. Her improvement
appeared to be more a matter of will than of anything
else. She must get well. Her daughter needed her.
It would have been impossible for the mother to die
then. And she remembered that she had always been
told that she had the Ware constitution. It was now
that the Ware constitution asserted itself.

The period of absolute physical rest had enabled
her to regain her grasp on strength. In a week she
could sit propped up in the bed. Moore was lavish
in his kindness. Strengthening delicacies, flowers,
everything the young man could think of which could
help the invalid or amuse her, he brought out to the
hut. And in all this week he had had no word alone
with Salome. She told him that she did not wish to
leave her mother for a moment. Her mother might
want something.

The girl shrank from her lover with a terror that
she could not conceal. And when she believed that
she was not observed she watched his face with an
intentness that was piteous.

And her mother watched her; and as she watched,
Mrs. Gerry prayed with a kind of imperious agony
that she might have strength, and yet more strength.
For she would need it all, she was sure.

The two women talked no more about the forgery during that week. But they talked a great deal in an impersonal, extremely cheerful manner.

And Mrs. Gerry gained every day. In the beginning of the second week she was able to "be about the house," as she would have said; but mostly she sat wrapped up in a blanket in the sunshine at the door. And Salome sat by her, sometimes reading to her, but oftener silent, looking out among the pine-trees.

It was here that Moore found them for several days. He also would sit down. He took his place on the other side of Mrs. Gerry. He would make several brave attempts at talk; then he would subside into silence. In this silence he tried not to look at Salome; but it always ended in his fixing his eyes beseechingly on her, and appearing to forget that he and she were not alone together.

One day, in the last of the week, while the three sat there in the sunshine, they saw a tall man making his way slowly to them.

Salome knew directly that it was Walter Redd, and presently Mrs. Gerry exclaimed:

"Why, it's Walter!"

Redd came and shook hands with them all in his somewhat ponderous fashion. He said he wouldn't sit down: he couldn't stop; but he had just come from his trip through Florida, and he wanted to know how Mrs. Gerry was. He was glad enough to find she was better; he had been sure she would pull through.

As he talked on about orange groves, and land and investments, he often gave a long, questioning gaze into Moore's face.

Moore began to resent this gaze, though there seemed to be nothing hostile in it. But Moore was by this time in a frame of mind when he felt himself hardly responsible for anything he might do. He had been suffering for many days. He had slept little. There were times when he was desperate with the uncertainty, and with the thronging, terrible thoughts upon him.

Salome was as evasive, as unsatisfactory, as if she were a sprite, and not flesh and blood at all.

In those days Moore felt himself growing old. He could hardly recognize himself. He gave up his business entirely. He could think of nothing but that girl, and what she had told him. His heart longed for her and turned towards her with an entirely ungovernable impulse. But his judgment—Moore resolutely thrust his judgment into the background, and it was only now and then that it loomed up too prominently, like a spectre that would some day assert itself.

His naturally chivalric feeling towards all women was now concentrated into an unspeakable tenderness towards one woman whom he wished to defend and protect, even against herself. What mattered it about his judgment?

And Salome held herself austerely aloof. Every morning and every night he asked himself how long she would be like that. He would have tried to break impetuously through this guard if there had not been a certain beseeching phase in the girl's attitude. It was as if she asked that he should be her ally in whatever she wished to do.

Now when Redd said he must go back to the city, he turned towards Moore and asked if he would go

then ; Redd added that he particularly wished to see
him.

Moore rose in a kind of sullen acquiescence ; and
to be anything like sullen showed how keenly he had
been suffering.

He turned towards Salome, but she only bowed
gravely to him, as if to intimate that he might better go.

As the two young men walked away Mrs. Gerry
took the girl's hand between her own hot, dry palms.

“ Salome,” she said, anxiously, “ what are you
doing ?”

Salome endeavored to draw herself up.

“ I ?” she asked ; “ I am doing nothing.”

“ But you don't let Mr. Moore have a chance.”

Salome shivered. Then she rose and stood with
her back to her mother.

“ I don't know how I can bear to see him alone,”
she said.

“ But he wants a talk with you ; an explanation.”

“ There can be no explanation,” was the response.

“ You cannot tell that. It is unfair not to let him
see you.”

“ Unfair ?” Salome wheeled about. “ Then I will
see him. But I know it all now.”

“ He loves you, Salome.”

The mother's voice, however, was very sad as it
pronounced those words.

The girl stood silent an instant before she was able
to say :

“ Yes, I think he does love me. And you love me,
mother, but you do not respect me.”

Notwithstanding all her self-command, Mrs. Gerry,
as she heard and saw her child at this moment, gave
an audible groan.

She leaned her head back and shut her eyes.

Salome drew yet nearer.

"Mother," she said, "you never lie; you never prevaricate. Answer me this: Do you respect me?"

Mrs. Gerry's lips grew stiff, but at last they obeyed her.

"Salome, I know you are not base. I am your mother, and I know you are not base."

The woman suddenly extended her arms, and with a swift access of strength she drew the girl into them.

Mrs. Gerry began to sob, and she could not at first check those sobs. Now at last she felt as if her heart would break because of Salome's unhappiness, and more because of the girl's lack of genuine rectitude.

In that brief time, while she feebly held the young head against her breast, a process of reasoning flashed through her mind. In these days she was always reasoning about the girl in the hope that she might arrive at some solid justification of Salome's actions. Was there not a moral diathesis as there was said to be a physical diathesis, and how accountable was one who—here the woman's thoughts grew incoherent. What justification was there for falsehood? What could one build upon a shifting foundation?

"You do not answer me," said Salome. She withdrew herself from her mother's embrace. "It is enough that you have hesitated."

She knelt by her mother's knees and put her face in her mother's lap. She appeared weak and prostrated.

With her face still in that position, she said:

"I can endure from you, because you are my

mother, what I couldn't endure from a lover. But it is hard from you."

Mrs. Gerry gasped in an agony of silence.

The vision of her child's future passed now plainly before her eyes. She was asking if Salome had that power of self-sacrifice which is so spontaneous, so almost involuntary, in some feminine natures.

And Mrs. Gerry could not say anything, for in her secret soul she sympathized with her daughter in this. First and foremost, Mrs. Gerry felt that she must be respected. But if she were not worthy of respect, she must do without love. She knew that this was what was in Salome's mind. But would it endure in Salome's mind? And she could say nothing. But this phase of character Salome had not inherited from that ancestor whose traits were so impressed upon her; this phase was a tincture of New England blood.

The two young men who had left the cabin together walked on for some distance without speaking. Moore had no wish to speak. He strode on with his head bent, brooding upon the one subject, and he almost forgot that he had a companion until Redd spoke.

"Maybe," said Redd, "you'll say I've no right, but I guess I'll venture to take the right, anyway."

He stopped in his walk in such a way that Moore was compelled to stop also.

"Well, go ahead," said Moore, impatiently.

His thoughts were a torture to him, but he was indignant if any one intruded upon him and prevented that constant dwelling of his mind upon the one theme.

Redd was very slow, and he did not speak immediately. Moore kicked at a palmetto stump with some viciousness as he stood and waited.

But nothing was likely to hurry Redd. When he was quite ready to speak he squared round upon Moore, taking in as he did so the bright attractiveness of Moore's aspect. That aspect was cloudy enough now, but Redd perceived, with a smouldering anger, how bright and winning it was natural for Moore to be. And as he took this in he had a crushing sense of the difference there was between them.

"I understand," he said, "that you are going to marry Salome."

"That is my intention," was the answer.

"I haven't got anything to say about that," returned Redd, heavily, "but I want to look into things a little. I ain't going home till she looks different from what she does now—that is, I don't think I shall."

"I don't know what right you have—" began Moore, hotly.

He found that his temper was like tinder in these days.

"It ain't worth while for you to get mad," now remarked Redd. "I don't know as I care particularly whether I have what you call any right or not. But I love Salome Gerry."

"I was sure of it!" interjected Moore, savagely.

"All right, be sure of it," was the response. "It doesn't harm her to have me love her; and she never pretended to love me any. She loves you. Now, what I want to know is: are you up to anything that is making her wretched? Tell me that."

Redd's eyes burned deeply as he spoke. But he stood with perfect quiet, his figure looking large in the sunlight.

Moore plunged his hands into his pockets. His face was crimson. He lowered himself to a subterfuge.

"You seem to forget that she is grieving for her father," he said.

He could no longer dispute Redd's right. And he was obliged to acknowledge that this somewhat uncouth man from the country had a power of presence and personality.

"It ain't that," said Redd; "you know it ain't that I mean. It's something about you. Something is wrong."

"Yes," exclaimed Moore, with some violence, "something is wrong; but it's nothing I've done. I am waiting and hoping to have a word with her. Can't you see I'm so wretched myself that I'm almost ready to put a bullet into my head?"

Moore, in spite of himself, was so conscious of the genuineness of the man before him that he spoke differently from what he had intended.

"You give me your word that it ain't any fault of yours?"

Redd looked at Moore with unswerving, stern gaze.

"I give you my word," said Moore. Then he laughed. "You see, I let you catechise me. But I should like to know what you would do about it, anyway?"

A dark flush came into Redd's face.

"It's no matter," he said at last, "what I'd do. But I'd make this world an uncommon bad place for anybody that did her any harm. But I believe you. A fellow's got to believe you, somehow. I'm glad of it, since she cares for you. It must be a solemn thing to be loved as Salome loves you."

Redd turned away. After an instant of silence Moore came closer to him. He held out his hand.

"Will you shake hands with me, Redd?" he asked.

The two men clasped hands.

Then they walked on towards the city.

But Moore could not stay in Augustine. He tried boating as a panacea which sometimes had power. To-day, however, he could not endure to stay on the river, and in half an hour he was at the wharf and had thrown his oars down with relief.

As he stood there a party came down to go out in a yacht. He saw Miss Nunally among the group. She looked towards him and smiled. He suddenly walked up to her. She knew, and she was a woman with exquisite perceptions. Women understood; and they were so sympathetic. It would be a great relief to him, Moore thought, if he might spend the next hour with Miss Nunally. Perhaps he could then endure the time until he could go out to that cabin again.

There was very little of the stoic about Moore. He craved sympathy almost as a woman might crave it.

"Are you going with all these people?" he asked, abruptly.

"I was going," was the answer.

"Then do a deed of charity and come with me. Please come with me. I shall be a miserable companion, though; I warn you of that."

Moore was conscious of a decided feeling of gratitude when Miss Nunally turned to her friends and explained that she was asked to do a deed of charity, and that a deed of charity was something that brought its own reward.

The next moment Moore had handed her into the boat he had just left. He pushed off into the river, while Portia waved her handkerchief at the yachting party.

"This is so kind of you," Moore said, when they were well away.

"It is not so difficult to be kind to you, Mr. Moore," was the response.

Miss Nunally met his rather absent gaze with a look of simple well-wishing which had a faint comforting power upon the young man.

Moore endeavored to rouse himself. He must not be merely a lump of flesh in this girl's presence.

"Why do you try to talk?" asked Portia, kindly. "It is not necessary. You look as if you were suffering, Mr. Moore. Let us be silent. Row wherever you please; it is always a pleasure for me to be on the water."

For a long time Moore simply obeyed her. He was soothed by her mere presence and by the knowledge that she understood. He need not tell her; she understood.

The lines in his forehead grew less deep. His whole attitude relaxed. He was not thinking of Miss Nunally at all. She knew this fact perfectly. She did not look at him, but she saw the change in him.

She sat leaning against the side of the boat, her parasol over her head, her face calm, a faint glow in her eyes, the white roses in her corsage moving gently in the wind and exhaling their fragrance lavishly.

At last Moore glanced at his companion with eyes that were a little less strained. Then Miss Nunally spoke.

" Does she know how you suffer ?" she asked.

The young man threw up his head as if a deep breath might have a restorative power. He looked wistfully at Portia.

"I don't know," he said, slowly, resting upon his oars. "She is very unhappy. But I don't know much about women ; they are so strange. I think Salome has some strange idea in her head. I can't tell what it is. I have a suspicion, though."

Moore now drew in his oars and leaned his arms on his knees. He was gazing steadily just beyond the girl in front of him.

" And what are your suspicions ?" she inquired.

" That she will want to break our engagement," was the reply.

Portia suddenly lowered her eyes. She put her handkerchief to her lips. But she responded directly :

" Not because she does not love you ?" she said.

" No," he said, slowly: "it is not conceited in me to think she loves me. But women are so different from men. Sometimes I think they don't know how to love."

No answer to this remark. Moore still continued to gaze beyond Miss Nunally ; and Miss Nunally, who was not accustomed to having men gaze beyond her, still continued to bear this attitude of her companion with apparent calm.

" Do you believe that women know how to love ?" questioned Moore.

But he did not wait for any reply. He went on immediately :

" I have suffered more within the last few days than I can ever suffer again. My mind is one hor-

rible chaos. There is only one thing I clearly know—
only one thing."

" And that is—" as the speaker hesitated.

" That I love her. No matter what she has done,
I love her."

Miss Nunally bent down as if to pick up something
from the bottom of the boat.

" Have you assured her of that?" she inquired, in a
clear voice.

" I have had no opportunity. You know how ill
her mother has been."

Moore took his oars and began to row again.

After a time Miss Nunally said :

" Perhaps we might better go back to the wharf."

Without answering, Moore turned and began to row
towards the city. As they drew near he looked at her
with a glance which for the first time really saw her.

" How tired you are !" he exclaimed. " I can't forgive myself for having bored you so."

" You haven't bored me," she answered.

" Truly, haven't I ? You are so good, Miss Nunally. And you have helped me so much. You have
helped me so by just letting me be with you, don't
you know. And you know all about it. Miss Nunally," with vibrating earnestness, " I wish you were
going to be happy. But you never will be happy if
you marry that man. And you don't even pretend to
love him, do you ?"

" Oh no ; I don't even pretend to love him," now
meeting her companion's eyes. " And I am not going
to marry him, Mr. Moore."

" Ah !" with a start of interest.

Moore again pulled in his oars. He held out his
hand. As she put hers within it she said :

"I couldn't do it, after all. And I could not forget what you said, Mr. Moore, about such things. Now you will congratulate me, won't you?"

She did not allow her hand to remain an instant in his.

"Indeed yes, I congratulate you," impressively.

Then Moore began to row, and his face clouded over deeply again.

When the two parted on the Plaza the young man thanked the girl again for her kindness, his eyes dwelling on her with a half absent but wholly wretched expression. And she said nothing.

In an hour he was out at the cabin again, going this time with a well-defined resolution not to leave until he had had an interview with Salome.

He was somewhat surprised to see her coming to meet him. She left her mother sitting at the door of the cabin. She glanced back at that figure which now did not lean back in its chair any more. With the first strength she had Mrs. Gerry ceased "to loll." She sat now upright and watched her daughter as she went towards Moore. Salome had said nothing, and her mother had given no advice. She felt that this was a matter solely between these two, and that she could not advise.

She noted the subdued eagerness with which Moore greeted the girl. She saw them walk away among the trees, with Jack following sedately a few feet behind them.

Then, after a while, the woman went and laid herself on the bed. But she had been there but a few moments, she thought, when the hound came in his sober way in at the door. Mrs. Gerry rose hurriedly. She looked out among the pines and saw Salome coming alone. Jack went back to her and ranged himself behind her.

Salome came straight on until she reached the house. Her mother hastened to meet her.

"Well?" she said, her heart sinking.

"He has gone," said Salome. But she had hardly spoken when Moore came rapidly towards them. He went directly to Mrs. Gerry, taking both her hands. She had never seen him look like this in the least.

"I'm going," he began. He stopped suddenly. Then he began again. "I'm going, because she insists upon it. She says she knows she is right. She says she knows herself so well that she knows she is right. Well—" he again found himself unable to go on. But he waited until he could say, "I can't prove that she is wrong. But I love her. She cannot make me promise not to come back. Good-bye."

When he had gone, Salome, still standing by her mother, said, with an appearance of calmness:

"I want to say what I have to say now; for I can't go on talking about it. I knew he couldn't respect me fully; and he couldn't tell me he could. He said he was bewildered, confused. He said he was sure of one thing: that he loved me and wanted me for his wife." A pause. Presently the girl's voice went on again: "In his place I should have lied and asserted that I felt respect, that what I had done did not really stain me, and so on. But he could not. And I told him I had tendencies which I could not control, and which were not—I think I said were not—honest, and that they would make him unhappy. I told him—but it makes no difference. He has gone. Mother!"—with a sudden sharp intonation—"he has gone!"

"But he will come back?" said Mrs. Gerry.

"Will he? But how can I change? How can I be a different woman?"

Salome looked at her mother with a tremor of passionate inquiry.

But the tremor subsided instantly. She was too spent with what she had just suffered to feel intensely now. Before Mrs. Gerry could think of any reply, Salome said, with a kind of dull abruptness:

"Miss Nunally loves him."

"How do you know?" quickly.

"I don't know it; but I believe it."

There was nothing to respond to this.

The two stood there together at the door of the cabin. They stood in the full light of the sun.

Salome turned towards the woman beside her.

"It is you and I, mother," she said.

"Yes," said Mrs. Gerry, "you and I, with God to help us."

She stood erect. She put her arm about her daughter, who also stood erect, with a difference.

Above them some black spots came moving on from towards St. Augustine. Salome saw these moving things. She became yet paler.

"Mother," she said, "there are the crows. They fly between me and the sun. But it is no matter."

THE END

By MARIA LOUISE POOL.

KATHARINE NORTH. A Novel. Post 8vo, Cloth, Ornamental, $1 25.

"Katharine North" is, from an artistic and literary standpoint, Miss Pool's best work, and will take high rank among the novels of the year. The story is an intensely interesting one, and is most skilfully constructed.—*Boston Traveller.*

MRS. KEATS BRADFORD. A Novel. Post 8vo, Cloth, Ornamental, $1 25.

Miss Pool's novels have the characteristic qualities of American life. They have an indigenous flavor. The author is on her own ground, instinct with American feeling and purpose. —*N. Y. Tribune.*

The dialogues are very natural, and the book is very wholesome reading. No one who begins it will be able to give it up until the last page has been reached.—*N. Y. Journal of Commerce.*

ROWENY IN BOSTON. A Novel. Post 8vo, Cloth, Ornamental, $1 25.

Is a surprisingly good story. . . . It is a very delicately drawn story in all particulars. It is sensitive in the matter of ideas and of phrase. Its characters make a delightful company. It is excellent art and rare entertainment.—*N. Y. Sun.*

Like Rowena at her brush, Miss Pool may be said to have the "touch." By a few lively strokes of her pen, her characters are made clear in outline, and are then left to explain themselves by their own words and actions.—*Nation, N. Y.*

DALLY. A Novel. Post 8vo, Cloth, Ornamental, $1 25; Paper, 50 cents.

There is not a lay figure in the book ; all are flesh and blood creations. . . . The humor of "Dally" is grateful to the sense ; it is provided in abundance, together with touches of pathos, an inseparable concomitant.—*Philadelphia Ledger.*

WILLIAM DEAN HOWELLS.

THE WORLD OF CHANCE. A Novel. 12mo, Cloth, $1 50; Paper, 60 cents.

THE QUALITY OF MERCY. A Novel. 12mo, Cloth, $1 50; Paper, 75 cents.

AN IMPERATIVE DUTY. A Novel. 12mo, Cloth, $1 00; Paper, 50 cents.

THE SHADOW OF A DREAM. A Story. 12mo, Cloth, $1 00; Paper, 50 cents.

A HAZARD OF NEW FORTUNES. A Novel. 12mo, Cloth, 2 vols., $2 00; Paper, Illustrated, $1 00.

ANNIE KILBURN. A Novel. 12mo, Cloth, $1 50; Paper, 75 cents.

APRIL HOPES. A Novel. 12mo, Cloth, $1 50; Paper, 75 cents.

MODERN ITALIAN POETS. Essays and Versions. With Portraits. 12mo, Cloth, $2 00.

CRITICISM AND FICTION. With Portrait. 12mo, Cloth, Ornamental, $1 00.

A BOY'S TOWN. Illustrated. Post 8vo, Cloth, $1 25.

THE MOUSE-TRAP, AND OTHER FARCES. Illustrated. 12mo, Cloth, $1 00.

CHRISTMAS EVERY DAY, AND OTHER STORIES. Illustrated. Post 8vo, Cloth, $1 25.

A LITTLE SWISS SOJOURN. Ill'd. 32mo. Cloth, 50 cents.

THE UNEXPECTED GUESTS. Illustrated. 32mo, Cloth, 50 cents.

A LETTER OF INTRODUCTION. Ill'd. 32mo, Cloth, 50 cents.

THE ALBANY DEPOT. Illustrated. 32mo, Cloth, 50 cents.

THE GARROTERS. A Farce. 32mo, Cloth, 50 cents.

BY MARY E. WILKINS.

JANE FIELD. A Novel. Illustrated. 16mo, Cloth, Ornamental, $1 25.

YOUNG LUCRETIA, and Other Stories. Illustrated. Post 8vo, Cloth, Ornamental, $1 25.

GILES COREY, YEOMAN. Illustrated. 32mo, Cloth. Ornamental, 50 cents.

A NEW ENGLAND NUN, and Other Stories. 16mo, Cloth, Ornamental, $1 25.

A HUMBLE ROMANCE, and Other Stories. 16mo, Cloth, Extra, $1 25.

It takes just such distinguishing literary art as Mary E. Wilkins possesses to give an episode of New England its soul, pathos, and poetry.—*N. Y. Times.*

The simplicity, purity, and quaintness of these stories set them apart in a niche of distinction where they have no rivals. —*Literary World*, Boston.

The author has the unusual gift of writing a short story which is complete in itself, having a real *beginning*, a *middle*, and an end.—*Observer*, N. Y.

No one has dealt with this kind of life better than Miss Wilkins. Nowhere are there to be found such faithful, delicately drawn, sympathetic, tenderly humorous pictures.—*N. Y. Tribune.*

The charm of Miss Wilkins's stories is in her intimate acquaintance and comprehension of humble life, and the sweet human interest she feels and makes her readers partake of, in the simple, common, homely people she draws. — *Springfield Republican.*

The author has given us studies from real life which must be the result of a lifetime of patient, sympathetic observation. . . . No one has done the same kind of work so lovingly and so well.—*Christian Register*, Boston.

CHARLES DUDLEY WARNER.

AS WE WERE SAYING. With Portrait, and Illustrated by H. W. McVickar and Others. 16mo, Cloth, Ornamental, $1 00.

So dainty and delightsome a little book may it be everybody's good hap to possess.—*Evangelist*, N. Y.

Who but Mr. Warner could dangle these trifles so gracefully before the mind and make their angles flash out new and hidden meanings?—*Critic*, N. Y.

OUR ITALY. Illustrated. 8vo, Cloth, Ornamental, Uncut Edges and Gilt Top, $2 50.

In this book are a little history, a little prophecy, a few fascinating statistics, many interesting facts, much practical suggestion, and abundant humor and charm.—*Evangelist*, N. Y.

A LITTLE JOURNEY IN THE WORLD. A Novel. Post 8vo, Half Leather, Uncut Edges and Gilt Top, $1 50.

The vigor and vividness of the tale and its sustained interest are not its only or its chief merits. It is a study of American life of to-day, possessed with shrewd insight and fidelity.—GEORGE WILLIAM CURTIS.

A powerful picture of that phase of modern life in which unscrupulously acquired capital is the chief agent.—*Boston Post*.

STUDIES IN THE SOUTH AND WEST, with Comments on Canada. Post 8vo, Half Leather, Uncut Edges and Gilt Top, $1 75.

Perhaps the most accurate and graphic account of these portions of the country that has appeared, taken all in all. . . . A book] most charming—a book that no American can fail to enjoy, appreciate, and highly prize.—*Boston Traveller*.

THEIR PILGRIMAGE. Richly Illustrated by C .S. REINHART. Post 8vo, Half Leather, Uncut Edges and Gilt Top, $2 00.

Mr. Warner's pen-pictures of the characters typical of each resort, of the manner of life followed at each, of the humor and absurdities peculiar to Saratoga, or Newport, or Bar Harbor, as the case may be, are as good-natured as they are clever. The satire, when there is any, is of the mildest, and the general tone is that of one glad to look on the brightest side of the cheerful, pleasure-seeking world with which he mingles.—*Christian Union*, N. Y.

DATE DUE

GAYLORD

PRINTED IN U S A

www.ingramcontent.com/pod-product-compliance
Lightning Source LLC
Chambersburg PA
CBHW021534110726
47902CB00004B/870